PRAISE FOR JOEL C. ROSENBERG

"Joel Rosenberg has an uncanny talent for focusing his storytelling on real-world hot spots just as they are heating up. He has done it again in *The Kremlin Conspiracy*."

PORTER GOSS, former director of the Central Intelligence Agency

"Marcus Ryker rocks! Breakneck action, political brinksmanship, authentic scenarios, and sharply defined characters make Joel C. Rosenberg's *Kremlin Conspiracy* a full-throttle and frightening ride through tomorrow's headlines."

BRIGADIER GENERAL (U.S. ARMY, RETIRED) A. J. TATA, national bestselling author of *Direct Fire*

"Joel C. Rosenberg writes taut, intelligent thrillers that are as timely as they are well-written. Pairing a fast-paced plot with an impressive understanding of the inner workings in the corridors of power of the Russian government, *The Kremlin Conspiracy* is a stellar novel of riveting action and political intrigue."

MARK GREANEY, #1 *New York Times* bestselling author of *Agent in Place*

"*The Kremlin Conspiracy* is my first Joel C. Rosenberg novel, and I am absolutely blown away by how good this guy is. The story moves at a blistering pace, it's crackling with tension, and you won't put it down until you reach the end. Guaranteed. Simply masterful."

SEAN PARNELL, *New York Times* bestselling author of *Outlaw Platoon*

"If there were a *Forbes* 400 list of great current novelists, Joel Rosenberg would be among the top ten. . . . One of the most entertaining and intriguing authors of international political thrillers in the country. . . . His novels are un-put-downable."

STEVE FORBES, editor in chief, *Forbes* magazine

"One of my favorite things: An incredible thriller—it's called *The Third Target* by Joel C. Rosenberg. . . . He's amazing. . . . He writes the greatest thrillers set in the Middle East, with so much knowledge of that part of the world. . . . Fabulous! I've read every book he's ever written!"

KATHIE LEE GIFFORD, NBC's *Today*

"Fascinating and compelling . . . way too close to reality for a novel."

MIKE HUCKABEE, former Arkansas governor

"[Joel Rosenberg] understands the grave dangers posed by Iran and Syria, and he's been a bold and courageous voice for true peace and security in the Middle East."

DANNY AYALON, former Israeli deputy foreign minister

"Joel has a particularly clear understanding of what is going on in today's Iran and Syria and the grave threat these two countries pose to the rest of the world."

REZA KAHLILI, former CIA operative in Iran and bestselling author of *A Time to Betray: The Astonishing Double Life of a CIA Agent inside the Revolutionary Guards of Iran*

"Joel Rosenberg is unsurpassed as the writer of fiction thrillers! Sometimes I have to remind myself to breathe as I read one of his novels because I find myself holding my breath in suspense as I turn the pages."

ANNE GRAHAM LOTZ, author and speaker

"Joel paints an eerie, terrifying, page-turning picture of a worst-case scenario coming to pass. You have to read [*Damascus Countdown*], and then pray it never happens."

RICK SANTORUM, former U.S. senator

THE JERUSALEM ASSASSIN

JOEL C.
ROSENBERG

THE
JERUSALEM
ASSASSIN

Tyndale House Publishers
Carol Stream, Illinois

Visit Tyndale online at www.tyndale.com.

Visit Joel C. Rosenberg's website at www.joelrosenberg.com.

TYNDALE and Tyndale's quill logo are registered trademarks of Tyndale House Publishers.

The Jerusalem Assassin

Designed by Dean H. Renninger

The Jerusalem Assassin is a work of fiction. Where real people, events, establishments, organizations, or locales appear, they are used fictitiously. All other elements of the novel are drawn from the author's imagination.

For information about special discounts for bulk purchases, please contact Tyndale House Publishers at csresponse@tyndale.com or call 1-800-323-9400.

Library of Congress Cataloging-in-Publication Data

Names: Rosenberg, Joel C., author.
Title: The Jerusalem assassin / Joel C. Rosenberg.
Description: Carol Stream : Tyndale House Publishers, Inc., 2020.
Identifiers: LCCN 2019041032 (print) | LCCN 2019041033 (ebook) | ISBN 9781496437846 (hardcover) | ISBN 9781496437860 (kindle edition) | ISBN 9781496437877 (epub) | ISBN 9781496437884 (epub)
Subjects: LCSH: Political fiction. | GSAFD: Suspense fiction. | Christian fiction.
Classification: LCC PS3618.O832 J47 2020 (print) | LCC PS3618.O832 (ebook) | DDC 813/.6—dc23
LC record available at https://lccn.loc.gov/2019041032
LC ebook record available at https://lccn.loc.gov/2019041033

ISBN 978-1-4964-4605-3 (International Trade Paper Edition)

Printed in the United States of America

26	25	24	23	22	21	20
7	6	5	4	3	2	1

To my nephew, Luke,
for whom I have the deepest love and the fondest hopes.

CAST OF CHARACTERS

Americans

Marcus Ryker—special operative, Central Intelligence Agency

Richard Stephens—director of the Central Intelligence Agency

Martha Dell—deputy director of intelligence (DDI), Central
   Intelligence Agency

Peter Hwang—special operative, Central Intelligence Agency

Andrew Clarke—president of the United States

Barry Evans—U.S. national security advisor

William McDermott—deputy national security advisor

Margaret "Meg" Whitney—secretary of state

Kailea Curtis—agent with the Diplomatic Security Service

Geoff Stone—special agent in charge, Diplomatic Security Service

Carl Roseboro—deputy director, U.S. Secret Service

Robert Dayton—U.S. senator (D-Iowa), member of the Senate
   Intelligence Committee

Annie Stewart—senior foreign policy advisor to Senator Robert Dayton

Carter Emerson—pastor, Lincoln Park Baptist Church,
   Washington, D.C.

Maya Emerson—wife of the pastor

Russians

Oleg Stefanovich Kraskin—son-in-law to the late President
   Aleksandr Luganov

Mikhail Borisovich Petrovsky—president of the Russian Federation

Nikolay Vladimirovich Kropatkin—head of the FSB

Iranians

Grand Ayatollah Hossein Ansari—Supreme Leader of Iran

Yadollah Afshar—president of the Islamic Republic of Iran

Mahmoud Entezam—commander of the Iranian Revolutionary
Guard Corps

Dr. Haydar Abbasi—Iranian ballistic missile scientist and director of
Iran's missile program

Israelis

Reuven Eitan—prime minister of Israel

Asher Gilad—director of Mossad

Tomer Ben Ami—deputy director of the Shin Bet

Palestinians

Ismail Ziad—president of the Palestinian Authority

Amin al-Azzam—Grand Mufti of Jerusalem

Hussam Mashrawi—director of the Waqf and son-in-law of the
Grand Mufti

Saudis

Faisal Mohammed—monarch of the Kingdom of Saudi Arabia

Abdulaziz bin Faisal—heir to the throne and minister of defense

Abdullah bin Rashid—director of the General Intelligence Directorate

Turks

Ahmet Mustafa—president of the Republic of Turkey

Hamdi Yaşar—producer, Al-Sawt satellite television network

Others

Abu Nakba—commander of Kairos

Mohammed al-Qassab—member of Kairos

Maxim Sheripov—member of Kairos

Amina Sheripova—member of Kairos

Dr. Ali Haqqani—member of Kairos

"What enables the wise sovereign and the good general to overcome others and achieve things beyond the reach of ordinary men is foreknowledge. Now, this foreknowledge cannot be elicited from ghosts and spirits, nor by analogy with past events, nor by deductive calculation. It must be obtained from men who know the enemy situation."

SUN TZU, THE ART OF WAR

PART
ONE

They were coming, and he knew they were coming, and he knew why—they were coming to kill him and to kill the president and to kill anyone else who got in their way.

They were coming to settle scores.

The United States had inflicted too much damage in too short a time. Such actions could not simply be ignored. They had to be avenged. They had to be repaid at the highest levels, starting with the man responsible for issuing the strike orders.

What wasn't clear was when or where the attacks would come or how many were coming or precisely how they would strike. Despite vacuuming up untold terabytes of phone calls, emails, text messages, and other electronic communications over the past month, America's seventeen intelligence agencies had precious little to show for their efforts, and what few leads they had uncovered were infuriatingly inconclusive.

Yet why let threats of murder and chaos ruin a perfectly good evening? thought

Marcus Ryker as he stepped out of the shower and toweled off. He had never been one to let himself become paralyzed by fear, and he certainly wasn't going to start now. Growing up on Colorado's Front Range, he had lived to push the boundaries, especially as a teenager, to experience the rush of the unknown, to suck the marrow out of life. He wasn't repelled by danger; he was drawn to it, electrified by it. His sisters accused him of being an adrenaline junkie, and that was probably true. Still, he was no longer as reckless as he had been in his youth. That's what he told himself, anyway. Time and experience and loss and immense pain had, he hoped, refined his most foolish instincts and perhaps tempered them with a bit of wisdom.

Unlocking the wall safe in his bedroom closet, he removed his Sig Sauer P229, inserted a full magazine, chambered a round, and put the automatic pistol in his shoulder holster. Next he withdrew two spare magazines and clipped those to his belt before closing and locking the safe. Though there was plenty of disturbing chatter out there, there was no credible intel indicating attacks were imminent anywhere in the homeland, much less here in Washington. But one could never be too careful.

Opening the front door of his apartment building, he scanned the street. Traffic seemed light, but it was still early. Other than a few teens huddled on a stoop across the street, he saw nothing suspicious. Satisfied that all was clear, Marcus walked briskly down the street and around the corner to where his 1986 Nissan Stanza was parked. It was ugly and brown and rusty and almost as old as he was, but somehow it still ran, and—best of all—it was paid for. He got in and started the engine.

Two blocks away, Marcus pulled over at a florist and spent far longer than he should have picking out an appropriate arrangement. Too many varieties. Too many colors. He couldn't even remember the last time he'd bought flowers. He finally settled for a bouquet of daffodils and paid the clerk in cash.

They'd agreed to meet at seven. By the time he got to the town house, it was almost twenty minutes past. And there was no place to park. He eventually found a spot several streets away. He'd be even later now, but it gave him a chance to walk a bit, and that helped settle his nerves.

Finally reaching his destination, he stepped onto the front porch, knocked on the metal screen door, and waited under the porch light. The night was chilly, and there was a brisk breeze coming off the Potomac River. In faded blue jeans and boots, a black crewneck sweater over a white T-shirt, and a black leather jacket, he wasn't exactly cold. But he suddenly wondered if he should have worn a suit or at least a shirt with a collar. In all that had happened over the past few years, there were some things he could not forget, no matter how hard he tried. There were others he struggled to remember, and social graces were among them.

Marcus knocked again, harder this time, but still no one answered. The longer he stood there on the creaky wooden porch, the more he wished he were home, ordering Chinese food, throwing on sweats, and falling asleep on the couch watching ESPN. Pete Hwang kept saying he needed to get out more. Then again, Pete was an idiot. A friend, of course. The best one Marcus still had. But an idiot nonetheless. Divorced. Estranged from his kids. Living alone in a new city. Yet insisting he was enjoying his newfound "bachelor's life" and trying to get Marcus off his rear end and "back in the game."

And then, just as he was contemplating walking back to his car, the front door finally opened.

2

"You made it," Maya Emerson said in her distinctive Southern drawl.

"Sorry I'm late," Marcus replied. "But I brought you these." He held out the bouquet, and the old African American woman's face lit up.

"Ooh, I love 'em—aren't you sweet? And Marcy will be thrilled. She's been talking about you all week, and she just loves daffodils. How did you know?"

As Marcus shrugged—he most certainly *hadn't* known—the large woman stepped out on the porch and gave him a hug, kissed him on both cheeks, and insisted, as she always did, that he return the favor. Only then did she lead him inside. As Maya disappeared around a corner, Marcus took off his jacket and hung it in the front closet. At the same time, he removed the magazine from his pistol and cleared the chamber, slipping both the mag and the round into his jacket pocket.

The aromas wafting down the hall from the kitchen were heavenly, and they were beckoning him. Pot roast. Mashed potatoes and gravy. Sweet corn on the cob. Homemade chocolate chip cookies and a pot of freshly brewed coffee. From the family room, Marcus could hear the roaring fire and smell the crackling pine logs. And someone was playing the piano beautifully. That, he had no doubt, was Marcy.

Heading to the kitchen, he finally began to relax. He loved this home and he loved these people and he knew it was silly of him to have been anxious even for a moment. Somewhere in their midseventies now, Maya and Carter Emerson had been married for more than fifty years. Carter, a decorated Vietnam vet, had been pastoring Lincoln Park Baptist for at least forty. And since Marcus had started attending, they had effectively adopted him, constantly inviting him over for dinner on Wednesday nights before church and for lunch on Sundays after church. Given his schedule, he couldn't always accept, and even when he was free, he didn't always come. Mostly he didn't want to be a bother. These two had so many others who needed their time and affection. Yet his periodic refusals never stopped them from inviting him, and he never regretted coming. The Emersons were the only family he had east of the Mississippi, and they had walked with him through the darkest days of his life.

"Marcus, my boy, how are you?" Carter bellowed from where he stood at the counter, tossing a spinach salad in a large wooden bowl.

"Better than I deserve, Pastor."

"Ain't that the truth," Carter laughed as Maya, still swooning over the daffodils, put the flowers in a vase and set them on the kitchen table.

"Thanks again for having me over," Marcus said. "I probably needed a night out."

"'Course you did—and it sure as shootin' beats Chinese food and ESPN, don't it?"

Marcus shrugged and grinned. The man knew him too well.

"Well, I hope you're hungry," Carter said as his wife checked the roast. "Maya made your favorites to celebrate your big new job. Can't wait to hear all about it."

Before Marcus could respond, the prettiest girl in the world appeared in the doorway to the family room. She came sprinting into the kitchen and threw her arms around Marcus, squeezing him like she was never going to let him go, and for the first time all day—in too many days, actually—a smile broke across his face.

"Young lady," Carter said, "did I tell you or did I tell you, this here is the kindest boy in the entire church? Better snatch him up now before someone else snags him. And look—he even brought you your favorite flowers."

The Emersons' granddaughter was only nine, but she was smart as a whip and effervescing with a joy that hardly seemed real. Beaming, Marcus scooped up the wiry little girl and whirled her around. She squealed with laughter and gave him two big kisses, one on each cheek. Marcus immediately kissed her back before she ran to the kitchen table, bent down, smelled the flowers, and hugged him all over again.

Marcy wasn't Carter and Maya's only grandchild. She was, however, the one who lived the farthest away, and she was certainly the one who had experienced the most pain. Her father was nowhere to be found. Marcy had never even met him. Her mother lived in Seattle and had been in and out of jail and rehab more times than Marcus could remember. Each time, Gammy and Pop Pop had flown to Seattle to help out, then brought Marcy back to stay with them. So it was again. She was staying at least through Thanksgiving, Carter had said over the phone when he'd invited Marcus to dinner, and probably through Christmas.

"I drew a picture of you," Marcy whispered. "Want to see it?"

"I'd love to," Marcus whispered back.

He set her down and winked at Maya before following the girl into the family room. There they curled up in a big chair by the fireplace and reviewed Marcy's entire portfolio while Carter started a Duke Ellington album playing on an old Victrola in the corner. This was why Marcus had come tonight. For all the looming threats he and his country faced, how could he say no to Maya's cooking and Marcy's hugs?

Dinner, as usual, was all about Marcy. She barely ate. Instead, she speed-talked about all that she'd seen and done at the National Zoo that day with her grandparents. Marcus quipped she should be a correspondent for

Animal Planet, but Marcy thought that was ridiculous. She was going to be a veterinarian—"the best one in the whole wide world." Marcus had no doubt.

After dinner they played a compressed, one-hour version of Monopoly. Marcy cleaned their clocks. She bankrupted her grandmother in less than twenty minutes, and Carter and Marcus weren't far behind.

A bit after nine, Maya took the girl upstairs for a bath and bed. Carter brought Marcus a mug of hot coffee and a second round of cookies, fresh out of the oven. Marcus began to decline but instantly thought better of it. Who was he kidding? Maya's cookies were simply irresistible, and he caved to temptation.

"How are the ribs?" Carter asked as he settled into his favorite overstuffed chair and lit up his beloved pipe.

"Better," Marcus said, patting his side and wincing. "Well, not totally better."

"Still tender?"

"A little."

"But you're running again?"

"Five miles a day—just so I can eat Maya's cookies."

Carter chuckled and puffed away. "And how's Pete?"

"Pete's Pete—what can you do? But at least his arm is healing nicely."

"You two still having breakfast on Sundays?"

"Every week."

"Well, give him my regards."

"Will do."

"And tell him to come with you to church tomorrow."

"I ask him every Sunday."

"And?"

"And he's always got another excuse—he's a stubborn ole coot."

"Is it my preachin' or Maya's singin'?"

"Let's just say it ain't Maya," Marcus replied. "Beyond that, I plead the Fifth."

"Fair enough," Carter laughed as the cherry-scented smoke swirled about his head. "So tell me about this new job. You happy with it?"

The two men had barely seen each other in the last several weeks, much less had a chance to catch up on all the latest developments in Marcus's suddenly very different life.

"Bit of an adjustment, you might say, but I think it'll be a good fit."

"But the State Department?" Carter asked. "I don't really picture you at State, son."

Marcus shrugged. "Well, you know, it's not just State—it's DSS." Carter, a D.C. native, would know he was referring to the Diplomatic Security Service. "It'll be sort of like my days in the Secret Service, but maybe not as much travel and hopefully not as much stress."

The moment Marcus said it, he wished he'd put it differently. It wasn't a lie. Not exactly. But the truth was far more complicated. His job at DSS was real, but it was just a cover. The fact was, he had just been drafted into the employ of the Central Intelligence Agency.

3

Marcus got up early and went for a run, past the Capitol and down the Mall.

When he got back to his apartment, he showered, dressed, and headed to Manny's Diner, just a few blocks away. Pete wasn't there yet, so he grabbed a booth, ordered coffee, and began reading the *Washington Post*.

By twenty minutes after nine, Pete still hadn't arrived. When Marcus checked his phone and found no text messages or emails from him, he began to worry. Just as he was about to call Pete and read him the riot act, however, a woman he'd never seen suddenly dropped into the seat across from him.

"Hey, old man," she said, grabbing a menu. "What are we having?"

Marcus tensed, though he didn't take the woman for a threat. "And you would be?"

"Your new partner," she said without looking up.

"I beg your pardon?"

"Wow, Ryker, you really are old—lost your hearing, have you?" she quipped, now looking up as the waitress approached the booth. "Coffee—black; scrambled eggs—dry; and . . . do you have asparagus?"

"'Course," said the waitress.

"Good—then a side of asparagus instead of the hash browns, if that's all right."

"You got it." The waitress smiled and turned to Marcus. "And you?"

"Give us a minute, okay?" he said, and she shrugged and headed to the kitchen.

Marcus turned back to the mystery woman across from him. Younger than him by nearly a decade, she looked to be about thirty or thirty-one, with light-brown skin, chocolate-brown eyes, and jet-black hair tied back in a ponytail. She had an athletic build and struck Marcus as a runner. She wore no rings—no jewelry of any kind, actually—and her hands were calloused and strong. Her nails were unpainted and carefully trimmed. She wore a jean jacket over a black turtleneck, and he had no doubt that under the jacket was an automatic pistol.

Before he could speak, she slid a leather case across the table. Marcus recognized it immediately, as he'd recently been given one of his own. Sure enough, when he opened it, he found the woman's badge and ID. Her full name was Kailea Theresa Curtis, and she was a DSS special agent.

"Your buddy Pete won't be coming. He's in a meeting," she said.

"With whom?"

"The director."

"Why?"

"I'm afraid he's getting some bad news—he's not cleared for field duty."

"Why not?"

"His arm isn't healing properly. He needs another surgery. It's scheduled for Wednesday. So I've been assigned to you. We've got three days to prep for the NSA's trip to the Middle East, and we fly out Tuesday night."

She was referring to the president's national security advisor, General Barry Evans. This was the first Marcus was hearing about any trip. Neither the director of DSS nor his real boss, CIA director Richard Stephens, had said a word. But for some reason he believed her.

Suddenly his phone buzzed. He was getting a text.

"That's me," Kailea said. "Now you've got my number."

His phone rang. This time it was Pete.

"Where are you?" Marcus asked. "I thought we were supposed to—"

But Pete cut him off, and Marcus just listened as Pete relayed the same information Kailea had. A minute later, Marcus set his phone down on the table.

"You see, old man? I really was telling the truth." The woman smiled. "Now try to stay with me. We've got a briefing at Langley at eleven with the rest of the general's detail. So get yourself some breakfast and let's hit the road. Got it?" Then, raising her voice as if she were talking to someone in a retirement home, she said, *"GOT THAT? BREAKFAST NOW. BRIEFING LATER."*

Marcus held his tongue and sipped his coffee. "So, Agent Curtis, what's your story?"

Before she could answer, though, an explosion pierced the morning calm.

"Just a car backfiring," the waitress said as she arrived with a mug and pot of coffee. "Happens all the time."

But Marcus knew better. It wasn't a car backfiring. It was a Glock semiautomatic pistol firing a 9mm round. It was a sound he had heard a million times before, and it was close.

"Check the back door," Marcus said as he quickly slid out of the booth. "And make sure the manager locks it."

Kailea nodded and walked immediately to the kitchen. As she did, Marcus noticed her right hand move almost imperceptibly toward the bulge under the back of her jacket where she kept her weapon.

Brushing past the waitress, Marcus unzipped his leather jacket, giving him quick access to his Sig Sauer, though he didn't draw it yet. As he headed to the front door, he scanned the eyes of the various customers seated about the diner. None of them looked nervous. None of them seemed alarmed. Apparently none of them had even noticed the shot or cared, or they assumed like the waitress that it was a car backfiring. They were simply eating their omelets or reading their papers or doing their crossword puzzles or lost in their smartphones, oblivious to the danger or just numb to it, having lived in the southeastern section of D.C. all their lives.

Marcus stepped out onto Eleventh Street and looked left.

It was now almost nine thirty on a brisk, cloudless, spectacular Sunday morning, the kind of day that made him love living in the nation's capital, especially in the fall. The leaves still clinging to their branches were vibrant gold and maroon and yellow and orange. But nature would have her way. Even those were falling to the ground, swirling along the sidewalks and spinning down the streets amid stiff breezes that signaled winter was coming soon.

Seeing nothing out of the ordinary, Marcus looked right.

Again, nothing was obviously amiss. All was quiet. No cars were moving. No trucks. Barely anyone was on the streets, save a few young girls playing jump rope nearby. Marcus heard no pounding of running feet, no yelling, no screeching tires or approaching sirens. The only sound was that of an American flag, its colors now a bit faded, snapping sharply atop a tall steel pole outside the diner.

"All clear out back," Kailea said, coming up behind him. "What've you got?"

Marcus just stared up Eleventh Street, then started walking northward.

"What is it?" she pressed.

Marcus said nothing, but his pace increased. Soon he was jogging, with Kailea hastening to catch up. When they reached East Capitol Street, Marcus stopped abruptly in front of a dry-cleaning shop. He swept left to right, then turned his attention to the nearly barren trees of Lincoln Park. That's when he heard the Glock again. This time four shots rang out in rapid succession. A moment later, an automatic rifle erupted. It was an AR-15, or perhaps an M4, and the burst was followed almost immediately by bloodcurdling shrieks like nothing he'd heard since Kabul and Fallujah.

"The church!" yelled Marcus, and he broke into a sprint.

Kailea Curtis raced to catch up with Marcus, who was a good twenty feet in front of her.

She could see Lincoln Park Baptist straight ahead. The massive brick building—a historic landmark—took up nearly a city block. She saw a muzzle flash from the bell tower. Bullets began whizzing past their heads, and both she and Marcus ducked for cover behind enormous oak trees.

Drawing her weapon, Kailea tried to assess the situation. For starters, it was definitely an AR-15. That much was now clear. She could see someone lying in a pool of blood on the church's front steps. There was no sign yet of any law enforcement. The big question was, how many shooters were there? She could hear shots being fired inside the building, so that was one. The guy in the bell tower was two. Were there more?

Kailea spotted a minivan coming down East Capitol. Suddenly more gunfire erupted from the tower. Marcus pivoted around the tree and fired off three shots, trying to draw the man's fire. He did, but not in time. The windshield of the minivan was blown out. The vehicle smashed headlong into a lamppost. The driver—a Caucasian woman, her face covered in blood—threw open her door. She tried to make a run for it but was quickly riddled with bullets.

Next the shooter turned his fire on a sedan heading north on Thirteenth Street. Both Marcus and Kailea opened fire on the tower, but it wasn't enough. The shooter kept firing at the sedan and soon every window was blown out. The car rolled to a stop and the driver—a Hispanic male who looked no more than seventeen or eighteen years old—slumped forward onto the horn, which now wouldn't stop blaring.

Kailea glanced back and found Marcus on his phone. He had dialed 911 and was explaining their location and relaying everything they were seeing. When Marcus hung up, he motioned to Kailea to cover him. She nodded, took a deep breath, tightened her grip on the Glock, and pivoted to squeeze off six shots at the bell tower. This time the shooter responded with a volley of shots in her direction, and she pulled back just in time.

Seeing that Marcus had safely made it across the street, Kailea used the moment to reload. The moment the shooter did the same, she fired off three more shots, then bolted across Thirteenth Street and bounded up the front steps of the church. Marcus was kneeling beside the man sprawled out on the steps, checking his pulse, but she could tell it was too late. He was gone.

Inside the church, the shooting had temporarily stopped, but the screaming had not. On Marcus's signal, the two yanked on the handles of the huge oak doors, only to find them locked from the inside. An instant later, someone inside unloaded an entire magazine at those doors, forcing Kailea and Marcus to retreat around the left side of the building. There they found another set of locked doors and kept moving. Under the cover of a cantilevered roof, Marcus led the way around the corner to the back doors as Kailea guarded his six. Unfortunately, these too were locked.

Once again automatic weapons fire erupted inside. Kailea could hear sirens in the distance. They were faint, but she knew police units and ambulances would soon be approaching from every direction.

"Cover me. I have an idea," Marcus hissed.

"What are you, insane?" she shot back. "There's no way to get in, and the cops will be here any minute. We should hold here until they arrive."

"Agent Curtis, people are dying in there—*my* people. We have to go in now." Marcus didn't wait for an answer. He turned and bolted out into the parking lot.

Kailea tensed. Standing at the corner of the building, she'd be able to see threats emerging from either of two directions. Yet because she was still under the cantilever, she couldn't see the bell tower. Nor could she see any of the third- or fourth-floor windows. Thus she had no way to know who was lying in wait and no way to cover Marcus, who had just raced into the open without explaining his plan.

Sure enough, gunfire opened up above them. Kailea glanced over to see if Marcus was okay but quickly turned back. She knew a shooter could come out the rear doors or along the side of the building at any moment, so she had to stay focused. But it was hard. Behind her she could hear parked cars being shredded by round after round, and she feared for Ryker's safety. Despite the cool November air, sweat was pouring down her face and back. Yet all she could do for now was raise her Glock 22 and brace herself for whatever was coming next.

Just then, she heard the roar of a truck engine coming to life. An instant later came the squeal of tires and the blast of a truck horn. Kailea turned just in time to see a red Ford F-150 roaring across the parking lot and picking up speed. To her horror, she saw Marcus behind the wheel. The man was heading straight for the building.

Kailea dove out of the way just in time.

Marcus didn't slow, much less stop. Instead, as he came flying across the parking lot, he floored the accelerator. Kailea watched as the Ford smashed through the locked doors and screeched to a halt inside the church's rear lobby.

She stood there for several moments, staring at the gaping hole in the wall where the doors used to be. Then, hearing Marcus yelling for her, she forced herself forward, climbed through the wreckage, and found Marcus engaged in a firefight.

The hallway was filled with smoke and the dust of shredded Sheetrock. The overhead lights were flickering. Sparks showered down from exposed wires in the ceiling. Water from a ruptured pipe sprayed everywhere. Through the haze, Kailea spotted Marcus positioned behind the open driver's-side door of the truck. He had his Sig Sauer out, and he was squeezing one round after another at a shadowy figure wearing a ski mask on the other side of the sanctuary.

No one else was visible. Kailea assumed many were dead. But even the wounded weren't about to show themselves. If it were her, she'd have flattened on the floor and desperately tried to take cover under the rows of wooden pews. There was, of course, nothing she or Marcus could do for the wounded until they had neutralized the shooters. But how exactly were they going to do that?

They were completely outgunned. Whoever this guy in the ski mask was, he was using an automatic rifle with a high-capacity magazine capable of holding between sixty and one hundred rounds. All Kailea carried was her service pistol and two magazines, not counting the mag she'd already emptied. Each held fifteen rounds, giving her a total of only thirty shots. Marcus also had just two magazines left, but given that he was using larger, .357-caliber rounds, his magazines held only a dozen rounds. That gave him twenty-four shots, each one as precious as it was irreplaceable.

Kailea felt her Android vibrate. She ignored it and looked at Marcus, only to see him urgently holding up his phone and pointing at her. She pulled her phone out and found a text from him.

Draw fire, Marcus had texted. **Right flank, start shooting, quick. I need better position and angle.**

At first she found it odd Marcus was texting her rather than shouting out commands. Then again, they could barely hear each other in the cacophony, and even if they could, it probably wouldn't be smart to telegraph their precise moves.

Kailea didn't like the thought of being used as bait. Nevertheless, she crouched down and began advancing along the right side of the Ford, hopefully low enough not to be seen, yet high enough to see over the truck into the sanctuary as well as into the large hallway to their left. Every few seconds, Marcus squeezed off another round, then braced for an onslaught in return.

Another text came in from Marcus.

On my signal open fire, he wrote. **I'll crawl toward main doors, center aisle, take him out.**

Kailea stared at the message in disbelief. This guy really was insane. Shaking her head, but without a plan of her own, she texted back.

Fine.

What other choice did she have?

Crossing herself like she'd done as a girl growing up in Brooklyn, she opened the passenger-side door of the truck and, using it as a shield, opened fire.

The moment Marcus got her reply, he dropped to his stomach.

From this vantage point, he could now see dozens of people hiding under the pews. Some faces he recognized. Most he did not. Everyone was shivering in fear. Some were bleeding out. Others lay motionless. And then he saw Marcy.

The little girl was curled up in a fetal position in a beautiful pink dress, covered in blood. Marcus had no idea if it was her own or someone else's. He strained to see if either Carter or Maya were with her but couldn't tell. Regardless, he knew he had to move quickly. Suddenly Marcy's eyes met his. She began to reach out to him. She looked like she was going to call to him. But he immediately put his finger over his lips and motioned for her to stay quiet and still.

With bullets whizzing just above his head, Marcus put the Sig Sauer back in his shoulder holster and began crawling across the wooden floor toward the little girl. Her eyes widened, though she remained frozen and mute, just as he'd instructed. Before he reached her, however, he shifted directions, turning right and crawling down the left-side aisle of the sanctuary as quickly as he could. When he had nearly reached the edge of the main vestibule, he turned right.

Behind him, he could hear his new partner doing her job. She was drawing the shooter's fire and fury, but how long could that last? Kailea was in real danger of running out of ammo or being charged by the attacker with no way to adequately defend herself. Marcus forced himself to move faster, even while having to stay low and out of view.

When he finally reached the center aisle of the sanctuary, he stopped, but only for a moment. He drew his pistol, said a silent prayer, and took a deep breath. Then he popped to his feet, took aim at the shooter, and squeezed off four quick shots.

6

He missed.

The shooter was standing behind the pulpit at the front of the room, a good thirty yards away. He wasn't hit by the new shots, but he had been blindsided. He had obviously thought he was safe from Marcus's direction, since the front doors were locked. Now he was under fire from an unexpected angle.

Enraged, the man in the mask began charging down the center aisle, screaming, weapon up, hunting for a target. And that's when Marcus made his move. Scrambling back to the aisle along the left side of the sanctuary, he whipped around the corner, pressed his back against the side of the second-to-last pew in the row, and silently counted down from five. When he got to zero, he sprang to his feet, wheeled around, and aimed the Sig.

The shooter was exactly where he'd expected him to be. He was standing motionless, at the head of the center aisle, sweeping the vestibule with his AR-15, dumbfounded to find no one there. Marcus fired twice. Both rounds hit their mark. The first entered the shooter's right temple and blew out the other side of his head. The second pierced the man's neck, slicing right through his jugular.

The man instantly collapsed to the floor.

For several seconds, an eerie silence settled over the sanctuary. No one was screaming anymore. No one, in fact, made any sound at all. Marcus yelled, *"Shooter down."* His deep voice echoed beneath the domed ceiling and across the second-floor balconies. Then he called for Kailea, who emerged from behind the Ford and raced to his side.

Marcus motioned for her to check the body, just to be sure. Kailea kicked aside the AR-15, bent down, checked the man's pulse, and shook her head. She picked up the automatic rifle and handed it to Marcus before stripping the dead man of his ammo and giving that to Marcus as well. He told her to check the man's pistol. She did, clearing the chamber and ejecting the mag.

"How many rounds?" Marcus asked.

"Ten," she replied.

Marcus nodded and moved cautiously toward the front of the sanctuary. Sweeping his Sig Sauer from side to side, he scanned for anyone who could still pose a threat. All he found were the dead and wounded.

The nine o'clock service wasn't nearly as heavily attended as the ten thirty service. That had long been a sore spot with Carter and the board of elders. This morning, it was a blessing. The second service was typically standing room only, even in the balconies. Yet as bad as this carnage was, Marcus shuddered at what it could have been had twice as many people been in the building.

"Clear," Marcus said at last, convinced no other shooters were present. The guy in the bell tower could wait.

Then he remembered Marcy. He raced over and found the little girl slipping into shock. Putting his pistol back in its holster, he stripped off his leather jacket, wrapped her in it, and scooped her up, cradling her in his arms. She was trembling. Her eyes were glassy. They needed to get her to the hospital, and fast.

Marcus turned and saw Kailea holster her weapon and begin attending to the most severely wounded. As she did, Marcus thought about what she had just told him. *Ten rounds. Nine in the magazine. One in the chamber.* That was important information. He began visualizing how the brutal crime had likely played out. The man in the ski mask had to have been the one who had killed the usher on the front steps. That would have been his first shot—the shot he and Kailea had heard at the diner. Then the two men—if there were only two—had burst into the church building. One had proceeded to use the Glock to fire four more shots in rapid succession. That explained the four bodies lying in the vestibule.

Five shots.

Five people dead.

Five bullets missing from the magazine.

Ten remained.

At that point, Marcus realized, the lead shooter must have switched to his AR-15. He'd begun shooting up the sanctuary as his partner broke left and raced for the stairs heading for the bell tower to shoot anyone approaching the church building from any angle.

But why? Marcus wondered as he held this precious little girl. *Who were these monsters? And why had they come to shoot up a house of worship?*

He heard someone call his name and turned quickly, scanning every face of every person emerging from their hiding places. That's when he saw his pastor, Carter Emerson. The man was lying off to the right of the stage, and he was writhing in his own blood.

"*Carter!*" he cried as he rushed to the man's side.

Gently laying Marcy down on the front pew, Marcus bent and saw the massive gunshot wound in Emerson's stomach. The man's white shirt and black pin-striped suit were covered in crimson. Marcus immediately began applying pressure to the wound as he assured the man that everything was going to be all right. In truth, Marcus wasn't so sure. Emerson was one tough cookie. He hadn't always been an urban preacher. A million years earlier, he'd been a Green Beret. He'd done three tours in Vietnam and along the way had earned not one but two Purple Hearts for being wounded in battle, as well as a Bronze Star for demonstrating extraordinary valor during a covert operation behind enemy lines in North Vietnam. But that was more than a half century ago.

Just as Kailea reached them, the sound of automatic gunfire again erupted from the bell tower. Marcus directed his partner to continue applying pressure to Carter's wound. As she did, he got up and looked out the nearest window. At least a dozen police cars and several ambulances had arrived on the scene. But rather than racing inside to help, the first responders were having to back up to get out of range of the wrath being rained down on them from above.

"Marcus, I've got this," Kailea assured him. "Go take that guy down."

7

Marcus sprinted to the nearest stairwell.

He bounded up the steps two at a time, reached the second floor, then paused before entering the hallway. He was second-guessing himself now. *Was he absolutely certain there were only two shooters? What if there were more?*

Marcus stuck the barrel of his weapon into the hallway, then pulled it back, wondering if he might draw fire. Nothing happened. He chanced a quick peek around the corner. The hallway looked clear. Hearing heavy fire continuing from the bell tower, he knew he couldn't wait any longer. He took one final brief look but again found the hallway was clear in both directions.

Taking a deep breath, Marcus pivoted around the corner with the AR-15 out in front of him. He moved quickly though quietly down the hallway to the stairwell at the opposite end. As he went, he looked through the windows into each Sunday school classroom. He could not see a single child or teacher. What's more, the lights in every classroom were off.

These were good signs. Marcus had attended this congregation for years.

He'd helped Carter and the elders develop security protocols, and he'd personally taught each teacher what to do if there was ever an active shooter in the building. He knew, therefore, that the children and teachers were all sitting on the floor, huddled along the walls of their classrooms closest to the hallway, heads down, and thus out of immediate sight of anyone in the hallway who might be glancing in the windows. He knew, too, that all the classroom doors would be locked, and when he checked them one by one, sure enough they were. The teachers had followed his protocols to the letter.

Marcus wanted to assure them that everything was going to be okay. They knew his voice and would be grateful to hear it. But as he still didn't know for sure how many shooters he was up against, he couldn't afford to give away the element of surprise. For now, he had to remain silent. The teachers and kids would have to stay hunkered down a little while longer.

When he reached the stairwell on the north end of the building, Marcus worked his way up to the third floor. The shooting continued in short bursts from the bell tower, but each of the church's offices still had to be cleared one by one.

Marcus glanced into the hallway. Finding no one waiting for him, he took a moment and texted an update to Kailea. Then he crept into the hallway and into Carter Emerson's office, AR-15 at the ready. The phones were ringing off the hook, but Carter's private study and his secretary's area were empty. Marcus moved into the adjacent conference room. It, too, was empty. From there, he cleared the church administrator's office, the copy room, the supply room, the office of the Sunday school superintendent, and the "bull pen" where a half-dozen interns from various Baptist seminaries typically worked in cubicles. Fortunately, these were also empty. There was no third shooter. Everyone who was supposed to be in the building was in the sanctuary or locked away in the Sunday school rooms. Marcus could now turn his full attention to the one shooter that remained.

He carefully approached the doorway that opened to stairs leading to the bell tower. With every step closer, the sound of the gunfire grew louder. He reached out for the doorknob but found the door had been locked from the inside. He took the butt of his rifle and smashed it against the knob. It snapped off instantly, yet the door didn't open.

Marcus needed a new plan, and it came to him quickly. He had spent most of the summer as a volunteer, fixing leaks in the 137-year-old church's roof, stripping off old roofing tiles and installing new ones. That experience now came in handy. Removing his jacket and tossing it aside, he slung the rifle over his back and secured it with the shoulder strap. Then he stepped into the office of the Sunday school superintendent, where there were three large windows. The one on the far left was fitted with an air-conditioning unit. The other two were not only locked but painted shut. Marcus found a large metal stapler on the superintendent's desk and used it to punch out one of the windows and scrape away the remaining shards of glass in the large frame.

Tossing the stapler back onto the desk, Marcus climbed out onto the ledge. The November air was chilly, especially with strong breezes coming off the river. He quickly scaled the side of the building until he reached the roof, but there was no clear shot. The bell tower was a good fifteen feet higher than the roof on the main building. So Marcus ran to the center of the roof and scrambled over the large dome that covered the sanctuary, stopping only when he reached the base of the tower.

Three helicopters circled overhead. Marcus could see that one was from the D.C. Metro Police. The other two were from local TV stations. All of them were taking care to remain out of range of the shooter. Marcus sent another text update to Kailea. He told her to call 911 and make sure the cops were fully apprised of what he was doing. He didn't want the police mistaking him for an assailant and taking a shot at him.

A minute later, Kailea wrote back.

They want him alive.

8

Marcus stared at his phone in disbelief.

How exactly was he supposed to take this guy alive? His only objective was to get into that tower as rapidly as possible and take down the shooter at all costs.

Marcus glanced at his watch. It was 9:59 a.m. He wished he'd brought gloves, but in their absence, he blew warm air on his hands to try to keep them from growing stiff. Then he moved to the south side of the tower. There, just as he'd discovered while working on the roof that summer, he found the steel handles that had been bolted into the side of the tower, enabling repairmen to get up there when necessary and work on the bells and their supports and mechanisms. The handles were freezing cold. But he'd only need them for a moment.

Marcus glanced at his watch again.

Four seconds to go.

Three.

Two.

One.

The church bells began to ring out, as they did at the top of every hour. At that proximity, they were as deafening as they were beautiful, which was exactly what Marcus needed. Seizing his moment, he scrambled up the side of the tower, spotted the shooter, and lunged through the arched opening at the top.

Marcus landed directly on top of the man, catching him by surprise and causing his weapon to drop to the street. He grabbed the man's head and drove it hard into the wall, trying to knock him unconscious. He didn't succeed, but in the process he ripped off the man's ski mask. He was younger than Marcus, but it was impossible to tell how much. He had a dark complexion. His head was shaved bald. He was built like a beast, and there was both shock and murder in his eyes.

Seizing the initiative, Marcus thrust his knee into the shooter's groin and sent his right fist into his nose. Then Marcus drove his left fist into the shooter's jaw. That should have knocked him out cold. But it did not. Instead, the younger man fired one gloved fist into Marcus's stomach, the other into his ribs. The speed and power of the combination drove Marcus across the confined space and nearly knocked his wind out. He landed hard, sprawled out across the closed steel access hatch. His AR-15 dug painfully into his back.

The shooter immediately dove forward and drove his elbow into Marcus's chest so hard Marcus gasped for air. Roughly six-foot-three and well over two hundred pounds, this guy was taller than Marcus by at least a couple of inches, and heavier by a good twenty to twenty-five pounds, and he took full advantage of his larger size as he rained down blow after blow with his massive fists. Marcus tried to protect his head and face, but it was a losing battle. He knew he had to turn the tables. He had to go on offense before he was knocked unconscious. But he was pinned down and barely able to move.

Finally, in near desperation, Marcus shot his right arm up. He grabbed the back of the shooter's head, yanked it forward, and head-butted him as hard as he could. Then he drove his left thumb into the man's eye socket and squeezed. Marcus could barely hear the screams over the bells, but he could feel the man's body convulse and his head snap back, and in that instant, Marcus regained the freedom of movement he so badly needed.

Swiveling his hips and throwing his right leg violently to the left, Marcus managed to throw the shooter off-balance just enough for him to maneuver his back up off the steel hatch. From there, Marcus heaved his torso forward. The moment he reached an upright position, he grabbed the rifle, still strapped to his back, and swung it around with all the force he could muster. The butt of the rifle smashed directly into the man's nose. Marcus felt the cartilage implode. Blood sprayed everywhere, but Marcus wasn't finished. He flipped the man onto his stomach and smashed the butt of the rifle into the back of his neck. His face crashed into the steel hatch. Then, just as the bells stopped ringing, Marcus whipped the gun around, drove the barrel into the back of the man's left knee, and pulled the trigger. An instant later, he fired the gun into the back of the man's right knee. The sound of the two explosions echoed across the city, and as suddenly as it had all begun, it was over.

The man went limp. He was unconscious and bleeding profusely, and he wouldn't be walking again anytime soon, but he was alive. Marcus staggered backward, leaned against the inner wall of the tower, and fought to catch his breath. Finally he pulled out his phone and called Kailea.

"Shooter down," he said between gasps. "But alive. Get the medics up here."

"Will do," she said. "And then you'd better get back down here."

"Why? What happened?"

"I'm afraid I've got some bad news."

Marcus feared what she was going to say but made her say it anyway.

"Mrs. Emerson was wounded," Kailea said after a long pause. "They're taking her right into surgery."

Marcus winced. "And Carter?"

There was another long pause. "I'm sorry, Marcus," she finally said. "He didn't make it."

9

The twin-turbine Mi-8 helicopter touched down at almost 8 p.m. local time.

Even before its rotors had finished spinning, Nikolay Kropatkin bolted out the side door, briefcase in hand. With three members of his security detail flanking him, the forty-two-year-old acting director of the FSB raced up a freshly shoveled and salted pathway from the helipad to the back entrance of the personal residence of the newly installed Russian leader.

Once inside, Kropatkin was searched by members of the presidential security detail and asked to step through a magnetometer. His briefcase was put through an X-ray machine, and its contents were thoroughly searched by hand. Only then was he allowed to proceed, escorted by the chief of proto-col. His detail stayed behind. Following the triple assassinations of Russia's president, prime minister, and the former head of the FSB a little more than a month earlier, security procedures had been tightened considerably. No longer were any exceptions made. Not even for family or the president's most trusted advisors.

Working their way down the immense marble hallways of the sprawling palace—reportedly built for a cost of some $200 million (though Kropatkin knew the real figure was nearly twice that much)—the intelligence chief was surprised to see that they were not headed to the administrative wing but to the residential wing. He soon noticed the scent of chlorine and could feel the humidity in the air increase considerably. Kropatkin was led through a set of double doors and found himself standing before an Olympic-size indoor pool. A lone figure was methodically doing laps while six large and heavily armed men in business suits stood watchful and tense.

"*Nikolay Vladimirovich, come, join me. The water is warm.*" The baritone voice of Mikhail Petrovsky boomed and echoed across the cavernous domed annex.

Kropatkin demurred.

Petrovsky finished his lap and bounded out of the water, grabbed a fresh towel from a nearby stack, and dried off his face and dark-brown mop of hair. For a man rapidly approaching his sixty-fifth birthday, a man who not two months earlier was merely the nation's minister of defense, Petrovsky was in remarkably good physical shape. He not only swam a hundred laps a day, he also ran upwards of ten kilometers every other day.

"So what brings the nation's top spy for such an urgent visit on a cold and forbidding night—a Sunday, no less?" the Russian president asked as he wrapped a towel around his waist.

"Marcus Ryker," Kropatkin said.

"The American?"

"Yes, sir."

"Please tell me he's dead."

"Sorry, but no, Mikhail Borisovich."

"Then what?"

"Ryker is back in the news—a hero, it would seem."

"What are you talking about?"

"Details are sketchy, but a few hours ago, two men entered a church building in Washington, D.C., and began shooting up the place. Police were called. They were on their way. But it seems that Ryker and a woman were nearby and decided not to wait. They headed into the church, killed one of the shooters, and incapacitated the other. The media isn't reporting the name of the woman, but Marcus Ryker is now the lead story on every news service in the world."

"Incapacitated?" Petrovsky asked. "Meaning what?"

"Ryker blew the guy's kneecap off. Actually, he blew them both off."

"Was it a terrorist operation or something local?"

"It's not clear yet—the investigation is just getting under way."

"Then why come all the way out here to tell me?" the president asked as he headed into a locker room.

Kropatkin followed. "There's more to the story, sir. A senior American official was attending the church when the shooting began."

"Who?"

"Janelle Thomas—she was the deputy secretary of state."

"*Was?*"

"They killed her," Kropatkin said.

"Why was she there?"

"Reuters is reporting she was a member of the church. Lived close by. Attended every Sunday she was in town."

"Was she the target?"

"Hard to say. Early reports say the shooters were skinheads, fascists from the southern United States who hate blacks, Jews, and Muslims. Thomas was black, but so are most of the people who attend the church."

"I still don't understand why you couldn't have told me all this in our regular briefing tomorrow," Petrovsky said.

"It's Ryker. Reuters is also reporting that he now works for DSS."

"What's that?"

"The Diplomatic Security Service," Kropatkin replied. "It's a branch of the State Department, responsible for protecting American foreign service officers, embassies, consulates, and the like."

"I don't understand," said Petrovsky, still toweling off. "Didn't the

American president assure me just a few weeks ago that Ryker was a private citizen, that he was retired, on his own, with no government ties whatsoever?"

"He did, sir—and that's my point. Clarke also told you that Ryker couldn't have had anything to do with the assassinations here. He insisted that Ryker left Moscow with Senator Dayton's entourage, flew back to Washington, and had to be hospitalized with some mysterious illness. Now, suddenly, Ryker's well enough to be a federal agent, take down bad guys, and get his face plastered all over the news?"

"Clarke was lying to me?"

"I don't know, sir, but something isn't right."

"No, it's not—find out what, Nikolay Vladimirovich, and do it quickly."

10

"My sons, I have something very difficult to tell you."

It was nearly midnight when Hossein Ansari dropped the bombshell.

"I am afraid my days have come to an end."

No one spoke. The Supreme Leader's inner circle simply stared at their octogenarian spiritual guide in disbelief. As ever, he was dressed in his signature brown flowing robe and black turban. He sat on a mound of pillows covered with thick wool blankets. He had not looked well for some time. Tonight, he looked much worse. His skin was pale and slightly jaundiced. He had lost weight in the past week. His typically neatly trimmed gray beard now looked unkempt, even a bit wild, and the pale-blue eyes behind his wire-rimmed glasses had never looked more tired.

They had assumed his health had been affected by a series of wrenching setbacks, beginning with the triple assassination in Moscow just over six weeks earlier that had taken the lives of Tehran's three most trusted Russian allies.

This had been closely followed by disaster in the East China Sea. They were all reeling from these events, and the initial shock had eventually morphed into searing rage. For none of them was this truer than for Ansari, but he was now suggesting something worse was at play.

"Over the summer I received some disappointing news," Ansari said without emotion. "I was diagnosed with pancreatic cancer. Stage four. My oncologists advised me that surgery and chemotherapy were options. But they caught it late. Neither of these measures will spare me from the inevitable. They would merely prolong my agony, and thus I have chosen to decline such treatment."

The chamber remained eerily quiet.

Ansari continued. "My sons, I have no more than two months to live, if that. But I want you to know how deeply I cherish you all. We have been through a great deal. Together, we have carried on the Revolution in a manner, I believe, that would have made Imam Khomeini proud of us—very proud indeed."

Ansari suddenly lapsed into a coughing fit. He waved off their efforts to assist him. Rather, he reached for a nearby cup of tea, took a sip, then set it down again and wiped his mouth with a handkerchief.

"We have accomplished more than our adversaries could have imagined," he said softly. "Our Persian kingdom has seized no fewer than four Arab capitals. Through our Hezbollah proxies in Lebanon, we have effectively gained control of Beirut. Through our Houthi proxies in Yemen, we have all but consolidated our control of Sana'a. As a result of our strategic alliance with Moscow, we have gained operational control of Damascus. And of course, with the withdrawal of the Great Satan from Iraq, and after an enormous investment of funds into our Shia brothers there, we have come to dominate if not yet completely control the fortunes of Baghdad. Allah has granted us tremendous—*tremendous*—success, and these are by no means our only gains. Our investments in Hamas have paid spectacular dividends in Gaza, as have our investments in Turkey and Qatar. These, as well as our efforts to drive nearly all of the Great Satan's forces out of Afghanistan, I consider among my greatest joys. And yet there is one more objective I long to achieve before I go."

As commander of the Iranian Revolutionary Guard Corps, Mahmoud Entezam sat directly across from the Supreme Leader, and he did not like what he was hearing. Only fifty-three, Entezam was the youngest general ever to run the IRGC. He had been repeatedly promoted to reward his many operational successes, and in this, he had taken great pride, as had his bride, who happened to be the ayatollah's highly favored niece. However, the horrific events of the last months had been the most difficult of his entire life and career. After the catastrophe in the East China Sea, Entezam had immediately offered to resign. Privately, he had even contemplated taking his own life, so profound was his humiliation and his shame. Only the absolute insistence of the Supreme Leader that he in no way considered Entezam to blame for the Americans' perfidy—along with his robust private assurances that Ansari was grooming Entezam to one day serve in high elected office in the regime, possibly even as president—had brought the IRGC commander back from the brink of despair and given him the strength to continue in the regime's service.

But this stunning new development could change everything. The last thing they could afford right now was a power struggle if the nation's Supreme Leader really was dying. The country's economy was already far too fragile. Oil prices were too low and the American economic sanctions had taken a terrible, and continuing, toll. The regime was hemorrhaging cash. Inflation was spiking, as was the unemployment rate. Protests were breaking out all over the country. The people were demanding increased subsidies for bread—subsidies the government could not afford—and sweeping political liberalization the government would never accept.

In Entezam's assessment, it was only the moral authority and unparalleled leadership skills of Hossein Ansari, honed over decades of palace intrigue and tectonic shifts in the geopolitical sphere, that kept the regime intact and the country from exploding in a full-scale civil war. What's more, it was only Ansari's raw political power that had kept Entezam from losing his job and possibly his head. He had long suspected other senior officials were gunning for him, especially now. What would happen when Ansari was gone?

11

If Ansari was truly dying, a succession battle was coming, the first in decades.

And as the old man's thoughts drifted a bit, Entezam studied the faces of the wolves around him.

To his right was Yadollah Afshar. At sixty-one, the president of the Islamic Republic of Iran was a cruel and insanely ambitious man whom Entezam thoroughly despised. Yet he was beloved by the ayatollah and many of the mullahs, and Entezam wondered if the man—himself a Shia cleric who had studied in seminary in Qom under Ansari—might see himself as a potential successor to the Supreme Leader. That would be a disaster, but it could not be ruled out.

To Entezam's left was Ali Mansur, the newly appointed deputy director of the IRGC. Having served with great distinction leading his fellow Revolutionary Guards in one battle after another against ISIS and al Qaeda forces in Syria, Mansur, too, was a favorite of the Supreme Leader. Only forty-one years old, he was tall, fit, strikingly handsome, happily married, and the father of five sons and two daughters. Mansur was without question an exceedingly capable soldier and intelligence operative. But he was not Entezam's first choice as deputy commander. There were at least a dozen men under Entezam's command who were more capable and more experienced—men he himself had trained, men who were loyal to him. Yet when the position became open, in a rare act of intervention, the Supreme Leader had quietly summoned Entezam to his chambers and requested, as a personal favor, that he elevate Mansur to the role.

It was all but unheard of to have the nation's spiritual leader involve himself in such personnel decisions, and it immediately made Entezam suspicious. Why had Ansari made such a request? Did he have a connection to Mansur of which Entezam was unaware? Was it possible President Afshar was maneuvering a loyal ally into position before launching a decapitating strike against Entezam? The fact that Entezam had no idea bothered him all the more.

The only other man in the room was Dr. Haydar Abbasi. The Supreme Leader had asked the chief of the nation's space and satellite directorate to brief him and the others on the tremendous progress Abbasi and his team were making on upgrading Iran's long-range ballistic missiles, progress based entirely on stunning new test data from the North Koreans. Yet Abbasi was hardly a member of the inner circle. Why, then, would the ayatollah include him on a night when such important news was being revealed?

"Your Holiness, tell us what to do," President Afshar said softly. "How can we help you finish your journey?"

The gesture evoked a smile—weak but most sincere—from the eighty-four-year-old leader of the Revolution. "Thank you, my son," Ansari said, reaching for another sip of tea and swallowing with some difficulty. "I have summoned you to my private study, this place I have come to so love, to express to you all my dying wishes."

"Whatever you ask, my lord, we will do it," Entezam said before Afshar could.

"You are most kind," Ansari replied. "I have only three requests."

Each man leaned forward to catch every word.

"First, above all else, you must promise me you will continue in earnest our quest for the Persian Bomb. Build it. Buy it. Steal it. But do not settle for a single weapon. You must acquire an entire arsenal—no matter the cost. Is this clear?"

They all nodded.

"Understand this: Iran will never be a great power—nor shall we ever resurrect the glory of the Persian Empire—until we have this ultimate power in our hands. We cannot annihilate the Americans or wipe the criminal Zionist entity off the map until we have this power. Nor can we ever hasten the coming of Imam al-Mahdi, peace be upon him . . ."

"Peace be upon him," they repeated.

". . . until we have the arsenal of the apocalypse in our hands. Never lose sight of this divine mission."

All four men voiced their solemn assurances, Entezam loudest of all.

"Second, you must never allow the Palestinian people or their leaders to be lured into a false and final peace deal with the Zionists or the Americans. *Never.* Do not worry about our dear friend and brother Ismail Ziad. He has personally given me his oath. He will go to his grave without betraying our cause. We have paid him well. And I've assured him his widow and sons will be well paid too. But Ismail Ziad is an old man. Who will lead the Palestinian people after him? Will a warrior rise from the shadows to unify the people and lead them into an all-out jihad against the Zionists? Inshallah. Yet what if a Judas appears instead, ready to sell out his people for thirty pieces of silver? My sons, I fear that after Ismail's departure from this life, a new leader will emerge who is exhausted by the conflict, mesmerized by the Zionists' lies, bedazzled by the Americans' bribes, and ready to undermine all we have prayed, worked, and prepared for. You must never let this happen."

No one nodded. No one even spoke a word. Yet there was no doubt they had all received and accepted the message.

Then Ansari uttered his final request, and there was a fire in the man's eyes that Entezam had not seen in months. "Children, listen—listen to my voice. The desert sands are now slipping through my fingers. Soon I will face the Day of Judgment, where my good deeds must outweigh my sins. So as my third request, I ask you to grant me a gift I can take with me when I go to face Allah. Avenge for me the blood of Alireza al-Zanjani, our beloved son, who gave his life for our cause. Give no rest to those responsible for his murder. Send them to the fires of hell—and for the sake of Allah, do it soon, while I still can hear of it and smile.

"My final request, my sons, is this: do whatever is necessary to kill the Israeli prime minister and the American president. Kill Reuven Eitan and Andrew Clarke."

12

THE WHITE HOUSE, WASHINGTON, D.C.—17 NOVEMBER

"Gentlemen, POTUS will see you now."

At precisely 7 a.m. local time, President Clarke's executive secretary nodded toward the open door. The Secret Service agent standing post stepped aside, and four men rose from antique chairs and headed into the Oval Office.

Richard Stephens, the director of the Central Intelligence Agency, entered first. Almost sixty-five, the former three-term senior senator from Arizona had served for almost a decade as chairman of the Senate Intelligence Committee. Along the way, he had emerged as the widely respected dean of the U.S. intel community even though he was technically outranked by the director of national intelligence. The DNI, however, was not present that morning. He was traveling with Secretary of State Margaret Whitney on a five-country trip through Belgium, the Baltics, and Germany, still trying to calm Washington's NATO allies after the crisis the Kremlin had sparked just two months earlier.

Behind Stephens was Lieutenant General Barry Evans, the president's national security advisor. Now sixty-two, the retired Army three-star had first made a name for himself helping Norman Schwarzkopf plan and execute the liberation of Kuwait. From there, Evans had gone on to run U.S. Special Operations Command and later served as deputy commander of Central Command. Bitter at not receiving his fourth star, he'd retired and become a military analyst for FoxNews and written two military thrillers. The first had done quite well. It had even been optioned by Hollywood, though it had not yet been produced.

Bill McDermott entered next. The forty-six-year-old deputy national security advisor was a former Marine. He'd enlisted after finishing Yale and served three tours of duty in Afghanistan and two in Iraq. For a time he'd commanded the unit Marcus Ryker and Pete Hwang had served in. Upon returning to civilian life, McDermott had gone back to school, earned an MBA from Wharton and a master's in national security studies from Georgetown, before making a killing on Wall Street. Only then had he let himself be drafted back into government service.

Marcus was the last man in and the youngest of the four. The last time he'd been in the Oval Office, he'd been serving on the Presidential Protective Detail. Coming back stirred up memories he didn't care to revisit. He'd sworn to himself that he'd never return. Now, once again, events had changed everything.

The president was sitting behind the *Resolute* desk, absorbed in the *Wall Street Journal*. The four men walked over to the couches in the center of the room and waited. A moment later, Clarke removed his reading glasses, came around the desk, motioned for them to take their seats, and took his own by the fireplace. A steward entered through a side door and served coffee.

"Agent Ryker, America owes you a tremendous debt of gratitude," Clarke began. "Again."

"Well, it wasn't just me, sir," Marcus demurred. "Kailea Curtis did an incredible job. Just wish we'd gotten there sooner."

"A whole lot more people would have died if you two hadn't gotten there when you did. But let me extend my condolences to you on the loss of your pastor. From what I understand, you two were very close."

"We were, Mr. President. Thank you."

"I tried to call his widow . . ."

"Maya," Marcus offered.

"Right, well, I called her last night, but they said she was still in surgery."

"I just came from the hospital, sir," Marcus noted. "She's under heavy sedation."

"When will the memorial service be?"

"Probably Saturday, but I think Maya will have to make that call."

"I'd like to attend."

"That would mean a great deal to everyone, Mr. President."

Clarke then turned to his national security advisor. "Where are we with the latest casualty count?" he asked.

"Nine dead, not counting the shooter," General Evans said. "Twenty-seven wounded, including six critically, several of whom might not make it."

Marcus could see the anger in the president's eyes.

"And to top it all off, we lost Janelle Thomas?" Clarke asked.

"I'm afraid so," Evans confirmed. "It's a staggering loss to our team and to me personally, sir. Few people have worked more closely on crafting your Middle East peace plan than Janelle, and she was supposed to fly out with me Tuesday night to help sell it."

"So what was it?" Clarke asked. "Wrong place, wrong time?"

Evans turned to Marcus. "You were there," he said. "What's your take?"

"Mr. President, I believe Deputy Secretary Thomas was the intended target of the attack," Marcus replied.

"Based on what?"

"Well, sir, it's now clear these were professional terrorists. The guy I killed was from Qatar. He traveled to Iraq and joined al Qaeda after we liberated the country. Killed a lot of Americans. Then moved to Syria and joined ISIS. Bugged out to Europe just before the Caliphate fell. Apparently spent most of his time in Italy or Greece; then about six months ago he just disappeared off the grid."

"And the guy you took down in the bell tower?"

"He isn't talking, but his fingerprints are. Born in Turkey. Joined al Qaeda. Fought in Afghanistan. Later in Iraq. Then joined ISIS in Syria. Best we can tell, that's where the two met. Then he, too, drops off the grid. We have no idea where he spent the last year, but our operating theory is that they were together for part of that time."

"And Janelle?" Clarke asked.

"Interviews of surviving witnesses indicate that most of the killings appeared random. The Qatari was spraying machine-gun fire everywhere. But with the deputy secretary, everyone says the guy stopped, studied her carefully, and asked her name. When she gave it, he shot her four times in the chest and once in the head. No one else was singled out like that."

Thus far, McDermott had just been taking notes. Now he looked up and said, "Since then, sir, the FBI was able to crack his phone. They found emails he'd received from overseas—Greece, actually—with pictures of Janelle, the address of the church, and the starting time of the service."

The president set down the cup of now-cold coffee in his hands. He hadn't taken a sip yet, nor was he going to. He turned to the DCI. "Tell me why they went after her."

"I can't, Mr. President," Stephens replied. "Not yet."

"Is this part of the retaliation you guys have been warning me was coming?"

"Perhaps, but it's too soon to draw any conclusions."

"Has anyone claimed responsibility?"

"No, sir."

"Do we have any evidence the Russians were involved?"

"No."

"What about the Iranians or the North Koreans?"

Stephens shook his head. So did Evans and McDermott. Marcus had his suspicions, but for the moment he kept those to himself. Looking unconvinced, the president considered their answer as he flipped through the presidential daily brief, the CIA's morning summary of the highest priority global intelligence.

Then he suddenly turned and looked up at Marcus again. "You know, Ryker, it wasn't that long ago I thought you were a traitor."

"Apparently you weren't alone," Marcus replied before completely thinking it through.

"Quite right," Clarke said. "And now here you are. Guess we owe you an apology as well as our thanks."

"Not at all. Based on the intel you had at the time, I know my actions looked bad."

"They did," Clarke replied. "Very bad." The president studied Marcus's face.

"Sir, at the risk of sounding self-serving, may I change the topic?" Marcus asked after an awkward pause.

"It depends," Clarke said. "What've you got?"

"Two things, sir. One, I realize, is above my pay grade, but I'd like to recommend Tyler Reed to be your next deputy secretary of state."

"Our ambassador to Russia?"

"Yes, sir. With Luganov gone and Petrovsky now in power, a new ambassador to Moscow is probably in order. And I was quite impressed with Reed when I worked with him. He's smart. Savvy. Cool under pressure. And I think he gets what you're trying to do, sir. Just a thought, but given how important your peace plan is, I'm thinking you might need to replace Mrs. Thomas rather quickly."

"And the second matter?" the president asked, noncommittal.

"Well, sir, I need to recommend you give your speech unveiling your peace plan from here in the Oval Office, not from Jerusalem, and certainly not on the Temple Mount."

"Hold it right there, Agent Ryker. That's way outside your mandate," the CIA director admonished his newest hire.

"With all due respect, sir, I don't believe it is," Marcus replied. "You guys hired me to counter the blowback we all knew was coming after our recent operations against North Korea and Iran. Let's be clear: that blowback started yesterday, and it's going to get worse. Mr. President, I respect your commitment to forging Mideast peace, and your plan deserves a hearing, but strictly from a security perspective, the idea of putting you in Jerusalem right now is a mistake."

"Noted," Clarke said with an edge of irritation. "Now if you'll excuse us, Agent Ryker, you're dismissed."

13

When Marcus was gone, Clarke turned to Stephens.

"Not exactly a wallflower, is he?" the president asked.

"No, sir," said Stephens.

McDermott had to agree. Marcus had never been shy about speaking his mind.

"But he's right about Reed," General Evans interjected. "Bill and I discussed him last night on a secure call to Berlin with Secretary Whitney. We all think he'd be ideal."

The president looked to McDermott. "Meg's already on board?"

"One hundred percent," McDermott said. "And she recommends we move fast."

"How fast?"

"She'd like to order Reed back to Washington immediately and make a formal announcement in the next few days."

"Why the rush?"

"She believes it would send a strong message that you won't be intimidated by terrorists or let your agenda be derailed."

"And you agree?"

"I do, sir."

"Any red flags?" Clarke asked the CIA director.

Stephens shook his head. "None. Reed was thoroughly vetted before being sent to Russia, and he's performed ably every day since."

"Fine. Get him and his family on a plane pronto," Clarke said.

"Will do, sir," Evans responded. "Now can we talk about your speech?"

"Forget it," Clarke said. "I'm going to Jerusalem, and that's final."

"Sir, Ryker does have a point," Evans noted.

"I don't want to hear it, Barry. You guys do your jobs and I'll be just fine," Clarke pushed back. "You leave for the region tomorrow night?"

"Yes, sir."

"Jerusalem first?"

"Actually, I go to Ramallah first, then double back and meet with the Israelis."

"Then what?"

"Amman, Manama, Doha, Abu Dhabi, Muscat, Riyadh, and Cairo—followed by London, Paris, and Moscow."

"Twelve cities in ten days? Goodness," said Clarke. "You're certainly working awfully hard for a peace plan you don't really believe in."

McDermott was stunned by how cold the comment was.

"I do believe in it, sir," Evans said calmly.

"No, you don't, Barry, and you haven't from the beginning."

"With respect, sir, I believe the plan is not only impressive but historic."

"And yet . . . ?"

McDermott shifted in his seat. He'd spent hours discussing the general's deep concerns with him, even encouraging Evans to be more forthcoming with the president about those concerns. But this hardly seemed the time or the place. Shouldn't the president discuss this with General Evans one-on-one?

"Permission to speak freely, sir?" asked the general, ever the military man.

"Come on, Barry—just say what you have to say," the president ordered.

"Sir, my team and I drafted this plan, just as you asked. But I've maintained from the beginning that the timing is wrong. Neither the Israelis nor the Palestinian leadership are ready to make peace. But honestly, it's not the Israelis I'm most worried about at the moment. It's the Palestinians."

"Why?"

"Because they have no interest in coming back to the negotiating table right now. And frankly, to Ryker's point, I'm worried we could see an explosion of new terrorism, perhaps even another Palestinian intifada."

"That's where you're wrong, Barry. This is *precisely* the moment to unveil this plan. The Russians, North Koreans, and Iranians are back on their heels. The Gulf States are warming toward Israel. The Israelis know I love them and won't let any harm come to them. And the Palestinian regime is weak and divided and desperate to give something concrete to their people. That's why we need to go on offense—*now*. So I don't want to hear any more of this talk about changing venues. I'm going to Jerusalem. And that's final."

14

Marcus climbed into the passenger side of a black Chevy Impala.

"Where to, chief?" Kailea asked from behind the wheel of the government sedan.

"DSS headquarters."

Kailea nodded. They pulled away from the curb and drove in silence for a few minutes, weaving in and out of rush-hour traffic, until she asked, "How'd it go in there?"

"POTUS still wants to go to Jerusalem."

"And you think that's crazy."

"He's the president, not me."

"So we're still heading out tomorrow night with Evans?"

"Apparently."

"And yet we missed all of yesterday's briefings."

It was true. They had an enormous amount of material to absorb and internalize, and barely thirty-six hours to do it in. They had spent most of the previous day at the crime scene, interviewing witnesses and being interviewed themselves, not just by D.C. detectives but by the FBI and the investigators from DSS's department of internal affairs. Only well after nightfall had they had time to get a quick bite to eat, then head to George Washington University Hospital to see how Maya Emerson was doing. But Carter's widow had just gotten out of surgery and had still been in recovery. There was no way they were going to be able to see or talk with her that night. So Marcus had insisted that they visit everyone who had been wounded at the church and taken to G.W. Some were still in surgery themselves or under heavy sedation. One patient they were able to see was nine-year-old Marcy, grieving her grandfather and waiting for word on Maya. Marcus held the sobbing girl for more than an hour before returning her to the care of Carter's secretary.

Then there were those who had succumbed to their injuries. Marcus and Kailea had sat with their husbands and wives, children and grandchildren, cousins and friends and neighbors. They'd apologized for not being able to do more. It was nearly two in the morning when Marcus, drained and exhausted, had gotten back to his apartment.

When they arrived at DSS headquarters in Arlington, Virginia, Kailea parked in a reserved space. The two cleared security and found a glum-looking Pete Hwang waiting for them in the lobby. Pete was not flying with them to Israel the following night. Instead, he was scheduled for another surgery on his wounded arm. After that, he'd be assigned to the DSS operations center, he said. In the meantime, he was supposed to get up to speed with the rest of them.

"Haven't spent this much time in hospitals since I left medicine," he said without humor as he led them to a conference room where they joined the rest of the detail. The three of them sat together. Marcus and Kailea were singled out by the director, who praised their heroism and led the team in a standing ovation. Then the briefing got started.

"Hey, will you do me a favor? Take good notes," Marcus whispered to his best friend as the group took a deep dive into logistics for the London leg of the trip. "I need a moment."

Marcus excused himself and found a men's room down the hall. He washed his hands thoroughly and splashed warm water on his forehead, cheeks, and neck, then dried himself off with several paper towels and looked at himself in the mirror. Though he was tired, his eyes were no longer bloodshot, as they'd been the night he'd jumped out of the G4 over St. Petersburg. He was sleeping well these days, eating better, working out, and overall feeling far healthier than he had in years. He ran his hand through his sandy-blond hair. It was short again, the way he liked it, though not nearly as short as the buzz cut he'd gotten at boot camp on Parris Island.

His rugged, chiseled face—the gift of his father's Dutch DNA—was freshly shaved, though the scars he'd acquired over the past several weeks were clearly visible, reminders of his violent reentry into the service of the U.S. government. One ran just above his right eyebrow. Another ran down the left side of his face, near his jawline. Two more crossed his neck. There were days he wondered if he should grow a beard. That would cover all but the scar over his eye. Elena had always hated beards. So had his mother and his then-mother-in-law. He'd never been sure he'd look good with one anyway, so there had been no percentage in offending the three most important women in his life. On the other hand, he hadn't had these scars when Elena was still alive. But he had no idea if DSS agents were allowed to grow beards, and he didn't want to embarrass himself by asking around. All the men back in that conference room were clean-shaven. Why rock the boat so soon after climbing aboard?

As he stood alone in the men's room, he couldn't help but wonder if all this was a mistake. Maybe everything was moving too fast. Maybe he wasn't ready to head back into the field. Besides Pete, he didn't know a single person on the detail—not even Agent Curtis, though he'd been impressed with her skills so far. The truth was, Marcus had been out of the protection business for too long. He wasn't familiar with DSS culture or protocols. And the stakes could not be higher. Whoever had just taken out the deputy secretary of state wasn't finished. They were coming back for more, and in this game, there was no margin for error.

15

Dark thunderheads were rolling in.

The winds were picking up. The temperature was dropping. There were no tourists to be found. Few locals either. It wasn't a particularly significant day on the Muslim calendar. It was merely a Monday, and a late-afternoon storm was bearing down on the city where the old man and nine generations of his family had been born and raised.

Amin al-Azzam exited the Al-Aqsa Mosque with the help of his most trusted aide and a hand-carved wooden cane that his father had bequeathed to him on his deathbed. Together, the two men—the eighty-one-year-old Sunni cleric and his forty-one-year-old son-in-law—worked their way across the plaza. With some difficulty, al-Azzam climbed the steps and passed a small grove of olive trees that he had planted in his youth.

"Come, father, let us sit for a spell," said the younger man. "You need your rest."

"It is not rest that I need, my son," al-Azzam replied, though winded and experiencing great pain in his knees. "It's privacy. I have something important to discuss with you. But it is very sensitive, and we must be alone, far from prying eyes or ears."

"Then let me get you inside."

They soon stepped out of the chilly autumn air into the relative warmth of the octagonal shrine known in Arabic as *Qubbat al-Sakhrah* and in English as the Dome of the Rock. They were certainly alone now. The guards employed by the Jerusalem Islamic Waqf—the foundation tasked with administrating the entire thirty-seven-acre plaza and its various buildings—had not only cleared the ancient facility of all people but had swept every nook and cranny for listening devices, as they did three times a week.

The younger man helped his elder to his favorite corner, and together they sat on the thick, handwoven carpet, behind an immense marble pillar. It was here that the Grand Mufti of Jerusalem—one of the most revered Muslim clerics in the region—liked to come to think and pray and read and meditate. It was here that Amin al-Azzam came to get away from all the noise and the pressures of daily life. And more than any other place, this was where he liked to whisper instructions to the man who had married his beloved youngest daughter, Yasmine.

Hussam Mashrawi was more than family and far more than a mere aide. He was an impressive scholar in his own right, a faithful scribe and personal secretary. He served as the Grand Mufti's emissary to the rest of the Muslim world. Though they had graduated four decades apart, they were both alumni of Al-Azhar University in Cairo—the Harvard of Sunni Islam. Both had graduated at the top of their class. Both had gone on to earn doctorates in Sharia law. Indeed, al-Azzam had hired the young man fresh out of Azhar, and the two had worked side by side for nearly two decades.

In big ways and small, the two men seemed almost supernaturally aligned. Aside from Arabic, their mother tongue, both men were fluent in Farsi, Hebrew, English, French, and Greek, both classical and contemporary. Both had married after finishing their education, and both at the age of twenty-five. Both had purchased modest apartments in Jerusalem's Muslim

Quarter, within walking distance of the Al-Aqsa Mosque, shortly after getting married, and both still lived in the same homes today. Both of their
wives had suffered two miscarriages each. Yet for both couples, the sorrow
of unfulfilled pregnancy had been followed by the healthy, joyful births of
five children—one boy and four girls each.

Several years earlier, a writer for the *New York Times Magazine* had
shadowed the two men for a profile she was working on. When the eight-
thousand-word cover story was published, al-Azzam had chuckled at one
particular line, that he and his son-in-law "must have undergone a Vulcan
mind meld at some point, so unified are their views on theology and politics
and even where in the Old City to buy the best baklava.

"Study the wedding pictures of al-Azzam and those of Mashrawi, and—
setting aside the fact that one set is in black and white and the others are
in color—one would swear that the two men even looked alike on the day
they took their vows," the profile continued. "Even today, both men sport
narrow goatees and pencil-thin mustaches that look so similar, one might
be forgiven for thinking they go to the same barber (though, for the record,
they don't)."

The Grand Mufti had had the article framed and mounted on the wall in
his office. No foreign visitor left without being shown the story. Indeed, the
older man often mused that the similarities between himself and Mashrawi
must be why his beloved Yasmine had fallen so madly in love with the boy.

In reality, however, there were far more differences between the two than
al-Azzam cared to notice. Among the most superficial: Hussam Mashrawi
actually knew two more languages than his father-in-law—Spanish and
Russian. Yet he very purposefully never used either language in the older
man's presence, not wanting to risk upstaging one of the most esteemed
leaders in the Islamic world.

Far more importantly, the Grand Mufti was secretly a moderate when it
came to relations with the Jews. In public, al-Azzam positioned himself as a
hard-liner. Privately, however, he strongly supported a two-state solution to
the conflict between the Israelis and Palestinians and even met from time
to time with senior Israeli government leaders and intelligence officials,

discreetly providing them much-needed insights into the latest trend lines and fissures in Palestinian society and sometimes even privately fuming against Palestinian leaders who had turned down every offer of statehood since the U.N. Partition Plan of 1947.

Hussam Mashrawi, by contrast, positioned himself in public as a voice of reason, yet the truth was far darker. Hussam Mashrawi was secretly far more radical than either his wife or father-in-law could possibly have imagined.

16

Hussam Mashrawi was not poor.

He was not uneducated. Neither was he an orphan or someone who had been physically, emotionally, or sexually abused as a child or in his teenage years.

To the contrary, he had been born to a large and well-to-do Palestinian family in Nablus, the third-largest city in the West Bank. The baby of the family—the youngest of nine siblings—Mashrawi felt close to every one of his three brothers and five sisters and closer still to the taciturn yet well-meaning parents who worked hard to instill in him and all their children the religious and cultural values they held so dear.

Mashrawi's mother, veiled and pious, was the eldest daughter of a prominent sheikh from the city of Jenin, whose population of some thirty-four thousand was a mere fraction of that of Nablus. Though she had little formal education, she had memorized the Qur'an by the age of twelve. As a teenager she was highly regarded as one who took her Muslim faith seriously, and as an adult she served as model and mentor to the young women in their community.

Mashrawi's father was the dominant force in the house. He, too, was devout in his faith and religious duties, having been raised by one of the most respected sheikhs in Nablus. He, too, had memorized the entire Qur'an and for a season in his youth had seriously considered following in the footsteps of his father and grandfather and becoming a cleric. He had even applied and been accepted to study at Al-Azhar. However, his dreams had been crushed when he was denied an exit permit by the Israeli government. He had been forced to take a job working for the small construction company started by one of his uncles.

As it turned out, he had a knack for the business, and soon he began helping his uncle chart a path to extraordinary growth. At first they had merely built small homes and shops and gas stations. Before long, however, they were winning contracts to build apartment complexes and hotels and hospitals. More recently, they had been selected to build the new palace for the president of the Palestinian Authority, a contract that brought the company a tremendous financial windfall and widespread respect throughout the P.A.

Hussam Mashrawi was far too young to have experienced the trauma of the 1948 war with the Jews, widely known among the Palestinians as Al Nakba—"the catastrophe." Nor had he experienced the humiliations of the '67 war or the one in '73. He didn't remember the election of Ronald Reagan in the States or the Soviet invasion of Afghanistan or the Israeli invasion of Lebanon in '82. The First Intifada, the violent popular uprising against the Israeli occupation that had erupted in the West Bank in December of 1987 and spread like wildfire to Gaza, had barely made an impact on him. Such events were mere legends for Mashrawi. He'd studied them in school and absorbed the stories from countless dinnertime conversations with his father and his older brothers. But at the time they'd meant little to him.

It was the Second Intifada, which erupted in the fall of 2000, just as he was preparing to complete his undergrad degree, that changed everything. All these years later, he could still remember the acrid stench of the tear gas the Israeli soldiers had fired into his neighborhood. He could still feel his eyes sting and his nose run. He could still hear the rumble of Israeli Merkava battle tanks roaring down the streets of his city and the chain saw–like buzz of machine-gun fire and the chilling *snap, snap* of Israeli sniper rifles as night fell and the curfews began. Even now he could see the bloody, shredded body of his oldest brother, Ibrahim, after he was shot to death running from an IDF patrol. He had never learned why his brother had been running that night. But for as long as he lived, he would never be able to silence his mother's blood-curdling shriek from echoing in his ears.

Mashrawi's father had moved quickly to send him out of the country—to Cairo, then Al-Azhar. He had no idea how much his father had paid to secure him an exit permit in such tumultuous times. But in his heart, Mashrawi knew his father didn't simply want his youngest son to get the elite religious education he never got. The man could see his son's pain turning so rapidly into rage and was desperate to prevent him from joining Hamas or Islamic Jihad or the Al-Aqsa Martyrs' Brigade or any one of a number of other extremist groups in order to avenge Ibrahim's death.

Looking back, Hussam Mashrawi knew that single decision had saved his life. Rather than throw himself into the fight against the Jews, Mashrawi had thrown himself into his studies. The Muslim Brotherhood, the parent of Hamas, had been banned in Egypt during the reign of Hosni Mubarak. University campuses were closely monitored by the secret police. It was difficult, if not impossible, therefore, for Mashrawi to find like-minded conspirators in Cairo who shared his seething anger. The only place he could find solace, it seemed, was in the library. His only source of peace was the writings of the Qur'an and the hadiths, and so it was to these that he turned his full attention.

By the time he returned to Palestine, Mashrawi was no longer the grieving teenager with the volcanic temper. He had instead become a disciplined and highly focused young man. He had learned in the suffocating political environment of Cairo what was acceptable to say and what not to say, whether around the family dinner table or in the mosque or café or with his closest friends hanging out on a street corner. Upon reentering Nablus, he had no desire to draw the attention, much less the wrath, of the IDF or the

Shin Bet—Israel's equivalent of the FBI—or even the Palestinian Authority, whose intelligence services were on high alert for Hamas sympathizers and were determined to prevent Hamas from attracting new recruits.

Hussam Mashrawi, in short, had learned to be circumspect. Yet no one could tell him what to think. Nor could they prevent him from striking when the moment was right. And Mashrawi had come to believe that moment was very near.

17

Hussam Mashrawi was biding his time.

He was convinced that Hamas was not nearly pious nor extreme enough. His placid, unassuming exterior hid his true sympathies, which lay far closer to ISIS and the teachings of Abu Bakr al-Baghdadi than to Osama bin Laden or Sheikh Ahmed Yassin.

Mashrawi was not simply opposed—and vehemently so—to the prospect of a two-state solution to the Palestinian-Israeli conflict. The truth was he believed the Jews' days in the land of Palestine were numbered. He had no doubt that by the time his children were grown, the State of Israel would be no more. That said, it should *never* be replaced by a State of Palestine. Why simply transpose one corrupt, temporal state for another? Only fools and heretics set their sights so low.

What Mashrawi truly longed for, what he prayed for silently, privately, five times a day, was the arrival of the Caliphate. He hungered for the day that the Mahdi, the long-awaited Promised One, would finally be revealed upon the earth, with the prophet Jesus at his side, to usher in the global Islamic kingdom. He hungered for the time when Sharia would be the law of all the lands and the full justice of Allah would prevail. The savior of the Muslim people was coming—the signs of the times were so vivid to Mashrawi—and when that savior came, he would finally judge the Jews, the Christians, the atheists, the agnostics, and the pagans. Indeed, the Mahdi would judge every infidel and do so with fire and fury such as the world had never seen nor imagined.

There were moments when Mashrawi was tempted to confide such thoughts to his father-in-law, the Grand Mufti of Jerusalem. If anyone would understand him, surely it was Amin al-Azzam. Yet something in Mashrawi's spirit warned him to keep his mouth shut and his head down and simply keep quietly praying and diligently preparing for the moment when his part in the divine drama would finally be revealed.

"What is on your heart, my father?" Mashrawi asked after several minutes of silence. "You seem troubled. Is there something I can do for you?"

"I am not troubled, my son, but yes, I have something we must discuss," al-Azzam replied. "But first you must promise me you will not utter a word of what I am about to say to anyone—not until I give you permission."

"Of course," Mashrawi replied. "You have always had my discretion."

"And I have loved you all the more for your loyalty. But this is very sensitive."

"You have my word."

"Good—now listen carefully," al-Azzam said, his voice barely above a whisper now. "The White House is getting ready to release its peace plan."

"I have heard the rumors," Hussam replied, fighting not to grit his teeth. He hated the American president and whatever pathetic scheme he was about to propose with every fiber of his being. The road to peace crossed through Mecca and Medina, not Washington and Ramallah, much less Jerusalem.

"It's more than rumors, Hussam. My sources tell me that emissaries of the administration will be dispatched to the region this week to explain the plan and build support for it. But that is not all. The president is coming here."

"To al-Quds—to Jerusalem?"

"Yes, and not just to the holy city," the Grand Mufti replied. "He is coming *here*, to Ḥaram al-Sharif, to the Noble Sanctuary."

"Here . . . to these . . . these sacred walls?" Hussam stammered, sickened at the prospect yet trying his best not to betray the depth of his emotions.

"Yes, my son."

"You are certain?"

"Yesterday I received a call from the White House. Then this morning I received a call from the Shin Bet. An advance team will visit us in a few days. For now, this is all hush-hush. No one can know. Indeed, not even President Ziad. Not yet. Do you understand?"

The younger man did not, but he nodded anyway.

"Hussam, it will be our job—yours as well as mine—to greet the American leader, give him a tour of the great treasures entrusted to our keeping, and serve as faithful ambassadors of our people and our beloved religion," the Grand Mufti continued. "You must know how conflicted I feel about this. Andrew Clarke shows no evidence that he loves our people. In too many ways, he acts like a puppet of the Zionists. But we must welcome him anyway. We must show him what it truly means to be a follower of Muhammad, peace be upon him, and explain to him the pain and humiliation that we bear as Palestinians, and the justice we and our people not merely seek but demand."

"You think he will listen to *us*?"

"Perhaps not. But in receiving him in the best traditions of Arab hospitality, we will earn the right to speak truth to him, whether he wants to hear it or not."

Mashrawi struggled to focus. A near-blinding rage was rising within him. Beads of perspiration formed on the back of his neck, and his hands grew clammy. He could hear the older man speaking, see his lips moving, but he could not absorb the words; whatever meaning they held was completely lost on him. All Mashrawi could hear at that moment was the refrain "*No, never*" pounding in his head and rising into a deafening roar.

Suddenly it was as if everything went silent. Mashrawi's pulse began to slow. An unnatural calm began to sweep over him, and a new thought entered his mind. *This was it. The moment he had been told to wait for. The moment for which he had so long prepared. The president of the United States was coming. Here. To this place. This holy place. Perhaps the Israeli premier would join him. Perhaps even the Palestinian president. Imagine. All three in the same room. At the same time. How it would happen, he did not know. But he had no doubt in his mind that these three men were going to die. And he would be the one to kill them.*

18

It was 4 a.m. when the Antonov An-148 touched down.

The aging Ukrainian passenger plane taxied down the runway, then came to a stop outside the nearly deserted terminal. The pilots shut down the two turbofan jet engines. A ground crew rolled a set of stairs into position. But the plane's door remained shut until all of the airport's external lights were also shut down.

Once the ground crew sped away, a convoy of four SUVs emerged from a dilapidated hangar on the far side of the airfield and roared across the tarmac. Pulling alongside the jet, the drivers cut their headlights, and armed men dressed in black exited their vehicles and took up defensive positions around the motorcade and the plane.

Only then did the door of the plane open and a single bodyguard emerge. He scanned the scene looking for threats and received the "all clear" message from the team's sharpshooters positioned on several nearby roofs.

Then he headed down the metal stairs. A moment later, General Mahmoud Entezam emerged, wearing a dark suit and sunglasses, despite the fact the sun would not be up for several hours. Surrounded by a phalanx of IRGC operatives, Entezam hustled down the stairs and into the second of the four waiting SUVs. The rest of the team followed, and once every door was closed, the headlights of each vehicle flicked back on, and the convoy roared off into the predawn darkness.

The city of Ghat wasn't exactly a jewel in the Libyan crown. Situated in the country's southwestern corner, tucked against the Algerian border, it was once an important stop on the trans-Saharan trade route, the site of a fortress built by Italian fascists during the First World War, and occupied by the French during the Second. But in the modern era, it had long since ceased to be important to anyone but drug runners and terrorists.

Ghat wasn't a tourist destination. It was home to no Muslim or Christian holy sites. It had no oil or gas, no precious minerals or other natural resources. And it was hardly suitable for growing cash crops, given its proximity to the world's largest desert and thus the near-complete absence of rain. Most of the year the city was nothing but a blast furnace, inhospitable to man or beast. Entezam had been told the entire population comprised some twenty-four thousand residents, but that estimate seemed high to him. Ghat, he surmised, was a place you lived only if you couldn't afford to move or didn't want it known where you lived.

The rickety, sunburnt buildings of the airport had been built eighteen kilometers north of the city. But the convoy did not head south. Instead it headed west toward the Algerian border for about twenty minutes until it reached an enormous, walled, and completely desolate compound. Even if it had been daylight, no other houses or structures of any kind would have been visible in any direction. The road to get there wasn't even paved. Nor were there power lines or telephone poles or gas or water pipes connecting the compound to civilization.

This was not Entezam's first visit to Libya. To the contrary, he had invested a great deal of time and an even greater amount of his regime's money in this post-Gadhafi world of chaos and carnage. Afghanistan had once been the failed state of choice where he could fund, arm, and train jihadist proxy groups to do his bidding without leaving Iranian fingerprints. Then the Americans and NATO had come and fouled it all up. They'd tried to seize control of Syria in a joint venture with the Russians, to mixed results. In the view of the commander of the Iranian Revolutionary Guard Corps, however, it was Libya that was now proving the most ideal environment to recruit and deploy warriors for Allah. It was just as failed a state as the others. Lots of weapons. Lots of angry people. No functioning central government. And for the moment at least, no great powers trying to take it over. After Gadhafi's violent death, NATO hadn't had the stomach to stay. After the catastrophe in Benghazi and the murder of their ambassador, the Americans had effectively bugged out, as well. The Russians, the Chinese, and the Turks were certainly looking for ways to seize Libya's significant oil reserves. But that kept them operating in Tripoli, mostly. Rarely did Russian intelligence operatives—much less politicians or businessmen—venture outside the capital. Nor did almost anyone else, for that matter. That left the playing field almost entirely to Iran, and nothing could have suited Entezam better.

As the massive steel gates of the compound opened, the convoy turned off the dusty dirt road onto a beautiful paved driveway. They followed it, snaking through the sprawling complex until they arrived at a four-story villa painted a pale yellow. Parked out front were two armored personnel carriers, each fitted with a .50-caliber machine gun that was manned and ready to engage. On the roof, Entezam could see snipers eyeing them warily. On the balconies of each level, men stood guard with AK-47s. There were manned guard towers in every corner of the compound, and while Entezam could not see any attack dogs, he could hear German shepherds barking out back.

As the motorcade came to a stop, the Iranians exited their vehicles and set up a perimeter. Once this was done, Entezam's personal bodyguard got out of the front passenger seat of the SUV, scanned the environment, then entered a code into the handle of the rear passenger-side door. Entezam heard the click of the lock disengaging. The moment his bodyguard yanked open the heavy, armor-plated door, the general stepped out in the moonlight and was whisked inside.

The Iranian and his detail entered a spacious elevator and emerged on the top floor. They were led into a dining room far more elegant than might have been expected in the otherwise-spartan facilities. There was a long, antique mahogany table surrounded by a dozen ornately carved wooden chairs. Overhead was a crystal chandelier. Under their feet was a thick Persian carpet.

Entezam was shown a seat near the far end of the table. He sat down and set a small file folder on the table while the guards—both the Iranians and the Libyans—took up their positions around the room. Then an aide rang a small silver bell.

The elderly man who entered through a side door did not look like a killer. But Entezam had no doubt he was.

19

The IRGC chief stood out of respect.

He had heard a great deal about this man. They had exchanged numerous coded messages. This, however, was their first time to meet in person.

The jihadist's long, flowing hair was entirely gray, almost silver, as was his beard. He was stooped and walked with a simple wooden cane. He wore leather sandals and a white tunic covered by a classic Libyan robe known as the *jard*. As it was nearing winter, this one was made of wool, not cotton, and it was brown instead of white, as was standard in the blistering heat of the rest of the year.

"Commander, welcome," the old man said in almost-flawless Farsi.

"Abu Nakba, it is my honor," Entezam replied.

They embraced and kissed one another on both cheeks.

"Come, my friend, rest your weary feet," the elderly Libyan said as he was helped by aides into a chair—not at the end of the table, as Entezam had expected, but directly across from him. "Are you thirsty from your long journey? Of course you are. Let us have tea."

"You are most kind," said the Iranian, retaking his seat once his host was settled. "I see that you received the gift. I am glad it arrived safely." Entezam's eyes turned to the carpet with its rich greens, royal blues, deep burgundies, and wisps of lavender.

"Ah, yes. It arrived last week, and it is most lovely. I am humbled by your generosity."

"Please, my friend, I neither want your credit nor deserve it," Entezam clarified. "The carpet was entirely the gift of the Supreme Leader. It is a family heirloom which has adorned his estate for more than six centuries."

"Then I am touched all the more," came the reply. "Please assure the ayatollah that I am his most humble servant. I hope to one day tell him in person."

Entezam was careful to maintain his composure as a young servant poured both men piping hot mint tea. He was still reeling from the news that Hossein Ansari, the leader of the Islamic Revolution in Iran for nearly four decades, had only weeks to live. He could, of course, say nothing of this, not even to an ally as highly regarded as Abu Nakba. The condition of Ansari's health was one of his government's most closely guarded secrets. The truth would be known soon enough. Until then, there was much work to be done, all of which required every actor to believe that the absolute power of the Supreme Leader was absolute indeed.

"Inshallah," Entezam said, looking his host in the eye and smiling.

"Inshallah," the old man replied. "Now, my friend, how can I be of service? The impression I received from your request for a personal meeting was of a sense of urgency. I trust everything is well?"

"It is indeed," Entezam lied. "But yes, I have come with a very urgent request, one that His Holiness asked me to deliver to you face-to-face."

"Your servant is listening," Abu Nakba said, setting down his tea and leaning in.

"First of all, the Supreme Leader asked me to convey his gratitude and congratulations for the success of your first operation," Entezam said.

"The attacks inside the church in Washington and the assassination of the American deputy secretary of state were most impressive and generated tremendous headlines around the world and great fear among the American people. That said, we also wish to express our condolences at the death of one of your operatives and the capture of the other."

"The price of jihad," Abu Nakba replied without emotion.

"Should we be concerned that your man will talk?"

"Eventually they all talk," the Libyan conceded. "But there is not much he can say. Neither of the men we sent knew anything about Kairos or about me. They're not Libyans and have never been here to the compound. They were contract killers, pure and simple. I am not worried, nor should the Supreme Leader be."

"He will be pleased to hear this, as am I," Entezam said. "In light of this success, the Supreme Leader has commanded me to inform you that he is ready to dramatically expand his support for you and your community, providing you with the funds and the arms you need, on the terms your deputy expressed to me when I met with him last month in Rome. That said, His Holiness has two names that he needs added to the list."

"More names?" the old man asked. "How senior?"

"Quite."

"I need not remind you that the list you gave us is already quite complicated," the Libyan replied. "And you of all people know that we are still a very young organization, still recruiting good people, still building our assets, still positioning them in a most careful manner."

"And yet you have just proven your capabilities."

"The Washington operation went well, I grant you," the old man acknowledged. "But remember, this was a soft target. The deputy secretary had no security detail. That will not be the case with the rest of the names on the Supreme Leader's list. Each is more challenging than the one before."

"We are fully aware of the risks. But let me be clear: these two are personal. And thus, we are prepared to double your fee if you achieve success in the next thirty days."

"*Thirty days?*" asked a stunned Abu Nakba. "Why so quickly?"

Entezam remained silent.

"Such haste could put at risk all that I have built."

"Only if you fail," Entezam said. "If you succeed, trust me when I tell you that you will be rewarded beyond your wildest expectations."

The two men stared at one another.

"Of whom, then, are we speaking?" the old man finally asked. "Who exactly is the leader of the Revolution so keen on dispatching from this life to the next?"

Entezam slid the folder in front of him across the table and lowered his voice.

"The prime minister of Israel and the president of the United States."

20

MOSCOW, RUSSIA

Ambassador Tyler Reed boarded the Lufthansa flight just before 9 a.m.

With him were his wife and two daughters. Unfortunately, there were no direct flights from the Russian capital back to the American one. They'd have to route through Frankfurt.

Reed had no idea why he'd been asked to return to Washington on such short notice, nor why he'd been ordered to bring his family. The girls were giggling with excitement at the prospect that their father might be getting a new assignment, one that would finally liberate them from such a cold and dreary and dangerous city so far from family and friends. Reed's wife was even more excited than the girls. To her, there was something frighteningly sinister about Moscow to which she'd never been able—or willing—to acclimate.

Still, Reed had made it very clear he didn't want them speculating in public. They lived in a fishbowl. People were watching them. They would find out what was happening soon enough. Meanwhile, he told them to watch a few movies, read a few books, and keep their mouths shut.

Marcus's alarm went off precisely at 4 a.m.

He rolled out of bed, made coffee, and did his devotions. Then he threw on some sweats and headed out for his daily five-mile run.

It was ugly out. Fall had beaten a hasty retreat. Winter was coming with a vengeance. It was pouring, and temperatures across the capital region were dropping fast. By nightfall, this would all be snow, Marcus knew, and the streets and sidewalks would be sheets of black ice. He got back to the apartment chilled to the bone and indulged himself with a long, hot shower just to jack his body temperature back up to normal. Then he made himself a plate of eggs and more coffee.

Kailea Curtis picked him up at six. They planned to drive across the Potomac to DSS headquarters in Arlington, heading first to the gym to work out, then down to the gun range. Afterward, they would tackle the daunting stack of work ahead of them before they were wheels up. Despite the busy schedule, Marcus asked if they could stop at the hospital to check on Maya on their way to the office. Kailea made a show of checking her watch, but some things were more important than briefing books.

Marcus was pleased to find a spot to park right across from the hospital's main entrance. He invited his partner to join him, but Kailea begged off. She had calls to return. Snagging a gift bag off the backseat, Marcus exited the Impala, pulled up the collar of his jacket, trying in vain to protect himself from the elements, and dashed across the street. Inside, he rode an elevator up to the fifth floor, then checked in at the nurses' station.

"How is she?" Marcus said to the head nurse, who recognized him immediately both from his several visits and from his picture being all over the front page of the papers.

"Awake, but not exactly in the mood for visitors."

"I won't be long," Marcus promised, then headed down the hall to Maya's room and knocked twice.

"Hey," Marcus whispered after poking his head inside. "Thought you might like some company."

The drapes of the private room were shut, and the lights were dim. Pulling from the gift bag an aqua tin of Royal Blend tea from Fortnum & Mason in London, her favorite, he set it on the nightstand next to her. Maya was awake, though hooked up to oxygen, an IV, a heart sensor, and all manner of other devices and monitors, but she did not smile. Nor did she say thank you.

"This ain't a good time," she said, her voice weak and raspy.

"I just wanted to see how you were holding up."

"It would be best if you left."

"Left? Why?"

There was a long silence.

"*Maya?*"

"Ain't it obvious?" she finally said, her eyes moist and red. "Ever since you entered our lives, you've brought us nothin' but heartbreak. Carter and I welcomed you into our church. Into our home. We loved you like a son. And this is how you repay us?"

Marcus was floored.

"Son, ain't you never thought of anyone but yourself?" she continued. "You ever once think about how much danger you put everyone in who gets near you?"

And she was not finished.

"Your wife, Elena. Your son, Lars. Nick. And now Carter, not to mention all the others on Sunday. How many more, son? How many family and friends must die before you give up this ridiculous life and start thinkin' about others instead of yourself?"

Marcus was dumbfounded, unsure how to respond or if he even should. What hurt most was that Maya didn't seem to be saying any of this in anger but rather in profound disappointment. Stung, he looked down and stared at the floor for the better part of a minute. When he looked up, Maya's eyes were shut. She had turned away from him, and a single tear rolled down her cheek.

"I'm sorry, Maya," he said at last. "I never meant to . . ."

But his voice trailed off.

Maya refused to open her eyes or even acknowledge that she'd heard him. Twice more he started to speak, then stopped himself. In the end, he just turned and left the room as quietly as he had come.

21

"Well, that was quick," Kailea said when he got back to the car.

She said it in a lighthearted way, but he didn't respond. When she started the engine, he made no move to put his seat belt on. He just sat there, staring out the rain-streaked window.

"What happened in there?" Kailea asked.

Again, Marcus didn't respond.

"You okay?" she pressed. "Is she okay? Did something happen?"

"Just drive," Marcus finally said.

When they pulled up to DSS headquarters, Marcus got out of the car without a word and walked rather than ran through the deluge to the building. Kailea watched him go in, wondering what in the world had just happened. The challenge was she didn't really know him yet. That was going to have to change, and fast. But it wasn't going to be easy. The man wasn't exactly an open book. And those who knew him well weren't talking.

When the director of DSS had called Kailea early on Sunday morning, he'd told her that Pete Hwang needed surgery, that Marcus Ryker was going to be her new partner, and that she needed to meet Ryker at Manny's Diner and take him to Langley to prepare for the trips with General Evans. Beyond that, he'd really only given her two pieces of useful information. The first was that Ryker was a legend in the Secret Service, but she shouldn't let that intimidate her; Ryker knew nothing about the culture of DSS, and it was her job to get him up to speed. The second was that Ryker was a widower and a borderline burnout who no one was entirely sure was ready to come back.

Late Monday night, after their marathon briefing sessions, after everyone else had gone home, Kailea had stayed at her desk, logged into the DSS mainframe, and pulled up Ryker's files. She'd spent hours reading about his time in the Marines and his work for the Secret Service. She'd read about his medals and the reasons for each. She'd also read everything she could find on the murder of his wife and only son, including local newspaper accounts in the *Washington Post* and the *Times*.

That, however, was where she'd hit a dead end. She was stunned to find that Ryker's records since then—pretty much everything that had happened in his life since the murders, including how he'd come to work for the State Department—had been classified far above her security clearance. This piqued her curiosity all the more. Who was this guy? Who were the friends he had in such high places? And what secrets were they all hiding?

After a short layover in Frankfurt, the ambassador and his family boarded a United flight to Dulles.

The nine-hour flight would put them on the ground just after 3 p.m. Eastern. By the time they cleared passport control, retrieved their luggage, and met their government driver, Reed figured they could be checked into the apartment State had rented them at the Watergate by six, even if there was traffic. His dinner with Secretary Whitney at the Monocle on Capitol Hill wasn't until eight. But Reed was dying to know why he'd been recalled to D.C., and that was way too long to wait.

The sun had long since set over the British capital.

"Are you absolutely certain, my love?"

In a sparse, one-bedroom apartment in the heart of the East End, Maxim Sheripov looked into his sister's eyes, searching for any sign of doubt but finding none.

"I am," she said. "I've never been more certain of anything."

"There is still time to back out, you know."

"*No,*" Amina Sheripov responded with a vehemence her brother had not expected. "We must go through with it, together."

"Very well," he said. "The doctor's waiting."

Minutes later, the siblings were whisking across town in a hackney carriage—the black taxicab so distinctive to London—that Maxim had been driving for the last several years. Born and raised on the outskirts of Grozny, the forty-nine-year-old veteran of the brutal Chechen civil wars had been ordered by emissaries of Abu Nakba to relocate to the British capital, settle in, lie low, and await further instructions.

A welder by training, Sheripov knew he could not go back to his trade, no matter how well it paid. Operating with forged papers that indicated he was a Catholic from Ukraine, the Muslim mujahideen quickly concluded he needed a job that allowed him to learn the city thoroughly, that gave him access to airports, train stations, and bus terminals, and that allowed him to interact with all kinds of people at all hours of the day. Driving a cab had proven ideal. It had also helped him with his language and covered their living expenses.

Amina had taken their father's death at the hands of Russian special forces particularly hard. Maxim had vowed revenge, learning how to make roadside bombs and plant them for maximum impact. Amina, by contrast, had become almost immobilized by fear. Six years younger than her only brother, she had rarely ventured out of doors. Rather, she clung to her mother's side when she wasn't sitting motionless in her room as their putrid apartment shook from the Russian bombs that fell day and night.

Maxim vividly remembered the frigid December night when that had all changed. Their mother gathered them in the kitchen. The room was lit only by a single candle. It was snowing something fierce. They had almost no food. They no longer had running water. Electricity was available only two or three hours a day in Grozny. They had run out of firewood and were huddled together under thick wool blankets. Amina was twenty-one. Maxim had just turned twenty-seven. And that night their mother told them she had come to the conclusion she must avenge their father's death.

"Avenge?" asked Amina. "But how? What could you possibly do, Mother?"

"Become a Black Widow, of course, my love," she replied.

Neither Maxim nor his sister had ever heard the term.

"A Black Widow?" asked Maxim. "What is that?"

"Tomorrow night at this time, I will be smuggled out of Chechnya," the woman explained, "and taken to Moscow."

"What will you do in Moscow?" asked Amina.

She replied without a hint of emotion. "You will find out soon enough."

22

Two months later, Maxim and Amina had learned the truth.

They'd expected to hear through a close friend or operative. Instead, they read about the operation on the front page of the local newspaper.

Their mother had become a suicide bomber. She'd blown herself up just outside the terminal of one of Moscow's busiest train stations at the height of the afternoon rush hour. The blast had left forty-one Russians dead and another 120 injured, the paper reported. Maxim felt sick to his stomach as he read the account, but it was the last sentence of the article that undid him.

The bomber—an as-yet-unidentified Chechen woman—was decapitated by the blast, and police later found her head on the roof of the train station.

Maxim had begun vomiting uncontrollably. Then he'd bolted out of the apartment and spent all the money in his pockets to drown himself in vodka and the company of a prostitute. Hours later, he'd woken up alone, shivering and without shoes, these having been taken by the woman whose name and face he could not remember.

It was Amina who had found him and brought him home. Maxim assumed his sister would dissolve into unquenchable grief. But their mother's decision not to die as a wastrel but as a martyr for a cause electrified Amina. She not only snapped out of the depression that had nearly suffocated her, she threw herself into nursing Maxim back to health and hustling to make enough money to put food on the table, clothes on their backs, and even a new pair of shoes on her brother's feet.

In time, Amina shared with Maxim the wellspring of her newfound grit. She had devoted herself completely to the teachings of the Qur'an. She had been raised a Muslim, to be sure. They both had been. But neither sibling had taken religion seriously. Neither had their mother, really, until their father's death. Only when racked by immense pain over her husband's death had she found new admiration for his religious piety and the strength of purpose it had given him in his latter years.

Now Amina was wearing a headscarf and praying five times a day. She joined a group of women in the basement of the bombed-out neighborhood mosque to study the holy writings and implored her brother to follow.

Maxim had been slower to come around. Yet over months of watching his sister tap into such vast reservoirs of courage and fire, Maxim was persuaded to join a men's study group in the wreckage of the mosque and soon became convinced that Islam was the answer to his problems and that jihad was his path to immortality.

It was dark and late as they pulled into a deserted underground parking garage on the other side of London. Upstairs, they found a suite of medical offices tucked away on the ninth floor. The door was locked, so they rang the bell. Soon a woman in a headscarf led them to a waiting room in which no one was waiting. They sat and flipped through old magazines until a phone rang. The woman answered it, then asked the Sheripovs to follow her down a darkened corridor to a small but sterile operating theater. When the receptionist left, in walked a diminutive, swarthy-looking man in his sixties, from India perhaps or maybe from Pakistan.

"Dr. Haqqani?" Maxim asked.

"Please do not use my name," said the man, scrubbing his hands with hot water and pungent disinfectant.

"Forgive me," Maxim said. "It won't happen again."

"Be sure it does not."

"Did you receive the wire transfer?" Maxim asked.

"I did," said the doctor, putting on a pair of sterile nitrile gloves and turning to Amina. "So then, are you ready?"

"I am."

"I trust you have been told this procedure is irreversible."

Amina nodded.

"I want to be clear," said Haqqani. "Once I install the device, it cannot be removed. Is that understood?"

"Yes."

"There are no second chances."

"I want none."

"And no one is pressuring you?"

"No."

"Not your brother?"

"No."

"No one else in your family?"

"I have no other family."

"No one else in Kairos?"

"No."

"And knowing everything, you have no reservations?"

"None whatsoever."

"Very well, then," replied Haqqani. "My nurses will come in and make preparations. May Allah reward you."

23

JOINT BASE ANDREWS, PRINCE GEORGE'S COUNTY, MARYLAND

Marcus flashed his government ID and was cleared onto the base.

He found a parking spot for his Nissan Stanza, cut the engine, and then dialed a number from memory. It was a call he should have made Sunday, but he'd simply been too busy.

"Stravinsky & Sons Accounting and Tax Services, may I help you?" said the voice on the other end of the line.

Marcus couldn't help but smile each time he heard his Russian friend say the words. The man's name was not Stravinsky. It was Oleg Kraskin. And he was hardly an accountant. He was a Russian mole and an assassin who had taken out both the Russian president and the head of the FSB, then fled his country with a thumb drive containing the Kremlin's most prized secrets. Now he was living in the U.S. under an assumed name and working for the CIA, known to senior American officials only as "the Raven." And while his cover story was that he ran a tax preparation service, the truth was the Raven was working on two highly classified projects at the moment, with Marcus as his handler.

For starters, Oleg was helping the CIA identify European members of Parliament, journalists, political analysts, and businessmen who were secretly on the Kremlin's payroll. Already Oleg had put together a list of forty names of people surreptitiously paid in cash to provide the Kremlin with intelligence on NATO's military capabilities, steal trade secrets from key European businesses like Airbus, disseminate Russian propaganda, and recruit other people of influence. For weeks Oleg had been combing through the computer files he'd smuggled out of Moscow and building dossiers on each mole with proof of monies paid, means of payment, and what each traitor was tasked to do for the Kremlin.

The CIA had long suspected that both the EU parliament and NATO headquarters had been penetrated by Russian intelligence. Now they had proof. National Security Advisor Evans was urging President Clarke to have these people arrested immediately. Marcus, however, was urging Clarke to let the Agency keep monitoring these folks. Would the new Russian president try to use them? If so, to do what? If that happened—or more likely, *when* it happened—the president could decide whether to arrest them, feed them disinformation, or flip them into becoming double agents.

CIA director Stephens had sided with Marcus and taken his recommendation to the president, and for now, at least, Clarke agreed.

Then Stephens had asked Marcus to task the Raven with an even more urgent project: sifting through mountains of NSA intercepts, helping to scan for any evidence that Moscow, Pyongyang, and/or Tehran were planning revenge attacks after all the ways the U.S. had thwarted them over the past two months. Oleg had found nothing useful yet, and Marcus was sure Sunday's attack had hit the Russian hard.

"Hey, it's me," Marcus said, careful not to use either of their names.

"I'm so glad you are safe, my friend," Oleg replied. "I've been dying to call, but you gave me strict orders never to contact you except in an emergency."

Marcus smiled, if only to himself. Surely a man becoming involved in a mass casualty event qualified as an emergency. But he had no time to quibble. "I'm sorry I didn't call right away."

"It is I who am sorry. I should have found something, anything, that would have told us this was coming, but—"

"No one saw this coming. That's why I'm calling."

"You think it's just the beginning," Oleg said.

"Don't you?"

"Unfortunately, yes."

"Look—I'm heading to the Mideast tonight."

"With Evans, the national security advisor?"

"Right."

"I read about his trip."

"As has every terrorist," Marcus said. "So on top of everything else, keep your eye out for signs that any attacks are being planned."

"I will, my friend. Just watch your back."

"Will do," Marcus said, grabbing his bag and hustling to security. "Listen, I gotta catch my ride. Text me if you find anything."

As it happened, he was the last person up the metal stairs before the door was shut.

The military version of the Boeing 757-200 was painted blue, white, and gold. The words *United States of America* were emblazoned on both sides of the fuselage in black letters three feet high. The plane bore an American flag on the tail, along with the number 80002. Similar models of the VC-32A were used for the VP and the secretary of state. This one had been assigned to the national security advisor, and over the past two years the man had racked up an impressive number of frequent flyer miles.

As Marcus moved through the cabin to the cheap seats, he nodded to General Evans in the first-class area. The NSA was hunched over a laptop and chatting in a low voice with one of his key deputies, Dr. Susan Davis, the senior director for Near East affairs on the NSC. Evans nodded back. Davis did not.

Kailea was already settled into the window seat next to his. "Thought you'd never make it, grandpa," she quipped as he settled in. "Trouble with your wheelchair? Or filling up on Geritol at the PX?"

"Good to see you, too, Agent Curtis."

It was going to be a long flight.

24

The dark-haired Turkish woman checked her watch.

It was 7:36 in the evening.

She was dressed in ripped blue jeans, a GW sweatshirt, a brown leather jacket, and brown boots—with a canvas courier bag slung over her back. She was only twenty-six years old. But having cut her teeth helping smuggle ISIS operatives through her homeland into northern Syria, she'd been recruited by Kairos early—practically the day of its inception—and she had proven herself reliable.

Positioned at a gas station on the corner of Rock Creek Parkway and Virginia Avenue, next door to the Watergate, she had an unobstructed view of the building's front door. She bent over and pretended to check the air pressure in the front tire of her BMW motorcycle, then watched as Ambassador Tyler Reed emerged from the building and got into the backseat of a black Chevy Suburban, two DSS agents at his side, a third behind the wheel.

She immediately speed-dialed her commander. "Honey, I'm leaving for the office."

"Great; see you soon, sweetheart," the commander of the first cell replied in heavily accented English. "Stay safe."

As the woman donned her helmet and adjusted the visor, her commander speed-dialed the head of the second cell.

"Morning, Bob—I just got off the phone with Julie. Apparently Tony's flight just took off and should be on time."

"I'll be sure to pick him up when he arrives," came the reply.

Outside the Watergate, the Turkish woman revved her engine but did not pull out. Instead, a blue Dodge Grand Caravan idling across the street pulled away from the curb, did a quick U-turn, and began heading southeast on Virginia Avenue. The driver could see the Suburban. It was only three cars ahead. Yet when the Chevy made a left on Twenty-Third Street, the Caravan did not turn with it. Instead, it continued straight until it reached Twenty-Second Street, at which point it made a left.

The Suburban with Reed in it headed north, past the Foggy Bottom Metro station on the left and the campus of George Washington University on the right. As it approached Washington Circle, it bore right, flowing with traffic, took the third exit off the circle onto New Hampshire Avenue, and then almost immediately veered right onto L Street, heading east.

The moment the Suburban crossed Twenty-First Street, a white, four-door Ford Festiva pulled out of a driveway. It was also heading east on L Street, four cars back. By the time they crossed Connecticut Avenue, two of the three Kairos vehicles had turned off onto other streets. The Festiva was only one car behind the Suburban. In its front passenger seat sat the commander of the second cell. He could not see through the Chevy's tinted windows, but he speed-dialed the commander of the first cell and asked, "Just to be clear, is the shop located on Vermont Avenue or Twelfth Street?"

There was no shop. Rather, this was to inform the commander of the first cell that they were about to pass Vermont Avenue. It also signaled that the Festiva should break away from the Suburban, taking a left on Twelfth.

The Turkish woman, meanwhile, raced eastward down H Street. She was running directly parallel with L Street and receiving updates by phone through her Bluetooth earpiece every few moments. Zigzagging through traffic, she was making far better time. By the time she reached Chinatown, she was three full blocks ahead of the Suburban, stopped at a light.

Taking a hard left on Seventh Street, heading north, the Turkish woman accelerated until she reached L Street. Making a slow right on a red light onto L, she pulled over and checked her mirrors. At that instant, another call came in. The commander of the first cell told her she was in sight, all the cameras were rolling, and that "the FedEx truck" was just two blocks back. Glancing at her left mirror again, she saw the flashing red-and-blue lights of the Suburban. The ambassador's vehicle was coming up fast.

The moment Reed passed, the BMW accelerated again, pulling back into traffic, but three cars back. One block later, the BMW was two cars back. Just before Fourth Street, the Turkish woman made her move. She gunned the engine and quickly caught up to the Suburban. At the same time, the driver of the Festiva, heading south on Fourth, slammed on his brakes and screeched to a halt in the middle of the intersection, forcing the driver of the Suburban to hit his brakes as well.

Now the Turkish woman braked hard too, stopping on the rear left side of the Suburban as the DSS driver laid on his horn. In a well-rehearsed motion, the woman's right hand grabbed for her courier bag. She flipped open the cover, reached inside, and pulled out a thirteen-pound limpet mine. Typically used by Navy divers to sabotage ships, the device consisted of a cylindrical shell housing devastating explosives. It also contained powerful magnets, allowing the woman to easily attach the mine to the side of the vehicle, right over the gas tank. An instant later, she had set the fuse, revved her engine again, and taken a hard left on Fourth Street. The driver of the Festiva followed suit, hitting the gas and racing away from the scene.

Three seconds later, an enormous explosion shook the capital.

PART
TWO

Hamdi Yaşar struck a match and lit a candle.

"We need to talk," he said. "Father has added two names to the list. Wait for me to leave and then meet me at the hotel."

The two men stood close to the main altar of the cavernous cathedral. Yaşar considered it highly unlikely that any undercover police officers or intelligence operatives were monitoring them. They'd been diligent to make sure no one was following them, and no one could have known in advance about their meeting, given that he had chosen the location at the last possible moment.

Yaşar closed his eyes and breathed in the incense, allowing the aroma to overwhelm his senses. Then he turned and walked out into the moonlight. The sun had not yet risen over the Greek capital, nor would it for another several hours, and Yaşar preferred working in the shadows.

A young-looking twenty-nine, Yaşar had a fair complexion and a mop of dirty-blond hair. In ripped jeans, a black T-shirt, and a tweed jacket, he looked more like a graduate student in philosophy at the University of Athens than an award-winning field producer for Al-Sawt, a satellite news network based out of Doha, Qatar, known in English as "The Voice of the Arabs." But television was not his first love. Nor was journalism. These were merely tools. They provided him a cover, and a useful one at that.

What truly animated Hamdi Yaşar—what drove him to take ever-more-dangerous risks—was the dream his father had spoken of for so long, always in hushed tones. Now that dream was poised to become reality. It was time to restore the one true Islamic Caliphate on earth—not the pitiful version that had been such a colossal recent failure in the deserts of Iraq and Syria but the once grand and glorious Ottoman Empire.

At its zenith, the Ottoman Empire had controlled half of Europe, nearly all of North Africa, and most of the Middle East, including the holiest cities of Mecca, Medina, Jerusalem, Damascus, and Baghdad. Admittedly, it had collapsed after being subverted and betrayed by the pagan Western powers, particularly the Americans and the Brits. But the Ottoman Empire had ruled supreme for six centuries, and it would soon rise again. Allah's judgment of the atheists and the polytheists was imminent. So, too, was the dawn of the new era of Muslim might and glory. This was the cause that ran so deep in Yaşar's genes and so hot in his blood, and by the mercies of Allah, Hamdi Yaşar now found himself at the vortex of the Caliphate's prophetic rebirth. For unbeknownst to his family, friends, and colleagues, Yaşar was Abu Nakba's senior aide and chief courier and thus one of the most pivotal men in Kairos, the organization the great leader was building in the deserts of North Africa.

At a pace at once deliberate and relaxed, Yaşar walked nine blocks, never glancing back. Stepping into the lobby of the Royal Olympic Hotel, he took an elevator to the fourth floor and entered his palatial suite with the expansive and stunning views of the Acropolis, National Gardens, and Lycabettus Hill. Then he unlocked the door to the adjoining suite and grabbed a bottle of mineral water from the mini fridge.

Minutes later, someone rapped three times.

"It's open," Yaşar replied.

In walked Mohammed al-Qassab.

At thirty-four, the Syrian Arab wasn't that much older than the Turk. But with prematurely graying hair, a salt-and-pepper beard, and sporting a pin-striped, two-thousand-dollar suit, handcrafted Italian leather shoes, a crisp white cotton shirt with French cuffs, and a four-hundred-dollar turquoise silk tie, he could easily have passed for someone at least a decade older, possibly two. The man's ability to look significantly older than he really was might not have been his most important asset, but it certainly made the list. Al-Qassab rarely struck people as too young to be in the room. Typically they regarded him as the man who ought to be running the meeting.

"Has the room been cleaned to your liking?" al-Qassab asked as he stepped over to the glass doors leading out to a large balcony.

He was not referring to the handiwork of the housekeeping staff. He was asking whether Yaşar had thoroughly checked both of their rooms to iden-tify and remove any eavesdropping equipment and whether he had, in turn, installed appropriate electronic countermeasures to ensure their conversa-tion could be neither monitored nor recorded.

"It has, indeed," the Turk replied, watching his colleague pull the open drapes farther back to reveal the small black disk he had positioned in the far-left lower corner. The device created continuous vibrations across the glass, thwarting any long-distance laser microphones from monitoring the sound of their voices. "Come, have a seat," Yaşar said. "We have much to discuss."

The Syrian scanned the lights of the city for another full minute, then walked over to a control panel on the wall and pushed a button to shut the drapes. Only then did he take a seat on the plush crème-colored couch on the far side of the living room.

"You are to be congratulated for your hit on Ambassador Reed," Yaşar said. "Father is very pleased, and the money has been wired to your account. Now he has two new targets for you."

"Who?" the Syrian asked.

"Brace yourself. These are not ambassadors."

"My team can kill one as easily as another."

"No," said the Turk. "These two are different."

"Then tell me," the Syrian pressed. "My train leaves in an hour."

Yaşar leaned forward and despite all of their precautions whispered the names. "Reuven Eitan and Andrew Hartford Clarke."

26

The Syrian was visibly stunned.

For a moment, he sat across from Yaşar and said nothing. Then he got up and began pacing the room. Yaşar studied the man closely. He had advised Abu Nakba to choose someone else for this mission. The old man had been insistent that al-Qassab was the right man, but the old man was clearly wrong.

Part of Yaşar's distrust of the Syrian stemmed from their profound ethnic differences. Yaşar was a Turk and deeply proud of his heritage. Al-Qassab was merely Arab. And for a mission as vital as this, did they not need a Turk?

To Abu Nakba, however, Mohammed al-Qassab was, on paper, the perfect man to serve as the head of operations for Kairos, at least in Europe. Born and raised in Damascus, the son of a prominent general, he had served in Syrian military intelligence and been steadily promoted through the ranks before deciding against becoming a career officer. Moving to Lebanon after receiving his honorable discharge, al-Qassab completed his undergraduate studies at the American University of Beirut, then headed to the U.K. to earn his MBA from the London School of Economics. There, he'd discovered he had a knack for arbitrage and worked for a series of boutique financial firms before landing a job with a major investment banking house located in the Canary Wharf area.

Along the way, al-Qassab had changed his name to Michel al-Jalil and had taken great pains to suppress his Syrian ancestry and Muslim religion. His immigration papers from Lebanon and the bio on his firm's website both listed him as a Palestinian Catholic. They indicated his family had fled the Galilee region during the 1948 war, settled briefly in one of the many teeming refugee camps in southern Lebanon, and finally found their way to Beirut, where "Michel" was born and raised.

All of it was a lie, of course. Al-Qassab had no Palestinian roots. Neither he nor his parents had ever set foot on the shores of the Sea of Galilee or anywhere close. Yet he had convinced everyone he'd met at the London School—the administrators, his professors, his fellow students, and even his various girlfriends and one-night stands—that this was his story. No one had ever questioned it nor felt any reason to do so. They had simply accepted him and his story, and in time Mohammed al-Qassab had morphed into Michel al-Jalil.

When Abu Nakba had found and recruited him, the founder of Kairos had been pleased to discover that the wealthy Londoner was already in possession of two completely different legal identities and two complete sets of credit cards, driver's licenses, and other legal documents to go with them. It was just one more reason Abu Nakba had taken a liking to the man and made him such a generous offer to join Kairos and be assigned a prominent position in the fledgling terrorist organization.

Within the upper echelons of Kairos, he would be known by his actual, given name. To everyone else, and certainly everyone on the outside, he was known as Michel al-Jalil. His French was as flawless as his English and his Arabic. He was even learning Mandarin Chinese to pursue more Asian connections. He was intimately acquainted with both Western and Eastern banking and financial institutions and operated untraceable numbered accounts in various banks throughout Europe and the Caribbean.

Even his British fiancée had no idea who he really was. Al-Qassab had met the stunning coed at the London School in his second year. They'd started dating almost immediately, and after graduation he'd helped her get a job in the human resources department of the investment firm where he was a rising star.

Still, for all al-Qassab's formidable assets, Yaşar remained worried that the man might not truly be up to the job. As he continued to eye the Syrian closely, Yaşar removed from his jacket pocket a beautiful sterling silver lighter and small silver case engraved with his initials. He next removed a cigarette, lit it, and replaced the items in his pocket as bluish smoke flowed from his nostrils and encircled his head.

"Should I find someone else?" Yaşar finally asked.

"Don't be a fool—of course not."

"Perhaps you and your team are not as capable as you boast."

"I am building the greatest team the world has ever seen," al-Qassab snapped. "But what you are asking for is nearly impossible."

"Your father is not asking. He's giving you a direct order. Will you do it or not?"

"I will do it, but it will be costly—very costly."

"Get me a budget. I will get you the money. But you must be certain the evidence will lead here, to Greece, not to Father's home."

"What do you think I've been doing for the last few months?" the Syrian demanded. "We have painstakingly laid clues like breadcrumbs all across Europe, North Africa, and the Middle East. Once the name Kairos becomes public and the hunt begins in earnest, every spy service in the world will pick up the trail, and it will lead them here, just as Father has requested. The world will conclude that Kairos is responsible not only for the new attacks but for the slaughter of the Mossad team here this past summer as well, and they will begin tearing this country apart for us. Only there will be no one to find."

"You'd better be right," Yaşar said. "Father has great confidence in you. I have my doubts. Prove me wrong. Take out Eitan and Clarke, and do it fast."

"How fast?"

"Let me put it this way," Yaşar said. "In the next thirty days one of two things will be true—Eitan and Clarke will be dead, or you will be."

27

Hussam Mashrawi woke early.

He rubbed the sleep out of his eyes—or tried to—and put on his wire-rimmed glasses. He glanced at the clock on the nightstand beside him. The green digital display read precisely 4:15 a.m. Getting out of bed quietly so as not to wake Yasmine or the children, he washed and got dressed for the day. Then he put on his overcoat, grabbed an umbrella from the front closet, and slipped out the front door of their cramped third-floor apartment located less than twenty yards from the Damascus Gate.

Thunder rumbled overhead as he moved down the stairs. It was dark and it was pouring, and on any normal day he would have felt miserable, especially before his first piping hot cup of coffee. Yet this morning, Mashrawi's heart was pounding in his chest. As he headed to morning prayers at the Al-Aqsa Mosque, he hustled down nearly empty alleyways, past all the closed and shuttered shops, cafés, restaurants, and hostels. It was far too early for any but the truly devout to be stirring.

Not far from the Monastery of the Flagellation, however, Mashrawi saw a lone light on in a room above a shoemaker's shop. He ducked into the doorway and knocked twice. A moment passed, then another, but finally the door opened a crack. The shoemaker studied Mashrawi's face, then quickly opened the door more widely and allowed him to enter before shutting and locking the door just as quickly.

The man said nothing, just turned and walked down a long, narrow hallway. Mashrawi followed, past a workroom that smelled of leather and stale cigarettes, through a doorway, and past a darkened kitchen and two darkened bedrooms. Finally, in the back of the flat, they reached a small room cluttered with books and old newspapers. The man nodded to the antique desk and chair. Then he left, closing the door behind him, and Mashrawi was alone.

Removing a painting from the wall, Mashrawi found a wall safe, just as he'd been told by his handler. He entered the combination from memory, opened the safe, retrieved a mobile phone, and powered it up. Next, he opened the WhatsApp feature, so popular in the Middle East as a texting platform, not least because its communications were encrypted end to end and thus remarkably secure for a commercial app. Entering another number from memory—this time the mobile number—Mashrawi double-checked his watch. He wished he could have done this sooner, given the importance of the information he had, but certain preparations had to be made. Some things couldn't be rushed. Satisfied that the timing was right, he typed as quickly as he could.

Urgent: POTUS is coming to Jerusalem. Will give major, televised speech on the Haram al-Sharif. Advance team coming shortly to start planning. Don't have exact dates yet, but mid-December. Will send update once I get more.

Everyone was devastated by news of Reed's murder, but no one more than Marcus.

The American delegation had gotten the news not long after taking off from Andrews, yet to the surprise of many, General Evans had not turned the plane around or canceled the trip. The speculation was that the president had personally insisted that his national security advisor stay focused on the mission ahead while letting his deputy deal with the crisis.

No one on the flight was getting any sleep. Marcus certainly wasn't. Devastated for Reed's wife and daughters, he was battling feelings of tremendous guilt. It was he who had recommended that the president reassign the man. Kailea tried to talk to him about it, but Marcus shut her down. The last thing he wanted to do was bare his soul to a woman he barely knew.

Despite the countless trips he'd taken on the vice president's detail, and later on the Presidential Protective Detail, Marcus had never visited the Holy Land. It had long been a dream of his and had been for Elena and still was for his mother. Be it a lack of money or time, they had never made it. Now he was finally going, though this was hardly the itinerary he and the women in his life had prayed for. And Marcus was certainly in no mood to enjoy any of it. He and his team were going to be on the highest possible alert. Two senior American officials were dead, and they had no idea what might be coming next.

With a heavy security detail, Bill McDermott headed to the crime scene.

With him was the secretary of homeland security, who informed him that along with Ambassador Reed, three DSS agents were dead, as were three other Americans—one pedestrian and two more who had been driving a large moving van directly behind the Suburban. Four more pedestrians—tourists from Wisconsin—had been wounded by flying shrapnel, one of them quite seriously. All were being treated in local hospitals.

As their motorcade of armor-plated SUVs arrived on scene, McDermott could see a huge crowd of reporters and photographers and banks of satellite trucks. A row of D.C. squad cars and police barricades and dozens of uniformed officers were blocking the street and the sidewalks on both sides. After showing their badges, however, the drivers of the White House convoy were finally allowed to enter.

McDermott could smell the wreckage before he saw it. The street was still clogged with fire trucks, ambulances, and any number of FBI vehicles. The place was swarming with crime scene investigators wearing blue jackets with *FBI* stenciled on the back in large yellow letters. Given that the sun had set hours earlier, banks of floodlights powered by gas generators had been brought in, bathing the entire area in a white phosphorescence.

Coming around an FBI tactical unit truck, McDermott suddenly spotted ground zero. There was no evidence that a Chevy Suburban had ever stood there. Instead, McDermott found himself staring into a massive smoking crater as firemen continued to shower the area with water. Around the crater were the scorched hulks of at least eight cars and motorcycles that apparently had been parked along the street, three on the north side, five on the south. There were also the burnt remains of the moving truck that the SHS had mentioned—the one that had pulled up just behind the Suburban. Small plastic cards with numbers on them lay everywhere, marking each key piece of evidence.

As he tried to take in the full magnitude of the horror before him, McDermott heard someone approaching from his right. He turned to find the director of the FBI standing beside him.

"What are we looking at here?" McDermott asked.

"I can tell you what happened," said the director. "I can't tell you why or by whom yet."

"IED? Car bomb?"

The director shook her head. "This was a limpet mine."

"You're not serious."

"Wish I weren't, but it's all on video."

The director explained that in the hours after the explosion, the bureau had pulled video from the traffic cams and from every single surveillance camera located up and down L Street and Fourth Street. She described the woman on the motorcycle, the Ford Festiva screeching to a halt in the intersection, the Suburban slamming on its brakes, and the woman attaching the mine to the Suburban, directly over the gas tank. She said her team had captured the license-plate numbers of both vehicles. Both sets were stolen plates, but they'd still actually found the vehicles, also both stolen. Both abandoned a few miles from there, in locations where there were no surveillance cameras present. Thus far they'd found no usable fingerprints in or on either the Ford or the BMW. They'd found no witnesses who said they'd seen the vehicles being ditched.

"What you're telling me, Director, is that you have no suspects and no usable leads; am I right?" McDermott asked.

"I'm afraid so, sir."

"Have you found anything that would suggest this attack is connected to the one at the church?"

"Gut instinct? Yes," she said. "Hard evidence? No."

McDermott turned and stared again at the smoking crater. "You've sent more agents to protect the ambassador's widow and children?"

"Yes," replied the director. "My deputy is also there with the family at the Watergate, as is their priest and several friends. They're safe, but grieving and scared."

"Anything else I should know?"

"Not yet."

"All right. I'll go over and give my condolences to the family, then head back and brief the president. Call me the minute you have anything new."

29

Hamdi Yaşar stared at his phone.

He recognized the city and country codes. The text had come from occupied East Jerusalem. The number belonged to an elderly cobbler whom he was
paying $10,000 a month via a Swiss numbered account to establish a Kairos
cell in Jerusalem. But the message itself was from the shoemaker's first serious
recruit, Hussam Mashrawi, the executive director of the Waqf.

The cobbler and Mashrawi had been talking secretly for the better part of
a year. The conversations had gone so well that the cobbler had asked Yaşar to
meet with Mashrawi in Cairo. The meeting had taken place just two months
earlier, and Yaşar had been astonished by the man's passion for the cause and
eagerness to help. He wanted no money. Nor, after this initial meeting, did
he desire any direct contact. He said he felt it would be more suitable to pass
messages through the shoemaker. Yaşar had agreed.

But now this. Was it really possible that the American president was
heading to Jerusalem? If true, it was surely a gift from Allah. But how could

they possibly take advantage of it? Yaşar's hands were full. He had multiple complicated operations under way, and he needed to maintain his cover as a senior producer for a major Arab news network. The murders of the American deputy secretary of state and her would-be replacement were making a big splash. The next attacks, if they succeeded, would be even bigger. But this? The leader of the Great Satan in Jerusalem—at the Al-Aqsa Mosque, no less? If they could really take out Clarke—or even seriously wound him—in al-Quds of all places, they would accomplish more than al Qaeda or the Taliban or Hamas or Islamic Jihad or Hezbollah or ISIS or any of their competitors ever had.

Yet how? Kairos had only the beginnings of a cell in Palestine. Al-Qassab could coordinate. They had eyes and ears on the ground. They had some logistical support. But it was hardly enough. They needed more manpower. They needed someone to pull the trigger. But who?

It was almost 4 a.m. in London when the door to the operating theater finally opened.

"How is she?" Maxim Sheripov asked.

"Fine," said Dr. Ali Haqqani, still in his surgical garb.

"May I see her?"

"Not yet, but soon."

"Where is she?"

"In our recovery room and still unconscious."

"How soon can I take her home?"

"I'd like to keep her here for observation at least until tomorrow morning. By that time, we'll know if there's any unusual bleeding or signs of infection."

"And then?"

"Then we'll see."

"Can't you be more precise? Our window is very narrow."

"Perhaps you should have brought her sooner."

"You have your orders, Doctor. I have mine."

"Your sister needs to rest. We'll know more tomorrow."

"When can she go to work?"

"Monday at the earliest, maybe Tuesday. But she will still have pain."

"Will it affect how she walks, how she moves, how she speaks?"

"If she follows my instructions to the letter, then most likely no."

"You're certain? Because the stakes—"

"I understand the stakes, young man—far better than you," Haqqani snapped.

"I'm just saying that—"

"Your sister is healthy, and her faith is strong. But recovering from surgery is not an exact science. Every person reacts differently. It cannot be rushed."

Maxim bristled. They had one chance at their target, and only one, and that moment was coming up way too fast.

"Doctor, I must ask one more thing."

"What?"

"Is there any danger of the bomb going off . . . accidentally?"

"None whatsoever," said the surgeon, walking over to a wall safe. He spun the tumbler back and forth several times, and the door popped open. He withdrew a small cardboard box and handed it to Maxim.

"What's this?" Maxim asked.

"The detonator. The number is preset. You don't know it. She doesn't know it. You can't share it with anyone else. Nor can she. Nor can I. When you're both in position, all you have to do is power up the phone and hit speed-dial number five."

"Five."

"Yes—then you will have less than three seconds."

"How close to the target does she need to be?"

"Your sister has almost four kilos of plastic explosives inside her. It's the most I have ever used. She should get as close as she possibly can, but if everything works properly, everyone within a ten-meter range should die instantly."

"Anything else I should know?"

"Make sure you're not followed leaving this place," Haqqani said. "Or I swear to Allah, I will come and kill you myself."

30

TEHRAN, IRAN

Dr. Haydar Abbasi rarely left the base during daylight hours.

He certainly never went home for lunch. But the sun was high as he unlocked the driver's-side door and climbed into his decrepit Volkswagen Passat. He turned the key and felt the diesel engine roar to life. Then he worked his way out of the parking garage and exited through the heavy steel gates.

Soon the military complex was in his rearview mirror and he was threading through midday traffic, his stomach churning, his temples throbbing. Abbasi cursed himself for allowing more than two full days to go by. Two senior U.S. officials were dead. Scores more Americans were dead or injured. And it would soon get worse. This he knew full well. He also knew he was being watched. They were all being watched. And Abbasi shuddered to think of the consequences if he made a single misstep.

A few minutes later, not thinking clearly, he made a wrong turn and found himself driving past the city square where the bodies of six Iranians dangled from construction cranes. That very morning, they had been executed by hanging for crimes against the state. Abbasi felt his stomach tighten. He could taste the gastric juices in his mouth. He rolled down his window and gulped in the cool November air.

He had no idea what offenses these six people had supposedly committed. Nor had he any idea if they were truly guilty. But it didn't really matter. The regime didn't bother itself with such minor details. Iran's leaders meted out vengeance on whomever they willed. They had already executed 332 people that year, most by hanging. That worked out to more than one execution per day, and there was still more than a month of the year to go.

Tehran was on a war footing. The regime's spending on war efforts in Syria and Yemen was skyrocketing. The treasury was also pumping huge amounts of cash into arming Hezbollah and rearming Hamas and Palestinian Islamic Jihad after their repeated rocket wars with the Israelis. And of course, they had just spent most of the $150 billion the Americans had given them for agreeing to the Joint Comprehensive Plan of Action (aka the Iran nuclear deal) to buy nuclear warheads from the North Koreans, only to watch that investment sink to the bottom of the East China Sea.

Meanwhile, the economic sanctions the U.S. had reimposed after pulling out of the JCPOA were having a brutal effect. Iran's economy had already contracted nearly 6 percent, and projections for the coming year were worse. Unemployment was rising, as was inflation—particularly food and gas prices—not to mention the deficit. The value of the rial, on the other hand, was plunging. So were the nation's foreign currency reserves, and fewer countries were buying Iranian oil and gas. People were suffering. Protests were breaking out all over the country, many of them violent. Yet the already-bloodthirsty regime was cracking down even further.

A feeling of paranoia was palpable within the highest echelons of the regime. Since the Americans had discovered the shipment of the warheads from North Korea, pinpointed the exact ship, and blown it to kingdom come, Iran's intelligence services were beside themselves trying to figure out how the information had leaked and how to make sure it would never happen again. Only a handful of people at the top knew anything about the warheads, of course. But even low-level employees in sensitive agencies were being forced to take lie-detector tests. Some were disappearing. They simply wouldn't show up for work, and neither their friends nor families had any idea where they had gone.

Finally pulling up to his efficiency flat on the north side of the city, Abbasi parked in the lot behind his building. He glanced around to see if anyone was following him before exiting the Passat and heading inside. Seeing no one but the doorman upon entering, he took the elevator to the ninth floor and locked himself inside his room. He closed all his curtains before turning on the lights. Then he turned on his stereo, tuned to a government-run radio station playing classical Persian music, and dialed up the volume somewhat louder than usual.

He headed for the walk-through closet that connected the main room, which doubled as his bedroom when he opened his foldout couch, with the bathroom. His heart pounding, he moved aside several suitcases and boxes filled with books and lifted a loose floorboard. There lay the satellite phone he'd been ordered by his handler to use only when absolutely necessary. He grabbed it, powered it up, and dialed the only number he had been given. When a voice answered at the other end, he provided his fourteen-digit clearance code from memory.

"Take this down, every word," Abbasi said, nearly in a whisper. "I don't have much time."

31

It was hot and getting hotter as the three black Suburbans turned off the main road.

With Ramallah in their rearview mirrors, the American convoy sped north and soon arrived in a neighborhood known as Surda. Marcus checked his watch. It was precisely 1 p.m. local time as the massive steel gates opened and the vehicles entered the heavily fortified compound, pulling to a stop directly in front of the presidential palace.

The compound was surrounded by eighteen-foot-high walls and miles of barbed wire.

The gleaming, sprawling facility with its red-tiled roofs and massive marble columns was perched on a large hill, situated on six and a half acres of prime real estate. The largest building served as personal residence for the Palestinian leader. Adjacent wings housed offices and guest quarters. There were sprawling gardens and working fountains, a luxury swimming pool, and not one but two helicopter landing pads. The project had cost the treasury well over ten million dollars at a time when many Palestinians lived in dire poverty, often on the equivalent of less than five dollars a day.

No honor guard greeted the national security advisor. There was no marching band playing, as was usually the case for other foreign dignitaries. No one had rolled out a red carpet. Nor were any media present. A lone protocol officer and two policemen dressed in tan khaki uniforms and red berets stood outside the front door as the guests arrived. Marcus glanced at Geoff Stone, the special agent in charge of the detail, and at Kailea. Neither looked surprised. This wasn't an oversight. It was a message. But it wasn't directed at Evans. It was directed at the American president.

"Your Excellency, welcome," said the protocol officer, a young man of about thirty, as he shook hands with the general and led the American entourage inside.

Like his colleagues, Marcus unbuttoned his suit jacket, making it easier to reach his Sig Sauer. Of all the places they'd be visiting, the detail had been told this one would be the tensest. The briefers had certainly been on the mark. The territories were seething with discontent. The reigning political faction known as Fatah was widely seen by Palestinians as hopelessly corrupt and pathetically weak toward both the Israelis and the Americans. As Fatah's popularity plunged, Hamas's popularity was skyrocketing. This made it easier for Hamas leaders to raise funds in Turkey, Qatar, and beyond. It also made it easier for them to recruit jihadists from Jenin to Hebron. And that had been before Reed's death.

Marcus and his team had been told by a CIA briefer that if Israeli special forces weren't raiding Palestinian warehouses and safe houses every night all across the West Bank, grabbing terrorists and scooping up caches of weapons, the situation would be far more dangerous. But it still wasn't good. The Palestinian security forces were American-trained and equipped but at times seemed less than motivated to maintain maximum vigilance on their own people.

When they reached the office of the chairman of the Palestine Liberation

Organization, who served simultaneously as president of the Palestinian Authority, they found he was not actually there. They were greeted instead by Foreign Minister Jamal al-Hamid, who apologized that his boss was wrapping up a call with the newly installed Russian president Petrovsky and would join them shortly.

General Evans took his seat. Next to him sat Dr. Susan Davis, one of his trusted deputies. Behind them sat two additional NSC staffers serving as notetakers. Meanwhile, in the east and north corners of the room stood Agents Stone and Curtis, warily eyeing Ziad's bodyguards in the adjacent corners. Marcus took up his post just inside the closed door through which they'd all entered.

Evans and al-Hamid were served hot mint tea. Then their aides were as well. The principals drank slowly and made small talk. They kept it up for quite a while. Twenty-two minutes passed before the Palestinian leader deigned to arrive.

32

Ismail Ziad finally entered the room through a side door.

Marcus did his best to look not at him but at the eyes of the four Palestinian security men who entered with him. Still, it was impossible not to notice that Ziad, now in his mideighties, walked slowly, was hunched over slightly, and had never looked so frail. His shock of white hair was thinning, and he struck Marcus as gaunt and unusually pale.

"General Evans, President Petrovsky sends his greetings," Ziad said with a thin smile as he settled into a large leather chair in the center of the room. "He looks forward to welcoming you at the Kremlin next week as you wrap up your journey."

Ziad offered no kiss, no handshake, not even condolences for the recent murders of two senior American officials. The message was unmistakable. The man counted the Russians, certainly not the Americans, as his trusted friends and allies.

"I'm looking forward to meeting the new Russian leader," the general replied, "and wishing him our condolences on the tragic loss of three great leaders."

"Tragic, indeed," Ziad said coolly. "Especially with the gunmen still at large."

"Mr. Chairman, thank you for agreeing to see me," Evans began.

Ziad merely nodded.

"President Clarke asked me to bring you his personal greetings," Evans continued. "He recognizes there has been no small degree of tension between our two governments, particularly in the wake of our decision to relocate the U.S. Embassy from Tel Aviv to West Jerusalem. But he wants to begin a new chapter."

This was a carefully constructed opening line, designed to suggest that Ziad and his team had no reason to be so angry that the U.S. Embassy was now located in a section of Jerusalem to which the Palestinians made no formal claim. It wasn't East Jerusalem; it was West—close to the line, to be sure, but not over it. Again the chairman did not respond, so Evans moved on.

"The president wants you to know that after two years of meticulous work, his peace proposal is finally complete. He wants you to be the first to see it, and thus you're the first leader in the region I have come to brief."

Now Ziad nodded, almost imperceptibly.

"I can tell you that the president wholeheartedly believes you will welcome his proposal, which he hopes can serve as the starting point for robust negotiations and lead to a final, fair, and comprehensive settlement of the conflict between your people and the Israelis."

The tension in the room was palpable and intensifying.

"Before I walk you through the particulars of the plan, the president wants you to know right up front that two of the central concepts in his proposal are ones that you and your government have insisted upon from the beginning," the NSA continued. "First, the president is ready to help the Palestinian people establish a sovereign state—a real state with established borders, a flag, an anthem, a recognized government, passports, embassies, and so forth—based on the formula of land for peace, as stipulated in

U.N. Resolutions 242 and 338, so long as both parties negotiate in good faith and come to a conclusion satisfying to both sides. And second, as the president has stated repeatedly, he stands ready to help the Palestinian people establish the capital of the state in East Jerusalem. Furthermore, he would be happy to open an American Embassy in such a Palestinian capital as part of an overall effort to pursue strong U.S.-Palestinian relations."

The general clearly expected a reaction to this, and he paused for it. Ziad, however, remained silent and stone-faced.

"Mr. Chairman, our internal polling shows that two out of three Palestinians believe their society is going in the wrong direction. Well over half say their financial situation is worse than last year. The same percentages fear their dream of having a sovereign Palestinian state is further away than ever. And yet there is a ray of hope. A solid majority of Palestinians say they support resuming negotiations with the Israelis, and President Clarke believes the time is now."

Evans turned to his colleague Dr. Davis, who drew several items out of a large legal briefcase.

"On Tuesday, December 16, President Clarke will arrive in Jerusalem and address the American people and the world from the Haram al-Sharif," the general continued, referring to what the Israelis called the Temple Mount. "He will lay out the core principles of his peace initiative. He will also call for the commencement of immediate bilateral negotiations at the Camp David presidential retreat center, beginning on Wednesday, the seventh of January. Simultaneously, the president's 247-page plan will be posted on the White House and State Department websites in English, Arabic, Hebrew, French, Russian, Spanish, and Chinese so that anyone interested may study it carefully."

Davis handed Evans three black three-ring binders, each with the presidential seal embossed in gold leaf on the front cover. Evans proceeded to give one to Ziad and one to the foreign minister while keeping the third for himself.

"For the purposes of our discussions, I have brought you both a still-classified copy of the president's proposal," the general explained. "When we finish today, I will need to take your copies with me. But I assure you that multiple copies will be delivered to you next month, a few hours before the president begins his address."

Davis fished out of her briefcase two envelopes bearing the seal of the White House with each man's name handwritten in calligraphy.

"I have also brought you both personal invitations from the president to attend the summit he is planning for January," Evans added. "He would be grateful for your reply no later than December 1. Now, before I begin walking you both through the plan in detail, are there any initial questions I can answer?"

33

"How long ago did this come in?" the watch officer asked.

"Within the hour," said his deputy. "I brought it directly to you as soon as it was translated."

"And you're absolutely certain of the source?"

"The source? Yes. The accuracy of what he's telling us? No."

The watch officer, dressed in military fatigues and combat boots, quickly exited the operations center and headed for the elevators. When one of the doors opened, he entered, inserted his passkey, and pressed the button for the top floor. As the door closed, he stood there alone, his mind racing. The implication of the message was chilling. So was the risk to the source they had code-named *Kabutar*, which in Farsi meant "pigeon." If *Kabutar* were found out, he'd be slaughtered—that was, if he hadn't already been found out and was even now being used to feed them disinformation. How much longer could they keep him in place? Then again, how could they pull him out? They had no contingency plans for this.

Two minutes later, the watch officer was standing outside the immense corner office of Prince Abdullah bin Rashid, Saudi's director of the General Intelligence Directorate, or GID. When the officer informed the prince's aide-de-camp that he needed to speak with the man immediately, he was told the director was on an important call and had given explicit instructions not to be disturbed.

"He will want to be disturbed for this," said the officer calmly.

The aide stared into the officer's eyes, then told him to wait. He rapped twice on the door to the director's office and entered alone. Thirty seconds later, he reemerged and nodded for the watch officer to enter.

"I understand you have heard from *Kabutar*," said the prince, standing behind his massive oak desk.

"Yes, sir."

"Just now?"

"Correct."

"How long has it been since we heard from him last?"

"More than a month—that's why I thought you'd want to know immediately."

"Has anyone else seen the transcript?"

"Just my deputy, the translator, and myself, per your explicit orders."

"Give it to me," the prince ordered.

The watch officer approached the desk and handed over the handwritten transcription. The prince read it quickly, then waved the man out of the room.

WEST BANK, PALESTINIAN AUTHORITY

Marcus remained expressionless.

His eyes were trained on the eyes and hands of the two Palestinian bodyguards he'd been assigned to monitor. Thus far, the tensions in the room were as serious as any official meeting he'd ever witnessed. They were political tensions, the product of a seemingly unbridgeable gulf between two governments. They seemed unlikely to erupt into violence, yet all of Marcus's training had prepared him to expect the unexpected.

Ziad finally looked up. "General Evans, do you really expect my government to accept a proposal from an administration which has shown nothing but hostility toward me and my people?"

"Mr. Chairman, with respect, we have shown no hostility toward you or toward the Palestinian people. Since the midnineties and the signing of the Oslo Accords, the American government has provided the Palestinian people more than $5 billion in economic assistance through USAID. Since 2012, we've provided another $1.7 billion in economic grants to improve Palestinian health care, water, sanitation, infrastructure, and security assistance. This is far more than any other country, including any Arab country. Does not this generosity attest to our respect for both you and your people?"

"You know full well, General, that most of that aid predates the Clarke administration, the most hostile American White House we've ever encountered."

"To the contrary, President Clarke took office reaching out his hand to you in friendship and cooperation. He immediately invited you to the White House and treated you with great honor. He followed up by coming to meet with you here. Secretary of State Whitney also came to meet with you repeatedly in the early months of the administration, as did I. It was your decision, Mr. Chairman, to cut relations with us and refuse to meet with any senior American officials, the president included, until the exception which you made today. Rather than show gratitude to the American people and our elected leaders as your single greatest benefactors, you chose a path of hostility and disrespect. Perhaps such actions were rewarded by previous administrations. But President Clarke asks me to assure you, as a friend, that those days are over."

"*Disrespect?*" Ziad fumed, leaning forward. "*How dare you accuse me and my government of disrespect. Aside from your little preamble a few moments ago, your president has steadfastly refused to acknowledge the pain and suffering of the Palestinian people, refused to acknowledge our universal right of self-determination under the U.N. Charter, and refused to unequivocally declare his support for a Palestinian state, though he has been pressed on this issue time and time again. What has he done instead? He has slashed economic assistance to the P.A., slashed funding to UNRWA, unilaterally moved the U.S. Embassy to Jerusalem, publicly declared Jerusalem the capital of the Jews, and repeated over and over again that Jerusalem is 'off the table.'"*

"West Jerusalem *is* off the table," the general said quietly. "East Jerusalem, on the other hand, is most assuredly *on* the table."

"That's *not* what the president has been saying."

"With respect, Mr. Chairman, that's *exactly* what he's been saying. I have talked about this with him at length. He has stated clearly that the precise boundaries of Jerusalem are subject to negotiation. On this point he could not have been clearer. Indeed, every final status issue is on the table, but only if you come back *to* the table."

"Why should I come back to the table?"

"Because you'll never get what you want—what your people want and deserve—if you don't."

"I'm a patient man," Ziad said. "We are a patient people. We can wait. Time is on our side."

"No, my friend, it's not. You and your predecessors have said no to every single proposal for a Palestinian state since 1947. What do you have to show for it? You've lost control of Jerusalem. You've lost control of Gaza. Seventy percent of your own people want you to resign immediately. And why? Because a third of them are unemployed. Most of them live in poverty. Far too many of them live in squalor. Meanwhile, the Israelis have become a global technological superpower. They have the most vibrant economy in the region. The most powerful army. With every year that goes by, Israel grows stronger and the Palestinians grow weaker. The train is leaving the station. If you don't get on board now, it may very well pass you by forever."

34

"I won't dispute your facts," Ziad countered. "But I entirely reject your analysis."

"I'm listening," said the general.

"In 1947, the total Arab population of Palestine was about 1.2 million," the chairman began. "Today, there are 2.5 million Arabs living just in the West Bank alone. There are another 1.7 million in Gaza. There are yet another 1.6 million Arabs living in Israel. That means there are some 5.8 million Arabs living in Palestine. That, *my friend*, is a 483 percent increase in our numbers since 1947."

"And?"

"And given that there are only about 6.5 million Jews in Israel today, we Arabs comprise no less than 47 percent of the total population living between the Jordan River and the Mediterranean Sea. *Forty-seven percent.* Given our birth rates, plus the number of Palestinians living outside the land who long to return to the homes of their parents and grandparents, the demographics are working in our favor—soon we will outnumber the Jews. They can try to ignore us—you can too—but we have rights, and mark my words, they will be honored."

"How?" asked the general.

"What do you mean, *how*?" Ziad snapped.

"How will your rights be honored if you refuse year after year to come to the table to negotiate a comprehensive and final treaty?"

"You forget, sir, that every offer made to date has been better than the one before."

"Meaning what?"

"At Camp David in '78, Sadat and Carter abandoned us," Ziad insisted. "At best we were offered limited autonomy, not our own state. But this was ridiculous, so of course we refused to dignify such a travesty."

"What about in Oslo?"

"What about it? We were offered what we have now—the formation of the Palestinian Authority, on the road to a full state. And we said yes in good faith. It's the Israelis who haven't kept their end of the bargain."

"What about Camp David in 2000?" the general asked. "Prime Minister Barak offered you all of Gaza, 90 percent of the West Bank, and a good portion of Jerusalem."

"He wasn't serious, and it wasn't nearly enough," Ziad insisted. "Besides, he was a weak leader, and his government fell soon thereafter."

"In 2005, Prime Minister Sharon gave you all of Gaza. Why didn't you engage in peace talks with him right then for the rest of your claims?"

"Sharon handed us Gaza on a silver platter, for nothing. We didn't have to give him anything. So we took his offer, of course. We're not idiots. But do you really think the man who orchestrated the massacres at Sabra and Shatillah was going to negotiate a final agreement in good faith? Don't be ridiculous."

"Fine, then what about Olmert in 2008? He offered you 95 percent of the West Bank and *half* the Old City—the Muslim and the Christian Quarters. Your government didn't even reply."

"Why should we?" Ziad asked. "This is my point exactly. None of them offered us 100 percent of the land we possessed before the '67 war. None of them were willing to surrender the Haram al-Sharif, home of our most precious jewels, the Dome of the Rock and the Al-Aqsa Mosque. And what about the right of return? Are the Israelis really so arrogant as to deny all of our refugees their God-given right to return to the homes that were illegally and immorally stolen from them in '48? But this is my point. The Zionists still deny us what is rightfully ours. Yet the longer we wait, the more they offer. So we will continue to be patient, knowing that Allah—and time—are on our side."

"Look, Ismail—if I may—please believe me when I tell you that I understand your anger. You don't feel President Clarke is treating you fairly. I get that. And you don't trust Prime Minister Eitan to negotiate in good faith with you. I'm sympathetic—I truly am—on both counts. After decades crisscrossing this region, I have come to understand and, I would say, appreciate your narrative, just as I have come to understand and appreciate the Israelis' perspective. I readily acknowledge there is bad blood, and I'm not here to cast blame. It's based on years of history between your peoples and between you two personally. I get that. I do. But you and I have known each other—and, I believe, respected each other—for a long, long time, since we first met at Camp David back in 2000 during the Clinton Peace Initiative. So I truly hope you will believe me when I tell you that Olmert's offer in 2008 was the high-water mark. You and your people will never again receive an offer that generous from the Israelis. But President Clarke's plan is a good one. It's fair. It's balanced. And it's achievable. But only if you don't reject it out of hand. Now, may I walk you through the particulars?"

When the watch officer was gone, the Saudi prince picked up the phone and speed-dialed the private, secure number of the king's chief of staff.

It took nine rings before the man picked up. When he finally did, the prince explained both the content of the message and its source. The chief of staff began asking questions.

When had the message come in? Were they absolutely certain the translation from Farsi to Arabic was precise? Was there any doubt as to who'd sent it? Could it really be true, or had the Pigeon been compromised? Why did the prince regard it as real? And what did he propose they do next?

The prince had anticipated each question and answered with directness and precision. The chief of staff then told the kingdom's top spy he could brief His Majesty the king and His Royal Highness the crown prince at precisely 3 p.m. "And call AG," he finally instructed before hanging up.

The prince paused a moment, took a deep breath, and then dialed a second number. Like the first, this call was also encrypted and completely secure. Unlike the first, however, this one was routed by the GID's computers through multiple satellites, then through a maze of fiber-optic lines from Patagonia, to Mexico City, to Marseilles, through the island of Cyprus, and eventually to the private mobile phone of the director of the Israeli Mossad, Asher Gilad.

"Asher, it's Abdullah. Do you have a moment? We have a problem."

35

It was just before 8 a.m. when Reuven Eitan stepped outside to the carport.

The November air was chilly and damp. It had rained much of the night, not only in the Israeli capital but in Tel Aviv and up and down the Mediterranean coast. The driveway was wet and slick, and the Israeli leader, dressed in a new dark-blue suit, crisp light-blue shirt, and paisley tie, could see his breath.

Now in his midsixties, Eitan had been serving in public life since his midthirties. His hair was grayer now and a good deal thinner. He had put on a few pounds since then; actually, more than a few. His face bore more wrinkles, and today he needed reading glasses, while his eyesight back in the day had been perfect. Beyond that, he mused, what else had really changed when it came to the ever-elusive hunt for a final resolution with the Palestinians? As far as Eitan was concerned, his neighbors—their leaders, anyway—were as intractable as ever. Yet they never seemed to pay a price for saying no to peace year after year, decade after decade. To the contrary, the world was obsessed by a process that never produced peace. It was a never-ending hunt that perpetually failed to find the Holy Grail, and the blame was always pinned on the Jews.

Predictably, every new peace plan was announced with trumpets and so much fanfare. Yet they were all dead ends, producing nothing but raised expectations, immense frustration, and often more violence, not less. Yet Eitan would once again go through the motions. The United States, after all, was Israel's most important ally.

Marcus saw the prime minister through the window as the fleet of armor-plated black Suburbans pulled up the curved driveway, blue-and-red lights flashing, American flags fluttering in the morning breeze.

As the convoy pulled to a stop, DSS agents emerged and took up their assigned positions, as Israeli bodyguards maintained a close cordon around the PM. Special Agent-in-Charge Geoff Stone opened the back door of the third vehicle. General Evans climbed out and greeted the Israeli premier with a bear hug. Dr. Susan Davis, closely flanked by Marcus and Kailea, came around from the other side of the Suburban, and Davis was greeted by the prime minister with a kiss to both cheeks.

"I'm so sorry about Janelle," said Eitan. "I liked her very much, and Tyler . . . well, he was a rock star."

Evans nodded. So did Davis. But neither said a word. They were still shaken by the events of the last several days, and the fact that as of yet there was no one to blame, no one to go after, made it even worse.

The prime minister quickly ushered the Americans out of the chill and into his official residence. Heading through the vestibule, they entered the formal dining room, where the PM took meals with most foreign dignitaries. There a breakfast of egg-white omelets, grilled asparagus, freshly squeezed Jaffa orange juice, and rich Brazilian coffee awaited.

Eitan and Evans had known each other for most of their professional lives, through countless previous jobs and titles and incomes—and several wives, as well. Their children had grown up knowing each other. Now their grandchildren knew each other too. Eitan considered the national security advisor one of his closest personal friends, and he was not a man who made friends easily. Today, however, they didn't discuss family. Nor did they eat. They discussed the two attacks in Washington.

Finally Evans shifted gears. "Ruvi, as hard as it is for me to focus on anything but the situation back in D.C., I think it's probably time for me to share with you the president's plan."

"Of course," said the prime minister. "But first, how is the mayor of Ramallah?"

Judging by his reaction, it was clearly a term Evans had heard before, and not one he liked, Marcus noted.

"You're referring to President Ziad?" Evans asked.

"President of what, exactly?" Eitan asked.

"Don't get snarky, Ruvi," the general replied. "It doesn't become you."

"Actually, I'm completely serious. Ismail Ziad is the president of what, precisely? A sovereign state? He could be, but he's refused every deal we have ever offered him. He's completely lost control of Gaza to Hamas and done precious little to regain it. His approval rating clocks in at no more than 20 percent. Nearly eight in ten Palestinians want him to step down. He hasn't held free and fair elections since he came to power almost two decades ago. He has no plans to hold a free and fair election anytime in the foreseeable future. But I'll give you this: he's certainly built a lovely palace for himself—one that must have cost an absolute fortune for a regime that claims it doesn't have enough money to pay its own police officers, firemen, and teachers. So, again, I ask in all seriousness, how exactly is the mayor of Ramallah these days?"

36

Marcus was posted at the far end of the dining room.

Kailea was posted at the other end, near the fireplace. Geoff Stone was standing directly behind the general. Three of the PM's bodyguards were in the room as well, mirroring the Americans. In sharp contrast to the previous day, however, Marcus felt no significant tension in the room, other than the fact that it was clear neither the general nor Davis were happy with the PM's characterization of Ziad.

Marcus was intrigued by the Israeli leader and had been in multiple meetings with him during his years in the Secret Service, protecting the previous American president. As a champion of Israeli security, few other Israeli politicians were in Eitan's league. He had not only served in the IDF, he'd been recruited into Shayetet Shalosh-esray—the Israeli version of the Navy SEALs. Eventually he had served as commander of the elite commando unit, and a decorated one at that. What's more, he'd served multiple terms as the nation's prime minister, not to mention stints as foreign minister, intelligence minister, minister of industry and trade, and finance minister before that. He could pick up the phone and get almost any leader in the world on the line because he had worked with them for decades. He knew them. He understood them. And one by one, he was beginning to persuade them that Israel was not one of the problems in the Middle East, but one of the answers.

As a businessman, Eitan had had a storied career in the "start-up nation." Upon retiring from the IDF, before entering politics, he'd helped launch a tech company that he'd sold a decade later for a cool $400 million. That had helped him become a champion of Israeli commerce and put him in a position to relentlessly hack away at tax, regulatory, and trade barriers in order to maximize growth, particularly in Israel's high-tech sector. Under his leadership, the economy was now humming along at between 3 and 4 percent growth a year, a good one-third higher than most European countries. Unemployment was below 4 percent every quarter. Inflation was virtually nonexistent.

Of course, not every Israeli felt part of the new economy of which he'd been the architect. There were far too many Arabs, ultra-Orthodox families, and elderly Russians and Holocaust survivors who subsisted at or below the poverty level. Many young couples fought to make ends meet despite double incomes, and saving up enough to buy a first apartment was a pipe dream for all but those who had wealthy parents or grandparents willing to help out in a significant way. But somehow Eitan kept winning one election after another.

Marcus knew General Evans held enormous respect for the prime minister and appreciated his gifts more than most in Washington. At the same time, however, the NSA seemed fully cognizant of the man's shortcomings. Marcus watched the general pick up his cup of tea, take a sip, then set down the china cup on its saucer. He dabbed his mouth with a freshly starched white cloth napkin and set the napkin back on his lap. Only then did he look up and meet Eitan's eye.

"Ruvi, may I offer you some friendly advice?"

"Of course."

"This is not a tack I'd recommend you take with President Clarke."

"Am I wrong?" the PM exclaimed, throwing his hands in the air for effect. "Tell me how I'm wrong about our friend."

"Let me put it this way, Mr. Prime Minister," Evans replied. "Most of the governments of the world regard Mr. Ziad as the president of the Palestinian Authority. The U.S. government regards Mr. Ziad as the president of the Palestinian Authority. Most importantly, President Clarke regards Mr. Ziad as the president of the Palestinian Authority. Thus, I will refer to Mr. Ziad as the president of the Palestinian Authority, and for the purposes of our discussions, I recommend that course for you, as well."

"Fair enough, fair enough," said Eitan, putting his hands down and pouring himself a fresh cup of coffee. "So, then, in all sincerity, how was your time in Ramallah? I woke up half-expecting to hear the meeting had been canceled."

"Sorry to disappoint you."

"All in due time."

"You might be surprised. This round may be quite different from the past."

"I'm not holding my breath."

"The meeting actually went quite well."

"Ziad liked the plan?"

"I wouldn't go that far," replied the general. "He bristled at first. But over the next few hours, as I walked him through our proposal, I think he came to understand that this really is his best shot—and possibly his last—at creating a better life for his people and going down as his nation's single most consequential leader."

"Barry, come now," Eitan laughed. "I know you don't believe that."

"Actually, I do."

Eitan laughed again. "No, you don't. I've known you for a very long time, and I assure you, you neither believe that Ziad will take this plan seriously, nor that the time is ripe for a deal."

"Times are changing, Ruvi. The winds are shifting."

"Not in Ramallah, my friend," Eitan insisted. "Ismail Ziad doesn't want to go down in history as the man who made peace. He wants to be remembered as the man who refused to surrender to the 'criminal Zionists,' and you know it. But aside from all that, something quite serious has come up, and we really need to discuss it before we go any further."

37

Six hours later, the general was headed to Amman to brief the king.

Marcus and Kailea, however, headed straight back to the embassy. For the next few days, they'd work with the White House advance team, laying the groundwork for the president's upcoming visit. After that, Kailea would fly to London to link back up with General Evans for the European leg of their trip. Marcus would fly home to Colorado. From the day he'd joined the CIA, he'd requested the opportunity to be home for Thanksgiving. Director Stephens had readily approved the request for two reasons. Ryker certainly needed some R & R after the intensity of the past month. And there wasn't a snowball's chance that Stephens was going to let Marcus get anywhere close to Moscow, the last stop on the general's itinerary.

Each agent headed for a SCIF, a sensitive compartmented information facility. Kailea called DSS headquarters. Marcus dialed the Global Operations Center at Langley, requesting to speak with Stephens.

"I'm afraid the director is on another call, Mr. Ryker," said the watch commander. "May I put you through to the DDI?"

"Fine, but let the director know I called—it's urgent."

"Of course, sir. Standby one."

Soon, Martha Dell, the deputy director for intelligence, came on the line. "Make it fast, Ryker."

"Of course—I just got out of a meeting with Prime Minister Eitan," Marcus began. "He said the Saudis have credible intel that the Iranians have ordered a hit against himself and President Clarke."

"I'm not sure how credible it is, but yes, we've heard," Dell replied. "The director has been on several calls with the Saudis over the past few hours."

"And?"

"And Prince Abdullah is telling us the same story he's telling the Israelis."

"You sound like you don't believe him."

"I wouldn't say that, but he won't give us the source, so it's a bit hard to know how much credibility or weight to give it."

"The Saudis told Prime Minister Eitan their source was 'as good as it gets,' someone very high and deep inside the regime."

"Yeah, they used the exact same line with us. But he won't say anything more."

"You really expect him to?"

"For a threat against the president of the United States? You bet I do."

"Martha, not to reopen old—or not-so-old—wounds, but as you'll recall, I didn't give you guys my source when I told you Luganov was about to invade the Baltics."

"That was different."

"Was it?"

"Of course," said Dell. "We didn't just have your word or your source's word. We had other intel streaming in—Russian troops massing on the borders of the Baltics and Ukraine, whole divisions being transferred from Russia's Eastern Military Districts to the Western Districts, radio and telephone and other electronic intercepts backing up what you were saying. Plus we had the photos your source gave you of the war plans."

"You guys still didn't believe me."

"I did, and so did Stephens."

"Not the president. Not General Evans. Not Bill McDermott. Not at first, especially not given all the disinformation Luganov was pumping out," Marcus noted. "It took days to get the president to take the threat seriously and even more time to start acting. That was time we didn't have. And even once U.S. forces started flowing into Poland and then the Baltics, Luganov wasn't persuaded to cancel his plans. In fact, he was preparing to accelerate them. If the Raven hadn't acted, it's very likely Luganov would be sitting in control of one, two, or possibly three NATO countries right now."

"What are you saying, Marcus, that someone needs to take out another world leader?" Dell asked, her tone thick with derision.

"Of course not," Marcus countered. "I'm saying the best way to make sure another world leader—our own, not to mention Eitan—isn't assassinated next would be to encourage him to give this speech from the Oval Office, not from the epicenter of the most explosive region on the planet."

"Marcus, let me remind you that you're not in Jerusalem to make policy. You're there to make sure that when your commander in chief arrives there next month, nothing—and I mean nothing—goes wrong."

"Why are you so quick to rule out what the Saudis are telling us, especially in light of all that's happened back in D.C. in recent days?"

"Do I really have to remind you how sullied Riyadh's reputation has become in this city?" Dell asked. "Trust in the Saudis on Capitol Hill is at or near record lows. I haven't seen it this bad since 9/11. The king is an enfeebled dinosaur who's long past his prime. The crown prince is dangerously young and inexperienced. Some of my analysts describe him as a 'wrecking ball.' Others say he's 'as reckless as he is ruthless.' I had lunch last week with one prominent senator, whose name you'd recognize, who told me the crown prince is 'a madman who shouldn't be anywhere near the reins of power.'"

"Martha, I'm fully aware of the serious mistakes the Saudis have made in recent years in Turkey, Yemen, Lebanon—believe me, I get it," Marcus pushed back. "But do I really have to remind you how helpful Riyadh's intel was when I was hunting those North Korean warheads? Without the Saudis, we may very well have missed that oil tanker, and those warheads could be sitting right now atop a new breed of long-range Iranian missiles capable of hitting the Eastern Seaboard of the United States."

"Enough, Ryker. Let me handle the Saudis and their intel. Just do your job and let me do mine."

They were late, and they were never late.

Maxim Sheripov resisted the impulse to lay on the horn. There was no point annoying the neighbors at this early hour. Whatever was slowing down the couple, impatience wasn't going to make them move any faster. Besides, they were valuable customers. More valuable than they knew.

The husband was one of the assignment editors on the news desk at the British Broadcasting Corporation. The wife was one of the BBC's top political reporters, typically covering Parliament but occasionally the goings-on in the prime minister's office as well. Both on their second marriages, they had good incomes, no children, and could have easily afforded one of those car services that would pick them up in a Mercedes or even a Bentley. But Maxim had them pegged as the types who wanted to feel like they were in touch with the average working bloke. Just as likely, they had been born to families with very little money and couldn't imagine wasting resources on such frivolity. Whatever their reasons, the couple took his hackney carriage to work every morning, and quite often back home in the evenings too, though their return trips were far less predictable, given the variations in the news cycles.

He still remembered the day he'd received their names. His handler had been insistent that Maxim not rush things. Under no circumstances could it look like Maxim was pursuing this couple. To the contrary, he had to make them come to him. That's how trust would be established.

Finding the couple's home address had taken less than five minutes on the Internet. Meeting them in such a way that seemed innocent and casual had taken a bit longer, but it hadn't really been difficult. Maxim had simply begun to frequent their neighborhood pub. On some evenings, he'd stop in for a pint of beer. On others, he'd order dinner. Nothing fancy. Fish-and-chips or shepherd's pie. Some evenings he'd arrive around six. Other nights he'd come in between seven and seven thirty. Every few days, he'd come by closer to nine. He'd chat up the locals, tell jokes, play darts, and tip generously. In time, he began to win one client after another. It was an upscale neighborhood. Most of the folks in the pub were lawyers or accountants or somehow involved in financial services or the media. When someone had too much to drink, he'd even give them a ride home for free.

One summer night, the pub's owner, by then a pal, had introduced him to the Sullivans and talked him up as the best driver in the city. Every few days after that, Maxim would run into the couple again. He'd say hi, ask if they had a light, ask if they could pass the ketchup, whatever. They were friendly people, classic extroverts. They had interesting jobs, and they loved to talk about the people they met and the stories they covered. It wasn't long before they made Maxim an offer that he would never have refused. Yes, he would handle their morning commute, at a discount because they were "genuinely nice chaps," and he grew quite adept at feigning total fascination over every name they dropped and every tale they spun as he drove them to the BBC's main studios.

Finally the bright-red door opened and Giles Sullivan emerged. He opened a large golf umbrella and held it for his wife, Meryl, as she locked the door behind her. They hustled down the steps and into his cab.

"So sorry to be late, old boy," said Giles. It was nine minutes after the hour.

"Not at all," Maxim replied. "Everything okay?"

"Just a last-minute call from the office. Again, so sorry. Couldn't be helped."

"Broadcasting House?"

"Yes, and a big tip if you can get us there by eight, Maxim."

"I'll do my best." Maxim pulled onto Fulham Palace Road. With the rain and the rush hour, he doubted they could make it to BBC headquarters before a quarter past eight, at best. But he certainly didn't let on to the fact.

"The tabloids are saying the queen is hosting some of the Grammy winners for tea this afternoon," Maxim said as he used an old cloth to wipe condensation from the inside of his windshield. "Will you be covering all the festivities, ma'am?"

"That's a different team," Meryl replied, her head buried in her phone.

"I thought you covered politics."

"The royals aren't considered political."

"I can never get used to your system," Maxim confessed. "Where I'm from, if we had a royal family, they would be nothing if not political."

"Well, let's not get started on the differences between Grozny and Whitehall."

"Indeed—so, anything fun on the docket today?"

This one was directed at Meryl's husband, but just then Giles's phone rang and he took the call.

Meryl sighed and set her own phone down. "I'm afraid not, Maxim. We need a nasty election or a good scandal. Of course, the Americans are getting ready to roll out their big Middle East peace plan. That could get spicy."

"You think they still will, after all those attacks?"

"Well, their national security advisor is crisscrossing the region as we speak. He's coming here to brief the PM sometime next week."

"Quite right—what's the bloke's name again?"

"Barry Evans."

"And he's coming here?" Maxim asked, doing his best to bait the hook.

"That's what I'm told."

"When?"

"Not sure," Meryl confessed. "But I'm having drinks tonight with a senior aide to the foreign secretary. Hopefully I can pry something out of him."

Maxim said nothing.

JERUSALEM, ISRAEL

The advance team landed at 4:41 p.m. and came straight to the embassy.

At six thirty, Marcus and Kailea met them on the upper parking deck and led them inside the compound to a conference room just down the hall from the ambassador's office, where they had a working dinner of sandwiches, chips, and a variety of cold soft drinks.

To Marcus's relief, the group was headed by a consummate professional. At fifty-one, Carl Roseboro was the deputy director of the United States Secret Service. A twenty-five-year veteran of the agency, he was also the organization's highest-ranking African American. Roseboro would be responsible for all the security arrangements for POTUS's visit to the Holy Land, from his arrival and departure through Ben Gurion International Airport, to his ground transportation, to his overnight accommodations and food and beverage services, to his meetings with the Israeli and Palestinian leaders. He would also, of course, be in charge of designing the plan to protect POTUS during his big speech on the

Temple Mount. There was no one Marcus trusted more to protect the president than Roseboro, and he was grateful for the chance to reconnect with the man personally. The last time they'd seen each other was at Lincoln Park Baptist Church during the memorial service for Elena and Lars.

Marcus and Kailea would essentially be assisting Roseboro on all the security planning and arrangements while also keeping an eye out for any specific needs or concerns that Secretary of State Whitney and National Security Advisor Evans might have, since these two were also coming and fell under the responsibility of the Diplomatic Security Service.

The rest of the team members were mostly new to Marcus. But they seemed to know what they were doing, and he liked them from the moment they all met. Among them were the director of the White House Office of Presidential Advance, a rep from the White House Press Office, and another guy Marcus knew.

Noah Daniels, thirty-four, ostensibly worked as a staffer from the White House Communications office. He was responsible for ensuring that the president and his senior aides had safe and secure phone lines and data links back to the White House, the Pentagon, and all intelligence and other national security offices. In truth, however, Noah worked for the CIA. That's where Marcus had met him and been told that there was no system he couldn't hack or crash. Marcus saw a flicker of recognition in the man's eyes when they shook hands. For the time being, however, they acted as if they were meeting for the first time.

The group spent much of the evening discussing the latest intel from the Saudis. Yet no one was talking about why the president's trip should be scrapped. Not even Roseboro.

Why not? Marcus wondered. *Had the man lost his mind? Or was he just waiting for the right moment to tell the bigwigs in Washington that the idea of bringing POTUS to Jerusalem in this threat-filled environment was certifiable?*

Marcus had known and admired this man for years. Today he couldn't read him. But rather than speak up, he decided the best course of action was to sleep on his fears and see what tomorrow held.

Two Suburbans departed from the U.S. Embassy just before 9 a.m.

They left the Jewish suburb of Arnona on the capital's south side, working their way through morning traffic. Passing the Yes Planet movie theater complex, the mixed Jewish-Arab neighborhood known as Abu Tor, and then Mount Zion, they slowly approached the Old City. Pulling off of Ma'ale HaShalom Street, they took a right, and soon the armor-plated SUVs drove through the stone archway known as the Dung Gate, making their way up Batei Mahase Street. At 9:21 they stopped just before the entrance to the Western Wall Plaza and the covered wooden walkway visitors took up to the Temple Mount. The American advance team exited the vehicles and stretched their legs and were met immediately by their Israeli escort.

Tomer Ben Ami had spent nearly thirty years working for the Shin Bet, the Israeli security agency roughly equivalent to the American FBI, and was now the agency's number-two man, responsible for the protection of visiting foreign dignitaries. A sabra, or native-born Israeli, he was fluent in English, though his accent was thick.

Marcus was the first to shake his hand and appreciated his firm grip and thick, calloused hands. He'd read the highly classified version of Tomer's bio, a version to which he and Roseboro alone had been privy. Thus he knew something even Kailea did not. During his years in the IDF, Tomer had begun as a sniper and later was recruited into an elite but highly secretive unit known as Kidon. There, he had been directly involved in the targeted killings of some of the most dangerous terrorists Israel had ever faced. When he'd joined the Shin Bet, he'd shifted roles. No longer was he pulling triggers. Now he was tracking terrorist targets in Judea and Samaria—the territories more commonly known around the world as the West Bank—and relaying the hard, actionable intelligence that he and his team developed to younger men who arrested or eliminated the targets. It was no wonder, Marcus thought, that Tomer's superiors had eventually shifted him into VIP protection. The man thought like a killer and thus could anticipate and thwart a killer's every move. Who better to help keep the Israeli prime minister and the American president alive as serious new threats were rising?

With Tomer setting the pace, the group pushed to the front of a long line of tourists. They showed their government IDs and badges to the Israeli soldiers running the security checkpoint, then walked through the metal detectors and set them off over and over again. They didn't stop, however, to remove any of their sidearms, ammunition, radios, mobile phones, or keys. Instead, they headed up the wooden walkway, cleared a second security checkpoint, and soon stepped through a stone archway that Tomer said was the Mughrabi Gate, or the "Gate of the Moroccans."

Suddenly Marcus found himself walking on the Temple Mount for the first time in his life.

As an evangelical who read the Bible every morning when he woke up and every night before he went to sleep—or tried to, anyway—he found the experience far more moving than he'd ever expected. It was overwhelming to think that King David and Solomon had once walked across these very stones. So had Jesus and the apostles. The first and second temples had once stood on this very site, and one day a third temple would as well. This was the very mountain that God had said he had chosen for himself, to set his name there, to send forth his Word into all the world. Even for someone as scarred and jaded as Marcus had become in his line of work, there was something almost electric about walking on these stones. It was nearly too much to take in.

No longer, of course, was this a sacred Jewish site alone. For the past fourteen centuries, it had been controlled by Muslims. Tomer warned the group not to pray, not to pull out a Bible, not to do anything overtly religious. None of that was permitted by the Islamic police that patrolled the grounds.

Straight ahead of them stood the Dome of the Rock with its dazzling octagonal structure and gleaming gold-plated roof. To their right was the famed Al-Aqsa Mosque, the third-holiest mosque for the world's 1.8 billion Muslims. Marcus knew the mosque was first built in the late seventh century and had been destroyed repeatedly by earthquakes but always rebuilt bigger and grander. Now there it stood, right before them. Marcus couldn't help but be impressed by the architecture of both structures and by the sheer weight of the history their walls had witnessed.

Such emotions turned out to be short-lived. Marcus suddenly felt his phone vibrate and was surprised to see a text message from Oleg Kraskin.

I need to talk to you—in person, not over the phone, it read. **It's urgent. How fast can you get here?**

Just then, their Arab host approached and introduced himself. "Good morning, everyone. My name is Dr. Hussam Mashrawi—I am the executive director of the Islamic Waqf, and it's my honor to welcome you to the Haram al-Sharif." Mashrawi smiled broadly as he shook everyone's hands. "Today I will be your guide, and I will be your point man as we prepare for the president's visit. As we begin, let me say on behalf of the Grand Mufti and the rest of my colleagues that we extend our deepest condolences for all that has happened in Washington."

Roseboro thanked the man for his concerns, and Mashrawi continued.

"Now, as you know, there is a great deal of concern among Palestinians about the peace plan your president is about to unveil, whether it will be fair and provide justice for our people. But none of us believes violence is the answer. All of us here in the Waqf condemn terrorism in all its forms. And I want to assure you personally that I am not a political person. My sole concern is the care and operation of this sacred site."

Most of the group nodded their appreciation. Then a veiled woman at Mashrawi's side handed each person a three-ring binder. Marcus casually flipped through his and found it filled with details about the site.

"The Waqf is an Islamic charitable trust," Mashrawi continued. "Under the peace treaty between the Kingdom of Jordan and the State of Israel that was signed in 1994, the Waqf is responsible for administering this site, but this is not a new role for us. To the contrary, it is a role that we have been playing since the year 1187, and it is one we take very seriously. Please be assured, therefore, that I will endeavor to make your visit, and the president's, as safe and smooth as I possibly can. In a moment, I will take you on an initial walk-through of the site. But before we start, are there any questions?"

Everyone was silent. But not Marcus. "I have one," he said.

"Of course. And you are?"

"Special Agent Marcus Ryker, Diplomatic Security Service."

"Yes, Agent Ryker. What can I do for you?"

"Would you show us the exact spot where the king was assassinated?"

41

Kailea thought Mashrawi looked stung by the question.

His eyes narrowed. His smile dampened, though only for a moment. "Well, it didn't take long to bring up our worst moment, now did it?" he replied.

"I mean no disrespect, Dr. Mashrawi," Marcus assured him. "But we're not here as tourists. At least one world leader has been assassinated on this site. It's our job to make sure it doesn't happen again."

"Of course. And unfortunately, it is true. His Majesty King Abdullah I—the man who served as the first ruler of Transjordan and soon thereafter as the first monarch of the Hashemite Kingdom of Jordan—was tragically murdered here, on this mountain, on July 20, 1951. However, I cannot show you the exact spot, nor take you on a tour of the mosque or the Dome of the Rock. Not right now. Trust me, you will have access to everything. But you have to understand, these two facilities are usually off-limits to non-Muslims. So we have to do things in as low-key a manner as possible. The last thing we want to do is draw the attention of the locals or the press."

Mashrawi explained they would come back later that night, when the entire plaza was closed to visitors and thus deserted. From 10 p.m. until 4 a.m., they would walk through both sacred structures and discuss anything and everything they desired. For now, however, he led them to a conference room in the offices of the Waqf and introduced them to the Grand Mufti.

"Welcome to al-Quds," said Amin al-Azzam, using the Arabic word for Jerusalem. "Dr. Mashrawi and I are humbled by your visit, and we stand ready to help you in any way we can. I trust he has expressed my profound regret at the murder of so many Americans, including members of your government, at the hands of terrorists in recent days. We are praying to Allah for the speedy recovery of all the survivors and for the comfort of all the families and friends of the deceased. We know what it means to suffer such great loss, and it pains us to see others go through what we have."

The Grand Mufti then apologized that there had been a scheduling confusion and that he was supposed to leave at that very moment for Ramallah to meet with the president of the Palestinian Authority. But he invited them all to dine with him at his home the following night and promised they could talk late into the night on whatever topics they wished.

"That is very kind," said Deputy Director Roseboro. "We look forward to that."

Everyone around the table smiled and nodded. Everyone, that is, except Marcus, who now cleared his throat and inquired as to whether he could ask one quick question. "I understand that you're pressed for time, but this will only take a moment," Marcus promised.

"Of course," said al-Azzam. "What is your question?"

Kailea braced for impact. She didn't know exactly what was coming, but she could see anger in her partner's eyes.

"Over the past few days, I've been reading your sermons, interviews you've given to the media, articles you have written, and so forth," Marcus explained. "And I have to admit, I'm concerned by your history of denouncing Israeli prime ministers as 'brutal and bloodthirsty occupiers.' You have repeatedly attacked American Jewish and evangelical leaders and their support of Israel as the 'racist rantings of ultra-wealthy imperialists and colonialists.' And you've had no shortage of criticism of our current president as 'thoroughly anti-Palestinian' and a 'cancer on the international body politic that must be eradicated if there will ever be peace.'"

It was as if the wind had been sucked from the room. Even though it was all true, was this the place of a DSS agent, Kailea wondered, particularly one who had been on the job for less than a month?

"In other words, you have a history of stoking anti-American and anti-Israeli sentiments while refusing to denounce the actions of Palestinian suicide bombers, rocket attacks against Israeli civilians, and other forms of Palestinian violence over the years," Marcus added, deepening Kailea's anxieties. "My question is, in light of your deep-seated hostility and support for violence to achieve Palestinian objectives, is there a reason we should *not* be concerned for the safety of our president if he were to visit here in the next few weeks?"

Kailea wasn't the only one to visibly stiffen, though Tomer seemed nonplussed. Roseboro looked furious. So did Dr. Mashrawi, the director of the Waqf. To Kailea's surprise, however, the Grand Mufti himself did not seem bothered. He rather welcomed the question.

"I appreciate your candor, Agent Ryker," al-Azzam said softly. "I make no apology for my displeasure with Israel's military occupation of my people's land. And I would be less than honest with you if I said I haven't been deeply concerned by President Clarke's attitude and actions toward my people and their aspirations."

It occurred to Kailea that Marcus had not introduced himself to the Grand Mufti. None of them had. So she found it curious that al-Azzam already knew who Marcus was.

"That said, I am choosing to keep an open mind about the president's plan until I have read it thoroughly and can judge it for myself," the Grand Mufti continued. "Many of my friends and colleagues have chosen a different path. They have already concluded that they cannot trust your president. They are highly cynical about his motives, and they cannot begin to imagine that he will bring justice to the plight we have suffered under the occupation for so many decades. Perhaps I am in the minority when I say I hope your president proves us all wrong and truly offers us a peaceful way out of this painful and perennial conflict. At present, I am no fan of your president. But in the hopes of a better future, I will welcome him and afford him the respect that he and his office demand."

The room was silent, but for an unanswered phone ringing in a nearby office. All eyes shifted back to Marcus, who finally nodded and conveyed his appreciation to the Grand Mufti for providing a reply.

Roseboro seized the brief moment of détente to thank the Grand Mufti for his hospitality and end the meeting.

Smart move, thought Kailea. Roseboro wasn't just good at protection; he had over his years in the Secret Service become an effective diplomat as well. Still, the problem remained. What were they going to do about Ryker? Their mission here was already sensitive enough. Why was this guy so seemingly intent on making it that much harder?

42

United flight 1889 touched down just after 10 a.m. Mountain time.

Marcus had checked no bags, so after clearing passport control, he immediately caught a shuttle bus to pick up his rental car. By 11:45, he was in a brand-new black Corvette, racing west on I-70 under gray skies and a light snowfall.

As he headed further into the mountains, the skies grew darker and the snow fell harder. Marcus cranked up the heater and the windshield wipers full blast. His GPS system pegged the entire trip at four hours and ten minutes. But in this weather, he knew he'd be lucky to make it in six. He found himself remembering a sign from his childhood, one that used to welcome travelers arriving at DIA. *Welcome to Denver,* it read. *A change of altitude, a change of attitude.* The sign was long gone. Unfortunately, so was the feeling.

He should have loved being back in the U.S., back in the state where he'd been born and raised, where he'd come of age and fallen in love. But the

murder of so many Americans in so short a time—first the church shooting, now the D.C. bombing—weighed heavy on him. So did the fear that
something worse was coming. And even though he longed to see his family,
it seemed somehow wrong to be going home for Thanksgiving when his
colleagues were still in harm's way, not knowing what the next minute held.

Determined to drown out such worries, he turned on the car radio to
find some good tunes. That proved a mistake. The dial was set to KOA
NewsRadio 850 AM out of Denver, and before he could change it, their noon
broadcast opened with breaking news out of Ramallah. Palestinian Authority
Chairman Ismail Ziad had just held a press conference blasting President
Clarke's peace plan as "an abomination" that "shows no respect whatsoever
for the Palestinian people, our dreams, our aspirations, or our quest for justice." In remarks translated into English, Ziad called the plan the "mother
of all disappointments." He said his cabinet had just voted unanimously to
reject the White House's invitation to attend a peace summit in January at
Camp David—an event that hadn't even been made public yet—and called
on every member of the Arab League to "condemn the American plan as a
naked attempt to institutionalize the racist, apartheid nature of the Zionist
regime, its illegal and unjust occupation of the Palestinian lands, and its
unmitigated cruelty toward the Palestinian people."

"No reaction yet from the White House or State Department," the news
anchor noted. Then she added, "National Security Advisor Barry Evans is
currently en route from Riyadh, Saudi Arabia—where he just briefed the king
and crown prince on the plan—to Cairo, the capital of Egypt."

When the anchor switched to a story about the search for a new head
coach for the Colorado Rockies, Marcus turned it off, trying to process what
he'd just heard. He called Pete Hwang back in Washington but got voice mail.
He tried Kailea but didn't get her either. He even tried to call Bill McDermott,
both on his direct line and his mobile phone, but to no avail.

It was then that he realized he didn't have anyone else to call. Senator
Dayton's perspective would be interesting. Few Democrats knew the Middle
East better, and he'd read in the papers on his flight back to the States that
the senator and his top aide, Annie Stewart, were fresh back from the Gulf.

But Marcus was hesitant to call the ranking minority member of the Senate Intelligence Committee just to chitchat.

His thoughts shifted to Jenny Morris. The CIA's station chief in the Russian capital was smart. Experienced. Feisty. Opinionated. But serious. Focused. Willing to listen. And willing to act. She'd been a handful in Moscow. They'd gotten in some rip-roaring fights. But he liked her moxie. She'd become a real ally. And they'd have never gotten out of Russia without her. The more he thought about it, the more tempted he was to call her. Then again, he'd been forbidden to have any contact whatsoever with her while she was still in Moscow and on the FSB's watch list.

The guy he really wanted to talk to, of course, was his closest friend from his first days in the Corps, even closer than Pete. But he couldn't. Not now. Not ever. Nick Vinetti had been killed the month before. He'd been shot in the North Korean city of Tanch'ŏn, on a mission that Marcus had been on too, and Nick's death had hit him harder than most. Not a day went by when Marcus didn't think about his friend or wonder what would have happened if Nick had stayed home with his wife, Claire, like he should have.

It was dark and his stomach was grumbling when he reached Glenwood Springs. He took exit 116 onto Highway 82 and stopped briefly at a diner where he had a burger, coffee, and a slice of pumpkin pie. Using his phone, he scanned the latest headlines on Twitter, focusing primarily on coverage of Ziad's rejection of the peace plan. For the life of him, Marcus couldn't understand why Ziad had rejected it so quickly and so viscerally. How exactly did blistering the American plan help the Palestinian cause?

On second thought, however, there was a potential upside. Almost certainly now the president would not be going to Jerusalem. What would be the point? For this Marcus breathed a bit easier. The politics of the peace plan were not his responsibility, after all. Keeping the president and his senior diplomats safe was, and Chairman Ziad had just given this mission a huge gift.

Marcus gassed up the Corvette and got back on the road. Another two hours passed before he reached the Aspen city limits, and twenty minutes more until he reached the A-frame house tucked away on an obscure little road, which to his relief had been freshly plowed. He hoped the guy was home. He hadn't called. He hadn't been exactly sure when he'd be arriving.

As soon as he got out of the car, he caught a whiff of smoke pouring out of the chimney. He saw lights on in the front windows and wondered anew why he'd been summoned.

43

Oleg Kraskin looked stunned to see Marcus outside his door.

"You came!" said the Russian, welcoming him with a giant bear hug.

"I was in the neighborhood, so . . ."

"I am so glad to see you alive and well."

"Likewise, but I can't stay long. What's so urgent it had to be in person?"

"Come, sit down and I'll show you."

The house looked like something Marcus had built with Lincoln Logs as a boy. It was small, just a living room, kitchen, and bathroom on the first floor, and a wooden ladder leading up to a loft that he guessed was Oleg's bedroom. The living room had a stone hearth before a roaring fire that was giving off a great deal of heat. Marcus noticed no framed photographs on the walls, just a small one on the desk, next to three large computer monitors. In it, Oleg had his arm around his wife, Marina, who was holding their infant son, Vasily, at what appeared to be the boy's baptism.

Oleg noticed his friend staring at the photograph.

"Simpler days," the Russian said wistfully.

Marcus nodded, and Oleg walked over to the desk, picked up a manila folder, and handed it to Marcus.

"What's this?" Marcus asked.

"Your answer."

Marcus opened the folder and glanced through sixteen pages of what appeared to be intercepted phone and email transcripts, all in Russian and Arabic.

"What exactly am I looking at here?" he asked.

"Ah, sorry, I gave you the wrong one." Oleg took the folder back, grabbed another one off his desk, and handed that to Marcus. This one contained the same pages, stapled to sixteen additional pages of English translations.

"The Russians are funding some kind of new terrorist organization," Oleg said as a kettle on the stove whistled and he began making chai.

"The Russians?"

"*Da.*"

"Not the Iranians?"

"That, I can't say. I'm not hacking into the Iranians' computer, only those of my old friends and colleagues in the Kremlin."

"When did you finally break in?"

"Just before I called you."

"With the help of the NSA?"

"Of course."

"So who exactly have you hacked?"

"Two people so far," Oleg said. "The first is Petrovsky's personal secretary. Her name is Batya. She sits right outside his door. She worked for him at the Defense Ministry. I used to talk to her all the time."

"And the second?"

"A colonel. His name is Yvgenny. He was Petrovsky's military secretary over at Defense. He's basically doing the same job I did for Luganov."

"And you're sure no one at the Kremlin can tell you're inside their system?"

"Your people at Fort Meade and Langley have been very helpful in that regard."

"Good—so what can you tell me?"

"Well, as we'd both guessed, Petrovsky is fuming and looking for revenge. Kropatkin is warning him they have to be careful, that if there are any Russian fingerprints, it could lead them into war with the U.S. and NATO after all."

"Is Petrovsky listening?"

"It seems that way—the very fact that they are covertly funding a new terrorist group suggests that they're looking for deniability, a way to cover their tracks."

"Who's leading the new group?"

"I don't know; they don't say—not even with code words."

"Where is this new organization based?"

"Greece, it would seem. I can't figure out where exactly, but all the emails and phone calls emanate from or return to Greek area codes. And the group's name is Greek—Kairos—it means 'a time when conditions are right for the accomplishment of a crucial action.' Wherever they are, they're flush with cash—rubles, to be precise. The FSB has transferred at least twenty million into various accounts of theirs."

"Any chance they mention the specific banks and SWIFT codes?"

"Afraid not."

"Are they behind the hit on Reed?"

"I'm guessing so, but I haven't found any specific kill orders. The initial messages go back at least two years, when Petrovsky was defense minister and Kropatkin was deputy director of the FSB. Those talk mostly of building infrastructure throughout Europe and the U.S."

"Infrastructure?" Marcus asked. "Meaning what?"

"They don't spell that out," Oleg said. "Presumably they're hiring operatives, renting safe houses, buying vehicles and phones and weapons, and the like. But at this point, I can't say for sure."

Marcus sifted through the English translations, scanning them quickly. "This is good work, but you could have told me all this over the phone."

"Not this," said Oleg, handing over a separate folder.

He gave Marcus a moment to glance through another five pages of translated text messages between the Russian president and his spy chief but didn't wait for the American to read it all cover to cover.

"These are the conversations that have me really worried," Oleg explained. "These come from the last few weeks. Some from the last few days. Kropatkin is trying to keep the Kremlin distanced from the new terror group—fund it, encourage it, but let them do their own thing—while Petrovsky is pushing for more active and direct involvement. Now turn to the last two pages."

Marcus did.

"*That* is why I called you," Oleg said, pointing at the pages in his friend's hands. "Three days ago, Kropatkin tells his boss they are playing with fire if they get too close to Kairos. Then he tells Petrovsky that 'the big one' is coming soon, 'by the end of the year,' and he warns that the leaders appear to be 'taking orders from someone.'"

Marcus found the section Oleg was referring to and kept reading.

Petrovsky: **Who?**

Kropatkin: **I don't know, but it's certainly not us.**

Petrovsky: **How can you be sure?**

Kropatkin: **Because I'm hearing talk of a kill list, and we've never given them such a list.**

Petrovsky: **Who are the targets?**

Kropatkin: **Apparently, there are nineteen. We don't have all the names. But we do have two.**

Petrovsky: **Who?**

Kropatkin: **President Andrew Clarke and Prime Minister Reuven Eitan.**

44

"What do you mean he's trashed my plan?"

The president was beet red as he stared at the large plasma screen on the far wall of the Situation Room. On-screen was General Evans via a secure videoconference from the U.S. Embassy in Cairo. On a smaller, adjacent screen was the image of Susan Davis, also in Egypt.

"Mr. President, what he's saying publicly is that he's furious that the plan doesn't give him full and undisputed control of the Temple Mount, doesn't give him sovereignty over the Muslim and Christian Quarters of the Old City, and doesn't roll Israel back to the pre-1967 borders," said Evans. "He also says he's incensed the plan doesn't give Palestinian refugees the right of return and that it gives the Israelis sovereignty over all but a handful of what he calls 'illegal Jewish settlements' on the West Bank."

Deputy National Security Advisor Bill McDermott looked around the room. Clarke sat at the head of the table. To his right was Secretary of State

Meg Whitney, fresh back from Europe, and an empty chair where Janelle Thomas or Tyler Reed should have been seated. To the president's left were CIA director Richard Stephens and Martha Dell. What confused McDermott most was that Clarke seemed so surprised by the Palestinian leader's rhetoric when they had all warned him this would likely be Ziad's reaction. Yet Clarke had been adamant that given the enormous amount of money the U.S. and Gulf States were putting on the table to jump-start the Palestinian economy, Ziad would finally come to his senses and play ball.

"Have you spoken with him?" Clarke asked, barely containing his anger.

"Yes, sir."

"And what does he have to say for himself?"

"I've never heard him so angry," Evans said. "I was genuinely afraid the man might have a heart attack and drop dead on me in the middle of the call."

"Is there anyone around him suggesting he may be making a mistake?"

"Just the opposite, Mr. President—Ziad told me his cabinet is even more furious than he is."

"Fine, they don't like all the particulars. But why reject it outright? Why not come to Camp David and participate in direct negotiations? You told him he's not getting a dime if he doesn't come to the table, right?"

"I did, sir, but he says the plan makes such 'preposterous concessions' to the Israelis on Jerusalem and settlements, among other things, that Prime Minister Eitan will simply try to pocket these things and have no incentive to compromise."

"How does he know unless he tries?"

"Ziad insists the plan is a giant trap, one he has no intention of walking into."

"Tell me this is just their opening position, Barry," the president insisted. "Tell me that next week Ziad will soften his position and we'll find a way to move forward."

"I wish I could, Mr. President. But I don't believe that's the case. I'm sorry. I know you've invested a lot in this. We all have."

Clarke thundered a curse. "You better believe we have! And there's no way I'm going to surrender to—what did Prime Minister Eitan call Ziad?"

"The mayor of Ramallah."

"Exactly, *the mayor of Ramallah*—I'm running the world's sole superpower, and I am not going to just surrender to the *mayor of Ramallah*. We're going to move forward. We're going to roll this thing out just like we've planned. And we're going to make our case directly to the Palestinian people."

The silver-haired Secretary Whitney was writing something in her notebook, but at this she removed her reading glasses, set them down, and turned to Clarke. "Mr. President, just to be clear, you're not suggesting that you still want to go to Jerusalem after all that's happened, are you?"

45

"I'm not suggesting it, Madame Secretary. I'm stating it outright."

McDermott stiffened.

"Let me be clear: I'm going to release this plan," Clarke continued. "I'm going to invite the Israelis and Palestinians to come to Camp David. And then I'm going to announce that the U.S. will end all financial assistance to any party that refuses to accept and come ready to participate in serious, sustained, direct negotiations that result in a just and comprehensive end to the conflict once and for all."

"With all due respect, Mr. President, I'm not sure that's the wisest course of action," Whitney replied. "For starters, you could see a serious backlash against you throughout the Arab world. Imagine if anti-American protests break out in Arab streets from Amman to Baghdad to Cairo to Riyadh—then what? That would seriously impair our efforts to build a stronger coalition against Iranian nuclear ambitions. And then, of course, we're going to see backlash from our European allies as well."

"That's not all, Mr. President," Martha Dell interjected. "We could see an escalation of violence in the West Bank and Gaza. One spark, and the whole thing could erupt in a Third Intifada. It could take five years or more to tamp this thing down."

"I'm not going to let the terrorists or threats of violence intimidate me," Clarke almost shouted, slamming his fist on the table. "This is a good plan. It's good for the Israelis, but it's even better for the Palestinians. Sure, they don't get everything they want. But that's the price of saying no to every peace deal for three-quarters of a century. I can guarantee it's a far better deal than they'll ever get again. It's going to create real security and jobs and opportunity for the Palestinian people. It's going to put these terrorists out of business for good. And that's why I'm going to Jerusalem to stand on the Temple Mount and make my case, and I guarantee you—mark my words—at the end of the day we're going to change hearts and minds."

CIA director Stephens now spoke. "Mr. President, I believe it's important for you to give this speech and make an impassioned case that you truly care for the Palestinian people and that you are committed to working day and night to help them build a better life for themselves and their children and grandchildren," he said. "But from an intelligence perspective, I have to implore you not to give the speech in Jerusalem. Agent Ryker has just contacted me with new intel."

"Saying what?"

"He and the Raven have uncovered evidence about a new terrorist organization taking shape. As best we can discern, it's based in Greece. It's very well-funded. And Ryker and his team have picked up evidence that the group is making plans to attack senior U.S. officials in the coming weeks, including you. Whether this is connected to the Iranian threat I cannot say at this point. But Martha and I have just set up a crisis task force at Langley to find out everything we possibly can about this new group. And in light of all these developments, I have to strongly advise you not to go to Jerusalem at this particular time. The dashboard is blinking red, Mr. President. An attack *is* coming. And we've got to make sure the terrorists don't have a clear shot at you."

46

LONDON, ENGLAND—25 NOVEMBER

It was three minutes before 7 a.m. as Maxim turned left onto Averill Street.

By the time he slowed his cab to a stop, the Sullivans were already coming out the red front door. Meryl entered first with a cheery "Morning!" Giles climbed into the backseat after her, somewhat surly, his face buried in his smartphone.

"The usual?" Maxim asked, already pulling away from the curb.

"Actually, no," Meryl said, taking a sip from the to-go mug in her gloved hands. "Could you be a dear and drop me off at the U.S. Embassy, then take Giles on to Broadcasting House?"

"Of course, ma'am. Whatever you need."

Maxim looped around and got back on Fulham Palace Road, heading toward Putney Bridge. "Is that General Evans bloke still coming?" he asked, looking back in the rearview mirror. "I figured with what the Palestinian leader has been saying, the trip would be off."

"Me, too, but he's still coming," Meryl said before taking another sip. "I all but begged the embassy for the first exclusive interview in which he will articulate the American reaction, and they've said yes."

"Brilliant, ma'am—good for you."

"Well, we'll see. I'm having breakfast with the ambassador in a few minutes to nail it down."

"For tomorrow?"

"Most likely."

"Wouldn't that be exciting?" said Maxim. "Will you need my services? I can clear my schedule and take you and your crew anywhere you need."

"That would be marvelous. Let's see how this breakfast goes; then I'll ring you."

Mohammed al-Qassab was about to lose it.

He could think of nowhere he wanted to be less just then than a breakfast meeting in Canary Wharf with a room full of Chinese CEOs. One of the partners had been droning on for a good ten or fifteen minutes about exchange rates. All the Syrian could think about was the fact that he was currently responsible for three of the most complicated operations of his life, all officially sanctioned by Kairos, all with a very high chance of failure. If they did fail, his freedom, and likely his very life, were in danger. Yet there he sat, trapped in a twenty-fifth-floor conference room with people he didn't know, preparing to make a presentation he cared nothing about.

Just then, his smartphone vibrated.

Must talk now, read the text.

"Excuse me," he said, catching everyone in the room by surprise. "I wonder if we might take, shall we say, an environmental break?"

Smiles of recognition broke out all around the room. Al-Qassab got up and moved quickly out of the conference room, down the hallway, and into the stairwell at the far end. He bounded up the steps two at a time, then spilled out into a smartly appointed vestibule two flights up. He fished a set of keys out of the pocket of his trousers and unlocked the door, which opened to a rooftop lounge. It could be rented for parties and meetings by tenants of the building. At the moment, it was devoid of another soul. Punching in a series of numbers on his phone from memory, he paced nervously as he waited for the call to go through. Then he heard Dr. Ali Haqqani on the other end.

"We have a problem," the Pakistani blurted out.

"Not exactly the best time to chat," al-Qassab replied, hoping the tone of his voice would remind the surgeon that they were on an unsecured line.

"It cannot be helped. I'm leaving tonight."

"Leaving?" al-Qassab asked.

"A friend has a home in the country. He won't be there for several weeks. I thought I might go there for a break."

"What about your staff?"

"I have given them the next two weeks off."

"What about your patients?"

"We are rescheduling all of them."

With that, the call was over. Al-Qassab stared at the phone, then out over London. This was an ominous development. The two men had discussed the possibility of Haqqani leaving the country before the operation was complete. Yet in the end they had concluded that leaving might draw undue attention. The better play was for Haqqani to stay put, go about his daily routine, and act horrified and bewildered when the bomb went off.

Why, then, the sudden change of plans?

Maxim's mobile phone rang.

Meryl Sullivan's number came up on the screen. "Maxim?"

"Yes?"

"We're a go."

"You got the exclusive?"

"I did."

"*Brilliant.* How can I be of service?"

47

In the Rocky Mountains, it was still Monday night.

Well, technically Tuesday morning, Marcus realized, glancing at his watch. It was also snowing something fierce. He was supposed to be heading to his mother's house. Now many of the mountain roads wouldn't be cleared for hours, at best.

Without another option, the two men rolled up their sleeves and went to work. Stopping only for a late-night snack of leftover borscht, they carefully reviewed all the intelligence Oleg had gathered on the Russian connection to this shadowy new terrorist group. They also reviewed everything Oleg had gathered on the Russian moles operating inside NATO and the E.U.

Marcus pressed Oleg to brief him on the dozen folks the Russians had on their payroll who worked for the Greek parliament, in the Greek prime minister's office, or within the Greek military. Was it possible that one or more of these were involved in establishing this new terror front? Oleg searched for each name in all the computer files he'd smuggled out of the Kremlin. He also sent the names to Martha Dell and her team back at Langley to cross-check them against everyone in the CIA's and NSA's databases. Thus far, both agencies had come up empty. There was nothing to suggest that any of the compromised Greeks were involved in terrorism, though Dell vowed that her people would keep looking.

Well after three in the morning, bleary and bloodshot, the men called it quits. Oleg found Marcus a set of clean linens and a pillow, then stepped into the bathroom to change into a pair of red silk pajamas and brush his teeth. When he was done, he climbed up to his loft and disappeared. Marcus said nothing but smiled to himself at how ridiculous the Russian looked, before stepping into the bathroom himself. He changed into navy-blue running shorts and a gray T-shirt, brushed his teeth, and gargled some mouthwash. Then he came back into the living room, made up the couch, turned out the lights, and tried to settle down.

Rather than sleep, however, Marcus found himself staring at the dying embers in the fireplace, replaying in his mind's eye the painful conversation he'd had with Maya Emerson and bracing himself for the exact same conversation he was about to have with his mother. This, he knew, was why he hadn't come home in so long. He couldn't bear to be told he was disappointing her. On top of everything else, it was simply too much. For much of the last two years, he'd struggled every morning just to get out of bed. Most days, in fact, having stayed up until the wee hours of the morning watching ESPN or listening to music, he hadn't gotten up until well after noon. What was the point? After Elena and Lars's deaths, he'd been consumed by utter loneliness and wrenching grief. The last thing he needed was his mother's guilt trip. But it was coming, and Marcus was grateful for the storm that had given him a reprieve from the inevitable for one more night.

As it happened, Oleg was also too keyed up to sleep. As the Russian lay there in the loft, no doubt staring up at the sloped ceiling of the A-frame, he suddenly called out in the darkness, asking Marcus if he was still awake.

They started talking and didn't stop until dawn. At first they traded theories on why Ziad would shoot down the White House peace plan rather than use it as a basis for negotiations. Oleg was particularly astonished that the Saudis, the Emiratis, and the Bahrainis had already assured the Clarke administration that they would invest upwards of $100 billion over the next ten years to help build a viable Palestinian state, yet Ziad still wasn't biting.

Eventually, though, they recounted their miraculous escape from Russia and how close they had come to never getting out at all. Oleg said he didn't believe in miracles. It had all been luck, he argued, a fortunate twist of fate.

Marcus knew better.

48

The talk shifted to Jenny Morris.

Oleg asked how she was doing and seemed stunned to learn Marcus had no idea. Oleg was under strict orders not to contact her, but apparently no one had told him Marcus was too. Oleg was actually under legal prohibition from contacting *anyone* in the U.S. government other than Marcus, Martha Dell, and one technical guy in the CIA's Office of Information Technology. But Oleg would be forever grateful to the woman who had helped save his life and his country, and he wanted to know how she was faring. "Don't you want to know?" the Russian asked.

"Of course."

"Then why haven't you hacked into her computer?"

"Very funny."

"Surely there's something you can do to find out, someone you could ask."

Marcus didn't answer, just let the statement hang in the air. He knew Oleg was right, though, and felt a sudden twinge of guilt. He could be resourceful when he wanted to be. Why hadn't he found a way to get an update on Jenny Morris?

"Can I ask you a question?" the Russian asked after a long silence.

"Haven't you been doing that all night?" Marcus replied.

"A personal question."

"Maybe."

"What do you mean, *maybe*?"

"You can ask, but only if I can ask you something first."

"Ask whatever you want," the Russian replied.

"Fine, here's my question," Marcus said. "Can you ever imagine that you could believe that God exists and that he loves you and wants you to know him personally?"

"That's an easy one," Oleg answered. "Not in a million years."

"Why not?"

"I'm a man of science, my friend—a man of logic, reason."

"And you don't believe a serious, educated, logical thinker can believe in God?"

"If he's truly honest with himself intellectually? No—no chance."

"You don't stare up at the stars at night or look into your wife's eyes and marvel at it and think maybe, just maybe, we're not all the product of random chance but the result of some kind of intelligent design?"

"No, not really."

"But you baptized Vasily, right?"

"True."

"Why?"

"Because my lunatic father-in-law insisted."

"Because your beloved *Marina* insisted."

"Well, of course," Oleg said, a wistfulness in his tone. "I may be an atheist, Marcus, but I'm not a fool."

"Have you ever read the Bible?"

"Of course not."

"You've never read the number-one bestselling book in the history of mankind?"

"Why would I?"

"How can you rule out the existence of God without at least reading the book that two *billion* people believe are his very words?"

"I don't know. I just never had any interest."

"Would you read it?"

"Why would I bother?"

"As a favor to me."

"You're serious?"

"I am."

"You're not going to change me—I'm unconvertible."

"Maybe, maybe not."

"It's never going to happen, Marcus—100 percent, no."

"But will you at least read it? The New Testament, even?"

"In exchange for what?"

"For me answering your question."

"I haven't even asked it yet," the Russian protested. "You have no idea what I'm going to ask."

"I'm an open book, my friend," Marcus replied. "If you'll promise to read just one of the Gospel accounts in the New Testament, I'll answer any question you have."

"Really?"

"Really."

"Okay, then, I will read just one of the Gospels."

"You promise?"

"Do you?"

"Of course."

"Then so do I."

"Great," Marcus said. "That's settled. Now, what is your question?"

There was a long pause. The last of the embers in the fireplace were dying. The snow was still coming down hard. Oleg cleared his throat and spoke softly.

"Marcus?"

"Yes?"

"Do you think you'll ever remarry?"

49

LONDON, ENGLAND—26 NOVEMBER

The alarm went off at precisely 5 a.m.

Typically Maxim hit the snooze button and slept another twenty or thirty minutes, but not today. His heart was racing. This was it, the day for which they had prayed and planned for so long.

Amina was already up, showered, and dressed. To Maxim's surprise, she had even made them breakfast. He couldn't remember the last time she'd done so. They sat down to steaming plates of scrambled eggs, bangers, brown bread she had gotten up early to bake herself, and strong black coffee. They said very little as they ate their last meal together. Neither had any more questions. They had been over the plan a thousand times. Every detail was tattooed into their psyches. All that was left was to execute.

"Are you ready, my love?" Maxim asked as he finished eating.

"Inshallah," she said with a genuine smile.

Wiping his mouth with a napkin, he kissed his sister on the forehead, then headed out. He bounded down the five flights of stairs, too full of energy to take the lift, then bolted out the back door of the building, unlocked his cab, and fired up the engine.

Maxim never stopped on his way to Averill Street. But today he did. He pulled up at a newsstand not far from his apartment on the East End, purchased a fresh pack of cigarettes, three tabloids, and a copy of *The Times*. Setting down a fifty-pound note, he told the man to keep the change. That was his signal back to his Kairos handlers. The operation was a go. The vendor nodded and picked up a mobile phone to relay the message to others as Maxim dashed back to his still-running cab.

At precisely seven o'clock, the red door opened. This time, however, only Meryl Sullivan emerged from the town house.

"Where's the mister?" Maxim asked as Meryl climbed into the backseat. "Is everything okay?"

"Giles won't be coming today—a wee bit under the weather, I'm afraid."

"So sorry to hear that, ma'am."

"Never you mind—he'll be fine. I made him a fresh pot of tea and tucked him back into bed. I'm sure he'll be back with us tomorrow. Now listen, we need to stop by the studio and pick up Thomas before heading to Downing Street."

"Of course, ma'am," Maxim said. Thomas Gibney, Meryl's cameraman, was a frequent rider in the hackney cab.

The main studios of the British Broadcasting Corporation were located on Portland Place in the Marylebone district of London. Maxim pulled up to the front entrance, idled, and turned his blinkers on. A moment later, Thomas got into the cab, carrying two large cases of equipment.

"Morning, Tommy," Maxim said cheerfully.

"Maxim, Meryl," the cameraman replied, tipping his plaid cap.

"Downing Street, ma'am?" Maxim asked.

"Yes, Maxim, right away."

The morning traffic was more congested than usual, but neither Sullivan nor Gibney paid any mind. They were completely focused on discussing the logistics of their day. Their voices were animated, full of anticipation about the interview with Evans and the headlines it might generate not only in the U.K. but around the world.

Neither the journalist nor the cameraman even noticed at first that Maxim had turned off the main road and into an abandoned underground parking garage. Only when Maxim took the car down three further levels did Tommy ask where on earth they were going.

"To hell, my friend," Maxim said, pulling the cab to a stop. He drew a silenced pistol from under his raincoat, pivoted quickly, and double-tapped the man to his forehead.

Meryl Sullivan's eyes went wide.

"You, too, my love," he said, then shot her once in the head and once in the chest before she could let out a scream.

A moment later, Amina stepped out of the shadows.

"All set?" she asked.

"Absolutely," Maxim replied.

He exited the driver's-side door and grabbed some blankets out of the boot while Amina stripped the two corpses of their wallets and press passes. When she was done, Maxim covered the two bodies with the blankets and removed the two cases of equipment Gibney had brought with him. Then they climbed into a nearby van that had been painted to look exactly like those used by the BBC News division.

50

It was on to Whitehall.

Along the way, Amina removed Thomas Gibney's driver's license from his wallet and replaced it with a falsified license bearing Gibney's name but Maxim's photograph. She made the same swap in Meryl Sullivan's wallet, replacing the British woman's real license with a fake one bearing her own photograph. Next, she removed family photos from both wallets and put them in an envelope with their legitimate press passes. The envelope she sealed and slipped into the glove compartment, hidden under a stack of other papers. Then she slipped over her neck a falsified BBC press pass dangling from a thin chain. It bore her picture and Sullivan's name and details. She handed her brother a similar pass bearing Maxim's photograph and Gibney's details.

They arrived early to the Foreign Ministry. Parking the van in a special lot for the media, they unloaded their equipment and headed inside. Once there, they handed over their documents to the security division for verification.

The process seemed to take forever. With every minute that passed, the risk was rising that either or both of them would break out in perspiration or in some other way look guilty. They had been assured by their handler that both of their press passes were masterful, flawless forgeries, as were their driver's licenses.

They had better be, thought Maxim. He had great confidence in his handler. The man was a stickler for details and always seemed flush with cash. He wasn't going to cut corners. Kairos would pay for the best money could buy. What still worried him, however, was that they might be asked questions they were not adequately prepared for.

One of the security guards asked Amina for her national ID number. She flawlessly rattled off Meryl's from memory. A moment later, Maxim was asked his home address. He gave the guard Gibney's without hesitation. A grueling two additional minutes passed, but in the end, they were each given a curt nod and waved forward.

Next they had to pass through the magnetometers, Maxim first, followed by Amina. Dr. Haqqani had insisted that the amount of metal used both for the detonator and the internal phone-call receiver was so minuscule as to eliminate all concern. They had even run several tests, putting Amina through both a metal detector and a bomb sniffer that al-Qassab had purchased and stored at a safe house in Haggerston.

To their relief, they both passed through the metal-detection equipment without triggering an alarm. But they weren't done yet. Each was now wanded. Once again, they cleared without drawing any attention.

Finally the two submitted their camera equipment, all of which was run through an X-ray machine and then thoroughly checked by hand. To Maxim's astonishment, this, too, went without a hitch. Less than fifteen minutes after entering the press center, they were fully cleared through security.

Amina excused herself and headed toward a nearby ladies' room. Once inside, she stepped into a stall and locked the door behind her. Opening her purse, she took off the press pass stating that she was Meryl Sullivan and replaced it with yet another falsified pass. This one used her real name and personal details. Maxim was in the men's room going through the same process.

The theory was this: the security guards working at the Ministry of Foreign Affairs couldn't possibly know every British and foreign journalist who covered Whitehall. There were hundreds of them and new ones coming and going every month. The press pool, however—the mere two dozen reporters and producers who would actually be standing out in the freezing cold on Downing Street to cover a simple "coming and going"—was a more intimate group. They would definitely know Sullivan. They might even know Gibney. That, al-Qassab had informed them, was a risk they could not take. They needed to act as if they were a crew newly assigned to Whitehall by the BBC and just helping out for the day.

As they were among the first of the TV crews to arrive on Downing Street, Maxim found a prime location on the risers across from Number 10 and the famed black door. He set up the tripod, mounted the video camera upon it, then put on his headphones and tested all of his equipment. Next he pulled out the mobile phone the surgeon had given him, powered it up, and slipped it into his raincoat pocket.

Over the course of the next hour, more crews arrived, and by ten o'clock sharp, everyone was in position.

51

Several of the reporters asked about Meryl.

The utter implosion of the American peace plan even before it had been publicly unveiled was a huge story. It wasn't like Meryl to be late. Where could she be?

Maxim kept his mouth shut. He was just supposed to be a cameraman, after all. Amina took the lead. In her nearly flawless English, she explained that she had no idea where Meryl was but that she fully expected the veteran correspondent and her crew to be there any moment. She even pretended to text the woman several times to figure out where she was.

Meanwhile, Maxim was growing more anxious by the minute. One of the heavily armed bobbies was eyeing him suspiciously. How long would it be until someone came over and interrogated him and Amina and blew their covers? Amina could see that he was growing anxious. She patted him gently on the arm and whispered that everything would be fine.

"Stand by!" a protocol officer suddenly shouted.

A moment later, a black BMW sedan with red-and-blue flashing lights mounted in the front grille pulled up Downing Street from their right, followed by two black, armor-plated Suburbans. The motorcade stopped about twenty yards from Number 10. Out of the front passenger door of the BMW emerged a tall man wearing a dark suit, sunglasses, and a small earpiece. Maxim knew him immediately to be Agent Geoffrey Stone, head of General Evans's security detail. Kairos had sent him dossiers on everything that was known about the detail and their procedures, and Maxim had memorized the entire file. Beside Stone now stood a rather striking woman of Indian extraction. This had to be Agent Kailea Curtis, Maxim told himself. Both agents swept the faces in the crowd. Then Stone opened the back door of the BMW, and out stepped the U.S. national security advisor, a broad smile plastered on his face.

"General Evans," shouted one of the reporters from Sky News. "What's your response to the Palestinians' rejection of the president's plan?"

"What do you have to say to Chairman Ziad?" shouted another.

"Has President Clarke betrayed the Palestinian people?" yelled a third.

The general smiled and waved to the press corps as he helped Susan Davis out of the backseat of the BMW.

Maxim was riveted as he stared through the viewfinder of the video camera at the two walking the twenty yards up to the famous black door marked Number 10 and stopping. So far everything was going as planned. The Chechen was not surprised that Evans and Davis were standing there without their security detail, nor that Agents Stone and Curtis were standing behind the BMW, nearly out of view of the reporters. It was, after all, the first of two photo ops. DSS agents were never supposed to be in the picture. Maxim had watched at least a hundred videos on YouTube of various world leaders visiting this famous house, and rarely if ever had he seen bodyguards in close proximity to their protectees.

Maxim had been explicitly instructed by al-Qassab not to detonate the bomb until Evans and Davis reemerged from the building with the British prime minister at their side. The PM was the primary target, the Syrian had said, and chances were good that he would accompany Evans and Davis outside after the meeting and smile at the cameras. But Maxim simply could not wait. He was now sweating profusely, even in the November cold, and increasingly terrified that he and Amina would be found out and that all their painstaking preparations would come to naught.

This was it, Maxim decided. It had to be now. Besides, Amina was not expecting it. She was calm, relaxed, sure she had at least another hour or more to wait. How much more merciful and efficient, he thought, not to have her even the slightest bit worried?

Slipping his right hand into his coat pocket, Maxim gripped the mobile phone, felt for the number five, which he had covered with a bit of masking tape. The Americans weren't answering any of the media's questions. They were just standing there, smiling like imbeciles.

Maxim sniffed. What a perfect moment.

Just as the Americans were about to turn and step inside, the Chechen hit the speed dial and shouted at the top of his voice. *"Allahu akbar!"*

The massive explosion came a split second later.

PART
THREE

52

As Abu Nakba lay prostrate on the floor, there was a knock at the door.

He had been praying all night in his private study and reading the Qur'an by candlelight, and he had not stopped when morning came. No food had touched his lips in ninety-six hours. Nor had water or any other form of drink. His physician had warned him that at his age there could be grave consequences for fasting for so long, but the founder of Kairos refused to listen.

"Allah bids me to fast," he would say. "If he also bids me to leave this world and enter paradise, so be it."

Having left standing orders with his staff that he not be disturbed, he had no desire to see mere mortals. He longed only to enter the presence of Allah himself. The knock, therefore, startled him as he lay facedown on the prayer rug that had been shipped as a gift to him by Iran's Supreme Leader. The door opened a crack, and Hamdi Yaşar stuck his head in.

"It is I, my father, and it is finished," his closest aide said quietly. "Come and see."

The old man lifted his head. Could it be over already? Had that much time truly passed? With much difficulty, he grabbed his cane and used it to pull himself back to his feet. Then he padded into the adjoining conference room. Yaşar was waiting for him and helped the old man into his favorite chair. As Abu Nakba fumbled to put on his glasses, both men looked up at the large screen on the far wall.

The TV was tuned to Al-Sawt and showed footage from a rooftop camera pointed at Number 10 Downing Street. The image showed billowing smoke and flames leaping into the air. The anchor, a veiled woman back in the studio in Doha, was explaining what had happened, but Abu Nakba wasn't listening. He already knew, and tears of joy began to streak down his face.

"You have done well, my son," the old man said after several minutes, when he had composed himself and wiped his eyes dry. "With three strikes against the Great Satan in less than two weeks, Allah will be well pleased. And for what it's worth, so am I."

"That means a great deal to me, my father," Hamdi Yaşar said as he turned off the television and sat down beside the man. "Thank you."

They sat quietly together for a while, eyes closed, savoring the moment.

"As you know, I grew up in the desert," the old man said after some time. "An orphan. Poor. Very little education. No prospects for a better life. But Allah saw me. He saw my heart and knew my soul and took pity on this little orphan boy. He had a plan for me. He raised me far above my station, enabled me to become a warrior for his name. And everything in me is shaking, telling me that the time of the Mahdi's arrival and the rebuilding of the once-and-future Caliphate is fast approaching. This is what drives me. This is what gives me joy and such strength in the season of my sunset—the hope of striking a fatal blow to the Crusaders and the Zionists and ushering in the End of Days."

"Your vision has always inspired me, my father," Yaşar said. "But never more than today."

"Come, join me on the veranda," said Abu Nakba.

The younger man helped his elder rise to his feet, and the two walked out of the private study to a spacious balcony. They settled down in cushioned chairs beside a small glass table. The sun was high and bright over the vast expanse of desert. The sky was a brilliant blue, and there was not a cloud to be seen to the very edge of the horizon. The air was cool. The thermometer read twenty-three degrees Celsius, about seventy-three degrees Fahrenheit. A slight breeze was coming from the north. Abu Nakba felt there would soon be rain, and he said as much to his protégé.

"Rain, my father?" Yaşar looked doubtful.

Winter was approaching, to be sure. There were typically only six or seven days of any rain in a year in Libya, usually in November and December. Today it did not look as if rain were imminent. Yet Abu Nakba had always been able to feel precipitation coming, rare though it was. In childhood he'd astounded the adults in the madrassa by his uncanny ability to predict the first day of rain every year without fail. It would not be today, though, he said; of this he was certain.

After a time, the old man asked, "What progress have you made on our Iranian friend's request?"

"I have good news there, too," Yaşar replied.

"You have my undivided attention."

"Very well, here is the short version. At your command, I have been setting up a Kairos cell in Palestine. We began last year, recruiting a few low-level people, building a bit of infrastructure, but it has been slow going. Until now."

"Go on."

"Last week, I received a message from a man you may have heard of, a Dr. Hussam Mashrawi—he lives in Jerusalem."

"The son-in-law of Amin al-Azzam? The director of the Waqf?"

"The very same," Yaşar said. "So you know him?"

"Not personally," said the old man. "I certainly know of them. Al-Azzam is a good man from a good family. Devout. Brilliant. The son-in-law, I'm not so certain."

"Actually, Mashrawi portrays himself as a moderate, but that's a facade. In truth, he is one of us."

"How do you know?"

"I met with him a while back in Cairo. We spent several hours together.

I went back to Doha convinced, and we have stayed in touch ever since. He's ready to help us in any way we ask. In fact, he's already been recruiting people, acquiring assets. As a result, I now have a dozen Palestinians and Israeli Arabs on the Kairos payroll. On my orders, they are lying low for now. But they are itching for battle."

"And?"

"And last week he contacted me with incredible news—he said President Clarke was planning to come to Jerusalem in mid-December to deliver a major speech outlining his so-called peace plan on the Haram al-Sharif."

"You cannot be serious."

"I am," Yaşar said. "The intel is good. An advance team came last weekend from Washington to make all the preparations for the trip. Mashrawi even sent me pictures of him meeting with them. Here, take a look."

As per their standard security protocols, Yaşar had turned off his mobile phone and removed its SIM card before coming to the compound. But he had brought a half-dozen printed images of the photos Mashrawi had texted him. They were in a sealed envelope, which he now handed over to the old man.

"Miraculous," said the Kairos founder, chuckling to himself. "The president of the United States. Very likely the prime minister of the Zionists as well. Standing together in al-Quds. Together on the Haram al-Sharif. A man on the inside of the Waqf. A team in place. And all within the window the Supreme Leader asked of us. How great and merciful is Allah?"

With this, the old man rang a silver bell. A servant appeared immediately. Abu Nakba instructed him to bring tea and some freshly baked bread.

It was time to break his fast. There was much work to be done, and he needed his strength.

53

Marcus awoke in a panic, his body covered in sweat.

He'd been having one nightmare after another about the president being shot and killed in the Holy City while Marcus just watched, frozen, unable to react. In one, Clarke's head was blown off by a sniper. In another, the assassin was a veiled woman hiding a handgun under her robe. In yet another, the president had just entered the Al-Aqsa Mosque when the entire building erupted in a tremendous explosion.

It had been months since he'd experienced such night terrors. In the past, his nightmares centered on the deaths of his wife and son and him just standing there paralyzed and unable to help them. In time, those visions had faded. Now they were being replaced by new anxieties that left him exhausted and disoriented.

Marcus rubbed his eyes and sat up. It took him several moments to realize that he wasn't in Jerusalem. He was seven thousand miles and nine time zones away. But he wasn't on the outskirts of Aspen anymore, either. He was finally back in Monument, back in the town of his youth, waking up in the very room—the very bed—he'd slept in growing up. He hadn't set the alarm on his phone. He'd even turned off the ringer. He was, after all, supposed to be on vacation.

The storm had broken. The Rocky Mountain roads had been plowed. After spending more than eighteen hours holed up in Oleg's A-frame, drinking tea and eating borscht because that's all the Russian had in the house, Marcus had finally been able to drive back down to civilization. His mother had welcomed him with open arms, grateful to finally see and hold her only son again. And the truth was, he was grateful to be back in his childhood home, eating her amazing cooking again, even if the conversation he dreaded having with her still hung over him like a cloud.

The sun was just coming up across the Front Range. Dawn's early light streamed through the curtains his mother had hand-sewn for him when he was a boy. He looked around at the faded family photos and movie posters and his high school and college diplomas on the walls. His eyes, bleary and red, swept across the dusty football and basketball trophies on the shelves, across the various knickknacks from summer camps and junior prom and senior ball and spring break trips and his four years at UNC Greeley. It was surreal to think that just a few days before, he'd been standing in the epicenter of the epicenter of the epicenter, and now he was so far removed from those exotic sights and sounds and smells.

Marcus couldn't remember a time he had seen his mother so happy. The moment he'd pulled the Corvette into the driveway just after nine o'clock the previous evening and shut down the engine, she'd come bursting out the front door and embraced him with kisses and tears. As they'd climbed onto the porch, he had smelled the lasagna she had baked for him. He'd quickly set down his luggage and washed his hands in the little restroom off the living room and joined her in the kitchen, where they'd had dinner together, just the two of them, with a bottle of cabernet and so many stories to tell.

His older sisters, Marta and Nicole, and their husbands and children had not yet arrived. They'd be coming Thursday morning. It would be the first time they celebrated Thanksgiving together in years, and Marcus was eager to catch up with them and watch movies together and play with his nieces, all of whom were growing so quickly. Yet he could see in his mother's eyes how much she needed time with him alone. The prodigal son had finally come home.

As Marcus came down the stairs and into the kitchen, he found his mother, clad in a smudged apron, already cooking up a storm.

"Wow, that's quite a production," Marcus said as he looked over all the pies and squash and stuffing that were in various stages of preparation as his mother was busy dressing not one turkey but two.

"Why, you're up early—I was sure you'd be in bed till noon, at least," she replied. "You sleep okay?"

He couldn't bear to lie to her. Instead, he simply went over and gave her a hug and a kiss on the top of her head.

"I'm good, Mom, thanks."

"Want some coffee? I just made a fresh pot."

"I'd love some," he said, opening a cabinet, grabbing a mug with the logo of the U.S. Marines emblazoned on it, and pouring himself the first of what he was sure would be many, many cups that day. "So how can I help you today, Mom? I'm all yours."

He could tell the question caught her completely off guard. It wasn't a sentence she'd heard from her son before. But before she could answer, the phone on the wall rang.

"Would you get that, honey?" Marjorie said. "My hands are all messy. It's probably Esther Kline. She wants to drop off some new toys for Nicole's kids."

Marcus took another sip of coffee, then set down the mug, crossed the kitchen, and picked up the receiver.

"Domino's Pizza, may I take your order?" he quipped, throwing in a lame British accent for no particular reason at all.

As his mother shot him a glance of mock disapproval, Marcus was shocked to find that the voice at the other end of the line was not that of Esther Kline, nor any of his mother's other friends. It was Pete Hwang, calling from Washington.

"Marcus, you need to get back here—now."

"Why, what are you talking about?"

"Haven't you heard what's going on in London?"

"I just woke up."

"Well, pack up and get to the airport. We just got hit again."

Marcus hung up the phone, went immediately to the family room, turned on the television, and found CNN.

"What is it, Marcus?" his mother asked. "What's the matter?"

The moment she followed him into the room and saw the images on the screen, she knew. They both did.

"You need to go," she said.

Marcus turned and looked at her, unsure if she'd just asked a question or was taking a shot at him. He tried to steel himself for the conversation he'd been dreading. He certainly had not intended it to happen so soon, and definitely not like this.

"Listen, Mom," he began. "I know that you—"

But she cut him off. "They need you," she said. "Go pack, and I'll get your clothes out of the dryer."

"But . . ."

She stepped closer to him and put her finger over his lips. "Marcus, when I look in your eyes, I see your father," she said softly. "He was a warrior, and so are you. Is that calling easy on a wife or a mom, to say so many good-byes, to see your man go into danger, not knowing if you'll ever see him again? No. It's not. But that's what you were born for. That's why God made you. That's why he wired you like he did. To take risks—crazy risks. Not for yourself. But to protect people. Me. Your family. Your country. I know it's not easy on you either. Because sometimes you can't always protect the people you love. But never think for one minute that I don't love you or support you 1,000 percent. Because I do. Your father had his calling. You have yours. And you're good at it. Really good. That's why they need you. So go—do what you have to do without any fear or hesitation—and God be with you. I'm so proud of you."

Then she kissed him on the cheek, wiped a strand of hair from his eyes, and held him one last time.

54

By sundown, Marcus was back in Washington.

Upon landing at Reagan National, he took a cab directly to the White House, a last-minute request of Director Stephens. Having no time to go home to change, Marcus found himself standing at attention in the Situation Room wearing not a suit and tie but ripped blue jeans, a black T-shirt, and a North Face fleece. The president, who had begun the morning speaking at a fund-raising breakfast in Los Angeles, had landed back at Joint Base Andrews less than an hour ago. His motorcade had just pulled onto the White House grounds moments earlier, and he now rushed into the room for his first formal briefing.

Around the table were Stephens, an ashen-faced Secretary of State Meg Whitney, Defense Secretary Cal Foster, and Bill McDermott, who was now serving as the acting national security advisor. The VP was on Air Force Two, returning from meetings in Brazil. The secretary of Homeland Security was also on a plane, coming back to D.C. from a visit to the Texas border. The FBI director was on a plane bound for London.

"Where are we?" Clarke said after asking everyone to sit.

Stephens nodded to McDermott, who pressed several buttons on the console before him, lowering the lights and turning on the large flat-screen monitor on the far wall. Displayed were pictures of each of the Americans killed in London.

"So far, we have eight Americans dead," he explained. "In addition to General Barry Evans and Dr. Susan Davis, six American journalists were killed in the blast."

Marcus stared at the faces, his fists clenched and jaw tight. Then he lowered his head in the darkness and said a silent prayer for their families and friends. After a full minute, Stephens called for the next slide.

"Twenty-three British citizens were also killed," the CIA director continued as more victims' faces were projected on the screen. "They included two police officers, but mostly they were journalists and photographers. Next slide. In addition, nine others died in the blast, a combination of reporters, producers, and cameramen, mostly from European countries."

"Injuries?" Clarke asked.

"Next slide," said Stephens. "Yes, sir, they were extensive. Another thirty-one people—Americans, Brits, and others—were injured, some quite severely. At the moment, at least six lives are hanging by a thread. We may not know for several more hours if they are going to make it."

"I don't see any DSS agents among the dead," said the president.

"That's true, sir. Not a single DSS agent was killed, but Agents Geoff Stone and Kailea Curtis were cut up pretty badly by flying glass and shrapnel."

"I don't understand," Clarke said. "How did Stone and Curtis survive if Evans and Davis didn't?"

"Protocol," interjected Defense Secretary Foster.

"I'm sorry?" Clarke asked.

"The Brits don't permit bodyguards to stand close to their protectees when they come down Downing Street," Foster explained. "It's partly tradition and partly optics. They want photos of principals entering Number 10 on their own, not with aides and certainly not surrounded by agents. It's been that way forever. I've seen it dozens of times myself."

"Could Barry and Susan have survived if their agents had been closer?"

"No, sir. They would all have been killed instantly."

"So where exactly were Agents Stone and Curtis standing?"

"Next slide," said Stephens.

On-screen now was a diagram of the site. The DCI used a laser pointer to show where the front door to Number 10 was and where the motorcade had stopped.

"The agents were at least twenty yards from Evans and Davis. Stone and Curtis were standing behind their vehicles, holding open the doors, when the explosion occurred. Other agents were still in their vehicles."

"That's what saved their lives?" Clarke asked.

"Yes, sir, it is."

"How long will they be in the hospital?"

Stephens turned to the secretary of state. "Meg, do you have that?"

"At least till this weekend, Mr. President," Whitney replied. "I spoke to each of the agents a few hours ago, beginning with Stone and Curtis. They're all doing quite well physically. Emotionally, of course, it's hitting them pretty hard."

"I imagine so," Clarke said. "Get me their numbers, Meg. I'd like to call them all myself."

"That would mean a lot to them, sir. We'll do that right away."

"Good, now talk to me about suspects. Do we have any?"

"No, sir," said Stephens.

"Has anyone claimed responsibility?"

"No, not yet."

"No one?" Clarke asked, incredulous. "Again?"

"I'm afraid not, sir."

"Then tell me we have some solid leads. I mean, how did they get the bomb past security to begin with?"

"Well, sir, the problem is the scene is a complete mess. The bomb went off in the press pool. It was so powerful, we don't have a single body intact.

To be honest, we have absolutely no idea how the attack was executed. Neither do the Brits."

"I don't understand."

"I can explain it to you, or I can show you the video that MI5 sent us."

"The video, of course."

"Are you sure, Mr. President? It's worse than anything I've ever seen before."

"Show me," Clarke said, looking Stephens in the eye. "I want to see exactly what these bastards have done to our people."

55

The acting NSA hit a button and the video began to play.

But McDermott could not watch. He had already seen the video twice.

The first images—all full-color—and accompanying sound track were hardly troubling. A chyron in the top right corner of the screen indicated this portion of video was courtesy of a Sky News feed to its satellite track.

The American motorcade arrives. DSS agents open the doors of the lead sedan. Evans and Davis emerge. The two walk unescorted up Downing Street, smiling at the media but refusing to answer any of the questions shouted by the press corps. As they approach the front door to Number 10, they stop, continue smiling. Suddenly a man yells, *"Allahu akbar!"*—"God is great" in Arabic—and then the video feed is cut.

The next portion of video was in black-and-white and silent. The chyron in the top right corner indicated that these images were from one of the British government surveillance cameras. McDermott winced as he heard the room gasp. In his mind's eye, he could see the images running in slow motion as an explosion erupted from the center of the press pool. There was a brilliant burst of light, and the lens of the surveillance camera cracked. Still, for about ten seconds one could see the devastation. No longer were Evans and Davis visible. No longer were any members of the media visible. Fires raged and thick black smoke billowed to the sky.

The scene cut to the angle of a dashcam in one of the vehicles in the American motorcade. This feed ran in slow motion. Very slow. And this time, the room was completely silent as they watched Evans and Davis vaporize, frame by frame.

Only then did McDermott reopen his eyes, though he still didn't look at the screen. There was no way he could watch his boss and one of his closest friends obliterated for the third time in one day. He did, however, want to watch the president's reaction as he watched the next set of images.

Video footage taken by an MI5 crime scene investigative team began to play, without any audio. Buckets of blood and small bits of body parts were everywhere. Occasionally a scorched shoe with part of a foot was visible or an individual finger wearing a wedding ring. Not once, however, could one find a head or a face or discernible limbs. This was worse than any moment McDermott had ever experienced in combat or any horror movie he had ever seen. Tears were streaming down Whitney's face, but to her credit she continued to watch. Foster watched stone-faced. Stephens, though he had already seen it four times, watched it again even more carefully this time, looking for clues he might have missed before. Clarke was white as a ghost. For the entire four minutes and twenty-seven seconds, he just stared at the flickering screen, at once mesmerized and horrified by the images that were unfolding.

Finally the nightmare was over. McDermott hit the Stop button and turned off the monitor, then brought the lights back up. For several minutes no one said a word. Then Whitney, wiping her eyes with a cloth handkerchief she'd taken from her pocketbook, asked the president if it would be all right if they said a prayer. Clarke nodded and asked Cal Foster, an elder in his Presbyterian church, if he would lead them. When he agreed, they all bowed their heads and closed their eyes.

"Amen. Thank you, Cal," Clarke said when they were finished.

Then he turned back to the director of Central Intelligence. "So clearly this was a suicide bomber—but you still haven't told me how they got the bomb past the Brits' security."

"Honestly, Mr. President, that's what has us all baffled," Stephens replied. "Every member of the press corps went through a standard security screening process, no less professional than what happens here at the White House every day. The Brits certainly would have spotted a vest filled with explosives."

"Could the bomb have been concealed in one of the TV cameras?" Foster asked. "That's how a team of al Qaeda operatives killed Commander Ahmed Massoud on September 9, 2001, just two days before the attacks on us, Mr. President. Massoud was a powerful Afghan warlord. He was vehemently opposed to the rule of the Taliban. Osama bin Laden decided to take him out, to complicate what he knew would be an American retaliation for what was coming. So he sent three jihadists to pose as a TV news crew, and boom, no more Massoud."

"All true, but highly improbable in this case," Stephens said. "Every piece of equipment brought by the media was run through X-ray scanners, bomb sniffers, and hand checks, just like we do here. I don't see any possible way the Brits missed a thing, much less a bomb large enough to do that much damage."

"What about a drone?" Whitney asked.

"No, not possible," Stephens answered. "The Brits have a very sophisticated antidrone system they bought from the Israelis years ago. Believe me, they're watching for this stuff, all of it. I spoke to the head of MI5 twice today, as well as to the head of MI6. They have absolutely no idea how someone pulled this off or who could have done it. And that's what's freaking out everyone in my office right now, because if these terrorists have figured out how to blindside the Brits, who's to say they couldn't do it to us?"

Once again, it was quiet for a while. Then Secretary Whitney spoke up.

"Mr. President, clearly Richard and his team and the FBI are going to do everything in their power to hunt down those responsible for these attacks and bring them to justice," she began. "But right now, what we in this room really need to discuss is your trip to Jerusalem."

"No," said the president. "That won't be necessary."

"Sir," said Whitney, "I know that you have very strong feelings about this, but—"

Clarke, however, cut her off. "I'm not going, Meg."

She looked stunned. They all were stunned.

"I've seen enough," the president said quietly. "There's no way I'm going to let the terrorists win. I'm still going to give the speech and lay out the plan, but I'm not going to put any more Americans in harm's way to do it. I'll give the speech here, in the Oval Office. But for now, I've got more pressing matters. If you'll all excuse me, I need to go call more grieving spouses and then address the nation."

"I'm afraid I have bad news," Hamdi Yaşar said.

Abu Nakba, sitting out on the veranda and enjoying a beautiful desert morning, looked up from his breakfast of coffee and boiled eggs.

"Yesterday I told you that President Clarke was planning to announce his peace plan on the Haram al-Sharif. I wish now I had brought you this intelligence the moment it arrived in my hands," Yaşar continued. "But I was so focused on the operation in London that I set it aside."

"What is the problem?"

"We have been too successful."

"How so?"

"Because London went so well, the American president has been frightened off. I received another message from Mashrawi early this morning. He's just learned that the president has quietly canceled his trip to Jerusalem and will instead give his speech from the White House. I fear I have failed you, my father, just when victory was within our grasp."

Abu Nakba took the younger man's hand and looked back out across the desert. "You have not failed, my son. Stop believing the lies of Satan. A week ago, this opportunity did not exist. And then it did. And now it doesn't. Does this stop the will of Allah? By no means. He has a plan. We just have to wait for it to reveal itself."

"How can you speak of waiting? With all respect, the countdown is ticking to zero, and I have no plan. Neither does Mohammed al-Qassab."

"But you have achieved so much success and so quickly. Was this not the hand of Allah guiding you?"

"Yes, of course, but those operations were easy compared with what lies ahead," Yaşar protested.

Abu Nakba held up his hand, silencing the young man. "I have shared little of my personal story with you. As you know, I am an intensely private man. This is for my safety. And the safety of others. But there are some things you should know, Hamdi. My father was a Libyan. An oilman. But a drunk. A wastrel. He betrayed his religion and his family. He drank away all of our money and left my mother and me to the streets, and I hated him for it. My mother, however, I loved with all my heart and soul. She was a girl from Palestine. Ramallah, in fact. Her father came to Tripoli to work in the oil fields, but he died in a drilling explosion. Her mother died a few years later from cancer. So my mother grew up without means. Without education. She had a simple faith, a pure faith. But she had no way to earn a living. And then one night she was murdered by bandits—her throat was slashed—right before my eyes. I was only seven years old. And now I had no hope. No prospects. No future. I was alone. Hungry. Unwanted. Destined to die young and forgotten, full of bitterness and rage. Yet look what Allah has done. Look what he has made me, where I am today."

Yaşar was quiet, and the old man continued.

"All that I am and have is Allah's. Was it not he who guided and protected me when I joined the Muslim Brotherhood and fought in Egypt against Sadat and his cronies? Should I not have died in the mountains of

Kandahar, fighting the Russians? Or later, in the streets of Mogadishu, fighting the Americans? Or in Fallujah and Mosul? Or in Raqqa and Aleppo? I can claim no credit for whatever successes I have achieved in my life, nor even for surviving as a Palestinian orphan boy to the ripe old age of eighty-three. I live because Allah has chosen me to live, and I serve at his pleasure. He could have taken me from this wretched earth. Instead, he has given me a bold new mission, and to accomplish it, he has given me you."

"The wind is at your back, my father. Allah's hand is mightily upon you, like one of the prophets of old. But perhaps I am not looked upon as fondly. Or maybe I was meant to help you get this far, but no further."

"Nonsense. Put away such foolish talk. Do you really think I could have built Kairos from a forgotten corner of the desert by myself? No, I needed you, so Allah gave you to me. And look what he has done. Just look. We have ninety-seven full-time operatives. A budget of more than $40 million. Three successful operations that have dazzled our investors beyond anything they could have imagined. The Russians think they created us and that they sustain us. So do the Iranians. And the Turks. They all believe they are running us, that we are agents in their employ. They have no idea that they are all pawns in our little game."

"It hardly seems little anymore," Yaşar noted.

"That is true. But how could all of this have happened—how could you and I have seen so much favor in just a few short years—unless Allah was smiling upon us both?"

It was quiet for a good long while.

"How, then, shall we read this setback?" Yaşar finally asked.

"What, Clarke canceling his trip?"

"Yes. It changes everything."

"Relax, my son. Allah will lead us—you must only have faith in the jihad to which we have both been called. In the meantime, you must go to Ankara and hold the hand of the sultan while we await a new door to open."

57

"Gentlemen, I present to you His Excellency, President Ahmet Mustafa."

The protocol officer stood ramrod straight. Hamdi Yaşar immediately rose to his feet. He had arrived from Libya two hours ago, and he and his crew had spent much of that time setting up their cameras, lights, microphones, and the many cables snaking back to the satellite truck parked outside. Now, with less than two minutes to go, the enormous double doors to the ballroom opened, and in walked the twelfth elected leader of the modern Turkish state, surrounded by a phalanx of bodyguards.

Now seventy, Ahmet Mustafa was a rather tall man with a long, gaunt face, thinning gray hair, a pencil-thin mustache, and large bags under his sad, cold eyes. Tonight, Yaşar noticed, he was wearing a charcoal-gray suit, a crisp white shirt, and a dark-maroon tie.

"Hamdi, my friend, what a pleasure to see you again."

"Mr. President, it is my honor," said Yaşar. "Thank you for speaking with Al-Sawt."

"Why not? You know it is my favorite news network."

"That is very kind, Your Excellency."

"Give my regards to your managing director—he is a good man."

"I will—thank you—but now, Your Excellency, we are a bit pressed for time."

Mustafa took his seat as one of the crew attached a microphone to the lapel of his suit coat. Another fitted him with an IFB earpiece, allowing him to hear both the anchor and the director back in Qatar. A moment later, Yaşar asked for quiet and put on his headphones as a red light atop the main camera lit up.

"Good evening, everyone, and thank you for tuning in to *Spotlight*, the region's number one most-watched evening newscast," Yaşar heard the anchor say in Arabic. "Tonight, amid the continuing news out of London, we are honored to speak with Turkish president Ahmet Mustafa, live from the brand-new presidential complex in Ankara. Mr. President, thank you for joining us tonight."

"Good to be with you," Ahmet replied in flawless Arabic, though it was his third language after Turkish and English.

"To begin," the anchor continued, "four senior American diplomats are dead in three separate attacks, along with scores of other casualties. What is your reaction to these terrorist attacks?"

"It is a shock to everyone, really," the president replied. "I knew General Evans well, though not the others so much. And I must say, we had many disagreements on policy. As your viewers know, I strongly oppose President Clarke's so-called peace plan. I oppose his administration's utter disregard for the suffering of the Palestinian people, his insensitivity to the dreams and aspirations of the Muslim world, and his blind subservience to the Zionist cause, no matter how egregious Israel's crimes. But that is a discussion for another time. This is a very sad day for the victims' families and friends."

Yaşar was at once intrigued and impressed with the Turkish leader. The man could somehow signal his devotion to the masses of Islamists around the world whom he considered his spiritual and ideological base while simultaneously sounding sympathetic to the American families who had lost loved ones in attacks he had helped fund. Yet all the while he was not actually denouncing such acts of terrorism much less calling for the perpetrators to be brought to justice. Abu Nakba was right—the man possessed a rare gift that needed to be both cultivated and flattered.

"Less than an hour ago, Mr. President, a communiqué was issued from a new organization based in Athens, taking responsibility for the attacks," said the anchor. "The group is calling itself Kairos. What can you tell us about this group, and will the government of Turkey invoke Article 5 against Kairos, given that two fellow NATO allies—the U.S. and the U.K.—were attacked today?"

"Well, let's slow down there a bit—it is far too premature to be assigning blame or talking about invoking Article 5," Mustafa said. "No one in our region wants another war. Let's see how this all plays out and where the investigations lead."

"And Kairos?"

"This is the first I've heard of such an organization," Mustafa said. "It's all very new to me—I really couldn't say."

"Fair enough. One last question, Mr. President."

"Of course."

"Would you care to comment more specifically on the new peace plan the White House is planning to unveil next month and on which these American diplomats were focused?"

"Well, to be clear, I have not yet seen or read the plan, nor been briefed on it directly by the Americans. But I was the first person that my great friend Palestinian Authority president Ismail Ziad called before he held his press conference the other night. He told me why he and his government had no choice but to oppose the plan, and I find myself agreeing with their decision. What President Clarke and his team are preparing to lay out to the world amounts to a declaration of war against the Palestinian people and their leaders and should be vigorously opposed by every Muslim nation and the entire world with every tool at our disposal and every fiber of our being."

58

"Strong words tonight from Turkish president Ahmet Mustafa," said the anchor.

The red light went off. The live feed was cut, and Hamdi Yaşar stood and helped the president remove his microphone and earpiece.

"Hamdi, might I have a word in private before you go?" Mustafa whispered.

"Why, of course."

"Good—come with me."

Yaşar told his crew he would be back shortly. As they began to pack up their equipment, he walked with the Turkish leader and his bodyguards out of the ballroom and down a long hallway. Taking a left, they entered not the president's formal office but a more intimate adjacent study. Mustafa asked Yaşar to make himself comfortable and for his aides to give them some privacy.

"How did you think that went?" the president asked when they were alone.

"I couldn't have asked for better," Yaşar replied. "I didn't expect you to blast the White House plan as a 'declaration of war' on the Palestinian people. But that will surely be the headline."

"It wasn't too much?"

"Not at all—it was perfect, Your Excellency. The Zionists, the Egyptians, the Jordanians—even the Gulf states—are tripping over themselves to denounce these attacks in the harshest possible language. Meanwhile Tehran is silent. Moscow is cagey. But step by step, you are becoming the voice of every Muslim man, woman, and child who is incensed by American imperialism, furious with Zionist occupation, horrified by the cowardice of the Arab leaders, and crying out for bold, courageous leadership."

"I want you to know, Hamdi, that your advice, along with that of Abu Nakba, has been most welcome. How is our friend the sheikh?"

"He is well, and he is most grateful for your vote of confidence in him," Yaşar lied. "He is forever in your debt."

"Our investment is finally paying dividends," Mustafa said, taking a deep breath and leaning back in his chair. "Now, how are plans coming for the next news story?"

"It's difficult to say, Your Excellency," Yaşar conceded. "It is not easy to kill an American president. It has happened only a few times in history."

"Are you saying you cannot do it?"

"I'm saying it hasn't been done since 1963—and never in this century. It will take a great deal of planning—meticulous planning—and such things take time."

"On the contrary, you must move quickly, with something far grander. This is how you will attract recruits and money and headlines and glory for Allah."

"With respect, Your Excellency, this week's actions have made things more difficult."

"*How dare you say that—how can you have so little faith in this cause?*" Mustafa suddenly fumed. "Yesterday no one had ever heard of Kairos. Today we have captured the attention of the entire world."

"This is my point exactly," Yaşar said. "Abu Nakba, as you well know, was opposed to issuing the communiqué and telling the world our name. But you insisted. And you are the money. You are the grand strategist. So he humbly assented. But now you have captured the full attention of the Central Intelligence Agency, the Defense Intelligence Agency, the United States Secret Service, the Diplomatic Security Service, MI5, MI6, Interpol, the Mossad, the Shin Bet, and the list goes on. It took months for us to plan these attacks, and we had the luxury of not being known, much less hunted. Now everything has changed."

"It took you months and many millions—*my millions*—because you had to recruit and train and build and deploy a team from nothing," the Turkish leader pushed back. "It always takes longer to lay the foundation of a great building. But once that foundation is in place, the rest of the structure goes up very quickly."

Yaşar fought to steady his breathing and his voice. His mission was not to rebuke this man but to hold his hand and keep the money flowing.

"That is true, Your Excellency," he said softly. "Forgive me for my lapse of faith. It was only temporary, I assure you."

"Let us hope so, Hamdi," said Mustafa. "I have a great deal riding on you."

59

It was the first time Marcus had set foot in the building in two weeks.

He had missed all of the memorial services for those killed in the shooting on the sixteenth, having been overseas or in Colorado, and he regretted this, given all that his church family had done to support him when Elena and Lars had died. Still, after what Maya had said to him, it was probably better that he had stayed away for a bit. He hoped that with the passage of some time, Maya would reconsider. He could bear her reproach if he had to, but he certainly didn't want to. He looked for her as he arrived at the service but didn't see her. It was possible, he thought, that she was still in the hospital or recovering at home. It felt odd not knowing or being able to ask her directly.

He headed for a pew in the back, thinking about Elena and Lars, and soon found himself recalling the conversation he'd had with Oleg the other night and the pointed question the Russian had asked him.

"Do you think you'll ever remarry?"

At first, Marcus had been angry at his friend for even broaching a subject so personal and so painful. He realized Oleg was lonely and missing his own wife and son back in Russia, yet the question was insensitive and over the line. Still, he'd promised to answer any question Oleg asked.

"No," Marcus had finally said. "That door is shut to me. Elena was the only girl I have ever loved. I gave her my heart—forever—and that was that. It's not possible to find a woman who could ever come close to her, so getting married isn't worth thinking about. Period. End of story."

Oleg had been skeptical at first. He had pressed Marcus with many follow-up questions. But in the end he had accepted Marcus's answer, however reluctantly.

Yet on the plane back to Washington, Marcus had become increasingly uncomfortable with what he had said. By the time he'd landed at Reagan, he'd been forced to admit, if only to himself, that the issue wasn't so cut-and-dried. Merely contemplating the concept of remarrying seemed like a betrayal of Elena. He felt guilty even thinking about it, much less discussing it. Yet he knew in principle it was not wrong.

Weren't the Scriptures clear? Wasn't a man whose wife had died free to marry again? One was not wed forever, after all, only "till death do us part." Wasn't that the vow he and Elena had taken so many years before? And hadn't God himself said, "It is not good for man to be alone"?

There were times since Elena's death that the loneliness he felt was nearly unbearable. And he was still a young man. It was possible he could live another forty or fifty years. Was he really going to rule out the possibility that the Lord could bring a godly woman into his heart that he could love and cherish for the second half of his life?

Yes, he conceded, it was possible. He could never replace Elena. Nor would he want to. But that didn't mean God couldn't or wouldn't provide someone new, someone different, to fill the wrenching void in his heart.

And yet how could he ever marry again if it meant putting his new wife—whoever she might be—at risk because of the life he led? Was that fair to any woman? And if he gave up this life and career to be with her, to care for her and keep her safe, what then would he do? Could he ever be happy in a job less interesting, where the stakes were so much lower?

The worship band began to play, and this snapped Marcus back to the present. He noticed the sanctuary was standing room only, and he was struck by all the media covering the service. A gaggle of reporters and a bank of video cameras mounted on tripods were set up in the back. Marcus couldn't help but think of Commander Massoud, killed in 2001 by a bomb hidden inside a TV camera. There were no magnetometers or X-ray machines screening people coming into the church. Could what had just happened in London happen here?

A new private security company had been hired by the church to keep everyone safe. Marcus had counted no fewer than a dozen uniformed and armed guards on the premises that morning, including two standing outside the front door and two in the vestibule, and there were likely others he was not seeing. In addition to the rent-a-cops, the D.C. Metro Police had positioned two squad cars out front and two near the parking lot in back. One officer was directing traffic, and several others were gathered on the front steps, keeping an eye on everyone coming in and serving, Marcus hoped, as a deterrent.

As he found a seat, his phone buzzed. It was Kailea, calling from London.

"Hey," he said in a whisper.

"Hey, old man," she replied. "Am I catching you at a bad time? What, are you at a bingo parlor or something?"

Marcus smiled, glad to hear she was regaining her strength and sense of humor.

"Hey, young lady, I'm fine. How about you?"

"They just released me from the hospital—Geoff, too."

"So you're coming back?"

"No, that's why I'm calling."

"Why—what's up?"

"The director wants us to help with the investigation."

"You sure you're up for it?"

"Honestly? No. But that's the job, right?"

"How long will you be?"

"As long as it takes to figure out who's responsible for this mess and put a bullet in their heads—I mean, you know, arrest them and bring them in."

"Right," Marcus said, just as someone began playing the organ. "I've got to go. But keep me up to speed on what you guys find."

"Will do, geezer. Curtis out."

The line went dead.

The service continued without a hitch, but Marcus struggled to concentrate, so consumed were his thoughts with Kairos and what they were plotting next. After the service, though, he was grateful to see so many people he knew. One by one, the men shook his hand and slapped him on the back. The women hugged him and a few kissed his cheek. All of them thanked him for saving their lives. Some cried on his shoulder. But he never saw Maya.

What floored him were the two people standing on the sidewalk as he exited the church—Robert Dayton and Annie Stewart.

"Good morning, Marcus," said the senator, tipping his fedora.

"Senator, Annie—what a pleasant surprise," he replied, shaking their hands. "I thought the Senate was out of session this week."

"It is," Dayton said.

"Then what brings you back to the swamp so early?"

"Something has come up. We wondered if we could talk."

"Must be serious for an atheist to show up at church."

"I'm here on Annie's Baptist credentials," Dayton conceded. "But yes, it's pretty important. You free for lunch?"

"Now?"

"Nothing fancy—how about Manny's?"

"That'd be fine," said Marcus. "My car or yours?"

"Could we walk?" Annie asked. "It's the first nice day in weeks."

As they crossed the street, Marcus whispered to Annie, "I thought you were a Methodist."

She laughed. "I am—he doesn't know the difference."

Soon, the three had hung up their coats and taken a booth.

"So, Marcus," Annie began after the waitress took their orders and stepped away.

"So, Annie," he replied.

"The three of us have known each other a long time, and we have a lot of history together."

"True."

"But the senator finds himself in an unusual position and not entirely sure how to proceed. I suggested he come to you, and after thinking about it for several days, he decided to fly back to D.C. last night."

"I'm happy to help you and the senator if I can, Annie. I consider you both friends, and I don't take that for granted."

"Thank you—and I trust that what we discuss will remain here, unless we come to an agreement on others to bring into the loop?"

"What is this, Las Vegas?" Marcus said, smiling.

Annie smiled back. It was easy to see why Pete Hwang was so infatuated with her, Marcus thought. They'd all met during one of his combat tours in the Marines. Annie had been a young press aide for the senator, fresh out of graduate school and no more than twenty-four or twenty-five years old. He could still remember her dazzling green eyes and short, blonde shag haircut. And that smile. That was well over a decade ago. Yet somehow, she looked better now. She was wearing a navy-blue dress with white trim at the collar. Her hair was longer now, below the shoulders with side-swept bangs. It was still blonde, but there were a few wisps of gray. And she wore glasses—black, narrow, flattop Ray-Bans that gave her a studious look—along with small, silver hoop earrings and a stylish black-and-gold watch.

"The topic," she said, suddenly growing serious, "is Saudi Arabia."

60

"Saudi Arabia?" Marcus asked.

"Let me start at the beginning," said the senator. "I understand the president has decided to cancel his upcoming trip to Jerusalem."

"How did you know about that?"

Dayton just sat back in the booth with a quizzical look, at which point Marcus realized what a ridiculous question that had been. The man was the ranking minority member of the Senate Intelligence Committee. He'd been in this town for a long time and had a lot of sources inside government and out. What's more, he was planning a run for the Democratic nomination for president. Of course he knew what Clarke's plans were, especially on such a sensitive matter of national security.

"Let me strike that from the record, Senator," Marcus laughed. "But yes, in light of last week's events, the president is going to deliver his address on the peace plan from the Oval Office."

"Not from the Temple Mount?"

"No, thank goodness."

"That's a mistake," Dayton said.

"I beg your pardon?"

"The president needs to go to Jerusalem."

"Senator, I know you want his job, but you can't really hate him that much."

Dayton ignored the comment. "The Saudis have had it with Ziad," he said quietly. "They're ready to make peace with Israel on their own. Furthermore, the crown prince is prepared to come to Jerusalem, but only if the president will invite him and facilitate the discussions."

"You're not serious."

"I am."

Marcus turned to Annie.

"He is," she confirmed. "Look, Marcus, we were just in Riyadh a few weeks ago. We met with the king and the crown prince. The senator read them the riot act on everything from the war in Yemen to the murder of that dissident to their completely unacceptable record on human rights. He let them know in no uncertain terms just how furious Congress is with them. But he also made it clear that he knew full well their strategic value as an ally. He told them that, unlike many of his colleagues in the Senate, he was not going to throw them under the bus. But 'business as usual' is no longer acceptable. They have to accelerate their social and economic reforms. They have to release prisoners, beginning with the highest-profile human rights activists. They've got to stop arresting everyone who disagrees with them. They've got to find a way to wrap up this war with the Houthis. And so forth. They weren't happy. But they listened. And then they told us things we've never heard Saudi leaders say before."

"Such as?"

"Such as that in light of the existential threat posed by Iranian mullahs, they've completely reconsidered their position on Israel. They've concluded that Israel is not part of the problem but part of the solution, and that if they were to make peace, Israel could be a vital ally for the kingdom militarily, economically, technologically, and beyond."

"I don't know what to say," said Marcus.

"Actually, there's more," said the senator. "On Wednesday, a few hours after the attack in London, Prince Abdullah bin Rashid—their intelligence chief—called me. He wanted to see if I would serve as a back channel to the president and to the Israelis. The Saudis don't want the president's peace plan to be delivered stillborn. He said they're ready for peace talks as soon as possible."

"Even after the Palestinians rejected the plan?"

"*Because* the Palestinians rejected the plan."

"We realize this is a bit of a surprise," Annie noted, seeing Marcus's skepticism.

"A bit?" Marcus replied. "Given the Saudis' history of anti-Semitism and radical Wahhabism, it frankly sounds preposterous."

"Nevertheless," said Dayton, "we think it's real."

"Then why come to me?"

"I want you to set up a meeting with the president—quiet, off the record."

"Why don't you just pick up the phone and ask him directly?"

"Because he hates me."

"I don't know about *hates*, but . . ."

"Don't sugarcoat it, Marcus. The man sees me as a competitor and would like nothing more than to squash me like a bug."

"Well, you have said some pretty tough things about him—and to be fair, you *are* a competitor."

"Not anymore."

"What's that supposed to mean?"

"Haven't you been watching the polls?" Dayton asked.

"My hands have been a little full of late."

"Then let me fill you in. Yes, nationally, my numbers look strong. But that's when you factor in independents and moderate to liberal Republicans. Among hard-core liberals, I'm tanking. I couldn't get elected dogcatcher in the Democrat Party right now."

"Why?" Marcus asked. "You were running strong before we went to Moscow. Then you took on Luganov face-to-face. You convinced Clarke to bulk up American forces in Poland and the Baltics to prevent a Russian invasion, and he completely followed your advice. The coverage was spectacular. You were a rock star."

"If he was running as a Republican, absolutely," Annie interjected. "But the activists in his party are furious he worked with Clarke at all. They feel betrayed, and they're abandoning ship."

"Because you put the interests of your country ahead of your party?" Marcus asked Dayton directly.

"Because I put Clarke ahead of my party," the senator replied.

"Well then, they're idiots."

"Maybe so," said Annie. "But they're the idiots that knock on doors and run the phone banks and raise the money. They're the idiots the senator needs to win the nomination, and after his lifetime of serving them, I'm telling you, they hate his guts."

Marcus considered that, then turned back to Dayton again. "So just to be clear, Senator, you're hated by Clarke for being too liberal and hated by liberals for being nice to Clarke?"

"Welcome to my world."

"And you're really not running?"

"No."

"Why haven't you made that public—or did I miss it?"

"I was actually scheduled to be on *Meet the Press* this morning. I was going to drop my little bombshell, as it were. But it hardly seemed appropriate under the circumstances, so last night I canceled my appearance. The producers went ballistic, but I told them that everything I knew about the attacks was classified and there was no point saying, 'No comment' to every question they asked me."

"And they bought that?"

"They didn't have any reason not to, though I'm not likely to be invited back anytime soon."

The waitress brought them steaming bowls of soup—corn chowder for Dayton, gumbo for Annie, and thermonuclear Texas chili for Marcus.

"Why not call Secretary Whitney?" Marcus asked when they were alone again.

"She's a little busy herself right now," Annie said. "And this is urgent. Look, Marcus, the Saudis are terrified of Tehran getting the Bomb. They know the Iranians and Russians have been knocked off-balance. They know they have a window of time, and it won't last forever. What's more, they like the president's peace plan. They're furious with Ziad for rejecting it before it's even been made public. And they believe now is the time to make their move. They saw how useful the senator was as a back channel during the whole Luganov thing, and they know I played a behind-the-scenes role with you with the whole warhead thing."

"And they could certainly use a little bipartisan cover in this town," Marcus was quick to add. "What could be better than to have a prominent Senate Democrat, one everyone believes is running for president, convince his incumbent Republican opponent to broker a Saudi-Israeli peace agreement in the ashes, literally and figuratively, of the last week's events?"

"Exactly," said Annie. "So will you help us? Will you call the president?"

Marcus looked at her, then back to the senator.

"I'd love to."

61

Marcus glanced at his watch as thunder boomed and it began to pour.

It was six minutes past closing time. He was the last customer sitting in the Starbucks near the corner of Pennsylvania and Seventeenth Street, a stone's throw from the White House complex. The staff were wiping down counters and mopping floors, but the manager told him as long as he kept buying, she'd let him stay.

Then she told him why.

She remembered him from his days with the Secret Service. He'd been a regular, after all. Moreover, she told him that she remembered the day he'd been awarded the Medal of Valor for defending the president and the White House staff through a terror attack she otherwise had chosen to forget. She'd watched the whole ceremony on TV, as had everyone in the store that day. If he wanted to sit in her coffeehouse after hours all alone, then so be it. He was always welcome.

Suddenly there was a knock on the door. Three men stood outside.

"Those your friends?" the manager asked.

Marcus nodded, and she unlocked the door and let them in.

"You gentlemen want anything?" she asked.

The two large men with earpieces said, "No thank you, ma'am."

Bill McDermott, on the other hand, asked for a cup of "something strong, as big as you've got." She obliged him, then gave them their space. One agent took up a position by the front door. The other checked to make sure no one was in either of the bathrooms before taking a post by the back door.

"What's this all about, Marcus?" McDermott asked.

"I need to see the president."

"What for?"

Marcus explained his lunchtime conversation. The acting national security advisor was as stunned as Marcus had been. He asked a flurry of questions. But in the end, intrigued if not entirely satisfied by Marcus's answers, he pulled out his government-issued BlackBerry and hit the first number on his speed dial.

"Maggie, I need fifteen minutes with POTUS—no, right now—and give the Secret Service a heads-up. I'm bringing in an old friend."

"Agent Ryker," said Clarke. "This had better be good. My plate's full."

"I understand, Mr. President," Marcus said as they sat down on couches in the White House residence. "And I'm sorry to bother you so late on a weekend."

"Bill here says you've got something pretty hot—too hot, apparently, to go through normal channels. That's not how I typically do business. But you've got your fifteen minutes. So let's have it."

"Thank you, Mr. President. I promise to keep this brief."

He proceeded to tell Clarke exactly what he had just told McDermott, which was exactly what he had heard from Senator Dayton and Annie Stewart. The Saudis liked his peace plan. They didn't agree with all of it. It wasn't how they would have written it. But it was serious. It was credible. And the Palestinian leadership was foolish for shooting it down like an

Iraqi Scud missile. Marcus then explained that the king was ready to make a bold move toward peace with the Israelis—sending the crown prince to Jerusalem, but only if the president would call and host a peace summit.

Clarke listened carefully. He neither interrupted nor asked any questions until Marcus was through. Then he got up and walked over to the rain-streaked crescent window overlooking the South Lawn and the Washington Monument. After a while, he turned back and looked Marcus square in the eye. "How do I know Dayton isn't setting me up?"

"Did he last time, with Luganov?" Marcus asked.

"That was different," Clarke said. "We were facing war with the Russians."

"We're facing war again, Mr. President, against Kairos and whoever is funding them." Marcus was not prepared to mention Moscow's apparent connection to Kairos. That was too explosive and as yet unverified. Indeed, it could very well be that Iran had a hand in the latest attacks as well, just as the Saudis had said. The CIA needed more time to work their sources and gather hard facts. For now, however, something else was at stake. "We're also facing what could prove to be the greatest breakthrough in the Middle East since Sadat went to Jerusalem in November 1977," he added.

"You think the Saudis are really serious?" Clarke asked.

"I really can't say, sir; I'm just passing on what I've been told."

"Did the king bring any of this up with Evans or Davis when they saw him?"

"I wasn't there, so I don't know."

"What about their detail?" McDermott asked. "Surely they heard the conversations with the king and crown prince."

"No, they didn't. I checked," said Marcus. "After I met with the senator and Miss Stewart, I called Geoff Stone and Kailea Curtis. As you'll recall, Geoff was the special agent in charge on the general's detail. Kailea was his deputy. They were wounded in London and only released from the hospital today. But they both told me there were no agents in the room at the palace in Riyadh."

"What about notetakers?" McDermott asked.

"No—not American ones, anyway. I checked. It was just Evans and Davis."

"Did Stone and Curtis know why you were asking?" the president inquired.

"No, sir. I asked them about all the meetings they had—made it look like routine fact-checking."

"Have you talked to anyone else about your conversation with Dayton?"

"No, sir."

Clarke looked to McDermott. "Bill, what do you think?"

"Well, sir, I don't like the idea of you being anywhere near the Temple Mount. But if the Saudis were really serious about making peace with the Israelis, that would pull your plan right out of the fire and put it in the history books. It would be a huge, *huge* story."

"It would, wouldn't it?" said Clarke, beginning to pace the room. "So do I meet with Dayton?"

McDermott turned to Marcus, but before he could respond, Clarke asked another question.

"Did Dayton really say he's going to shut down his exploratory committee?"

"He did, sir. He said he was planning to do it this morning on *Meet the Press*, but the attacks scrambled his plans. Look, I know you're concerned about the senator's motives. And he's a lib, don't get me wrong. But he's also a patriot. He proved that with the Russians. He has strong disagreements with you on domestic and economic policy, Mr. President. But on foreign policy, you two actually see eye to eye on more than you'd imagine."

"If he works with me again, he's finished in the Democrat Party."

"I suspect so, sir," Marcus said. "But actually that gives me an idea."

62

It was early and dark and pouring as Marcus finished his daily five-mile run.

His phone rang and it was Kailea in London, so he took it. "What's up?" he said, slowing to a walk and wiping the rain from his eyes.

"Got an update."

"Go."

"About an hour ago, some kids playing in an abandoned garage in the East End stumbled across a hackney cab. When they saw what was inside, they freaked out and called the police."

"What was it?"

"Two bodies, a man and a woman. We're pretty sure it's Meryl Sullivan and Thomas Gibney."

"Who?"

"Sullivan was a top political reporter for the BBC. Gibney was her cameraman. They were supposed to cover Evans's meeting with the PM. But they never made it. Instead, two people showed up in their place. The names were the same, but they'd changed the photos."

"Do you know who the substitutes were?"

"Not yet, but believe me, we're working on it."

"And how'd they get suicide vests through all that security? I still don't get that."

"No one does, but the Brits have detained everyone who was working the press security checkpoint that morning on suspicion of colluding with these imposters. I've got to go, but I'll get more as soon as I can."

Robert Dayton sat behind his large oak desk, his feet perched on a credenza.

Sporting his favorite brown linen suit, a crisp light-green Brooks Brothers shirt, and a dark-green silk tie with matching pocket square, the seventy-one-year-old senator was simultaneously listening to *Morning Joe* on MSNBC and reading the A section of the *Washington Post*. He was oblivious to the fact that three people had entered his office, even though they'd knocked twice and cleared their throats several times more.

Pete Hwang had been here countless times before. Yet this was his first time back in the senator's spacious corner office since stepping down from the employ of the man's political action committee and joining the Central Intelligence Agency. Dayton, of course, didn't know he worked for the CIA. Nor did Annie Stewart. Like all of Pete's family and friends, they believed he now worked as a physician for the Diplomatic Security Service. The real story, and Marcus's as well, was too highly classified even for a senior member of the Intel Committee and his most trusted aide.

"Senator," Annie announced in a loud and confident voice, "Marcus Ryker and our old friend Dr. Hwang are here to see you."

Pete hated when she called him "Dr. Hwang." Crazy about Annie but still too shy to ask her out, he had repeatedly insisted she simply call him Pete, but to no avail.

"Ah, yes, gentlemen, please have a seat," Dayton said, startled out of his thoughts and fumbling to find which of the four remotes on his desk would mute the television. Finally Annie walked over and took care of it for him.

Dayton exchanged pleasantries with Pete for several minutes, asking how his arm was recovering and how he liked being over at State. Then they turned to the matter at hand.

"I met with the president last night," Marcus began. "I shared with him what you and Annie told me, and he'd like to see you both right away."

"Really?" Dayton asked. "I have to say, I'm surprised."

"Well, sir, I admit it didn't come easy," Marcus conceded. "But in the end he asked the Secret Service to sneak you into the residence through the tunnel from Treasury so the press doesn't catch wind of anything."

"When does he want to meet?"

"At nine."

"Tonight?"

"No, in an hour," Marcus said. "But he has one condition."

"What's that?"

"He wants you to agree to be his new special envoy to the Middle East."

Dayton abruptly took his feet off the credenza. "I beg your pardon?"

"I told the president what you said about being finished in your party and about ending your presidential campaign."

"Did you now?"

"I said you remain a dyed-in-the-wool liberal. But I also told him you're an old-school patriot who believes in putting your country ahead of partisan politics."

"And?"

"And I suggested that he not simply listen to your counsel on how best to navigate a Saudi peace initiative but hire you to run the whole show."

The room was silent, so Marcus continued.

"Senator, let's be candid here. The president is prepared to put the entire weight of his presidency into making peace in the Middle East. If the Palestinians aren't ready, that's sad but not particularly surprising. But if the Saudis are ready to make peace with Israel, that would be absolutely historic. It could clear the way for other Gulf states to make peace with

Israel as well—the Emiratis, the Bahrainis, perhaps even the Omanis. But it's going to take someone with a tremendous amount of experience to thread this needle, and I told the president that you're just the man for the job."

63

Marcus paused a moment to let the thought sink in.

"The loss of General Evans, Dr. Davis, and Janelle Thomas is devastating—personally, of course, but also strategically," he continued. "Bill McDermott is a dear friend and a fine man. He's prepared to step into the general's shoes as national security advisor. But he isn't going to have the time to shuttle throughout the region to make this peace deal happen. Neither will Secretary Whitney—not while managing every other portfolio on her plate. So the president needs someone who . . . well, he needs you."

"I certainly wasn't expecting this."

"Neither was the president—but when I laid out the case, he loved it, and he wants to move on it quickly."

"I'll bet he does," said Dayton, rising from his seat and beginning to pace his office. "But you know what you're asking me to do, right? I'd have to resign my Senate seat, which I've held since the Stone Age. That, of course, would create an open seat. Then my governor—a Republican, mind you—will either take the seat herself or appoint some fire-breathing, pro-life, evangelical conservative who's the polar opposite of me. Then I'll have really burnt my bridges with the Democrats, and all for an appointment that will be quickly over if the president is not reelected?"

Pete saw his moment. "Senator, that's exactly what I told Marcus you'd say."

"Really?" asked Dayton. "And?"

"And I told Marcus that he and the president were getting way ahead of themselves. The last thing the administration needs right now is to send another high-profile official overseas to become a new target for this Kairos group. So, knowing you as I do, I told Marcus how this should work, if it's going to work at all."

The senator raised an eyebrow. So did Annie. But they were both listening, so Pete continued.

"The Senate doesn't come back into session until next Tuesday, right?"

Dayton nodded.

"Okay, so you and Annie make a secret trip back to Riyadh, not as an emissary of the president—not publicly or officially, anyway—but as a go-between, a back channel. Marcus and I come with you to watch your backs. You sound out the Saudis and find out just how serious they really are. Marcus reports everything back to Bill McDermott. That keeps everything quiet and deniable. But if it's real—if the crown prince is really prepared to go to Jerusalem—then the president brings you in to get your thoughts, and he has to promise to give you credit for helping broker a historic peace summit in Jerusalem with the Saudis and the Israelis. Specifically, he invites you to the summit as a key player in the negotiations. It's a huge story. It's bipartisan. Your base will hate it, but so what? You're not running anyway. And if the Saudis and Israelis really want to hammer out a treaty, then it's your choice—stay in the Senate or step down and be appointed the president's special envoy. The Republicans control the Senate, and your colleagues will want credit for something so huge, so your confirmation is guaranteed. But it would be your call, and there would be no pressure publicly or behind the scenes from the White House."

"That's not bad," said Annie.

"Thanks."

"Have you spoken to the president about this?" she asked Marcus, protecting her boss from having to ask.

"We called Bill just before we came here," Pete said before Marcus could answer. "He's already spoken to the president."

"And?" Annie pressed.

"Well, obviously he'd prefer it if the senator would come on board immediately, but he's ready to move either way that seems best to you."

The senator leaned back in his chair, smiled, and ran a hand through his hair. Then he turned to Annie. "What do you say?"

"I say we head to the White House, sir, and get this thing done."

64

Hamdi Yaşar landed at noon and was picked up by the Al-Sawt bureau chief.

Forty minutes later, he pulled his silver Mercedes onto the grounds of the Rome Cavalieri Hotel, a sumptuous, five-star property owned by the Waldorf Astoria group.

"Here are your room keys, some cash, and a local mobile phone," said the bureau chief, handing over a large sealed envelope. "I booked you in a king Imperial Room as you requested. You're already checked in, and I put down a network credit card to cover all of your expenses while you're here."

At precisely 2 p.m. local time, the knock came. Yaşar opened the door to the adjoining room and gave Mohammed al-Qassab an unusually warm embrace. He assured al-Qassab that his room had been "thoroughly cleaned." Then he praised the man profusely. "You have done a mighty deed, my friend."

"Praise Allah," al-Qassab replied, smiling broadly for the first time Yaşar could ever remember. "I only regret that the British prime minister was not among the victims."

"Even so, overall the operation could not have gone better," Yaşar continued as they sat in the living room of the spacious suite, looking out over the city of Rome and the Colosseum in the distance. "Father is very pleased."

"You talked to him?"

"I did, and he asked me to tell you there is a great reward awaiting you, not only in paradise, but in your numbered account in Zurich."

"This was a miracle of Allah. I can take no credit."

"Still, Father is counting on you to deliver an even bigger prize. Have you come up with a plan?"

"I'm working on one."

"Why is it not finalized?"

"Hamdi, you cannot be serious. Look, it is one thing to take out a national security advisor or a deputy secretary of state. But to kill the president of the United States? There is a reason it hasn't been done in this century. Not that it hasn't been tried. It has, many times. But the rules of the game have changed. The technology has changed. The training and procedures of the Secret Service have changed."

"Is it more money you need? I can get you nearly anything you ask for."

"No, no, it's not money I need—it's time."

"Time for what?"

"To think, to come up with a plan that has a reasonable chance of success, and then to train my teams properly."

"What did you do in London?" Yaşar asked. "It was brilliant, and the police are still completely baffled."

"That's just it," said al-Qassab. "I knew there was no way to get someone wearing a suicide vest through all that security, not at Number 10. So I tried a variation of something I learned when I was in Yemen on a recruiting visit last year."

"Go on."

"For several years, al Qaeda was experimenting with how to plant a bomb inside a human being. They tried everything but couldn't make it work.

I mean it worked in the sense that a person could blow himself up. But rarely was the explosion large enough to cause significant damage to others."

"Why not?"

"Several reasons. First, the human body is mostly water. And the bombs the al Qaeda guys were using were too small. As a result, most of the explosive energy released by the bomb was absorbed by the body of the bomber himself. Second, the bomb was typically inserted in the person's rectum so it wouldn't be detected by a pat down at an airport. The problem was that whatever explosive force wasn't absorbed by the body of the bomber was released through the rectum. This created enormous holes in the floors, but it didn't project the force of the explosion outward toward people standing nearby. In the end, the al Qaeda operatives I spoke to had all but given up on the idea."

"But not you?"

"No."

"Why not?"

"I was convinced they'd given up too early. So I recruited a doctor—a surgeon, a true believer, one of us—and asked him to run a series of experiments significantly different than what had been done before."

"How so?"

"First I asked him whether he could actually surgically implant a bomb *inside* a human body, and higher up—in the abdomen or near the rib cage."

"And?"

"I also asked him if he could use bigger bombs—implant several pounds of high explosives, not just a few ounces."

"And?"

"For months he practiced—on dogs, then on sheep, and finally on camels."

"Where?"

"In the mountains of Yemen."

"What were the results?"

Al-Qassab smiled. "Perfection. My theory was right, and the larger bombs worked."

"So this is what you used in London?"

"Yes. I flew the doctor—a Pakistani already living in England—to London last fall and placed him with a group of plastic surgeons I know there. They had no idea who he really was, and they never suspected a thing."

"You're sure?"

"Absolutely. We tapped the phones of everyone in the office. We monitor all of their emails. Everyone loves the guy. He's so good, so quiet, and makes them all so much money that they eventually let him hire his own nurses. I, of course, insisted that he hire people who work for us, and everything went beautifully."

"And who did you find to carry the bomb?"

"A brother and sister team from Chechnya. Their mother was a Black Widow years ago in Moscow. They both wanted to follow in her footsteps. I vetted them extensively and watched them closely for a full year. I didn't tell them until late in the game how I was going to deploy them, but they accepted the mission with great joy."

"And now they are *shahids*?"

"They are."

"And you think this same approach could be used against the president?"

"That's my hope," said al-Qassab. "But my fear is if we don't find a way to do it quickly, the Americans and the Brits will figure out what we did in London and develop a countermeasure against it."

"A moment ago you said you needed more time. Now you're saying we need to move quickly. Which is it?"

"I have the technique," said the Syrian. "I don't have a willing bomber, not in Washington, not yet."

"So you need someone willing to become a *shahid*, a true martyr for Allah?"

"Yes."

"I can help you with that."

"No, you don't understand. I can't use a Chechen again or a Syrian or a Yemeni. We're going to need an American, someone who can buy a ticket into a fund-raiser for President Clarke, walk right up to him, and detonate himself or herself. That will not be easy to find."

"Don't worry. We have nearly unlimited funds. We can do this."

"But finding the right person—an American we can totally trust—is only the beginning. We still need to get my doctor into the United States. And we need enough time for him to surgically implant the bomb, and for the person to recover from the surgery before the fund-raiser, or whatever event we deem appropriate, and all before the Secret Service figures this thing out, which honestly could be by the end of this week."

65

RIYADH, SAUDI ARABIA—3 DECEMBER

It was nearly two in the morning when the private jet touched down.

The Learjet taxied not to the private aviation terminal but to a military facility on the far side of the airfield. The hangar itself was nearly deserted. Just a single armed guard was posted outside. Inside, a small crew who worked directly for Prince Abdullah bin Rashid and serviced his private jet was standing by, along with the prince's chief of staff, a driver, and a black Mercedes SUV.

Both the timing and the low-key manner of arrival were intentional. Neither the Saudis nor the White House wanted anyone to know Robert Dayton and his entourage were in the country. Not airport staff. Not the usual ground crews. Not foreign intelligence agencies. Certainly not the Saudi media or foreign reporters. Not even other Saudi government officials. It was not unusual for American senators or congressmen or members of the executive branch to come in and out of the kingdom. It was, however, unusual for a senator to return to the kingdom so quickly after his previous visit, particularly a Democrat.

The senator climbed into the front passenger seat, while Marcus climbed in the far back, and Pete and Annie took the middle seats. Thirty minutes later, after a high-speed blitz down a maze of deserted highways, the Mercedes turned onto al-Diwan Street. They soon arrived at the al-Yamama Palace, stopping before two armored personnel carriers, each mounted with a .50-caliber machine gun and manned by soldiers in full combat gear. A commander of the guard, wearing a black uniform and black beret, requested everyone's passports and took them back to his guard station. While they waited, a K-9 unit worked its way around the vehicle, sniffing for explosives. Another soldier carrying a long pole with a large mirror attached at the end checked the underside of the SUV to be sure there were no bombs present. Two other soldiers checked under the hood and in the trunk while still two more searched their luggage.

Finally the commander returned their passports and requested they turn over all weapons and ammunition. Marcus and Pete had been informed by McDermott ahead of time that this would be the case. The attacks in London and Washington were being taken very seriously in Riyadh, and every precaution was being taken. Reluctantly the two men handed over what they had. Then they were all asked to hand over their mobile phones, as well.

Eventually the massive steel gates were opened. They drove into the walled compound under the wary eye of soldiers carrying automatic weapons and headed down a long driveway lined with palm trees on both sides. The beautifully manicured lawns and great fountains were all tastefully lit up, though it was the middle of the night. Finally they came around a curve and stopped under the portico at the main entrance, where they were met by more armed soldiers and the chief of royal protocol. They were greeted warmly, then led into a security station, where they passed through magnetometers. The few possessions in their pockets were sent through an X-ray machine. They were not permitted to bring their luggage inside.

After clearing security, they were led along elegant marble hallways, under gold-and-crystal chandeliers, and through ornately carved and painted wooden doors until they finally entered the empty royal chamber. At the far end stood a throne made of gilded wood and cream- and gold-adorned upholstery. The senator was shown to another gilded chair—though not nearly as nice as the king's—directly to the left of the throne. Annie was seated immediately to the senator's left, then Marcus, then Pete.

Across from them was a row of identical chairs, all empty. In the center of the room was a rectangular wooden coffee table, covered in gold, set on a thick, cream-colored carpet. The walls were beautiful, polished wood, which Marcus assumed was mahogany but couldn't be sure. There were large windows, as well, covered by royal-purple-and-gold drapes. There were two side tables, one on each side of the throne. On them were golden lamps with purple lampshades, a phone, a notebook and Montblanc pen, and a crystal glass filled with water. Behind the throne to the left and right were golden flagpoles, each bearing the green-and-white flag of the kingdom.

Once the Americans were seated, servants in traditional white robes and red-checkered kaffiyehs served them each small ceramic cups of Arab coffee. A few minutes later, the cups were removed, and they were served hot, sweet mint tea in small glasses with handles, on china saucers.

Suddenly the floor-to-ceiling doors opened. They all stood, and King Faisal Mohammed Al Saud entered, wearing his trademark yellow-and-white robes and red-checkered kaffiyeh. Now well into his eighties, he walked slowly, somewhat stooped, with the help of a black-and-gold cane. He shook each of their hands, beginning with Pete and working his way up the row. His face was oval and his eyes were brown. He had a black mustache and a black goatee; Marcus noted that neither had a hint of gray. His hands were soft, but his grip was firm. He looked them each in the eye and thanked them for coming, but when he reached the senator, he surprised them all by giving the man a brief hug.

Following the king was Crown Prince Abdulaziz bin Faisal Al Saud, the heir to the throne and the kingdom's minister of defense. Nearly fifty years his father's junior, he was a large man with a massive beard and a broad smile, and he wore a black robe with gold seams and gold piping. He, too, shook each of their hands and thanked them for coming, as did Prince Abdullah bin

Rashid, director of the Saudi General Intelligence Directorate, who followed the two royals wearing a far more modest all-white robe known as a *thawb* and a white linen kaffiyeh.

The king took his seat on the throne. The crown prince sat directly across from the senator. The intelligence chief sat beside the crown prince. Finally two notetakers from the royal court—who were not introduced—took their seats, opened their leather notebooks, and uncapped their pens.

"Senator Dayton, my good friend, thank you for returning to my kingdom so quickly," His Majesty began in perfect though heavily accented English. "You are a man of peace and always welcome here."

The senator nodded and thanked the king and crown prince for their warm hospitality and gracious spirit. The king asked Dayton to introduce his guests, which he did. Then they got to the heart of the matter.

66

"Were you able to speak to the president?" the king asked.

"I did, Your Majesty," said Dayton. "Actually, we all did."

"How did he respond?"

"Very favorably—he's ready to help in every way he can."

"Does he understand that I have not wavered in my views at all—that the Arab Peace Initiative is the right way to go forward, that the Palestinians deserve a sovereign state with East Jerusalem as their capital, and that the Israelis should pull back to the 1967 borders?"

"He does," Dayton confirmed. "And I told him that while you believe his plan reflects the spirit of the Arab Peace Initiative, you believe it is deficient in a number of important respects."

"This did not bother him?"

"Not at all. He said he expected as much. He said he never expected the Palestinians or you or any Arab state to embrace and approve every word of his plan. He recognizes that it doesn't comport precisely with the Arab Peace Initiative, but he argues that the initiative is two decades old and has not produced peace and therefore needs to be updated. Still, he said the initial goal of his plan is to jump-start the process and get the parties back to the table."

"Do you believe him, Senator?"

"Your Majesty, I do."

"Even though you're running against him and have had such harsh words for this president?" asked the king.

"Even so."

"Because I must say, my sons and I have been following the early stages of the presidential campaign in your country very closely. We have watched you both hit each other very hard. We also know we don't have many friends on your side of the aisle. Then again, as you so candidly articulated during our last visit, we have lost many friends on the president's side as well."

"Your Majesty, I've always tried to be honest with you, so I will be candid with you now as well. I do not have much respect for President Clarke personally or for his economic policies or his domestic and social policies. That's why I put together a presidential exploratory committee. That said, I do believe that he genuinely wants to forge a lasting peace between the Arabs and the Israelis and that he is committed to building an alliance in this region that can stand solidly against Iranian aggression. Perhaps more importantly, the Israelis trust him, and no one more so than Prime Minister Eitan. So if you convince President Clarke that you're sincere about making peace, no one is better positioned to convince Eitan."

The king looked over to his eldest son, then at his intelligence chief. Marcus noticed that neither spoke nor made any gestures that might indicate what they thought. Then the king looked down and folded his hands across his lap.

"I must say, I am deeply disappointed with my old friend Ismail Ziad," the monarch said softly, almost wistfully. "He has sat with me in this room many times, right in that chair where you sit now, sipping tea and telling me his troubles. So many times I have pleaded with him to get back into negotiations and secure the best deal he can, and I told him I will help fund the costs of building a viable, vibrant Palestinian state."

The king continued to stare down at his wrinkled hands.

"True, we once saw the Jews as interlopers, colonialists, occupiers, oppressors. But the Arab dream of driving them out of the region has not worked. The Israelis have built an impressive state, a powerful army and air force, and an even more powerful economy. And they've done it without a drop of oil and only recently with large discoveries of natural gas. I have told Ziad the Jews are not going anywhere. Israel is a fact of life. They are part of this region, this neighborhood, and it is time to accept this. Israel cannot be defeated. It cannot be wiped off the map. Nor can it be wished away. It is here and it is real and it is strong and getting stronger. Every day that passes, Israel grows mightier and the Palestinians grow weaker. 'How much longer will you resist reality?' I've often asked Ziad. I've told him, 'The longer you wait, the less you will get. You had the chance to have half of the Old City—the Muslim and Christian Quarters and the Haram al-Sharif. Olmert offered it all to you on a silver platter and you turned him down.' Ziad thinks he can get more. I say, 'No, you'll never get more than what Olmert offered. Now you'll get less. But at least you'll get something. I'll help you pay for it. And I'll persuade the Emiratis and the Bahrainis and the Omanis to chip in as well.'"

"What does he say?" Dayton asked.

"What can he say? Ziad is a stubborn old man," the king replied with no apparent malice in his voice. "He speaks endlessly about Israeli settlements and their expansion. I tell him, 'Yes, and the settlements could all stop expanding tomorrow. But only if you make a deal with the Israelis. You have to say yes to something—anything,' but he refuses to listen to me. He is determined to go to his grave as the man who refused to surrender to the Zionist occupiers. I will not judge him. I have not walked in his sandals. But nor will I wait for him. My kingdom has supported the Palestinian people for an entire century. No Arab nation has done more for them than the House of Saud. But we have other, urgent priorities—the Iran threat, the Muslim Brotherhood, the rise of a hostile new sultan in Ankara, and our own domestic challenges. Our oil is running out. We must fundamentally transform our economy. We must use our wealth, while we still have it, to build a high-tech superpower here in the heart of the Arabian Peninsula. We can do it. We want Israel as a partner. Now is the time, and we must move very quickly, before it is too late."

67

Marcus glanced over at Annie on his right.

She was taking notes as fast as she could. So was Pete. Neither seemed prepared to say anything, so he decided to address the "camel in the room."

"Your Majesty, may I ask a question?"

Everyone turned.

"Why, of course, Agent Ryker," the king replied. "You have my deepest respect for all you did to stop the madmen in Tehran from getting their hands on those nuclear warheads. I was moved by your courage and will never forget it."

"You are too kind, Your Majesty. There were many people—including those in this room—involved in that operation. I certainly cannot take the credit. But I want to say that I think what you are proposing here is extraordinary. I don't have to tell you how much distrust of the Saudi government there is back in Washington, whether it's regarding human rights and the lack of religious freedom here or the war in Yemen or—well, you know the list. Personally, I believe the relationship between the United States and the Kingdom of Saudi Arabia won't ever be as strong as it could be—and should be—unless you address those matters forthrightly and until far more bold reforms are made."

Marcus sensed his colleagues' unease, but he kept going.

"That said, if Saudi Arabia truly makes peace with Israel, this will be a huge signal of the dramatic change in direction that you and your sons are making from the old Saudi ways. It would be an immensely popular move to many in our country and in many countries around the world."

In his peripheral vision, Marcus noticed Senator Dayton shifting uncomfortably in his seat. But he was not finished.

"I'm not sure if you're aware of this, but Egyptian president Anwar Sadat was deeply unpopular in the United States, especially among tens of millions of Christians and Jews who love Israel and were horrified that Sadat launched a sneak attack against Israel in 1973, and on Yom Kippur, of all times, the holiest day on the Jewish calendar, when Jews were all fasting and praying and unprepared for war. Imagine if someone invaded you on the first day of Ramadan. I daresay there were many Americans who outright hated Mr. Sadat for that. But that all changed on November 19, 1977. Why? Because that was the day Sadat landed in Jerusalem and launched his peace offensive. He spoke to the Israeli people. He spoke to their parliament. He met with Israeli leaders at the highest levels and set into motion a chain of events that led to the signing of the Camp David Peace Accords in the fall of 1978. Whatever else Mr. Sadat had said and done before that, after Camp David he would be seen in the eyes of the vast majority of Americans as a man of peace, a man of great honor and courage. And personally, I think that's possible for you and for the crown prince and the people of your kingdom."

The king said nothing. His face was inscrutable, yet there was more Marcus wanted to say.

"I applaud what you want to do, and I believe all of us stand ready to help you make it happen. That said, I feel it is my duty to make sure you and your colleagues truly understand just how dangerous it could be to send the crown prince to Jerusalem. I don't think I have to remind you that Mr. Sadat paid for his courage with his life—assassinated by his own people, by fellow Muslims, in 1981."

"Not by his own people," the king corrected. "Sadat was murdered by members of the Muslim Brotherhood—by despicable men, *khawarej*, outlaws of our faith."

"Fair enough," Marcus conceded. "My point was simply that Sadat was murdered for making peace with Israel. Years later, Israeli prime minister Yitzhak Rabin was murdered by a Jewish extremist for making peace with Jordan and agreeing to the Oslo Accords with the Palestinians. The history of this region is filled with stories of attempted assassinations, some successful, some not. And unfortunately, I am reminded of another terrible tragedy, that of your great-grandfather, cut down by his own nephew, right here in Riyadh, here in this palace, on March 25, 1975."

At this the monarch winced. "I appreciate your concern, Agent Ryker. Nevertheless, let me assure you of two things. First, if we go down this road, we will not make peace with Israel to improve our image in the United States. We will do so because it is the right thing to do and because it is in our own national interest. We will do it to forge an alliance against the extremists in this region and to build an economic and security partnership that will benefit our people and make their lives better. Frankly, we want Israeli investment and technology, and we want to invest in Israel, as well. We cannot do that in the current environment, but as I said, I will not wait for the Palestinians any longer. If the Israelis are ready for peace on reasonable terms, then so are we, and I believe the time is now. Second, I want to assure you that we as a family and my inner circle have discussed the risks at length. We know what's at stake, and my son is willing, if necessary, to lay down his life for the cause of peace."

"I am," said the crown prince, "but I don't think it will come to this."

"That is very admirable," said Marcus. "But if, God forbid, your son were to die at the hands of an assassin, the entire peace process could die with him. Other regional leaders might be intimidated from following your lead for years, possibly decades to come. My job, and that of my colleagues, is to ensure the safety of our leaders and yours and, of course, the Israelis'. But let's not kid ourselves—there are agents of evil out there who would like nothing better than to have President Clarke, Prime Minister Eitan, and the Saudi crown prince in the same room at the same time and take them all out. Just look at what has happened in recent weeks."

"I have every confidence we can work together to make sure that never happens," replied King Faisal.

The room was quiet for a long while. Then Annie Stewart cleared her throat. She requested permission to speak, and the king granted it.

"Your Majesty, I share Agent Ryker's concerns. Yet I also share your confidence that our two governments and the Israelis will absolutely be able to ensure your safety," she began. "The last thing either of our leaders can afford is to allow a moment of historic peacemaking to end in tragedy."

"Thank you, Miss Stewart. I couldn't agree with you more," said the monarch, a twinkle in his eye.

"That said, I have a slightly different question, if I may."

"Please."

"Would it not send a more powerful signal, Your Majesty, if you made the trip to Jerusalem yourself?"

68

By dinnertime, the team was in Israel, dining with Prime Minister Eitan.

"He said all that?" asked the premier, setting down his glass of red wine.

"He did," Dayton confirmed.

"And the king really wants to come here himself, not the crown prince?"

"The king himself," the senator confirmed, winking at Annie.

Eitan turned to the only colleague he had invited to join them, Mossad director Asher Gilad. "What do you make of it, Asher?"

"Well, it's stunning—no question—but it's also entirely consistent with everything I know from my contact with the Saudis," Gilad said. "At your direction, I've been working very closely with my counterpart in Saudi intelligence, Prince Abdullah bin Rashid. We've been speaking regularly. We met in London earlier this year, together with the Emirati spy chief. It was the Saudis who provided us critical intelligence on the Iranian plot to buy the warheads from Pyongyang. It was the Saudis who helped us track and intercept the shipment. And when I met the crown prince secretly in Cyprus, you'll recall I came back and told you I thought he was ready to meet with you."

"Yes, but that was the son, not the father," said Eitan. "You've been telling me all along that the king was not as open-minded to making peace with us as the crown prince was—at least not until the Palestinians made a deal."

"Apparently I was wrong. Does it matter? This is a gift, Ruvi. Don't think about it. Take it before the father changes his mind."

It was after two o'clock in the morning when they finally left the prime minister's private residence. Once Eitan had said yes to the king's offer, they'd drafted a plan for his visit, incorporating all the requests the Saudis had made. As Marcus drove the team back to the King David Hotel, the mood was giddy. This thing was on, and they had precious little time to put all the pieces in place.

Still, at Marcus's insistence, they entered through the back and took a service elevator so as not to be spotted by anyone else in the hotel. They huddled in the senator's suite, divvying up assignments. Senator Dayton called Bill McDermott on a secure satphone to brief him on the day's events. Once McDermott was up to speed, he patched the senator through to a very happy President Clarke.

Pete, meanwhile, called the head of the Diplomatic Security Service, followed immediately by Carl Roseboro, deputy director of the Secret Service. He not only briefed them on the plan but requested that they reassemble the original advance team and put them on the next plane to Tel Aviv, followed by a larger team within the next twenty-four hours.

As he looked out over the twinkling lights of the Old City and the Mount of Olives, Marcus called Langley and asked to be put through to Richard Stephens. Two minutes later he was walking the CIA director through the plan. In two weeks—on Wednesday, December 17—the president of the United States and the king of Saudi Arabia would arrive at Ben Gurion International Airport, Marcus explained. They would both land in the morning, within minutes of each other. Israeli fighter jets would escort both planes in. Israeli airspace would be closed to all other flights for twenty-four hours, and Patriot and Iron Dome antimissile and antirocket batteries would be set up around the airport, just in case.

The Israeli prime minister would host a massive welcome ceremony for POTUS and the king. They would have to hold it indoors, probably in an El Al hangar, due to the winter rains. The Israeli president, members of the cabinet, members of the Knesset—Israel's parliament—foreign ambassadors, business leaders, religious leaders, and other VIPs would all be on hand, as would a seventy-two-member Israeli honor guard, just as when Sadat visited. The arrival would be covered by local and foreign media and broadcast live around the world.

Moving each entourage to Jerusalem would have to be discussed at length. Marcus said he and the advance team had drafted a plan using helicopters and motorcades, and they would prepare for both. The final call would be made at the last minute by U.S., Israeli, and Saudi security officials on the ground, based on weather and real-time threat conditions.

Marcus then explained that POTUS, the king, and the PM would visit the Dome of the Rock, and the king would take time to pray in the Al-Aqsa Mosque after their meeting with the Grand Mufti on the Temple Mount. All three principals also wanted to visit the Church of the Holy Sepulcher and Yad Vashem, Israel's Holocaust museum and memorial. That night, the prime minister would host a state dinner in honor of the king and the president.

The Saudi delegation would then RON—rest overnight—at the Waldorf in Jerusalem. In fact, the Saudis were planning to rent out the entire hotel for three days prior and one day after their departure to do security sweeps and bring in the king's favorite foods and drinks, linens, china, and cutlery. The president and the American delegation would take over the entirety of the famed five-star King David Hotel. All credentialed media would be housed at the David Citadel Hotel.

On the following day—Thursday, December 18—the prime minister wanted to host a working breakfast for the president and the king at his official residence. The three heads of state would get to know each other better and discuss the broad contours of a peace treaty, though both Faisal and Eitan asked the Americans to understand that this could only be a preliminary step. They could not possibly hammer out a final treaty so quickly, though both men said they would very much like to visit Camp David and hold further discussions there, as President Clarke had originally offered the Israelis and Palestinians.

The president, then the king, and finally the prime minister would address the Knesset, with gallery seating available by invitation only to foreign ambassadors to Israel. Finally, Marcus noted, there would be an elaborate departure ceremony at the airport, and both the Saudi and American leaders and their delegations would be wheels up no later than 3 p.m.

Director Stephens asked dozens of questions. The two men spoke for more than an hour. When they were finished, the director had only one more question. "What do you guys need from me to make this work?"

"Figure out who's running Kairos, and do whatever is necessary to take him down."

69

Marcus had no idea what time it was.

He could hear his phone ringing, but he'd been in such a deep sleep, he couldn't remember where it was or even where he was. The room was pitch-black, and when he rolled out of bed, he walked right into a wall. The phone was still ringing, and given that he'd been in a different room every couple of days for the last few weeks, he couldn't remember the layout of this particular hotel room.

He groped for a light switch, finally found one, remembered his phone was charging in the bathroom, stumbled over an ottoman, and got there too late. The screen indicated the missed call was from Kailea. He splashed some warm water on his face, toweled off, and returned the call. It was 4:22 in Jerusalem. That meant it was 2:22 in the morning in London.

"We know what kind of bomb it was," Kailea said immediately upon answering.

"Okay, what?"

"It was a suicide bomber, but not the typical kind. Ever hear of a BCB?"

"PCP?"

"No, BCB."

"Kailea, it's the middle of the night and I'm in no mood to play games. What in the world are you talking about?"

"BCB stands for a body cavity bomb," Kailea explained. "MI5 and the FBI have now determined conclusively that the explosives were surgically implanted inside the bomber. Not the camera. Not the tripods. They were implanted inside the woman."

"What woman?"

"The one impersonating Meryl Sullivan."

"The BBC reporter."

"Right."

"Is that a first, using such a bomb?"

"Actually, they've been tried unsuccessfully a number of times in recent years. This was the first time it worked."

"Why wasn't the bomb detected by the magnetometer?"

"That's not clear yet."

"Meaning what, that someone could enter the White House or Capitol Building later today and blow themselves to smithereens because our people might not be able to detect the bomb inside of them?"

"I'm afraid so."

"That's not good."

"Tell me about it."

"All right, good work," Marcus said. "Send me a summary of what you've got—"

"Already done."

"And make sure the Secret Service and all the intel agencies have it."

"Also done."

"Good—then learn everything you can about where these bombs have been used, by whom, for what, and most importantly, what doctors in London could have done the surgery to implant this thing."

"How do you know it was done in London?" asked Kailea.

"I don't, and if it was done outside London, we may never find the doctor. But if you had a live bomb in you, would you want to travel far to get to your strike point?"

"Probably not."

"Me neither," said Marcus. "So it's someone local. Or *was* local. They've probably left the city by now and possibly the country. But we need to find this guy—"

"Or woman."

"—or woman, and nab them before they try this thing again."

Marcus hung up the phone and tried to go back to sleep. But the thought of Kairos striking again, anywhere, at any time, made that impossible. He pulled out his notebook and reviewed his to-do list. He was plowing through it. The problem was, it wasn't getting any shorter. Just the opposite—for every item he crossed off, he had to add eight or ten more.

Throwing on a pair of workout shorts, a T-shirt, a sweatshirt, and running shoes, he went over to the wall safe and entered his personal code. He retrieved his Sig Sauer, two spare clips, and his badge and government ID. Then he loaded the weapon and made sure there was a round in the chamber. He put everything in a fanny pack, strapped it around his waist, and headed out the door.

It was still raining. It was so chilly he could see his breath. He asked the clerk at the desk how far the U.S. Embassy was and learned it was about two miles away. So that's where he headed. He'd work out at the embassy's gym for a while, do some target practice on the embassy's gun range, and then run back to the hotel and get ready for the day.

It wasn't the temperature that bothered him that morning. It was that more than two weeks had gone by since the first bombing in D.C. Eight days since the bombing in London. And not a single person had been arrested. They didn't have a single suspect. Meanwhile, the Greeks were tearing their country apart and still hadn't found any evidence of this shadowy new terror group. Oleg hadn't uncovered anything particularly useful either. The trail was cold.

70

Returning to the hotel, Marcus ordered room service.

He took a quick shower, shaved, dressed in a suit and tie, and donned his shoulder holster. When the eggs, fruit, and coffee came, he scarfed them down, brushed his teeth, put his Sig Sauer in the holster, attached the magazines and phone to his belt, and slipped his badge and ID in his pocket. Finally he put on his raincoat, grabbed his umbrella, and headed back down to the lobby.

Rather than drive and have to find parking, he asked a bellman to hail him a taxi. When the cab arrived, he told the driver to take him to the gate closest to the Temple Mount. Twenty minutes later, he had cleared security and entered the offices of the Waqf, where he asked a veiled woman if he could see Dr. Mashrawi.

"Do you have an appointment, Agent Ryker?"

"No, but I only need a few minutes of his time."

"I'm so sorry, but he's not in, and I don't expect him for another hour, but . . ."

Just as she said this, however, Hussam Mashrawi came through the door.

"Agent Ryker, I was not expecting you," said the Palestinian.

"Sorry for the intrusion. Is there a place where we can talk?"

"Of course—right this way."

They headed to his cramped office, and Marcus waited until he shut the door.

"Is something wrong?" Mashrawi asked.

"No, but what I'm going to tell you is highly confidential," Marcus said.

"I don't understand."

Marcus lowered his voice. "President Clarke is coming after all."

"Pardon?"

"He's not going to give the address here. That will be done from the Oval Office on Monday night in prime time. But he has decided to visit the dome and the mosque, along with Prime Minister Eitan and a guest."

"Who?"

"Again, this is completely confidential."

"I understand, but who's the guest?"

"King Faisal Mohammed Al Saud."

Mashrawi was stunned. "Here? All three of them?"

"Yes," Marcus said. "So there's going to be a lot of people coming here soon to make preparations. I'm going to need your help, and not just on all the logistics."

"I'm not sure I understand."

"Dr. Mashrawi, I'm trusting you with this information, as sensitive as it is, because you seem like a serious, reasonable man."

"Thank you," the Palestinian said hesitantly.

"But I have to trust you with something else, as well."

"What's that?"

Marcus paused again. He wished Pete were still with him. He always felt better with Pete at his side, but his best friend had been ordered to accompany Annie and the senator back to Washington.

"To be candid, we're not convinced we can trust the Grand Mufti," Marcus said.

Mashrawi looked puzzled. "May I ask why not?"

"Your father-in-law has made a number of inflammatory statements over the years, not just against Israel but against the U.S. and against the president," Marcus replied. "We've done a careful search of the record, and we don't find any such statements by you. So I'd like to think I can count on you in the days ahead."

"Whatever you need, of course, I'm at your service," Mashrawi said. "But I can assure you, you and your team have misjudged the Grand Mufti."

"How so?"

"It is true, of course, that he has very strong feelings about Palestine and the occupation and the biased role of successive American governments—not just the current one. He doesn't deny this. Indeed, he's quite open about his views. And why shouldn't he be? He loves his people. He grieves for their suffering. He sees it as his duty to be their voice—not as a politician, mind you, but as a cleric. He sees it as his duty to speak up for the poor and dispossessed, for all those who are suffering injustices at the hands of an occupier. Can you really blame him for this? Can you really hold this against him? Should he remain blind to such crimes, much less mute?"

"Don't get me wrong, Dr. Mashrawi," Marcus countered. "The Grand Mufti has every right to say what he wants. My concern is not his political views, per se. I'm here solely to see to the safety and well-being of the president, the prime minister, and the king. Obviously they will be sending representatives to meet with you as well in the coming days. But in light of the recent attacks, it is my job—along with my colleagues—to assess and mitigate risks. We're concerned that your father-in-law's views could encourage extremists to feel that they have the moral, even religious, duty to take some sort of hostile action against these leaders when they visit."

"I believe your concerns are ill-founded."

"Perhaps, but you'll forgive me if I inform you that we'll be taking every precaution to ensure that the visit here goes smoothly and without incident."

"And I hope you'll believe me, Agent Ryker, that the Grand Mufti and I want exactly the same thing," Mashrawi said.

"Then you'll help me with everything I need?"

"Of course. Do you have a list?"

"I do," said Marcus, reaching into his pocket and pulling out a sheet of paper. "Twenty-three things I'll need in the next seventy-two hours, beginning with another meeting with the Grand Mufti."

71

Early Friday morning, Hamdi Yaşar received a message he wasn't sure he believed.

He read it twice, then read it again. From anyone else, he would have dismissed it as preposterous. But this was coming from an impeccable source. Never once had Hussam Mashrawi told him something that hadn't proven true. Yet how was this possible? Was it a trick? A trap of some kind? Or a gift?

At heart, Hamdi Yaşar was a cynic. He was a journalist, after all, trained not to take things at face value. If something sounded too good to be true, it probably was. Still, as bizarre as this sounded, Mashrawi's note somehow rang true.

Yaşar read the note again. According to "a senior State Department source" who had ostensibly spoken with Mashrawi, President Clarke was going to give his big speech laying out his peace plan in a prime-time televised address on Monday night, just three days from now. In that speech, he would announce that King Faisal Mohammed Al Saud would join him at a peace summit in Jerusalem on December 17 and 18. The note did not say all the places the president, king, and Israeli premier would visit. Mashrawi could only say that they would definitely be coming to the Haram al-Sharif and that the king wanted to pray in the mosque.

The whole concept was at once so revolting that Yaşar wanted to vomit and so miraculously surreal that he wanted to dance. All three enemies in one place? At one time? And one of his own people was providing them real-time intelligence every step of the way? Assuming for a moment that Mashrawi was telling the truth, such plans might change. The king might get cold feet. Or the Israelis. Or the Americans. But Yaşar knew he had to set the wheels in motion. On the remote chance that this was real—and something in his spirit told him it was—Kairos had to be ready.

Heading up to the roof of the studios, where no one could overhear him, Yaşar made three very quick calls. The first was to Abu Nakba, relaying the message word by word, without details or commentary. The second call was to Mohammed al-Qassab, ordering him to get to Tel Aviv immediately and wait for further instructions. The third was to Dr. Ali Haqqani, currently hiding at a resort on the island of Mallorca, also ordering the Pakistani surgeon to get himself to Tel Aviv posthaste without telling a single soul where he was going or how long he would be gone.

United flight 72 nonstop from Washington landed in Tel Aviv at 4:30 p.m.

Stuck in traffic, Marcus pulled the U.S. Embassy's white Ford Transit 350 van onto the grounds of Ben Gurion International Airport twenty minutes late, but he wasn't worried—not about this, anyway. The advance team still had to disembark, clear passport control, and wait for their luggage. It would be highly unlikely he'd see them for another forty-five minutes to an hour.

In Colorado, it was nearly eight in the morning. Oleg had better be up and working, Marcus told himself. He pulled the van over to the side of the road, not far from the terminal, put it in park, and switched on his blinkers.

Then he pulled out his secure satellite phone and called the Russian to check in. "What've you got?" he asked.

"Nothing, my friend," Oleg replied. "Actually, less than nothing."

"What does that mean?"

"The Kremlin's IT folks found the back door I was using and patched it."

"Can the guys at Langley find a way back in?"

"They're trying, but they say it's going to take time."

"We don't have time," Marcus replied. "We've got a terrorist faction out there we know nothing about. We've got an American president and a Saudi monarch preparing to come to Jerusalem. I've got a partner who's in London rather than at my side. And now you're telling me you've got nothing?"

"I'm sorry—truly I am," said Oleg. "Believe me, I will call you when I have something useful—anything—but I have nothing right now."

Frustrated, Marcus nevertheless held his tongue. Hanging up with Oleg, he returned emails for the next forty-five minutes until he finally received a call from Secret Service deputy director Carl Roseboro. The team had their bags and were coming out of the terminal, Roseboro reported. Moments later, Marcus spotted them through the crowds and pulled forward to welcome them. Soon the team was headed back to Jerusalem. On the way, Marcus briefed the others on the events of the last few days, paying particular attention to his concerns about the Grand Mufti. Roseboro asked if Marcus had yet secured a list of everyone currently working for the Waqf and everyone who had in the previous ten years. Marcus directed him to a folder in his briefcase. In it, Roseboro found a printout of the names, titles, home addresses, home and mobile phones, and work and home email addresses, all courtesy of Dr. Mashrawi.

"When did you get these?" Roseboro asked.

"Just before I came to get you," Marcus said.

Roseboro studied the list carefully, then handed it to Noah Daniels, the team's high-tech whiz kid. "Send these to the Secret Service, CIA, and NSA," he instructed. "Have them run background checks on every person and start listening in on every phone call. I want intercepts of every email and text message and analysis of all their social media accounts, too."

"The Israelis are already doing this," Daniels said. "They started the moment we arrived last time."

"Nevertheless," Roseboro said. "We're not leaving the safety of our president in the hands of a foreign power. I don't care how close an ally they are."

"Got it, sir—consider it done," said Daniels, who began immediately scanning the documents into his secure phone and transmitting them in encrypted files marked "high priority."

72

Dr. Ali Haqqani woke before dawn, dressed, and took a pill to calm his nerves.

Then he packed and headed to the airport. He had never been to Israel, and the Pakistani was terrified. He had been given a new name, an elaborate cover story, new credit cards, and a fake passport, all designed to transform him into a wealthy, retired physician from New Delhi—a Christian and a widower—traveling to places he had always read about but never imagined actually seeing with his own eyes.

Hamdi Yaşar had thought of everything, or so he said. Yet Haqqani feared his nerves would betray him. He was not a Christian, of course. Indeed, he was a devout Muslim who considered Christianity a polytheistic religion of pagan dogs. He certainly did not live in the capital of his Indian enemies. He was, unfortunately, a widower, and this, perversely, gave him a shred of hope that he could pull this thing off. He'd studied Christianity and India. He could spout off all kinds of facts and statistics to any border guard who asked him. But his trump card was that he could well up with tears at a moment's notice at the thought of his dearly departed wife. It was no act. It was the cloud that hung over him every day. Were it not for having been recruited by Kairos to wage jihad against the Jews and the Christians, he could not imagine having the wherewithal to get out of bed each day.

Haqqani boarded Iberia Airlines flight 3917 without incident and sat in first class. The plane lifted off from Palma de Mallorca at 6:30 a.m. On the flight, the pill began to have its effect. Haqqani dozed off easily and was surprised how quickly the ninety minutes to Madrid passed. With a layover of nearly an hour and a half, he bought a newspaper and tried to read it over a leisurely breakfast of soft-boiled eggs and black coffee. Now he thought the pill had been too effective. He was having trouble concentrating. He drank three more cups of coffee. Then, checking his phone and finding no new instructions, he nervously walked to his new gate, cleared through a second security check, and boarded El Al Airlines flight 396.

He spent most of the four-and-a-half-hour flight trying to sleep or holed up in the restroom. Finally, at 3:05 p.m. local time, the Boeing 737-900 touched down in Tel Aviv. Haqqani, a ball of nerves, entered the terminal terrified of being singled out for interrogation. But as it happened, his flight arrived just after two jumbo jets from the U.S. filled with American tourists. Passport control was a beehive of activity, the day after the Jewish Sabbath. He showed his passport but was asked no questions. To his astonishment, he soon had an entry visa, had collected his luggage, and was hailing a taxi.

"The American Colony Hotel," he told the driver, and before he knew it, they were roaring up Highway 1 for the Holy City.

Haqqani sat in stunned amazement as he looked out the windows on the drive. He could not believe how green and fertile the land was and how many thousands upon thousands of trees he could see. He had always pictured Palestine as a vast desert. Where was the sand? Where were all the camels? None of what he saw could be reconciled to the images he had been raised with. Hadn't Allah cursed the Jews? Where, then, were the barren wastelands, the piles of refuse, the orphans plagued by flies, the beggars covered in sores?

Up, up, up the taxi climbed into the hills surrounding Jerusalem. Not only were Haqqani's ears popping with the pressure change, but he found himself more disoriented with every mile. The Jewish towns and villages and the homes they contained were so many and so beautiful. Everywhere he looked he saw construction cranes. New apartments and office buildings were being erected. Even the Muslim villages looked prosperous and bustling with commerce. Every minaret he saw—and he saw so many—confused him all the more. He'd heard there were many Muslims living as citizens in the so-called Jewish state, but he'd imagined them all oppressed and in hiding. He'd never considered the possibility that the followers of Muhammad, peace be upon him, could build their own mosques and worship freely.

Soon, Haqqani reached the American Colony and paid the driver. The moment the cab drove away, however, rather than check into the hotel, he walked down to the main street and hailed another cab, just as he'd been instructed. This one he took to the David Citadel Hotel, a ride of about fifteen minutes. Yet when he arrived and paid this driver, he again failed to enter the hotel and check in. Instead, he hailed a third cab to the Seven Arches Hotel, atop the Mount of Olives.

Twenty minutes later, Haqqani was dropped off for the third time. He nearly wept as he exited the cab and found himself staring down across a valley at the Haram al-Sharif, the gleaming gold Dome of the Rock and the glorious Al-Aqsa Mosque—the Mosque in the Corner to which Muhammad, peace be upon him, had ridden on his Night Journey to heaven. Never in his wildest dreams had the Pakistani physician ever expected to be there in person, and the scene was more beautiful than he could possibly have anticipated.

Fortunately, he'd remembered to text his handler that he was en route, and moments later, a rusty gray Mazda sedan pulled up. The driver engaged him in a series of prearranged code words, and only when the two men were convinced of the other's identity did Haqqani get into the car.

They did not drive far. To the Pakistani's surprise, the car slowed down about a thousand feet from the hotel and pulled through a steel gate and into a garage underneath a three-level compound overlooking the Kidron Valley and the city of al-Quds.

"Welcome, *habibi*, I am so grateful you made it safely," said an impeccably dressed man in a finely tailored British suit as Haqqani climbed out of the sedan. "What a joy it is—truly, an honor—to finally meet such a hero of the revolution. You have been in my prayers, day and night, for months. Come inside and settle in. We have prepared everything for your comfort and gathered all the supplies you requested."

The two men embraced, yet Haqqani couldn't hide his confusion. "You are most kind," he replied. "But I'm sorry—what was your name again?"

"Ah, forgive me. I know you so well. I have followed your work so closely. But I forget that you and I have only communicated by email and that my face you have never seen. Allow me to introduce myself properly. My name is Mohammad al-Qassab."

Kailea Curtis held her MP5 so tightly her knuckles were turning white.

Geoff Stone adjusted the chin strap of his Kevlar helmet, glanced down at his colleague's hands, and caught her eye. He took several exaggerated deep breaths, signaling for her to breathe, relax, focus. At first she seemed annoyed by the suggestion, but then she nodded, started breathing properly again, flexed her fingers, and waited for the command to go.

Stone was determined to keep a close eye on Curtis. She was an impressive agent, but it was clear that she'd been deeply shaken by the blast in Downing Street. She'd never served in the military, much less been deployed to a forward area or experienced combat. She'd been an NYPD beat cop in Brooklyn, and a good one, before joining DSS. She'd certainly seen her share of trauma and high-stress situations. But she'd never seen friends obliterated by a suicide bomber. The shrapnel wounds that had scarred her face and hands would heal in time. Stone wasn't so sure about the psychological scars. Curtis was tough, but only time would tell if she could work her way through all this.

The commander of SCO19—the special operations unit of the London police, roughly the equivalent of an urban SWAT team back in the States—gave the signal. Quickly and in complete silence, they moved into the high-rise apartment complex in a sketchy section of the East End. A half-dozen commandos entered the stairwell on the far side of the building. Another six took up positions in the vestibule, guarding the two lifts and each door. Two more operators, their commander, and the two Americans worked their way up the nearest stairwell, weapons up, safeties off.

On the fifth floor, still not speaking a word, they moved into the hallway as the second team also moved into position around flat 512. On the silent count of three, the commander nodded to the breacher, a hulk of a man who heaved an enormous sledgehammer-like battering ram into the door and ripped it off its hinges.

"*Go, go, go!*" the commander yelled.

Six commandos stormed forward. Stone was right behind them. Curtis remained in the hall upon his orders. As planned, Stone watched two officers pivot right into the kitchen. Two more pivoted left into the living room. The remaining two burst into the bedroom. One by one, Stone heard the men shout, "*Clear!*" Most of the commandos now climbed out of the bedroom window onto the fire escape and headed up to the roof to surveil the area. That's when the bomb squad entered the flat. They checked for evidence of explosives and other bomb-making supplies. When they found none, Stone lowered his weapon and called for his colleague to join him.

Kailea took off her goggles and helmet and carefully inspected each room.

There were dirty dishes in the sink. Sour milk in the refrigerator, along with some rancid halal meat. The bunk beds in the sole bedroom were not made up. Two unfinished cups of cold tea sat on the end tables by the couch in the living room. The lone bookshelf held two copies of the Qur'an, several travel books about London, and several more about Athens and Santorini.

On a lower shelf stood a half-dozen paperback copies of works by Sayyid Qutb along with what looked like a complete thirty-volume set of arguably the man's definitive work, *In the Shade of the Qur'an.*

Qutb, she remembered from an Islamic Studies course she had taken in college, had been born and raised in Egypt and was widely considered the intellectual and spiritual godfather of the Muslim Brotherhood in the 1950s and '60s. If Kailea remembered correctly, Qutb had been arrested in Cairo somewhere around '65 or '66, convicted of plotting the assassination of President Gamal Abdel Nasser, and executed by hanging. One of his most fervent disciples had been Aymin al-Zawahiri, the founder of Egyptian Islamic Jihad, who had later been the coconspirator behind the 9/11 attacks with his friend and fellow mass murderer Osama bin Laden.

As the forensics team began taking pictures and dusting for fingerprints, Kailea donned a pair of crime scene gloves and picked up one of the copies of the sacred Muslim scriptures. She was surprised to find it was an English edition, not Arabic. So was the other. She picked up one of Qutb's books, titled *Social Justice in Islam,* and began flipping through it. Like the Qur'ans, it was in English. Many passages were underlined or highlighted with green marker. She replaced it on the shelf and picked another, *The Battle between Islam and Capitalism.* It, too, was an English translation and heavily marked up. She wondered if the Chechens knew how to read Arabic. Most jihadists did. It seemed odd that they would not.

As she glanced through one of the thirty hardcover volumes, a particular passage caught her eye.

> The war the Jews began to wage against Islam and Muslims in those
> early days has raged on to the present. The form and appearance
> may have changed, but the nature and means remain the same.

Kailea replaced it on the shelf and began flipping through a dog-eared paperback copy of *Milestones,* the 1964 manifesto that had become required reading for Islamists from Morocco to Indonesia.

"Is that Qutb?" asked Agent Stone, coming up behind her.

Kailea nodded. "Real piece of work," she said. "Ever read any of his stuff?"

"Some back in college, but it's been a while."

"Same here. You should work your way through *Milestones* someday. It's something else. Listen to these first few sentences.

"Mankind today is on the brink of an abyss, not because of the danger of complete annihilation which is hanging over its head—this being just a symptom and not the real disease—but because humanity is devoid of those vital values which are necessary not only for its healthy development but also for its real progress. . . .

"It is essential for mankind to have new leadership! . . .

"It is necessary for the new leadership to preserve and develop the material fruits of the creative genius of Europe, and also to provide mankind with such high ideals and values as have so far remained undiscovered by mankind, and which also will acquaint humanity with a way of life which is harmonious with human nature, which is positive and constructive, and which is practicable.

"Islam is the only System which possesses these values and this way of life."

"A real bon vivant, eh?" Stone asked.

Kailea turned to the last few blank pages and found handwritten notes scribbled in Russian. Neither she nor Stone could decipher much of it. But what did catch her eye was a phone number written at the bottom.

74

It was exactly 4 a.m. in the Holy City.

Back in Washington, it was 9 p.m. on the dot. The advance team gathered in Marcus's sixth-floor suite, opening beers, colas, and snacks from the minibar and turning on CNN to await the president's prime-time address.

This was it. Clarke was about to lay out his Middle East peace initiative. The White House had released word of the speech over the weekend. It had been front-page news in Israel, throughout the Arab world, and around the globe. Most pundits and Mideast analysts were already savaging the plan they had not yet read as being "irrelevant," "overtaken by events," and "dead on arrival," given that Palestinian leaders had preemptively rejected it.

Still, Marcus and the team were grateful there had as yet been no leaks concerning the fact that Clarke was coming to Jerusalem to hold a peace summit. That would be the bombshell in his remarks tonight and the top news story for the next few days. It would also be topic number one for jihadists around the globe. The American intelligence community was on standby to monitor millions of phone calls, text messages, emails, and online chats, looking for potential threats to the summit and to POTUS. The good news was that the techies at Langley had broken back into the Kremlin's computer servers. Marcus had, therefore, ordered Oleg to pay close attention to what was being said by Petrovsky and his top advisors, and the Russian defector had promised he was on it.

Just as the anchor introduced Clarke and the picture switched from the CNN studios in Atlanta to the Oval Office, Marcus's phone rang. Annoyed, he apologized to his colleagues, scrambled to his feet, and headed to the bathroom, where his phone was charging on the vanity. He was about to silence it when he realized it was Kailea calling from London.

"We've got it, Marcus," she said immediately.

"Got what?"

"The names of the two people who impersonated the BBC crew."

"Who are they?"

"Chechens—Maxim and Amina Sheripov. Their mother was a Black Widow. She blew herself up in Moscow back in the nineties. We searched their flat yesterday afternoon and found a phone number. It led us to a medical clinic here in London and the name of the surgeon who placed the bomb in the woman, Amina."

"Give it to me," Marcus said, grabbing for a pen and notepad.

"His name is Ali Haqqani."

"One q or two?"

"Two. He's a Pakistani national. Born in Islamabad. Emigrated to the U.K. in 2010. That's all we've got at the moment."

"Focus on the money," Marcus instructed her. "Who paid him to do the surgery on the bomber? Where did the money come from? What banks did it route through? Search all of his phone records, too. He's got to have a handler, and that person might be based in the U.K., even in London."

"We're already on it—I'll send you everything as soon as I can."

"And he had to have nurses, right? Who were they? Where do they live? Where are they from? How long did they work for him? What do they know?"

"We're on that, too. The Brits are raiding all of their apartments as we speak."

"Great work. I've got to go, but keep me posted."

The president's speech was under way.

Typically, Ahmet Mustafa would be sound asleep at such an early hour.

The Turkish president loved to sleep late, rising around 9 a.m. and sometimes as late as 9:30. He usually joined his wife for a sumptuous breakfast at ten sharp each day, except Fridays, and rarely came to the office before noon. He was always back in his living quarters by six in the evening, unless he was traveling or hosting a foreign visitor for a state dinner. And he was in bed, lights out, no later than ten every night, without fail, wherever he happened to be in the world.

Hamdi Yaşar, therefore, was stunned to see Mustafa's private number show up on his caller ID. Sitting in the control room at Al-Sawt's main studios, he took the call and stepped out into the hallway. "Mr. President, is everything all right?" he asked as he headed back to his office. "It's a bit early for you."

"Are you watching this?" Mustafa replied, ignoring the question.

"The speech? Of course. What else?"

"Did you know this was coming?" Mustafa pressed. "Clarke, Eitan, and Al Saud together, in al-Quds next week?"

"We got an advance text of the speech, yes," Yaşar replied cautiously, suddenly realizing that the Turkish leader had accidentally called him on his work mobile phone, not his private satellite phone.

"Do you understand the implications of this—how huge this is?"

"It's a very big story, I agree, and our network would love to get your reaction to the speech on the record, but not right now," Yaşar said, desperately hoping Mustafa would not say anything incriminating on an open line. "May I send a crew later today once the Ankara bureau opens?"

There was a pregnant pause.

"Yes, yes, that would be fine—I would like to comment more extensively.

But for now, I'd just like to ask: Your network will be covering this peace summit from all angles, correct? This may prove to be a once-in-a-lifetime opportunity. I would hate to see it missed."

Yaşar started breathing again, relieved the Turkish leader had remembered the conversation was likely being recorded by the NSA, Israel's Unit 8200, and myriad other foreign intelligence agencies. But his message—however shrouded in euphemism—was crystal clear. Mustafa wanted Kairos to send its best assassin to Jerusalem.

Yaşar wanted to tell him that their best was already there, but that would have to wait for their next face-to-face meeting.

Ismail Ziad was apoplectic.

The longer he watched Clarke's speech, the more enraged he became. At one point, he threw a shoe at the TV set. A moment later, he picked up the phone on his desk and heaved it across the room, narrowly missing an aide who had just entered the office but hitting a mirror and smashing it to pieces.

"Get me al-Azzam," the Palestinian leader shouted. *"Now!"*

With Ziad's primary phone no longer functioning, the aide pulled out his own mobile phone, dialed the Grand Mufti's number from the phone's contact list, and waited until the old man answered. "Your Excellency, I have President Ziad on the line for you." Then he handed the phone over to his boss.

"Amin, are you there?"

"I am, Mr. President."

"Are you watching this travesty?"

"Yes, yes, of course, but I—"

"Blasphemy, I tell you—this is blasphemy against our people and against our holy city," the Palestinian president raged, cutting off the Grand Mufti in midsentence. *"And you must stop it, Amin—you must never let this thing come to pass."*

Prince Abdullah was still at his desk.

A bank of TV monitors on the far wall of his office showed President Clarke delivering his address on six different networks, but all were on mute. The chief of Saudi intelligence had already read an advance text of the speech that CIA director Stephens had sent him hours before. Right now he had more important matters on his mind.

Summoning his chief of staff, the prince demanded to know if they'd heard from their source in Tehran. He did not use the man's name. But the aide was one of the few people in the kingdom who knew exactly to whom his boss was referring—Dr. Haydar Abbasi, ostensibly the director of the Iranian space agency, though he was more precisely the head of Iran's ballistic missile program.

"No, Your Highness," the aide replied. "I'm afraid not."

"Do we even know if he's still alive?"

"Well, there was an item about him in the paper two days ago."

"Saying what?"

"It was small, just a picture and a caption, really. He welcomed a delegation from Moscow to discuss plans for a joint exploratory mission to Mars."

"Why wasn't I informed?"

"You have been so busy preparing for His Majesty's trip to al-Quds, I didn't think it necessary."

The prince stood, rubbed his bloodshot eyes, and took a swig of water from a bottle on his desk. "Fine, but we need more from him, and quickly. Can we contact him?"

"No, Your Highness—he was adamant from the outset that he will contact us, and we must never try to reach him."

Just then, the phone rang. The chief of staff answered it, then asked the caller to hold. He hit the Mute button and turned to the prince. "It's the American."

"Dayton?"

"No, Ryker."

"The DSS agent?"

"Yes, and he says it's urgent."

General Entezam had never seen Hossein Ansari so ill.

Even in the short time since their last meeting, the spiritual leader of the Iranian Revolution had lost weight. The man was emaciated. His skin was jaundiced. He could not get out of bed and could barely keep down a spoonful of broth.

Entezam had come to the residence to watch Clarke's speech with the Supreme Leader and to brief him on his latest conversation with Abu Nakba. But as he sat alone by the man's bedside, he knew it was not to be. Silently he prayed that Allah would have mercy on this giant he held so dear.

The man had accomplished so much in his lifetime. Now, in his final weeks of life, all Ansari wanted was to see vengeance exacted against the Americans and the Israelis for killing Alireza al-Zanjani and foiling his plans for Iran to have the Bomb. And all Entezam wanted was to share with Ansari the extraordinary news that Kairos, one of their most important proxies, would soon take out not only Clarke and Eitan but the Saudi monarch as well.

Privately, the commander of the Iranian Revolutionary Guard Corps wished he could do the deed himself. What he would have given to actually be in the city of al-Quds, on the Haram al-Sharif, the very martyr chosen to go to paradise and send these three devils straight to the fires of hell. He did not know the name of the one who actually had been chosen. Abu Nakba had been vague with the details, not even indicating whether the assassin would be a man or a woman. Yet rather than take offense at Abu Nakba's refusal to entrust him with the details of the very operation he was bankrolling, much less feed on the jealousy he felt toward the *shahid* or *shahida* preparing for glory, Entezam vowed to pray for this brave soul three times a day until the operation was complete. Whoever they were, they would need Allah's strength to overcome all the cunning traps of Satan.

"*Help me,*" wheezed Ansari, his raspy, thin voice barely audible. "*A basin— bring it quickly.*"

Entezam stood back up and looked around the room for something suitable. The best he could find on short notice was a wastebasket. He grabbed it and brought it to Ansari, asking if this was what he wanted.

But the Supreme Leader never replied. Instead, he began to cough and then choke and then to vomit his own blood.

76

Prince Abdullah picked up the phone.

"Agent Ryker, to what do I owe this honor?"

"Prince Abdullah, I'm sorry for calling so early and breaking the chain of command."

"Not at all. We owe you a great debt. You may call me anytime."

"You're most kind," Marcus said, then got to the point. "We've identified the bombers in London. They were Chechens, a brother and sister: Maxim and Amina Sheripov. I'm hoping you could run their names through your system and let me know whatever you can find on them."

"Absolutely. What else?"

"Have you ever heard of a BCB?"

"A body cavity bomb?" the prince asked.

"Exactly," said a surprised Marcus. "So MI5 and the FBI are now convinced that Amina Sheripov was the bomber and that Maxim pulled the trigger, as it were."

"And someone surgically implanted the bomb inside Amina?"

"Correct."

"Who?"

"A Pakistani by the name of Dr. Ali Haqqani."

"One *q* or two?"

"Two, we think. Would you run his name as well?"

"Of course."

"We can't say whether that's his real name or an alias, but that's the name he was using in London. MI5 and the FBI are tearing apart the medical clinic where he worked. We already have security footage from inside the clinic proving the Sheripovs came there and interacted with Haqqani."

"But you don't have him?"

"No. We're about to put out a warrant for his arrest."

"Don't—not yet," said the prince.

"Why not?"

"There's no way he's using the same name," said Rashid. "And you'll never find him in the U.K. He's gone. The question is what alias he's using now. If you put out an APB on him, the media will broadcast it across the world, and he'll go to ground. We don't have time for that. We need him in the open. We need him moving. That's the only way we'll spot him."

"The feeling here is different," Marcus said. "The more people who see his face, the more tips we'll get that can lead us to him."

"You'll be flooded with false leads. Again, we don't have time for that."

"Well, it's going to happen within the hour. The only way to stop it is if the king calls the president. I'm not sure that's the right call, but it's up to you."

"Listen, there's something I need to tell you, Agent Ryker."

"What's that?"

"Have you ever heard the name Abdullah Hassan Tali al-Asiri?"

"No—why?"

"Of course not," said the prince. "It's highly classified here in the kingdom. But I'm telling you so you understand how serious this threat is."

"Go on."

"Al-Asiri was a Saudi national. A terrorist. A member of al Qaeda. A real monster. Anyway, we were hunting him. You Americans were hunting him too. Turns out, he was hiding in the caves of Yemen. But in August of 2009, al-Asiri contacts Saudi intelligence. Says he wants to come in. Wants to see his family. Wants asylum in return for the names and exact locations of scores of other al Qaeda operatives. The man in my job at the time was Prince Mohammed bin Nayef. He's thrilled about the chance to bring in al-Asiri, so he approves the plan. But at the last minute, al-Asiri adds a condition."

"What?"

"He says he's filled with remorse and wants to repent to Nayef in person. Nayef agrees. He even sends his private jet to Yemen to bring al-Asiri back. They meet in the prince's home in Jeddah, on the Red Sea. Al-Asiri passes through two metal detectors. He's frisked—thoroughly—by the prince's security detail. He's declared clean, so he's brought to meet with the prince, face-to-face. That's when it happens."

"What happens?"

"Al-Asiri explodes right there in the parlor."

"A body cavity bomb."

"Precisely," said the prince. "It turns out al-Asiri had inserted the bomb in his—forgive me—his rectum. Most of the explosive force was focused downward. It created a huge crater in the floor. We found one of the man's arms in the ceiling. But Nayef, praise Allah, was not badly injured. Shaken, as it were, but not stirred."

"I've never heard that story."

"Few have. It was embarrassing to the Saudi intelligence and security services that we'd been duped by al-Asiri. Moreover, we wanted al Qaeda to think we still had him, that we'd detected his bomb and defused it. But you can understand why your news will be so disturbing to His Majesty the king, especially on the eve of the most politically difficult trip of his life. He's under enormous pressure not to go to Jerusalem, not to meet the Israelis. And this isn't going to help."

"Sorry to be the bearer of such news."

"Better now than later."

"True, which means I have to give the photo to the Israelis. We may not have a real name yet, but the Israelis have state-of-the-art facial recognition software. If Haqqani tries to enter Israel, you and I will both know why. We can keep it out of the media for now, but we need the Israelis to stop and interrogate him so he can lead us to the rest of Kairos."

"Very well," said the prince. "I will speak to the king. You must call Asher Gilad right now. Do you have his private number?"

"I do."

"Good—I'll call you the minute we run these names."

"Hello? Who is this?"

It was clear to Marcus that he'd just woken up the head of the Israeli Mossad. But it could not be helped.

"Mr. Gilad, I'm sorry to wake you, but this is Agent Marcus Ryker. We met at the dinner with the prime minister the other day."

"What time is it?"

"4:36, sir."

"This had better be important, Ryker," Gilad growled.

"It is, sir. The FBI and MI5 have figured out the identity of the man responsible for the bombing in London, or at least intimately involved in its planning."

"Who is it?"

"His name is Haqqani. I'm texting you his photo and details as we speak. We need to know whatever you have in your files on this guy. And we need you to put your people on the highest alert."

"Why?"

"We have reason to believe, sir, that Haqqani may be coming to Israel."

Hussam Mashrawi felt a sense of déjà vu.

Slipping out of bed as quietly as he could, he washed and dressed and put on his overcoat and slipped out the front door before the sun came up. It was not raining now, but it had been all night, and the stone sidewalks were slick. Still, Mashrawi moved as quickly as he could down the nearly empty alleyways, past the shuttered shops, cafés, restaurants, and hostels. As he approached the Monastery of the Flagellation, he saw a lone light on in a room above the shoemaker's shop. That was the signal.

Knocking twice, he entered quickly when the door was unlocked for him. He'd been told to call his handler at precisely six o'clock that morning. The clock on the wall told him he was three minutes early, and he breathed a sigh of relief. That would be just enough time to open the wall safe and—

Mashrawi's heart nearly stopped. As he entered the tiny room in the back of the flat so cluttered with books and old newspapers and smelling of stale cigarettes, someone was waiting for him. "Who are you?" he asked, trembling.

"Dr. Mashrawi, what an honor to finally meet you."

Mashrawi said nothing, though he slowly began backing away from the shadowy figure sitting in the chair at the antique desk.

"There is no need to be alarmed," the man said with a slight British accent. "The man you hoped to speak with sent me. He asked me to speak to you in person because the assignment he has for you is of the utmost importance, and no detail can be left to chance."

"How do I know that—?"

"That what? That I'm truly sent from Kairos?"

Mashrawi gasped. He'd never used the word, not even on a secure call.

"Who else could I be, the Shin Bet?"

"Perhaps."

"Then I'd be torturing you, not talking to you."

Asher Gilad finally called Marcus back.

"Are you somewhere you can talk privately?" the Mossad chief asked.

The speech was over. The party was over. The members of the advance team had all gone back to their rooms for a few hours of shut-eye. Marcus was alone in his hotel suite, trying to get some sleep himself. Now he switched on a lamp and sat up in bed. "Yeah, what have you got?"

"It's too late," Gilad said.

"Too late for what?"

"I passed on the photo you sent me to the Shin Bet and airport security services."

"And?"

"I'm afraid Haqqani's already in the country."

Stunned, Marcus was suddenly completely awake.

"Ryker, you there?"

"Yes, sir, I'm here."

"Apparently Haqqani entered Israel on Saturday via a flight from Spain. He used an alias—Mohammed Peshawar—but photos never lie. It's him."

"Please tell me you have some idea where he is."

"None whatsoever. We know he went to Jerusalem. One of our surveillance cameras picked him up getting into a cab. My men have tracked down the driver, showed him the picture. He says the man wanted to be taken to the American Colony Hotel and paid in cash. But the manager of the hotel says he has no reservation for a Haqqani or a Peshawar. We've run the CCTV footage and come up empty."

"So all you know for sure is he came to Jerusalem and vanished?" Marcus asked.

"I'm afraid so."

Marcus felt ill, but there was no time to slow down. He had calls to make.

The man in the shadows leaned forward so Mashrawi could see his face.

"My name is Mohammed al-Qassab. I am the director of operations for Kairos, and Father has sent me to ask for your help."

Mashrawi said nothing.

"You have provided us critical information about President Clarke's upcoming visit and about the king's visit and the prime minister's presence with them. You have pledged your loyalty to our father and told us you are willing to do whatever is necessary to achieve victory in our jihad, in our quest to rebuild the Caliphate. Is that true?"

Slowly Mashrawi nodded.

"Good. Then this is what Father asks. We need a *shahid*, a loyal and courageous martyr willing to kill the president, the prime minister, and the king. Will you lay down your life that the Caliphate may live?"

"I will—I am—I mean, I would if I could, but . . ."

"But what?"

"With all due respect, it would be impossible to bring a weapon onto the Haram al-Sharif, especially on that day. I am not a coward. I will do anything I am asked. But we must be realistic. Some things just cannot be done."

"Nothing is impossible with Allah, Hussam. Do you believe that?"

"Yes, of course."

"Good. There is a doctor I want you to see. He will perform a surgery on you. Tomorrow. And I will not lie to you. It will hurt. A great deal. For several days. But then you will be fine and ready for the most important and glorious mission of your life."

PART

FOUR

78

KING DAVID HOTEL, JERUSALEM—10 DECEMBER

A full day had gone by, and there was no sign of Haqqani.

Marcus's wake-up call came at 5 a.m. But he was already awake. He had been for more than an hour, trying to think of some way out of this mess and coming up with nothing. He rolled out of bed, threw on running shorts, a T-shirt, and a sweatshirt, and met Tomer Ben Ami, deputy director of the Shin Bet, in the lobby of the five-star hotel. No other guests were present, only the front desk staff and an older man mopping and polishing the floors of the grand vestibule. The rains had stopped, but the sky remained threatening, and it was cold and getting colder. Marcus wasn't particularly looking forward to a run, but he was glad the police agency veteran had offered to work out with him.

"So where are we headed?" Marcus asked.

"Ever done 'Murph'?" Tomer replied.

"Yeah, a million years ago."

"Welcome back." The Israeli smiled.

Marcus did not return the smile. "You're kidding," he said.

Tomer wasn't. "Murph" was a fairly grueling workout and one of the few things Marcus didn't miss about his Secret Service days. Designed in honor of Lieutenant Michael P. Murphy, a Navy SEAL who was killed in action in Afghanistan back in 2005, the CrossFit routine had become a favorite of U.S. Special Forces operators and the country's most elite law enforcement officers, who performed it as a way of honoring the memory of this heroic American warrior. Marcus was familiar with the workout but hadn't known its popularity had crossed the ocean or that a man nearly twenty years his senior could do it and wanted to.

They began by running a mile through the streets of Jerusalem. That was the easy part. Next, they did a hundred pull-ups, side by side, followed by two hundred push-ups, followed by three hundred air squats. By the end, Marcus was desperately sucking in oxygen. Tomer was drenched in sweat but beaming from ear to ear.

"Come on, Ryker, get the lead out," the Israeli shouted, swatting him on the butt as they headed out on another one-mile run.

As Marcus's feet pounded the pavement, trying to keep up, he realized he was hurting in joints and muscles he didn't remember having. Ever since joining the CIA under the guise of working for DSS, he'd been working out far more regularly than he had since his wife and son were killed. But not nearly this hard, and only that frigid Wednesday morning did he realize just how out of shape he still was. The one saving grace of the entire ordeal was that they hadn't done the hour-long workout wearing twenty pounds of body armor, as Marcus had back in the Secret Service.

They wound up at the Shin Bet's Jerusalem office. There, Tomer took him down to the agency's basement gun range. They toweled off, downed several bottles of water, and did target practice for an hour with handguns and submachine guns. Afterward Tomer drove Marcus back to the King David in his Range Rover.

After he showered, shaved, and dressed in a freshly pressed suit, Marcus found Secret Service deputy director Carl Roseboro waiting for him in the lobby. A few minutes later, Tomer pulled up out front, also showered and dressed for the day. Roseboro and Ryker climbed in, and they headed to the Old City.

"Anything on this Haqqani guy?" Roseboro asked.

"Not yet," said Tomer.

With just one week before Air Force One was wheels down in Tel Aviv, the Israeli prime minister's office was ecstatic, Tomer told them. The visit of the Saudi monarch was a huge diplomatic breakthrough, arguably bigger than Anwar Sadat's arrival in 1977. But Israeli security services were growing more nervous by the day.

"That's not exactly reassuring," Roseboro said.

"It's not supposed to be," Tomer replied.

"I want you to tell me you guys have this all under control."

"I wish I could."

"Israel has never lost a visiting head of state, right?"

"Right."

"And Rabin was the only Israeli prime minister ever assassinated, right?"

"Right again."

"And that was a long time ago."

"1995."

"And you guys have tightened up your protocols since then, right?" Roseboro pressed.

"Of course, but you don't understand," Tomer explained as they found a place to park and headed up to the Temple Mount. "The stakes are much higher now. Can you even begin to imagine how catastrophic it would be to Israel's reputation if a Muslim king gets popped while visiting our capital?"

79

The same young veiled woman as before greeted them and asked if she could help them.

"We have an appointment with the Grand Mufti and Dr. Mashrawi," Marcus said.

"I'm afraid Dr. Mashrawi had a dental emergency and won't be able to join you," the woman replied. "But the Grand Mufti is in his office and waiting for you."

The three men followed her down a series of hallways until they reached their destination.

Amin al-Azzam, decked out in his formal robes, stood up behind his large oak desk, piled high with books and papers of all kinds. Smiling warmly, he came around the desk and shook the men's hands as Marcus introduced his American and Israeli colleagues. Then he invited them all to sit on two well-worn beige couches in the corner of his office while he took a seat in an antique wooden rocking chair. Just then, the veiled woman knocked, entered, and served hot tea with a sprig of mint in each glass.

"I'm sorry to hear Dr. Mashrawi is not able to join us this morning," Marcus began. "I trust everything is okay?"

"Yes, yes, of course," said al-Azzam. "Hussam suddenly developed a severe toothache. He went to his dentist yesterday afternoon and found out he needed an emergency root canal. My wife is watching his kids, and his wife—my daughter—took him for the procedure this morning."

"I'm so sorry," Marcus replied, wincing. "That's no fun."

"No, it certainly is not. But I'm sure he'll be back on his feet in no time. So how can I help you gentlemen as the big day approaches?"

Deputy Director Roseboro set down his teacup. "Your Excellency, I want to thank you for getting back to us so quickly and thoroughly with the answers to the many questions Agent Ryker here posed."

"With pleasure."

"To be candid, that was the easy part," Roseboro continued. "Now, as Marcus no doubt mentioned, we need to begin a very detailed security sweep of every building, every office, every closet, every nook and cranny of the Temple Mount area, and we need to begin setting up metal detectors, video surveillance equipment, and so forth."

Marcus noticed the Grand Mufti tense ever so slightly at Roseboro's use of the Jewish term *Temple Mount* rather than the Islamic name, the Haram al-Sharif. Nevertheless, he also noticed that al-Azzam did not correct Roseboro but let the slight go.

"But of course, Director Roseboro," he replied calmly. "And I want you to know that I welcome all that is necessary to secure this place for the arrival of these three esteemed guests. This is our way. We want you and the rest of the world to see the hospitality we Arabs are famous for."

"You are most kind," said Roseboro.

"That said, I cannot allow you to begin your preparations until Saturday," al-Azzam added, surprising them all.

"I'm sorry—Saturday?" Roseboro asked.

"Yes, I'm afraid so," said al-Azzam. "The anticipated arrival of the

Custodian of the Two Holy Mosques has generated enormous interest—and passion, I might add—and thus we expect our numbers on Friday to be two to three times greater than normal. We are expecting upwards of a quarter million people for midday prayers on Friday. As such, we need every hour between now and then to prepare. Once they are gone, of course, and our own holy day is complete, then you and your people may make all the preparations you need. But not until sunrise on Saturday."

The news did not sit well at all with the two Americans, but when they began to push back, Tomer intervened. "Gentlemen, please; the Grand Mufti is only doing his job, and believe me, the last thing we want is to create a disruption ahead of Friday prayers," the Israeli explained to Roseboro and Ryker, then turned back to al-Azzam. "Can we count on you to encourage a peaceful and orderly day on Friday and calm in the territories between now and the end of the summit?"

"Absolutely," the Grand Mufti said. "So long as you respect my needs and those of my team between now and Saturday. Will this be a problem?"

"No, not at all," Roseboro said.

Tomer and the Grand Mufti then looked to Ryker.

"None whatsoever," Marcus replied.

Marcus's phone vibrated in his pocket. As the other men continued to talk, he pulled it out and glanced down at the screen, which read, *User ID unknown.*

"Excuse me for a moment," he said. "I'm afraid I need to take this."

When al-Azzam gave him leave, Marcus stepped out of the office and took the call. "Hello?"

"Agent Ryker, this is Prince Abdullah in Riyadh."

80

Marcus exited the building.

He walked across the plaza past the Dome of the Rock and found a quiet spot under a colonnade to take the Saudi intelligence chief's call.

"We ran the names you asked for—Maxim and Amina Sheripov and Dr. Ali Haqqani," Prince Abdullah reported.

"And?"

"I'm afraid we found nothing on the Sheripovs, just a report on their mother's perfidy in Moscow."

"What about Haqqani?"

"On him we found some very interesting material. I'm sending it all to you and your colleagues now, including phone numbers and email addresses. But here's the gist."

"Go—I'm listening."

"Haqqani's real name is Ghulam Salik. He was born to a devout Sunni family in Islamabad, the youngest of six children. His father was the personal physician to the president of Pakistan. His sisters are all married and still live in Islamabad. His eldest brother passed away of a heart attack about eighteen months ago, but before his death he was the personal physician to Turkish president Mustafa. Another brother is an investment banker living in Doha, Qatar. He keeps a very low profile, but we know he is closely linked to the ruling family and is a senior member of the Muslim Brotherhood."

"And Ghulam himself?"

"The black sheep of the family—a brilliant doctor who became a religious fanatic. Came here to the kingdom in the midnineties for medical school but also attended one of our most problematic mosques under an extremist cleric who was arrested and executed for subversive activities about ten years ago. On June 14, 2010, Ghulam Salik flew from Doha to Sana'a, Yemen. On August 1 of that year, he flew back to Doha and then to Istanbul, Turkey. But in 2010, our investigators determined that it was Ghulam who performed the surgery on Abdullah Hassan Tali al-Asiri."

"The al Qaeda suicide bomber?"

"Exactly."

"The one who tried to assassinate Prince Mohammed bin Nayef with the first body cavity bomb?"

"That's the one," the Saudi confirmed. "But by the time we put the pieces together, Ghulam Salik had vanished off the face of the earth. Frankly, I'd never heard of the name Ali Haqqani until you called me yesterday. It took us a while, but now it's clear to us that Haqqani and Salik are the same person."

"How do you know?"

"It's a long story and highly classified. Off the record, let's just say that about a year ago, the mainframe computers of the Turkish Ministry of the Interior were hacked. A half century of records of every birth, death, marriage, divorce, burial, and name change in the Republic of Turkey became available on the black market. I'm not saying we bought the files. But every now and then someone friendly to the kingdom may have the opportunity to peruse such collections and see what's available. Given that it's been about a decade since the Ghulam Salik case went cold, we never thought to ask these particular friends to run his name and see what popped up."

"But let me guess," Marcus said. "Yesterday you did."

"Again off the record, yes," the prince said. "We found that in the summer of 2010, while Ghulam was in Istanbul, he had his name legally changed to Ali Haqqani. A few months later, he emigrated to the U.K. That's where he's been living ever since."

"That's a huge break," Marcus replied. "Thank you, Your Highness."

"What are allies for?"

Marcus hung up, then received an incoming message. He opened the encrypted file from Prince Abdullah, reviewed it briefly, then immediately forwarded it to Oleg before calling the onetime Russian mole.

"Good to hear from you, my friend—what's up?" Oleg said.

"I just sent you a file of every known phone number and email address for Ali Haqqani," Marcus replied. "He used the name Mohammed Peshawar to get into Israel. But his real name is Ghulam Salik. Work your magic and get back to me as fast as you can."

81

Mohammed al-Qassab chambered a round in his silenced Glock pistol.

Then he pored over the image of the busy street three floors below.

Having arrived on Friday afternoon from London, this was now his sixth day in the flat above the dentist's office that served as the Kairos safe house. He had shaved his head and was now bald, but he had not shaved his previously clean face. His beard and mustache were coming in thick, the first of a series of steps he intended to take to change his appearance before the next stage of the mission. Even so, he did not yet feel comfortable stepping out on any of the three balconies or going up on the roof, for fear of being spotted and identified.

Obsessed with operational security, al-Qassab had made it his business to take hourly snapshots of Rabaa al-Adwaya, the street running below to the east, as well as the west-side service road that snaked up from the

Kidron Valley past the Tomb of the Prophets. He used a digital camera, putting the lens up to a small tear he'd made in two different curtains. Then, without pulling back or ruffling the curtains at all, he would take a photo and immediately study the images, looking for any threats as well as trying to establish what "normal" life looked like. He did this eighteen times a day.

Satisfied that they were not about to be raided by Israeli police or special forces units, al-Qassab glanced at his watch. It was almost ten in the morning. They had to get moving. Silently he gave Dr. Haqqani the signal. The Pakistani nodded, then whispered to the dentist and his two assistants—all of whom were on the Kairos payroll and building sizable nest eggs in their Swiss numbered accounts—that it was time to begin.

Two floors below, a lone secretary was on the phone rescheduling appointments for the following week, after the peace summit. Here in the dentist's personal flat on the top floor of the building, the dining room had been transformed into a makeshift operating theater. The dentist had sent his family away on holiday to Germany a week earlier. Neither his wife nor his four children had a clue as to who was coming to stay in their rooms or that anyone was coming at all. This gave them all the space and privacy they would need.

Already under general anesthesia and completely unconscious, Hussam Mashrawi lay on the dining room table, surrounded by pillows and covered by sheets. A large plastic tarp had been spread across the floor to protect the beautiful Persian rug from being stained by blood or other bodily fluids. Al-Qassab watched Haqqani's eyes scanning the medical devices that had been brought in and set up around the table. Mashrawi's vital signs were strong, and the oxygen machine was working properly. Haqqani donned his surgical gloves, took one last look at the size and shape of the bomb that was sitting on the kitchen table nearby, then picked up a scalpel and went to work.

★

Ryker and Roseboro were on hand as the first C-5M Galaxy landed at Ben Gurion International.

Tomer Ben Ami was right at their side as two Starlifters landed in succession, minutes after the first aircraft. No matter how many times Marcus had seen them in action, he still found himself in awe of the sheer enormity of these Lockheed cargo planes. They were among the largest military planes in the world, each seemingly capable of carrying a small city's worth of people and supplies.

Soon, the men watched as three Marine One Sikorsky helicopters were carefully removed from the hold of the first plane. Six identical versions of "The Beast"—the presidential limousine—rolled out of the second plane along with a fleet of armored Chevy Suburbans, other Secret Service vehicles, and unmanned surveillance drones. The remaining trucks, sedans, ambulances, and other vehicles needed for POTUS's motorcade and the Secretary of State's motorcade rolled out of the third plane, followed by yet more vehicles that would be pre-positioned along the primary motorcade route as backups. In addition to all these, the three men were overseeing the unloading of a veritable arsenal of Secret Service and DSS weapons, ammunition, radios, and communications gear, and a laundry list of additional equipment and supplies.

They were looking at the most bulletproof, bomb-resistant, RPG-impregnable vehicles on the face of the earth, thought Marcus. It was all very impressive. But none of them actually expected an attack against the motorcade. They were expecting a suicide bomber—more precisely, a homicide bomber—but they had no idea where. Or how to stop it.

It was well after 7 p.m. when the Red Crescent ambulance pulled up.

Two paramedics—both on the Kairos payroll—entered the first-floor office and found Hussam Mashrawi slumped in a dentist chair, unconscious. To maintain the cover of the operation, the dentist had actually conducted a completely unnecessary root canal on the man after the BCB surgery was successfully completed. He'd even pulled out a perfectly good wisdom tooth for good measure. As a result, both sides of Mashrawi's face were swollen, and drool was running down his shirt. The man's wife, who had dropped him off for what she thought would be a routine root canal that morning, would have questions.

Neither paramedic had any idea what Mashrawi had been through or who was staying in the flat two floors up. All they knew was that they were being paid to transport the executive director of the Waqf back to his home in the Old City.

With the dentist's help, the two men carefully lifted Mashrawi onto a stretcher. They wheeled him out and loaded him into the back of the ambulance. The dentist then said he'd like to accompany them all back to the Mashrawi residence, just to make sure everything went smoothly.

Al-Qassab peered through the curtain.

He watched as Mashrawi was placed in the ambulance. He watched to make sure the mobile phone he had placed in Mashrawi's jacket pocket did not fall out and go skittering across the pavement. That was the phone, after all, that Mashrawi was going to use to detonate himself when the moment came. Before the surgery, al-Qassab had taken the Palestinian into a private room, given him the phone, and walked him through every step, answering every question the man had.

Yes, there would be a slight delay, he'd told Mashrawi. *There could in fact be as many as three seconds between the moment he pressed the correct speed-dial number and the moment the bomb actually detonated. Yes, the explosion would be massive. It would kill everyone within ten meters, roughly thirty feet. No, he would not feel a thing. He would be obliterated instantaneously. One moment he would be shouting, "Allahu akbar!" The next moment he would be in paradise, remembered forever as a martyr and thus a hero back here on earth.*

Al-Qassab was impressed with just how calm Mashrawi was. Indeed, the man seemed eager to do his part for the Caliphate. He did not seem nervous. He did not seem worried about what would happen to his beloved wife and children. He accepted al-Qassab's assurance that they would be well cared for and provided for.

What al-Qassab did not tell Mashrawi, however, was that he had no intention of entrusting the Palestinian with so important a mission. The speed dial in the mobile phone had been properly programmed. But al-Qassab now looked down at the mobile phone in his own hands. He had programmed the speed-dial function on this one with the exact same number. There was no turning back, no room for hesitation. When the moment came, he would not be trusting Mashrawi to dial his own death. Al-Qassab would do that for him.

Red lights flashing, the ambulance pulled away from the curb.

It threaded its way through East Jerusalem and stopped as close as it could to the Damascus Gate. The two paramedics and the dentist unloaded the stretcher, cleared through an Israeli security checkpoint, and got Mashrawi to his third-floor apartment, where his wife, Yasmine, was waiting.

"What happened?" she gasped at the sight of her husband. "He looks like someone beat him up!"

"There were a few complications, but overall, everything went fine," the dentist replied, not exactly lying but certainly not telling the truth.

"Why isn't he awake?" she asked.

"I'm afraid he had an allergic reaction to the first type of anesthesia I used, so I had to use another kind," the dentist explained, following to the letter the script Dr. Haqqani and al-Qassab had given him. "I expect him to sleep through the night, but he should start feeling better tomorrow."

The paramedics hoisted Mashrawi off the stretcher and set him on the couch in the living room. The dentist gave Yasmine a bag filled with various kinds of prescription medications to manage the pain and reduce the swelling. He walked her through how much and when to give each pill, then promised to come by in the morning to check on his patient. With two of her young children grasping at the folds of her dress, Yasmine adjusted her veil, wiped her eyes, and thanked the men for their kindness, and with that they took their leave.

The first person Yasmine called was her father. The moment the Grand Mufti answered his mobile phone, she burst into tears. He had no idea what she was saying, but he promised to come to her side right away.

83

U.S. EMBASSY, JERUSALEM

"Agent Ryker, do you have a moment? I've got something you should see."

Marcus had just walked into the "war room," but he was in no mood to talk to anyone. He was hungry. He was thirsty. It was almost eight thirty at night. He hadn't had any dinner and still had hours of work ahead of him.

Roseboro had converted the conference room down the hall from the ambassador's office into a makeshift operations center for the senior members of his advance team, even as another forty lower-level Secret Service, DSS, White House, State Department, and Pentagon officials and staffers had arrived in recent days and had taken over the embassy's cafeteria to further prepare for the summit. Now, as Marcus poured himself a cup of coffee and tried to catch his breath from another brutally long day, Noah Daniels was asking for time he did not want to give.

It was all Marcus could do not to brush the guy off and tell whatever it was would have to wait. But he knew that the thirty-four-year-old communications whiz kid didn't actually work for the White House Communications Agency. In reality, Daniels secretly worked for the CIA. Stephens had confided to Marcus before leaving Washington that Daniels was one of the Agency's most valuable assets. So Marcus played along.

"What've you got?"

"Well, on Friday you asked me to make sure we were intercepting the calls and emails of every current and former employee of the Waqf, right?"

Marcus sighed, then took a sip of coffee so rancid he had to spit it back into his mug.

"Right—so?" he asked, wiping his mouth and dumping the sludge into the sink.

"We've picked up two calls I thought you would want to know about."

Noah handed Marcus two stapled sets of transcripts—one in Arabic, the other in English. The first was a conversation between Palestinian Authority chairman Ziad and the Grand Mufti, from the day after Clarke's speech. Noah pointed to the key sentence in the transcript, in which Ziad insisted that the Grand Mufti do everything in his power to keep the peace summit, which he called "blasphemous," from taking place.

Marcus winced. It was exactly what he'd feared. The Grand Mufti was a serious liability. The question was, how were they going to handle him and make sure he didn't act on Ziad's explicit instruction?

"Who else has seen this?" Marcus asked.

"So far, just the translator and me."

Then Noah explained that the second transcript, several pages longer than the first, involved a series of intercepts from the mobile phone of Dr. Mashrawi's wife, Yasmine.

"Was she even on the tracking list?" Marcus asked.

"No, but I figured if we were having the NSA intercept and record all of the calls, texts, and emails sent or received by Waqf employees, I might as well have them check spouses and children, too."

"Good idea. So what's this?"

"These are from the last twenty-four hours," Noah said. "Thirteen calls and text messages. They all relate to Dr. Mashrawi needing an emergency root canal. There are interactions with the dentist, conversations with friends, and finally a tearful call from Mrs. Mashrawi to her father, the Grand Mufti."

Marcus quickly scanned the pages. "Fine, but I already knew about the root canal. So what?"

"Well, sir, you radioed in this morning that Mashrawi wasn't at your meeting with the Grand Mufti and that the Grand Mufti said his son-in-law had to go get an emergency root canal. You wanted us to make sure that was really true."

"Apparently it is."

"Yes, sir," Noah said. "It would seem Dr. Mashrawi was telling the truth."

"Good to know," Marcus replied. "Write up a cover memo explaining exactly what you told me, and get both sets of transcripts to Roseboro, the director of DSS, and Director Stephens at Langley. Then get me every single thing you possibly can on the Grand Mufti. My worries about him are growing by the minute."

"Yes, sir," Noah said. "I'm on it."

As the young man stepped away, Marcus's satphone rang. It was Kailea in London.

"Please tell me you've got good news," Marcus said, ducking out of the war room into the hallway, where it was quieter.

"I do," she replied. "You're gonna like this."

"What?"

"After going through all of the computer files and phone logs for the medical clinic we raided, we found several odd emails and three phone calls from Dr. Haqqani to a banker by the name of Michel al-Jalil," Kailea explained. "According to everyone we've talked to so far, al-Jalil is a Palestinian Catholic. His family lived in the Galilee region of Palestine during the British Mandate. When war came in '48, they fled to Lebanon and settled in one of the refugee camps. That, supposedly, is where this guy, Michel, was born. But he was a sharp kid. He got out of the camps and earned an undergraduate degree from the American University of Beirut, then headed to the U.K. and got his MBA from the London School of Economics."

"And?"

"And there's simply no record of a Michel al-Jalil ever being born in Lebanon or going to AU in Beirut," Kailea explained.

"So?"

"So the guy's real name is Mohammed al-Qassab. As best we can tell, he's never set foot in Palestine or Israel. He was born and raised in Damascus. His father was a Syrian general under the Assad regime. Al-Qassab served in Syrian intelligence and was last stationed in Beirut."

"Cut to the chase."

"Early this morning, we raided an investment bank in the Canary Wharf section of London, where this guy worked, and the flat where he lived, a penthouse overlooking the Thames. We now believe al-Qassab is working for Kairos and has been acting as Haqqani's handler. The case is circumstantial at the moment but compelling. The laptop in his penthouse flat was wiped clean. But FBI technicians were able to recover his Internet search history off the cloud. You'll never guess what he's been into."

Marcus sighed. "I have no idea. Just spit it out."

"He's been studying the four assassinations of American presidents and dozens of failed attempts as well."

That got Marcus's attention.

"He's also been to Greece twelve times in the past two years," Kailea continued. "And two hours ago, MI5 picked up his fiancée. They're interrogating her now. I'll get you everything I can the moment they're done. But Geoff just sent you a photo and a quick dossier on this guy, everything we know so far."

"Any idea where he is now?"

"Unfortunately, yes, and that's the main reason I'm calling."

"Don't tell me he's in Israel."

"He got there Friday."

84

The secure video conference began at 5 p.m. local time, midnight in Israel.

As acting national security advisor, Bill McDermott had pulled the meeting together. The president didn't participate, as he was heading across town to speak to the National Governors Association. Nor did the VP or other cabinet members.

This was not a formal meeting of the National Security Council but of senior intelligence and security officials responsible for threat assessment and containment for the upcoming peace summit. As such, CIA director Stephens was joining from Langley; the directors of the Secret Service, the Diplomatic Security Service, and the FBI were joining from their respective operations centers; and Roseboro and Ryker were linked in from the embassy in Jerusalem.

"I appreciate everyone gathering on such short notice," McDermott began. "Let's get right to it. Agent Ryker, I understand you have new information for us."

"I'm afraid I do," Marcus began. "As I briefed you all yesterday, Dr. Ali Haqqani—the Pakistani surgeon who implanted the body cavity bomb in the woman who blew herself up on Downing Street two weeks ago—arrived here in Israel on Saturday. I've just learned that another Kairos operative is in Israel. Our team in London has identified a man named Mohammed al-Qassab as Haqqani's handler in London. According to the Mossad, al-Qassab landed in Tel Aviv on Friday at 3:00 p.m. Israel time on British Airways flight 165, direct from Heathrow."

"Using the name al-Qassab?" asked McDermott.

"No—using the alias he goes by in the investment-banking world in London, Michel al-Jalil. I'm sending you all a copy of the flight manifest. I'm also sending you a photo of the man clearing Israeli passport control, and I can confirm that al-Qassab and al-Jalil are one and the same person."

"Do the Israelis have any idea where he is right now?" asked the FBI director.

"Unfortunately, no—they do have CCTV footage of al-Qassab getting into a taxicab outside the airport, and they've determined the cab was heading for Tel Aviv," Marcus explained. "They've found the driver and are interviewing him as we speak. But so far it looks like the driver just dropped him off near the beach, not far from the American consulate, and that's where the trail goes cold."

"What's their working theory?" asked the director of the Secret Service.

"I just got off the phone with Asher Gilad," said Marcus. "He believes it's a better than fifty-fifty proposition that al-Qassab got into another cab and headed for Jerusalem. He thinks Haqqani may also have taken a series of cabs to keep changing his location once he was in Jerusalem. Gilad believes the two were planning to rendezvous, most likely in East Jerusalem, where they could blend in most easily."

"Didn't I see a report that MI5 was questioning al-Qassab's fiancée?" McDermott asked.

"You did, sir, and Agents Geoff Stone and Kailea Curtis—both with

DSS—helped interview her," Marcus replied. "Agent Curtis told me they believe the fiancée has no idea who al-Qassab really is and knows nothing about his involvement in Kairos or his current whereabouts."

"Is that MI5's assessment?" Stephens asked.

"It is, sir. And I should note that the investigation in London has effectively run its course, so I'd like to request that Agents Stone and Curtis be transferred to Jerusalem to assist in the hunt for both Kairos suspects."

This was approved without dissent.

"Gentlemen," Marcus continued somberly, "we are now facing an environment in which not one but two Kairos operatives are in Israel, likely in Jerusalem and likely within a mile of the Temple Mount, and all just days before the arrival of POTUS and the Saudi king. We still don't know a great deal about Kairos, but based on how we've seen them operate in Washington and London, we know they are highly sophisticated and effective at planning and executing attacks on senior American officials. When you add that to the threat reporting we've had over the last month—and sheer logic concerning the intentions of the Iranians and Russians—I believe I can say with high confidence that we're looking at an assassination plot against those involved in the peace summit."

Though the use of a body cavity bomb was a strong likelihood, Marcus went on to caution that Kairos might be planning other methods of attack as well. Then he shared the story he'd learned from the Saudi intelligence chief about the human bomb used against a member of the Saudi royal family several years earlier.

"Recommendations?" McDermott asked.

"Well, sir, Deputy Director Roseboro and I are divided on that topic," Marcus replied. "I'll let Carl speak for himself in a moment, but the short version is he feels the summit should proceed. I don't."

"But this was your idea, Ryker," said McDermott.

"Actually, it was the Saudis' idea, but yes, I was certainly supportive."

"And now you've changed your mind?"

"I have. Look, I've been doing threat assessments for a long time, and I'm telling you this is the most dangerous, most volatile environment I've ever seen. Setting the geopolitical implications aside for a moment, I would strongly advise that the president invite the king and prime minister to the White House or Camp David and delay a Jerusalem visit several weeks, at least until we can hunt down these Kairos guys and be far more confident the environment is secure."

"POTUS has taken trips to Baghdad and Kabul," said the FBI director. "Surely this situation isn't any more dangerous than that."

"Respectfully, I disagree," Marcus countered. "Those are always secret visits, announced only after Air Force One is wheels up and out of Iraqi or Afghani airspace. Here, we've announced not only who's coming and when, but the exact itinerary, including what time POTUS and the others will be at Yad Vashem, at the Church of the Holy Sepulcher, and so forth. Add to all this the chatter the NSA is picking up from terror groups around the region. Add the fact that the Raven has intercepted messages that two foreign governments—Russia and Iran—are pouring millions of dollars into Kairos. Then add in what Ziad told the Grand Mufti and the fact that the Grand Mufti has a long record of anti-American statements, and my assessment is that it's way too dangerous to bring POTUS into Jerusalem at this time, especially given that we don't have a proven way to guard against the use of a body cavity bomb."

85

KAIROS SAFE HOUSE, MOUNT OF OLIVES, EAST JERUSALEM—11 DECEMBER

Mohammed al-Qassab was growing anxious.

He'd spent the evening and much of the night so far in the living room, hunched over his notebook computer, scanning the latest headlines in Arabic and English and trying to gather every scrap of information he possibly could on the preparations that were being made for the peace summit. Many of the articles focused on the elaborate security measures being put into place. The Syrian had no doubt these were aimed at Kairos, to dissuade them from trying anything when the summit came to town.

What especially bothered al-Qassab was how few details the British government was giving out on the investigation back in London. So far as he could tell, not a single arrest had been made. Not a single home or office had been raided. That couldn't possibly be true. Surely MI5 was tearing up the city to find Kairos operatives and safe houses. But the Brits were being uncharacteristically quiet, forcing the Syrian to ask a series of questions—who was talking?

what were they saying? how close were authorities to tracking him down? how much time did he have before he had to run?—for which he simply had no answers.

Suddenly Haqqani was standing over him, offering him a bowl of something that looked like dog food and smelled indescribably worse. The man said it was lamb curry, his mother's own recipe. But there was not a chance al-Qassab was going to put something so putrid to his lips.

The two men were already on each other's nerves, cooped up in someone else's house, unable even to step outside for a breath of fresh air for fear of being spotted by a neighbor or an Israeli helicopter or drone. They had gotten into one squabble after another. Most were about petty matters—except one. Haqqani kept demanding to know the plan for getting him out of the country. *What was the plan? What was the plan?* If Haqqani had said it once, he'd said it a hundred times. Al-Qassab insisted the plan could not be finalized until they understood how the Israelis were going to handle the suicide bombing. Yes, they'd be leaving this safe house for another before the attack. For the rest, Haqqani would have to be patient, would have to trust him. Yet Haqqani persisted.

Maybe it was this galling lack of trust, not just the revolting food, that turned his stomach, al-Qassab thought. But he said nothing. He simply dismissed the Pakistani and his bowl with a wave and a sneer.

"What's your recommendation, Carl?"

"I agree with Marcus that the threat level is very high, and to be candid, I'd certainly support a decision to abort the trip," the deputy director of the Secret Service began. "However, if POTUS wants to proceed, it's certainly doable. But we will need to take some unusual, maybe even unprecedented steps to keep him safe."

"Like what?"

"For starters, we need to severely limit the number of people who have access to him, the PM, and the king, even more than usual. Second, we need to prevent anyone who will be anywhere near POTUS from having a mobile phone. Third, I'd recommend we jam all mobile phone signals within a mile of POTUS's location."

McDermott was jotting down notes, but when he looked back up, he saw Marcus shaking his head. "Agent Ryker, you disagree?"

"Absolutely—we can't take away the mobile phones of every reporter, producer, and cameraman. And we certainly can't jam all mobile calls for a mile out from the president's location. That would knock out phone service for the entire Old City of Jerusalem, and much of New Jerusalem as well, for two full days. Plus, we'd be interfering with police and other emergency communications systems. If we do attempt to impose such draconian security measures, that will become the story and drown out the message of the trip."

The director of the Diplomatic Security Service was the next to weigh in. "Bill, what if you guys lowered the profile on this thing and made it a meeting of foreign ministers rather than heads of state? It would still be a huge news story, but it would dramatically lower the threat profile. The Saudi foreign minister comes to Jerusalem. He and the Israeli foreign minister and Secretary Whitney hammer out the foundation for a future peace treaty. They lay the groundwork for a full-on summit in January. The three principals then meet at Camp David, as the president had originally discussed. It's a totally secure environment. And it buys us time to hunt down these Kairos operatives and figure out just what we're really up against."

"Believe me, I'd like nothing better," said McDermott. "But the president feels he's already too vested in this thing."

"Even with two known Kairos operatives in Israel, possibly in Jerusalem, along with undoubtedly many more that we don't know about?"

"Look, gentlemen, let me be perfectly clear," McDermott countered. "The president is going to Jerusalem. Period. End of discussion. I'm looking for recommendations on how to make this thing work, not how to deep-six it. Okay?"

"What are the Israelis saying?" asked the FBI director.

Marcus took that one. "They're worried, but honestly, they don't want to disappoint the president. And they definitely don't want to disappoint the Saudis." Marcus noted that Prime Minister Eitan had ordered all Israeli schools and government facilities in the municipality of Jerusalem to be shut down for the two days of the summit. He was also going to announce the following day that all nonessential businesses in the capital should close for two days, given the enormous number of road closures and the presence of up to fifteen thousand policemen and soldiers the Israelis were planning to deploy.

Roseboro pointed out that Patriot antimissile batteries were being set up around Jerusalem, as were Iron Dome anti-rocket batteries. Anti-drone snipers were being set up on the Mount of Olives, Mount Scopus, and the roofs of the Leonardo Plaza Hotel, the Knesset, and the King David Hotel. Army checkpoints would go up forty-eight hours before the summit on every road into the city. The IDF would be stopping every car, scanning every ID, checking for weapons, sweeping for explosives, and keeping a close eye out for Haqqani and al-Qassab.

"How long until the background checks are done for everyone working at each of the sites that POTUS will visit?" McDermott asked.

"Close of business on Sunday," said the Secret Service director. "That should still give us and the Shin Bet forty-eight hours to perform additional checks on anyone we have concerns about."

"What about the Saudis? How are they feeling?" asked the FBI director. "Richard, when was the last time you talked to Prince Abdullah?"

"Just this morning," Stephens replied. "We're doing a daily call now to keep each other up-to-date on all the latest developments."

"Are they nervous?"

"From the questions the prince is asking, yes, I'd say they are."

"But they're not talking about canceling or at least rescheduling?"

"Not a chance," Stephens said. "For them it's a shame-honor thing. The prince says they war-gamed this thing extensively before they reached out to POTUS. They know what they're up against, but they're committed. They gave the president and the Israelis their word that they're coming. To back out now, especially in light of a threat by the Iranians or their proxies, would be unthinkable. The prince told me, in confidence, that he has recommended against the trip, at least for now. But the king is determined to come to Jerusalem, come what may."

The knock at the door startled her.

It wasn't yet seven in the morning, and Yasmine couldn't remember the last time they'd had a visitor so early. She was covered with flour and pancake batter as she prepared breakfast for her children. But Hussam was still sound asleep on the couch and probably couldn't have gotten to his feet even if he had been awake. Grabbing a dish towel to wipe her face and hands and try to look somewhat presentable, she made her way to the door, peeked past the hand-sewn curtains covering the peephole, and unbolted the lock.

"Daddy," she exclaimed, "what are you doing here?"

The Grand Mufti stood outside surrounded by a half-dozen bodyguards. He was smiling and carrying an armful of freshly baked pita bread and chocolate pastries for the kids. "I brought you these, my love, and wanted to see your patient before I head to the mosque," he replied as he stepped out of the cold hallway and into the warm apartment. "Is that okay?"

"Of course, of course; come in," Yasmine said, taking the baked goods in her arms. "I didn't expect to see you on such a big day."

"It is a big day—we may have a quarter of a million pious souls coming to pray today," said al-Azzam. "But you and the kiddies come first."

Yasmine set the bread on the kitchen table, then hugged and kissed her father. She invited the security detail in for coffee, but they demurred and said they would wait outside. Even her father said he could only stay for a few minutes.

"Honey, sweetheart, hey, look—Daddy came to say hi," Yasmine said, kneeling down beside her husband and rousing him.

Hussam Mashrawi blinked hard, looked around the room, and tried, with much difficulty, to pull himself up to a sitting position. Both sides of his face remained swollen, and his eyes were puffy and bloodshot. He did look like he'd been beaten up, and as he came to, Yasmine went to get his medicine and a fresh ice pack.

"How are you, my son?" al-Azzam asked, standing over him.

"Fine, I'll be fine," Mashrawi replied. "Forgive me, I'll . . ."

"No, no, don't be silly," said al-Azzam. "Rest up. We need you at full strength next week when the president and king come to visit."

"But tomorrow is the big day," Mashrawi protested. "We have so many coming for Friday prayers. I must be there to help."

The Grand Mufti and his daughter looked at each other, perplexed.

"What day do you think it is, sweetheart?" Yasmine asked.

"Thursday. Why?" her husband replied.

Yasmine shook her head. "It's Friday," she said.

"But my surgery was Wednesday."

"And you've been sleeping ever since."

"You're saying I missed an entire day?"

Yasmine nodded, as did her father.

"All because of a root canal?" Mashrawi said, his thoughts still foggy.

"Well, you had to have a wisdom tooth removed, too, and the drugs they gave you knocked you out pretty good."

"But still," said an increasingly agitated Mashrawi. "I shouldn't have had to . . ."

"Had to what?" Yasmine asked.

But her husband said nothing more. He had simply stopped speaking in midsentence and now had a distant, troubled expression on his face.

"What is it?" al-Azzam asked.

"Nothing," Mashrawi said.

"What's wrong?" al-Azzam pressed. "I don't understand."

"Nothing. I'm fine. It's just . . ."

"Just what?"

"I don't . . . I can't . . . Never mind," Mashrawi stammered. "I just need to use the washroom. Please excuse me."

Yasmine and her father offered their assistance, but Mashrawi waved them off. He got to his feet with considerable difficulty, steadying himself at one point by putting his hand on the back of a chair and then against a wall.

"Do you think I should call a doctor?" al-Azzam asked his daughter. "This doesn't seem right, does it?"

"Not for a bit of dental work, no," Yasmine said as her youngest began to cry and she scooped her up and gave her a kiss on the cheek. "But you've got to go. You've got such a big day. I'll talk to him. Don't worry. I'm sure everything will be fine."

Hussam Mashrawi stumbled into the restroom and locked the door behind him.

Switching on the light, he looked at his face in the mirror as he steadied himself against the vanity. He could hear his wife and father-in-law talking about him. The last thing he could afford was the two of them worrying about him and insisting that a doctor come to their apartment and examine him. That was out of the question.

But how had he missed an entire day? He'd readily agreed to the dental surgery. Anything to throw family and friends off the scent of what he was really about to do. But no one had said the pain medication would knock him out so badly. Yet he couldn't imagine not taking it.

Mashrawi unbuttoned and removed the dress shirt he'd fallen asleep in almost forty-eight hours earlier. Then, with excruciating pain, he removed his undershirt to expose the large bandage that had been taped to his chest. Willing himself to ignore the nearly blinding agony, he pulled up the tape and looked under the bandage.

The scar was at least six inches long and a vivid red. They'd told him he'd be on his feet the following day, functioning like normal within another day or two after that and certainly able to go back to work. They'd said the incision would be tender to the touch and that he might feel pain when he breathed but that with some prescription medication and a bit of discipline he'd be fine, that no one would be the wiser. Further, they'd told him the explosive device now inside his chest could not be detected by metal detectors or bomb-sniffing dogs or any other external technology, only by a millimeter wave or MRI machine that had never and would never be deployed by the United States Secret Service.

Yet so much of what they'd told him was wrong, Mashrawi now realized. What else were they wrong about?

DOHA, QATAR—13 DECEMBER

Hamdi Yaşar sat on his balcony, enjoying the sun coming up over the Gulf.

The temperature was a comfortable seventy-five degrees Fahrenheit, and there was a gentle breeze coming from the east. Yaşar's wife and children were still sleeping. Normally, he'd already be in the Al-Sawt studios by now. But he found himself fielding too many calls from Abu Nakba and his inner circle to take all of them at the office. For much of the night he'd been briefing his superiors on the latest details. Now he was tired but perhaps more peaceful and content than he'd ever felt in his life. It was happening, all of it, and he was at the vortex, and he could hardly believe the good fortune Allah had bestowed upon him.

Yaşar missed the hustle and bustle and oriental mystique of Istanbul, the city of his youth. He longed to move his family back home to Turkey, and he sensed the time to make that shift was rapidly approaching. President Mustafa had been dropping none-too-subtle hints that as useful as it was for Yaşar to serve Abu Nakba and help build Kairos from an unknown entity into the world's most fearsome terrorist organization, perhaps it was time for him to come work for the next sultan and actually help build the Caliphate. Yaşar could think of nothing better. That was his dream. He had been made compelling offers by the emir of Qatar, by the commander of the Iranian Revolutionary Guard Corps, even—albeit indirectly—by the Kremlin. Men of wealth and power, men he greatly respected, not only saw but valued and coveted his skills, his connections, and the strategic guidance he quietly gave them all under the cover of being a senior producer for one of the Arab world's leading satellite news networks. But Mustafa was the man he respected most, and to serve as the Turkish president's consigliere, particularly at such a time as this, was as intriguing as it was intoxicating.

Yaşar sipped a chilled glass of pulpy orange juice he had just squeezed himself and marveled at the commanding view of Doha before him. He loved the newness of it all. Qatar itself hadn't even been born as an independent nation-state until 1971. The capital as a city dated back to the 1820s, but even by the 1920s it was little more than a scattering of mud-and-brick homes. The discovery of oil, of course, had changed everything. The Arab oil embargo against the Americans changed it even more. As the price of oil had soared, so had Qatar's wealth, and people streamed in from all over the region and all over the globe to make their fortunes.

By the fifties, the sleepy city's population had swelled to fourteen thousand. By the seventies, it had mushroomed to more than eighty thousand. Today, Doha was home to more than a million people. With more people came more construction. With such little land, the population couldn't spread out, so it shot upward. Out of the sands rose spectacular towers of steel and glass. All of it was impressive, a testament to man's engineering genius.

Yet none of it was enough to hold Hamdi Yaşar. When his operation in Jerusalem triumphed, he would be in a position to demand almost anything of the Turkish leader. Perhaps consigliere would not be enough, he mused. Why should he not be the nation's second in command, effectively the crown prince and thus the sultan's heir apparent?

His satellite phone rang. Yaşar set down his crystal glass and picked up the phone from the table beside him.

"It's me," said al-Qassab.

"Trouble?" Yaşar asked.

"Not really."

"Then what? I thought we'd agreed not to talk unless there was an emergency."

"There is a topic we've not discussed, and I need your advice."

"What's that?"

"The crew," al-Qassab replied. "How shall I compensate them when they are finished with their work?"

Yaşar considered the question carefully. Kairos's director of operations could only be referring to one person—Dr. Ali Haqqani. And he could only be asking one question. Was he supposed to kill Haqqani now that the man had finished operating on Hussam Mashrawi? Once the surgeon made sure Mashrawi was healthy enough to carry out his mission four days hence, would he be expendable? Or was al-Qassab supposed to help Haqqani slip safely out of Israel to perform future surgeries for Kairos?

"We did discuss it, thoroughly, in fact, when we were in Rome," Yaşar said, trying to contain his irritation.

"I'm not convinced we were thorough enough."

It was now clear what al-Qassab was recommending: taking out the good doctor either because he had not performed his duties satisfactorily or because al-Qassab was not convinced he could actually get the man out of Israel after all.

Either way, Yaşar decided, it wasn't his problem. He'd recruited al-Qassab to make such tactical decisions. Now was not the moment to second-guess his instincts. "It's your call, my friend," Yaşar replied. "Just make absolutely sure that whatever you start, you finish."

88

Marcus drove back to Ben Gurion International Airport.

Geoff Stone and Kailea Curtis were inbound from London, and he'd offered to pick them up at the airport. On the way, he called Oleg, hoping the Raven had come up with something useful, something that would help them crack this case and expose the Kairos network before it struck again. But once more Oleg had nothing.

The president met them in the Situation Room.

For the next forty-five minutes, McDermott, Stephens, and the directors of both the Secret Service and DSS again briefed the president on the high and rising risks of going to Jerusalem. They underscored the fact that they were still no closer to finding, much less capturing, Haqqani or al-Qassab or identifying anyone else that Kairos was working with in Israel generally or in Jerusalem in particular.

And there was more. Stephens explained that the head of Jordanian intelligence had called him the night before to express how worried he was about the upcoming summit and to ask for the opportunity to come to Washington to explain why.

"I told him not to bother," Stephens said.

"Why not?" Clarke asked.

"Because I already knew what he was going to say."

"Then enlighten me," said an increasingly exasperated commander in chief.

"For starters, the Hashemites are convinced the Saudis are trying to seize control of the Temple Mount from them."

"What's that supposed to mean?"

"Article 9 of the 1994 peace treaty between Israel and Jordan explicitly states, 'Israel respects the present special role of the Hashemite Kingdom of Jordan in Muslim holy shrines in Jerusalem. When negotiations on the permanent status will take place, Israel will give high priority to the Jordanian historic role in these shrines,'" Stephens replied, citing the treaty from memory. "The text goes on to state that 'the parties will act together to promote interfaith relations among the three monotheistic religions, with the aim of working toward religious understanding, moral commitment, freedom of religious worship, and tolerance and peace.' As such, while the Israelis provide overall security for the Temple Mount and insist they maintain sovereignty over the city, the Jordanians are in charge of the Waqf. What's more, the king of Jordan—who is himself a direct descendant of the Prophet Muhammad—sees the protection and oversight of these Muslim holy sites as his personal responsibility. But there is a real and growing concern in Amman that the Saudis, who of course oversee Mecca and Medina, are determined to persuade the Israelis to give them control of the Islamic holy places in Jerusalem. They're worried that if the Israelis say yes, this would not only violate their treaty but could set off a political explosion inside Jordan that could destabilize the region."

"How?" the president asked.

"Massive riots against Israel could erupt all across Jordan, calling on the king to rip up the treaty with Israel," Stephens replied. "If the king were to refuse, the fear is that the masses could turn on him and call for him to step down."

"Could any of that happen?"

"I certainly can't rule it out. Look, as you know, sir, I have the greatest respect for the king. The U.S. has no greater or more loyal friend in the Arab world. But let's be honest—he's sitting on a volcano, surrounded by a forest fire, waiting for an earthquake. At least 70 percent of his population is Palestinian. Plus, he's got more than a million Syrian refugees in his country. Most of them can't stand the fact that Jordan has a peace treaty with Israel. Every few months, the parliament demands the king cancel the treaty, close the Israeli embassy, send the Israeli ambassador home, cancel the deal by which Jordan buys natural gas from Israel—the list of demands goes on and on. On top of which, most Jordanians can't stand you, are furious to see our embassy moved to Jerusalem, and believe we are not treating the Palestinians in the West Bank fairly, to say the least. So, could that volcano blow? Yeah, it's possible. And could your summit with the Saudis trigger the political earthquake inside Jordan that could cause the volcano to erupt? I wish I could rule it out, Mr. President. But I can't."

Clarke leaned back in his chair for several moments, processing all that he had heard. Just then the secure phone on the table rang. Picking it up, he was told the Saudi king was on the line.

"All right, that's enough, gentlemen," the president said, calling the meeting to an end. "I'm going to Jerusalem. I'm holding this summit. You guys do your jobs, and everything will be fine."

Ali Haqqani lay on his bed in the Kairos safe house in Jerusalem.

The bed was piled high with blankets. The flat was not centrally heated, as his flat back in London had been. What's more, the space heater in the corner didn't work. As night fell, temperatures outside and inside the apartment building were dropping fast. The winds were picking up as well, rattling the windows and his soul.

Haqqani felt trapped. Actually, he clarified to himself, he didn't just *feel* trapped. He *was* trapped. He had done what had been asked of him. Now it was al-Qassab's job to get him out of harm's way. Surely al-Qassab had a new set of papers and passport for him, along with new credit cards and a new mobile phone. The airport in Tel Aviv wasn't safe. Haqqani knew that. But what about boarding one of the cruise ships that docked in Haifa every day? Barring that, his handler certainly had a way to slip him into Jordan or perhaps into Egypt via the border post south of Eilat, did he not?

Al-Qassab's refusal to lay out a plan, much less give Haqqani all the new documentation he would need, didn't make sense. Learning an entirely new alibi wasn't easy. It shouldn't be attempted in a few hours or even a day. It needed to be carefully thought through and precisely memorized, especially to get out of Israel, of all places. He was operating in the heart of enemy territory. It was not a matter of whether he would be questioned upon leaving the country, but for how long and how relentlessly. Haqqani could lie when he had to, but he was not particularly good at it. He was not a spy. He was a doctor—a surgeon—and there was no use pretending to be something he was not.

As he turned off the lamp beside the bed and lay there in the darkness, listening to the winter winds whistling across the mountaintop, he continued to mull al-Qassab's refusal to lay out an exit strategy. It was unnerving, to be sure, but it was more than that, Haqqani concluded. It was an act of professional irresponsibility. It could put the success of the entire operation in jeopardy, and—

Haqqani suddenly sat bolt upright in the creaking antique bed. A thought had just occurred to him that had never dawned on him before, and the more he considered it, the more he wondered how he had not seen it earlier.

What if Mohammed al-Qassab had no plan to get him out of the country? What if the Syrian was planning to escape on his own and leave Haqqani to the mercies of the Israeli Mossad?

89

Marcus woke earlier than usual, threw on sweats, and jogged to the embassy.

Keeping with the routine he'd established upon arriving in Israel, he worked out in the embassy gym, spent an hour in the basement gun range, then jogged back to the hotel to clean up. Every step of the way, his thoughts were consumed with al-Qassab and Haqqani. As he stood in the shower, the hot water pouring over his aching joints and muscles, the steam filling the bathroom, Marcus came to the conclusion that if they had any chance of finding the bomber in time, Haqqani was the key.

There was no way they were going to find al-Qassab. The man was a professional terrorist. He'd spent his entire life plotting mayhem and avoiding capture. He'd certainly made his share of mistakes, but he'd also be especially careful now not to repeat them.

Haqqani, on the other hand, was a physician by training, not a terrorist. Thus, he was much more capable of making mistakes—even likely to, given that he was now in unfamiliar enemy territory and under tremendous stress. If Marcus's operating theory of the imminent crime was correct, Haqqani had already performed the surgery on whomever al-Qassab had chosen to kill the president, prime minister, and king. The bomb was already in place. The assassin had already had several days to recover from the surgery. He or she was now operating at or near full strength, more or less. That meant that the Pakistani surgeon, while enormously valuable to Kairos, was no longer needed for this operation. If Haqqani was going to bolt, he was going to bolt now—today or tomorrow at the latest. This was their best chance to find him, trying to bluff his way through Ben Gurion, across a border into Jordan or Egypt, or onto a boat in one of Israel's shipping ports in Tel Aviv, Ashdod, or Haifa.

The smartest thing Haqqani could do was stay put and stay low. If he did that, they'd never find him in time. He'd be holed up somewhere at a safe house well-provisioned enough to allow him to stay in Israel—or the West Bank—for several weeks, perhaps several months, until the storm blew over and the manhunt ended. Yet based on every scrap of intelligence they'd pulled together on the Pakistani, Marcus felt certain the man would try to flee. He'd fled Yemen, after all, *before* Abdullah al-Asiri had blown himself up. He'd escaped London, too, just before the Sheripovs had blown themselves up. Why wouldn't he follow the same pattern now?

Haqqani was not a strategist. It was possible he didn't know the name of the so-called martyr in whom he had placed the bomb. But it was more likely that he did know the name, given all the other information he'd need to elicit about his patient before performing the surgery, from blood type and allergies to whatever medications the bomber was currently on, as well as the bomber's family medical history. It was also possible that he hadn't seen the person's face. Theoretically, the bomber's face could have been covered with a mask or a sheet or the like and Haqqani had never been allowed to see it at all. But Haqqani must have interviewed the bomber at length to build the medical profile, and certainly he had applied the oxygen mask and anesthesia himself.

Either way, the Pakistani would at least know if the bomber was a man or woman. He'd know the person's height and weight. And he was likely to know exactly what kind of device had been used, how big it was, how it worked, and what its blast radius was. He might also know where to find Mohammed al-Qassab, what his next movements would be, and what his plans were for escaping the country. And he would certainly have seen and interacted with other Kairos operatives here in Israel and perhaps in the West Bank. Subjected to the proper kind of interrogation, Haqqani would likely be able to provide names, ages, what types of vehicles they were using, and what types of weapons they had, among other critical facts, all of which could help stop the bomber and take down whatever cells Kairos was operating in the country.

Marcus turned off the shower and toweled off. As he lathered up and shaved his face, his thoughts turned to al-Qassab. More than likely, Marcus realized, it was this Syrian who was carrying the mobile phone that would be used to detonate the human bomb at just the precise moment. But if al-Qassab was playing Maxim Sheripov's role in this scenario, who was playing the part of Amina? Yet unless he wore some sort of masterful disguise, it seemed highly unlikely that al-Qassab could literally be at the side of the *shahid* as Maxim had been at his sister's side in the press pool at Number 10 Downing Street. Where would al-Qassab be standing? How would he know when his *shahid* was in position if he wasn't at or near his or her side?

When he finished shaving, Marcus took a suit, shirt, and tie out of the closet, then set up an ironing board and pressed them all. After he'd gotten dressed, he polished his shoes and put them on. Then he grabbed his Sig Sauer pistol and the rest of his gear and headed to the elevator.

It was between the fifth and fourth floors that it finally came to him. There was no way Mohammed al-Qassab was going to be at the side of his suicide bomber. For one thing, he had to know that the entire American and Israeli law enforcement communities were hunting for him by now, even though they'd been very careful not to let news leak that his office and apartment had been raided by MI5 and the FBI just days before. He'd know, therefore, that he'd never get into an event with POTUS and the other principals. But al-Qassab had also figured out that he didn't need to be in the room. Every move President Clarke made was going to be broadcast live on Israeli, American, and Arab television networks and probably European and Russian channels as well. That meant he could be sitting anywhere, watching television in any apartment in Israel or the Palestinian Authority, and know the exact right moment to make the call and blow the peace process and its participants to kingdom come.

They would never find al-Qassab, Marcus concluded. Not before the bomb went off, at least. Maybe Roseboro was right, Marcus mused as the elevator door opened. Maybe they *should* be jamming every cell tower within a mile of POTUS's location regardless of how big a fit the press and others would throw.

As Marcus entered the lobby of the King David, Roseboro was already waiting. A moment later, Kailea came up behind them, and Geoff Stone arrived shortly thereafter, followed by Noah Daniels and the rest of the senior team. At 7 a.m. sharp, they all loaded into two armored Suburbans and headed out on the short trip to the U.S. Embassy to gather in the war room and begin their daily working breakfast.

They had to figure this out. They had to find Haqqani, and they had just two days left.

90

Marcus showed up at the Waqf offices unannounced.

Agents Curtis and Stone were with him, as was Tomer Ben Ami. Dozens of Secret Service, DSS, and Shin Bet agents were also already on-site, along with several K-9 units, conducting security sweeps, testing the magnetometers and X-ray machines, and scrutinizing the IDs of every employee who was coming and going, even as the White House advance team set up and tested banks of lights, cameras, and sound equipment.

"We need to see the Grand Mufti," Marcus told the veiled woman at the desk.

"Is he expecting you?"

"He should expect us every few minutes until the summit is complete," Marcus said without a hint of humor in his voice.

The woman just looked at him for a moment. It was the first time in their numerous interactions that Marcus had spoken to her so brusquely.

"I'll see if he is free," she said, picking up a phone and punching several buttons. "Dr. Mashrawi, I have Agent Ryker and several colleagues here to see the Grand Mufti. No, they don't have an appointment. Yes, that's what I said. Of course. I will tell them."

The woman set down the phone and looked up at the four of them. "The Grand Mufti is on a call just now. But Dr. Mashrawi will be right out."

Marcus was not happy, but Tomer's eye told him to cool his jets and remember the importance of formality and decorum in the Arab world. Several minutes went by, and there was no movement. Marcus checked his watch repeatedly and was about to say something when Mashrawi finally came out of his office.

"I trust you're feeling better?" Marcus said as Mashrawi apologized for the delay.

Marcus had seen Mashrawi on Saturday morning when he and Tomer had stopped by the Waqf offices to begin their security preparations. He'd been taken aback by just how swollen the man's face had been and how glassy-eyed he'd seemed. Mashrawi had not even risen from behind his desk to greet them. By now most of the swelling was gone, though he seemed a bit shaky when he walked. His voice was still raspy, and he remained a bit pale.

"Let's just say I wouldn't recommend dental surgery on the eve of the most important event in your career, if not your life," the executive director of the Waqf replied, a mobile phone in his hand. "But yes, I'm feeling much better. Thank you."

After a few minutes, Mashrawi led them to the Grand Mufti. Agents Stone and Curtis stood post in the hallway. Marcus and Tomer entered and were greeted warmly by the old man. "Forgive me for taking so long on that call," he offered. "How can I help you?"

"For starters, Your Excellency, we brought you these," Marcus said, setting two lanyards on the Grand Mufti's desk. "These are your credentials—all-access passes—one for you, one for Dr. Mashrawi. Wear them at all times. You won't be allowed to enter the site otherwise."

"Understood," said al-Azzam.

"We need to discuss several people on the VIP list you submitted," Tomer added. "But there's another thing, too. Beginning tomorrow morning, no one will be allowed to bring a mobile phone or satellite phone onto the mount until the summit is completed."

Marcus noticed Mashrawi bristle when the Israeli mentioned the new security measure. The Grand Mufti, however, simply asked why.

"Those are our orders—that's all I know," Tomer lied.

37 HOURS BEFORE AIR FORCE ONE LANDS IN ISRAEL

"Where are we?" Reuven Eitan asked as he poured himself a cup of coffee.

"Nowhere," said Asher Gilad.

"Meaning what?"

"Meaning we've got a nationwide manhunt under way, but you've asked us not to give the names or photos of Haqqani and al-Qassab to the media, so we haven't," the Mossad director said. "But to be honest, that's severely limiting the number of eyes we have looking."

"If we release that information, we'll have a panic on our hands," the prime minister said, stirring in some cream and sugar and taking a seat at the small, round conference table in the corner of his office. "If there's a panic, the king will cancel. So will the president. We'll be embarrassed. And the summit will be ruined. You want that to be Israel's image to the world, right at the moment of the greatest diplomatic breakthrough of the century?"

"Ruvi, with respect, we have less than two days before President Clarke and King Faisal arrive, and we have at least one bomber out there whose identity we simply do not know. If either one of these men—or God forbid, both—are killed on our watch—"

Eitan suddenly looked up from his coffee and interrupted his colleague. "What do you mean, 'at least'?"

"Just what I said—the presence of both al-Qassab and Haqqani in the country strongly suggests Kairos is planning a suicide bombing. But Haqqani has already been here for over a week. Who knows how many surgeries he's performed?"

"You think there could be more than one bomber?"

"I cannot rule it out."

Eitan sighed and set his cup back on its saucer. "What would you have me do, Asher? I cannot cancel the summit—not now."

"I have not asked you to."

"Then what?"

"Let me put out a bulletin—two names, two pictures, no mention of Kairos, just say they are persons of interest, wanted for questioning for something, for a visa violation, anything; it doesn't matter."

"Doesn't that just alert Haqqani and al-Qassab that we're onto them? Doesn't that just drive them underground?"

"It's a possibility, but we're running out of options. The chances we find al-Qassab, even with the public's help, are minimal. The man is a professional. He's been hiding all his life. But Haqqani is another story. Agent Ryker thinks we can flush him out into the open, and I agree. But only if we act now."

The prime minister rubbed his eyes, then crossed his legs and smoothed out the creases on his suit pants. "Fine, Asher—as you've requested, I'm going to announce the closure of Judea and Samaria, effective immediately and through the end of the summit. No Palestinians come in or out of the territories. No work permits. No tourists. Nothing. Not until two hours after the summit ends and Air Force One is wheels up. Simultaneously, I'm going to shut down the border crossings with Jordan and Egypt until Sunday at 9 a.m. As I do this, you can put out a bulletin on Haqqani immediately— as a 'person of interest, wanted for questioning'—but only on him. Not al-Qassab. Not yet. And let's see what your team can do."

91

Hussam Mashrawi woke up early, determined to follow his normal routine.

He showered and dressed and made the kids' lunches, then straightened up around the apartment. But on this day, rather than slip out the door quietly, he stepped back into the bedroom before leaving for morning prayers and sat down on the bed.

"Yasmine, are you awake?"

She was not, but she smiled at the sound of his voice, yawned, and rolled over to greet him with a kiss.

"Yasmine, sweetheart, I need you to listen to me, okay?"

Though groggy, she nodded and took his hand.

"Tomorrow, as you know, is going to be a very important day, and security is going to be very tight, and all the schools are going to be closed," he began. "So this is what I need you to do. Are you listening? Look at me, sweetheart."

Yasmine had drifted off, but at this she roused herself and sat up in the bed.

"Are you paying attention?"

"Yes, yes, I'm sorry," she said.

"Good. Now, when you get up and dressed, I want you to take the children to your sister's, okay?"

"In Abu Ghosh?"

"Exactly."

"Why?"

"Because something very special is going to happen tomorrow."

"What?"

"I've arranged it so that you have an opportunity to join me at the VIP reception for King Faisal, President Clarke, and the prime minister."

At this, Yasmine brightened. "You did?"

"Of course."

"But why?"

"Because I love you, and I want you to be at my side on this historic occasion."

"But I thought you despised Prime Minister Eitan."

"This is history in the making. I'm going to be at the vortex of it all. And it wouldn't be the same without you."

Yasmine smiled sleepily and then hugged and kissed him. "You are so thoughtful, Hussam," she said softly. "Thank you."

"You're welcome—now there is something else you must do."

"Anything."

"Beginning today, no one can bring a mobile phone up to the Haram al-Sharif."

"Why not?"

"Who knows for sure? Something about security. Anyway, I actually bought a new phone the other day, and I'm giving it to you."

He pulled it out of his jacket pocket and set it in her hands. "Don't lose this."

"Of course not."

"I have to leave early tomorrow morning to get in place before the leaders arrive at the mosque. When you get up, I want you to put on your finest dress and your favorite veil. Then I want you to walk to Ahmed the shoemaker's shop—you know the one?"

"Near the monastery?"

"That's it."

"Why?"

"I want you to be close to the entrance to the Haram al-Sharif so you can get to my side quickly as it begins. Okay?"

She nodded.

"Ahmed and his wife will be expecting you. You can watch all the live coverage on Al-Sawt with them; just don't tell them why you're there. Bring several pairs of shoes that need to be repaired. That's what I told them you would be doing, but I also said you don't want to miss any of the coverage."

Yasmine nodded again.

"Now listen closely—this is very important—when you see me and your father meeting with the king and the president and the prime minister, at that very moment, I want you to turn on the phone and hit number five on the speed dial."

"Number five?"

"Exactly—and you must do it at precisely that moment."

"When I see you with Daddy and the leaders?"

"Correct, and not a moment before and not a moment after."

"Yes, of course, but why?"

"Because that number will put you through to the head of security at the entrance to the Waqf," Mashrawi lied. "When he answers, you'll tell him exactly who you are, and he will give you a security code. Write it down so you don't forget. Then hang up and walk immediately to the entrance. There will be a checkpoint. Give the officers your ID and tell them this code. They will bring you to me in the reception hall, okay?"

None of it was true, of course. There was no security code. There would be no VIP reception. But Mashrawi had been unable to think of anyone else he could trust to hold on to the phone and make the call at the precise moment. He was certain that al-Qassab held another phone and could, if he needed to, dial the number and trigger the explosion. But what if al-Qassab was distracted or, worse, detained? The leadership of Kairos was counting on Mashrawi himself to be responsible for this operation, and he would not let them down.

"There's one final thing," Mashrawi said.

"Yes, my love?"

"You cannot tell anyone what I just told you. Not a soul. Not your sister. Not your mother. Not the children. Not even your father."

"Not Daddy?"

"He has so much on his mind right at the moment, it would not be good to burden him with anything else. And it will be a surprise for him to see you arrive. Okay?"

"Yes—he loves surprises."

"So I can count on you?"

Yasmine kissed him gently on the lips. "You can count on me."

92

16 HOURS BEFORE AIR FORCE ONE LANDS IN ISRAEL

The sun was setting over Ben Gurion International Airport.

Kailea brought Marcus another cup of coffee; then they left the main terminal and headed to the hangar. It would be their final walk-through of the welcome ceremony before heading back to Jerusalem for the night. And they still had no leads on Haqqani or al-Qassab.

It had been another exhausting and infuriating day. They'd met with every agent and officer in charge of each sector, asking them if anything seemed out of place and if there was anything they needed. Everyone seemed confident they'd done all they could, but Kailea could see that Marcus's stomach was churning, and she certainly understood why. The president of the United States would be in the air in less than five hours, and the advance team was still no closer to ensuring his safety.

The folks from the White House advance team were still on-site, running through their checklists and making last-minute adjustments. The team from the White House Press Office was doing the same. It all certainly looked impressive. The stage had been built. The podium with the presidential seal had been set in place. A beautiful red carpet had been laid out, and someone was running a vacuum over it one more time. Enormous American, Israeli, and Saudi flags had been ironed and hung from wires attached to crossbeams in the roof. A row of flags on stands lined the back of the stage. Risers for the press corps had been erected, as had a section just for the IDF band and honor guard. Technicians were double-checking the lights and sound system. Around back of the hangar, row upon row of TV satellite trucks were parked and waiting. Each had been thoroughly checked by the Secret Service, DSS, and Shin Bet and then sealed off with eighteen-foot-high chain-link fences topped by razor wire and guarded by an elite Israeli police unit.

Meanwhile, K-9 units were working up and down the rows of white, wooden folding chairs set for a thousand VIP guests, sniffing for any trace of explosives. At the insistence of Roseboro—and over the vehement objections of the White House and Prime Minister's Office—the first row of seats had been set back a full thirty feet from the stage in the hopes of minimizing if not completely eliminating the damage that could be done to the principals onstage if a bomber were to detonate in the crowd.

Kailea was impressed that Roseboro had also won another victory: no phones of any kind would be allowed into the hangar. Advisors to the principals had been informed they would have to leave their phones in their cars. Guests had been emailed they should leave their phones in their cars or at home. Reporters had likewise been emailed that there would be lockers where they could leave their phones before entering the hangar.

Roseboro had even tried bringing in portable jammers to block all electronic signals coming in or going out of the hangar. Unfortunately, the systems had been so powerful they had interfered not only with the public-address system but with the radios the security officials were using. Thus, much to Roseboro's frustration, the jammers had, in the last few hours, been removed from the premises and from all the sites POTUS would be visiting.

As they continued their stroll around the grounds, Kailea noticed the teams of sharpshooters with night vision goggles stationed in every corner of every roof of the terminal and maintenance facilities. She could see hundreds of heavily armed Israeli troops in full combat gear posted around the perimeter fence and Humvees mounted with .50-caliber machine guns driving the service roads on patrol. She could hear helicopters overhead and pictured their pilots and crews using night vision goggles and thermal imaging to scan for threats.

What she could not hear was the sound of jet engines. For the first time in Israel's history, all commercial air traffic had been grounded for the two days of the summit and the full day prior. Flights would resume taking off and landing at 6 p.m. on Thursday, but not a moment before.

Convinced there was nothing more they could do, Kailea radioed back to the DSS command post at the embassy that they were heading "home." On the drive, Kailea tried to get Marcus's thoughts off logistics. She asked him how his cracked rib was healing. She asked him about his time with his mom in Colorado. She asked him if he'd found time to read any of his Dostoyevsky novel. But he didn't bite.

Marcus was all business. He wanted her to triple-check that extra supplies of POTUS's blood type—and the king's and Secretary Whitney's—had been delivered to all five of the hospitals that were standing by in case of trouble. She assured him that it had been taken care of, but he made her call Roseboro again just to be sure. Then he insisted she call the officer in charge of the motor pool and make sure tow trucks and plenty of spare tires had been pre-positioned along the motorcade routes just in case. Again she assured him she'd already done it, but that wasn't good enough for him. So she made the call again. Same answer. Same annoyed tone. But she dutifully conveyed it all to him and chose not to challenge him.

Technically, of course, Kailea outranked him. She had, after all, been in law enforcement all of her professional life. He'd been on the DSS team for, what, a couple of months? Yet Marcus Ryker was a legend among security professionals in Washington. He'd won the highest awards for courage under fire that could be bestowed upon a special agent of the United States Secret

Service. And then there were the rumors of what he'd done in Russia, North Korea, and the East China Sea.

Kailea still wasn't sure she believed the stories were true. Not all of them, anyway. Surely some of them, at least, had to have been embellished. But even if only a few were true, she knew she'd been partnered with the most interesting—and certainly the most dedicated—man she had ever met. Marcus was quiet. And there was a sadness to him. But how could there not be? she asked herself as they drove in silence up the Judean hills. After spending a lifetime protecting his country, he'd lost the two great loves of his life. Was it any wonder he was so determined not to lose any more?

93

A brutal winter storm was bearing down on the mid-Atlantic states.

With Marine One grounded due to high winds and snow, President Clarke, Secretary of State Whitney, Senator Dayton, and Annie Stewart traveled by motorcade to Camp Springs, Maryland. When they finally reached the base, the dedicated men and women of the Eighty-Ninth Airlift Wing—also known as the Presidential Airlift Wing—were ready to receive them, but they were already a half hour behind schedule.

The entourage was quickly loaded onto the gleaming blue, white, and yellow Boeing VC-25A. Moments later, Air Force One taxied out to the flight line, revved up to full power, and hurtled down runway 19R. They immediately hit severe turbulence. The modified military version of a 747 shook violently, and the pilots kept the Fasten Seat Belt sign on long after reaching their cruising altitude.

The senator gripped Annie's hand, though he tried not to crush it. Annie just smiled and closed her eyes. It wasn't the first time. It certainly wasn't going to be the last. Over their many years of working together, the South Carolina native had become more than a trusted advisor and friend. She'd become a daughter to him. They'd traveled all over the world together, to some of the darkest and most dangerous corners of the planet, and for all the man's political courage, Annie knew he hated to fly. That hadn't always been the case. Only since Afghanistan, the day she and Dayton had nearly been shot down by Taliban forces, the day they'd met McDermott, Ryker, Hwang, and Vinetti for the first time, the day those brave young Marines had saved their lives.

It was surreal to think of how much time had passed since that day, how much had happened in their lives. McDermott, married with three kids, was now the country's new national security advisor. Vinetti was dead. His beautiful wife, Claire, was a widow trying to raise two kids on her own. Hwang was divorced, wounded and working for DSS. Ryker was . . . Ryker. And what was she? A still-single advisor to a failed presidential candidate? Was that the best she could do? She wondered.

When the plane finally stopped shaking, Secretary Whitney poked her head in their cabin and invited the senator and Annie to come to the conference room.

"Robert, Annie, I wanted to take a moment and thank you both," the president said as they stepped past two Secret Service agents. "If it wasn't for your efforts, this summit wouldn't be happening."

"Don't thank us yet, Mr. President," Dayton demurred. "Not until we all get home in one piece."

Clarke laughed. Whitney did not. But both beckoned the two to join them for dinner.

"Any progress in hunting down Haqqani and al-Qassab?" Annie asked as she took a seat and a steward set an extra place for her.

"No," said the president, the smile disappearing from his face. "I'm afraid not."

4 HOURS BEFORE AIR FORCE ONE LANDS IN ISRAEL

Ali Haqqani turned off the shower and leaned against the tile wall.

It was 4:36 in the morning. He had barely slept, tossing and turning all night, trying to figure out his next move. Al-Qassab could not be trusted. That much was certain. The Syrian was still refusing to provide him a new identity, much less a plan to escape the country, and Haqqani had lost all hope that he would.

Pushing the shower curtain aside, he grabbed a towel off a nearby hook and dried himself off. Then he stared in the mirror and cursed himself for being so double-minded. His father would never be so cowardly. Nor would either of his brothers. They were men of conviction, men of action. He needed to be, too, and now more than ever.

Double-checking the bathroom door to make sure it was really locked, Haqqani reached into the pocket of his trousers and pulled out his mobile phone. Not the satellite phone the Kairos team had given him. That one he'd ditched in the Mediterranean before leaving Mallorca. This was his personal phone, one Kairos couldn't be monitoring because they had no idea he'd brought it with him.

Taking a deep breath, he powered up the phone. A moment later, it buzzed. A single text message was waiting for him. His hands trembled as he opened it.

Wire sent. Documents being prepared. Get to a secure location. Check back when you get there.

Haqqani found himself torn by conflicting emotions. His most trusted friend was moving heaven and earth to help him. But was it already too late?

94

2 HOURS BEFORE AIR FORCE ONE LANDS IN ISRAEL

Hussam Mashrawi didn't need the alarm on his phone.

He'd been awake for hours.

Now, hearing the *muezzin* call the faithful to prayer, he slipped out of bed and into the bathroom. He changed his bandages and performed his daily ritual wash. Then he dressed in the formal clerical robes of his office, went out into the living room, bowed down on the carpet facing Mecca, and said his morning prayers. The day was here. All his preparations had come down to this, and he had never felt more alive.

By force of habit, he stepped into the back bedroom to kiss each of his beautiful girls and his precious son as they slept, but of course they were not there. Surprised with himself for forgetting that they were staying with Yasmine's sister, he returned to the master bedroom and gave his wife a kiss and stroked her hair as she awoke. Then he set the mobile phone on the nightstand beside her and reviewed the plan with her one more time. What she would wear. The shoes she would bring to the cobbler. The moment she should call him. The speed-dial number she should press.

"Number five," she said, smiling. "Don't worry. I won't forget."

Kissing her one last time, Mashrawi exited his front door. The clouds were thick and foreboding, but it was not raining. The December air was chilly but fresh, with a stiff wind coming from the west. Mashrawi strolled down the narrow alleyways for the final time with a deep feeling of serenity. He was not nervous. He did not fear pain or death. Rather, he found himself almost giddy at the prospect of becoming a *shahid* and entering paradise. He would miss Yasmine and the children. But they would be well taken care of. Of this he had no doubt. Abu Nakba was many things, Mashrawi knew, but above all he was a man of his word.

Reaching the checkpoint, he showed the Israeli soldiers and American Secret Service agents his ID and the VIP lanyard around his neck. They scrutinized both and asked him many questions. But in the end, just as Agent Ryker had promised, they let him pass. His stomach tightened as he stepped through the magnetometer. But when no alarms went off, he relaxed again, smiled to himself, and headed onto the Haram al-Sharif to pray in the mosque and make his final preparations.

This was it, he realized, hardly believing it had been so easy.

1 HOUR BEFORE AIR FORCE ONE LANDS IN ISRAEL

Marcus and Kailea stopped at the checkpoint and showed their IDs.

A moment later, they drove through the Jaffa Gate, found a spot near Christ Church, and parked their embassy sedan on the curb, careful to place their special permit on the dashboard so it wouldn't be towed by the Israeli police.

Roseboro—working out of the war room at the embassy—had assigned them to serve as "free safeties." They did not have protective responsibilities for a specific leader or site. Rather, they had the freedom to go anywhere and quadruple-check any site they believed warranted it. This hadn't set well with Kailea. She wanted to be on Secretary Whitney's detail, but Geoff Stone had gotten that assignment instead. So she and Marcus headed into the *shuk*, then to the Christian Quarter and the Church of the Holy Sepulcher for a final walk-through of the fourth-century structure.

Kailea was finished with trying to engage Marcus in personal conversation, though she was more curious than ever as to who this guy was and what made him tick. An agnostic herself, the daughter of staunch atheists, she was now in the "Holy City" for the first time in her life. She knew Marcus was a devout, if tight-lipped, Christian. But though this was the ideal place to ask him why he believed what he believed, it was hardly the time. There was far too much radio traffic coming through their earpieces from agents on-site at Ben Gurion and along the motorcade route. There were still no leads on Haqqani or al-Qassab, and everyone was on the highest possible alert.

Upon entering the mammoth, ancient cathedral, the two agents met with the Roman Catholic, Greek Orthodox, and Armenian Apostolic priests who served as its caretakers. They chatted with the American and Israeli agents stationed throughout the facility, while saying nothing to the reporters and TV crews that were pre-positioned there. They strolled through the shadowy corridors, past the priceless artwork and empty tomb, breathing the incense and watching for anything out of place.

Just then, Tomer called from the Shin Bet mobile command center that had been set up in the basement restaurant of the King David Hotel. They hoped he had news, but all he wanted was a status report.

Air Force One was streaking across the Mediterranean.

95

30 MINUTES BEFORE AIR FORCE ONE LANDS IN ISRAEL

Ali Haqqani powered up his phone for the second time in four hours.

His friend had instructed him to get to a secure location to prepare to make his getaway. But where was he supposed to find a secure location—far from al-Qassab—at this hour? The West Bank had been sealed off. Most roads leading in and out of Jerusalem had been closed. Only emergency vehicles and official government vehicles were permitted through the myriad of army and police checkpoints that had been set up. Yet Haqqani knew he could not remain under the same roof as the Syrian and live to see another day.

Leaving now, he texted his friend. **Will call when I arrive.**

Then he shut down the phone, put it in his pocket, and strode to the bedroom door.

It was time to move.

Al-Qassab poured himself a cup of coffee and entered the living room.

He went straight to the chair he had nearly lived in for the past few days, sat down, and powered up the mobile phone the dentist had left for him. Then he dialed the number the dentist had scribbled on a napkin and leaned back in the chair.

"Yes, hello, can you hear me?" the Syrian said when someone finally answered. "Yes, I can, and there's been an accident. We need an ambulance—immediately."

Haqqani came around the corner. *"What are you doing?"* the Pakistani asked with alarm.

"My address? Yes, here it is," al-Qassab replied in nearly flawless Hebrew, holding up his hand to silence Haqqani and reciting the address to the flat where they were staying, then politely thanking the other person and ending the call.

"Who were you talking to, Mohammed?" Haqqani demanded. "You know we're not supposed to make any calls."

"It is time, Ali."

"Time for what?"

"Time for me to go, to switch locations while I still can."

"For *you* to go?" asked the Pakistani. "What about me?"

"Where I am going, Ali, you cannot follow."

"Enough, Mohammed, enough," Haqqani fumed. *"All this time I have been asking you for the plan to evacuate me, and now it's clear why. You want to cut me loose and save yourself."*

"Don't be ridiculous," the Syrian replied. "I have a plan for you. It's simply different than—"

Suddenly Haqqani pulled a 9mm pistol fitted with a silencer from behind his back and aimed it at the Syrian's chest.

"Enough of your lies, Mohammed. You're jeopardizing all we have worked for, all that Father asked us to do. But no more. I won't let you destroy this mission."

Al-Qassab looked at the pistol, then back at Haqqani's eyes. The man's hands were shaking, but his eyes were deadly serious. "Keep your voice down, Ali—someone will hear you."

"Shut up, Mohammed. I am done with you. You are a betrayer of the cause, and Allah will punish you for eternity."

With that, Haqqani pulled the trigger. But the gun did not fire. He looked down, aimed it again, and again pulled the trigger. Again it did not fire, and the Syrian burst out in laughter.

"Such a fool you are, Ali," he sneered as he picked up a newspaper on the coffee table beside him, revealing a pile of bullets.

Haqqani's eyes went wide.

"Did you think I didn't know that you'd brought a gun into the house?" al-Qassab asked. "I'm the director of operations for the world's greatest terrorist organization. Father did not choose me for my looks. He chose me because I am good at what I do. You should have stuck to medicine, Ali—murder does not become you."

"But when . . . ? How . . . ?" the Pakistani stammered, releasing the pistol's magazine and realizing to his horror that it was empty.

"*You*—not I—have betrayed our cause, and for this you will burn forever."

The Syrian reached behind him, pulled out his own silenced pistol, and shot Haqqani three times—once in the face and twice in the chest.

Five minutes later, a Magen David Adom ambulance—one painted to look just like those used by Israeli Jews, not Palestinian Arabs—pulled up out front. One of the paramedics came to the door carrying a large case. Al-Qassab let the man in, took the case from him, and stepped into the restroom. He quickly undressed and threw his clothes into a nearly full laundry basket. He opened the case, removed a Magen David Adom uniform, and put it on. Then he placed his weapon, a collection of mobile phones, and his satellite phone in the case, closed it, and carried it out the front door and into the back of the ambulance.

A moment later they were gone, lights flashing and siren blaring, heading for the Old City.

96

15 MINUTES BEFORE AIR FORCE ONE LANDS IN ISRAEL

Oleg Kraskin snapped awake.

After operating on fewer than three hours' sleep for each of the last six nights, the Raven hadn't realized that he had drifted off. But a series of audible pings on his computer got his attention.

Trying desperately to shake off the fatigue and refocus on his work, Oleg opened the two alerts on his computer screen. He read them both, then read them a second time. Confused, he looked at the time stamp on each and suddenly felt sick to his stomach. Fully awake now, he grabbed his satellite phone and pressed speed-dial one.

"Yes?" came the familiar voice at the other end.

"It's me. I've got something."

"What is it?"

"NSA just picked up a hit on one of Ali Haqqani's known phone numbers."

"Where?"

"An apartment complex on the Mount of Olives."

"You're sure it's him?"

"I'm sure it's his phone," Oleg said.

"Do you have the coordinates?"

"I'm sending them to your phone right now."

Oleg could hear Marcus relaying the information to someone—Kailea Curtis, he assumed—and trying to figure out the fastest way to get there.

"How many pings did you get?" Marcus asked.

"Two."

"In a row?"

There was a long pause.

"Hello? Hello? Are you still there?" Marcus pressed.

"*Da*, I'm here."

"Were the two hits back-to-back?"

"No, they weren't," Oleg confessed. "I'm so sorry, Marcus. I fell asleep at the desk. One came in hours ago, the other just twenty minutes ago."

Marcus ended the call and sprinted back through the Christian Quarter.

Kailea was right behind him.

When they got to the Jaffa Gate, Marcus tossed her the keys and ordered her to drive while he called Tomer. New to the city and still unfamiliar with the roads, Kailea put the address the Raven had just sent them into Waze, then gunned the engine, did a K-turn, and roared back through the gate and down the ramp. At the light, the GPS app told her to turn south on Hebron Road. She did, making an illegal left turn on HaMefaked Street. As they sped around the south side of Mount Zion, Marcus finally reached the Shin Bet officer and told him where they were headed.

"I'm on my way," said Tomer. "What's your ETA?"

"Waze says nine minutes."

"With all the checkpoints, it's going to take me almost twenty," said Tomer. "But hang tight and don't go in until I get there."

"Don't worry," Marcus assured him. "We'll be careful."

"I'm serious, Ryker. The place could be booby-trapped. I'll dispatch a bomb squad and a tactical unit from police headquarters. They're right on Mount Scopus, not far away. And I'll call in air support as well, in case Haqqani makes a run for it. But do not go in until I arrive."

"I'll keep you posted—gotta go," Marcus said, refusing to assure the Israeli that he'd wait for backup.

Kailea zigzagged up the mountain. She took a sharp right onto Gey Bin Hinom Street, then a left on Ma'alot Ir David Street. Soon they turned right onto Derech HaOfel, then right onto El-Mansuriya Street. Two minutes later they arrived. Kailea jumped the curb and slammed on the brakes. Marcus bolted out the passenger side and drew his weapon, telling Kailea to stay behind the wheel with the engine running.

Every instinct in his body was urging him to rush the building and kick in the front door, but Tomer's warning echoed in his ears. This wasn't his country or his show. Fortunately, four police cruisers and a tactical unit came roaring down the street. A moment later, the bomb squad was there as well, and though Marcus couldn't see them yet, he could already hear a pair of police helicopters approaching from the south.

Marcus speed-dialed Tomer as the Israeli units surrounded the house.

"We're here—all of us—how close are you?"

"I'm still twelve minutes out," he said.

"We can't wait," Marcus said. "We're going in."

Marcus hung up and gave the Israeli commander the order to move. Marcus wasn't sure why the man listened to him, but he did. The Israeli commandos simultaneously burst into the first-floor dental offices from the front, back, and side doors, then—encountering no initial resistance—sent bomb-sniffing robots in ahead of them. Marcus knew it was better than risking the lives of human officers, but it was also taking precious time they did not have.

97

10 MINUTES BEFORE AIR FORCE ONE LANDS IN ISRAEL

The Israeli ambulance had been Hamdi Yaşar's idea.

And it was a stroke of genius.

Not a single nonemergency vehicle was on the streets of Jerusalem, and as al-Qassab worked the radio in Hebrew, they were waved through every checkpoint until they pulled up to the Damascus Gate and screeched to a halt.

In his Magen David Adom uniform, al-Qassab jumped out of the ambulance with one of the Kairos paramedics. Grabbing cases of medical equipment, they ran down the steps to the gate, approached the IDF soldiers manning the checkpoint, showed their fake IDs, and cursed in Hebrew that they had a heart attack patient they had to get to. The young soldiers quickly stepped aside, and al-Qassab and his colleague sprinted into the Muslim Quarter. They raced down a labyrinth of empty alleyways until they reached the Old City branch of their man's dental practice.

Bursting through the front door, al-Qassab drew the silenced Glock and signaled for his colleague to wait by the front door. He worked his way down the main hallway, checking each examining room one by one. Finally he found the dentist and his assistants all laughing and talking and sipping tea in a back office.

They looked up in shock to see al-Qassab, but their shock didn't last long. The Syrian raised his weapon and double-tapped each one to the forehead. Checking to make certain they were all dead, and satisfied that they were, al-Qassab called for the paramedic waiting by the front door to come to the back office and help him. The moment he arrived, the Syrian double-tapped him, as well. Then he took the man's radio and held down the Talk button.

"Patient stabilized," he told the ambulance driver in Hebrew. "But we're going to be longer than expected. Return to base, and I'll get back to you."

"Affirmative," the driver radioed back.

Al-Qassab returned to the front desk. He pulled a piece of paper out of the printer and rifled through the desk drawers until he found a Sharpie. He wrote, *CLOSED UNTIL AFTER THE SUMMIT* in Arabic, taped the sign to the front window, locked the door, and pulled down the shades. When he was done, he stashed the cases of medical equipment in one of the examining rooms, stopping only to withdraw his collection of mobile and satellite phones and ammunition. These he stuffed in a backpack along with a spare set of clothes, then found the staircase and headed up to the two-level private apartment above the clinic.

The dentist was in his midthirties and married with a couple of kids. That much al-Qassab had learned from Hamdi Yaşar as they'd planned this mission. The family had been sent away. That was ideal, as it gave him the privacy he'd now need, along with a well-stocked refrigerator, running water, and a television on which he could watch the arrival of the president and king, which al-Qassab suddenly realized was happening right then.

98

Annie Stewart couldn't believe they were already on the ground.

It had been the smoothest touchdown she had ever experienced, and the most restful flight, after all the initial turbulence. It was her first trip on Air Force One, and she felt just a pang of regret that the senator wasn't going to run after all.

Pete Hwang sat in the DSS operations center, watching the live coverage.

Even as he texted and radioed steady updates to DSS agents in Israel, it was hard not to watch Air Force One come to a full stop outside the designated hangar without a stab of envy. But for his wounded arm, he would be there too, with his best friend, right in the thick of it. Yet as the door opened and the stairway was rolled into place and the IDF military band began to play "Hail to the Chief" and a smiling and waving POTUS emerged on a cloudy but dry day to roars of applause, Pete was five thousand miles away missing it all.

The Israeli commander was finally convinced the first floor was clear.

On his order, commandos poured into the building and confirmed the robot's findings. But the procedure had to be painstakingly repeated on the second and third floors. In the end, there were no booby traps, though the commander radioed to Marcus that they had found extensive traces of explosives on the third floor.

And a body.

Outside Aspen, the Raven was glued to the live coverage.

He watched as King Faisal's 747 touched down after the two-hour and two-minute flight from Riyadh. He was watching on RT, the Russian propaganda network, to see how they covered the story. So far they were playing it straight. The anchors noted that this was the first direct trip between the Saudi and Israeli cities ever flown by the Saudi national airline in history. It was going to be the first time a Saudi leader had ever met with an Israeli leader, at least publicly. It was also going to be the first time the remarks of an Israeli prime minister would be aired live on Saudi television and on Arabic stations throughout the Gulf region.

It was, Oleg knew, a day of many firsts. Yet, terrified by the immense danger the three world leaders were now in, Oleg Kraskin did something he had never done before—he bowed his head and prayed to a God he still wasn't sure he believed in to keep these men safe from all evil and harm.

Yasmine Mashrawi sat spellbound as she watched the coverage on Al-Sawt.

The anchors were using every opportunity to disparage the Saudi king for betraying not only the Palestinian cause but "that of every Muslim" for daring to "normalize" relations with the "criminal Zionists." The shoemaker and his wife, with whom Yasmine was sitting, meanwhile, wouldn't stop talking, wouldn't stop echoing every critical word the anchors uttered, and far worse.

Yasmine said nothing. She nodded her head occasionally, wanting her hosts to feel that she was with them. But privately, she couldn't help but think that just maybe the Saudi king was doing the right thing. Yasmine was not a political person. She would certainly never contradict her father, who was constantly blasting the Zionists and their American "enablers." And there was no question that the Israeli occupation of Jerusalem and the West Bank and Gaza grieved her. Yet secretly she could not understand why Ismail Ziad constantly refused every offer for peace and reconciliation that the Americans or Israelis proposed. Of course the Israelis' offers were ridiculous and unfair. But what did Ziad and his people expect? Why not go back to the bargaining table and bargain? How were the lives of the Palestinians ever going to get better if he didn't make a deal and start truly building their state?

Reaching into her pocketbook, Yasmine pulled out the phone her husband had given her. She powered it up and set it in her lap, full of anticipation of joining Hussam very shortly.

99

Amin al-Azzam sat in his office, watching the coverage with his staff.

All except his son-in-law.

"Where's Hussam?" the Grand Mufti asked as images of King Faisal's plane taxiing flickered on the screen before them. "Has anyone seen him?"

"He was here earlier," a young cleric said. "I think he was going to the mosque."

"Perhaps he's in the lavatory," said another.

"No, no, I saw him in the Noble Sanctuary," said a third. "He said he needed to make some final preparations."

Al-Azzam said nothing, but as he toyed with the lanyard dangling from his neck, he couldn't decide if he should be annoyed or concerned. All the preparations they could possibly make had been completed the day before. There was simply nothing left to be done. So where was Hussam? Why wasn't he here with the rest of the staff?

As the jumbo jet pulled to a halt next to Air Force One, al-Azzam found himself admiring the color scheme of the Saudi plane. The fuselage of flight 001 was painted beige on the top half and white on the lower half. The words *Saudi Arabian* were painted on the side in Arabic and English in a rich royal blue. The tail was painted the same shade of blue and featured the national symbol of the two crossed swords under a giant palm tree. The two planes looked good side by side.

A stairwell was rolled into position. The door opened. The king, stooped but smiling, appeared in the doorway. The Israeli crowd roared and applauded even more loudly than for the American president. Soon the aging monarch made his way down the steps and was greeted by Clarke and Eitan.

To al-Azzam's astonishment, the scene stirred something deep, something hopeful, in his soul. He could not say why, not even to himself. But at that moment, he found himself looking around the room and out the windows to his left, wondering what could cause Hussam to miss it.

Donning a Kevlar vest given to him by an Israeli officer, Marcus headed inside.

He bounded up the stairs and entered the flat where the commander and his team were waiting. It took only an instant to realize whom he was looking at—the bullet-riddled, bloodstained body of Ali Haqqani.

"That your man?" the commander asked, bending down to examine the bullet holes and the coagulated blood around them.

"One of them," Marcus replied.

"Nine-millimeter," said the commander. "Close range. Probably a Glock. And he hasn't been dead long. Less than an hour. But who shot him?"

"Mohammed al-Qassab," Marcus said, almost under his breath.

It wasn't a guess. It was a certainty. The Syrian terrorist was no novice. The man knew precisely what he was doing. He'd gotten all he needed from Haqqani. Now he was tying off loose ends.

Looking around the room, Marcus surveyed the medical equipment, the bloody sheets and pillowcases piled in the trash bin in the kitchen, and dried blood on the plastic tarp still on the dining room floor. Technicians were taking samples. They'd be sent back to a lab for analysis and DNA testing. All of it confirmed there was a bomber out there somewhere, and suddenly Marcus found himself wondering: Could it actually be al-Qassab?

As the Syrian watched the welcome ceremony, the rage within him was building.

Eitan's and Clarke's remarks were revolting but thoroughly predictable. Yet it was the speech by King Faisal Mohammed Al Saud that sickened him. Each line was more reprehensible than the last.

"What a joy it is to step foot on soil once trod by prophets, priests, and kings."

"I must say how disappointed I am in my brothers in the Palestinian Authority."

"The Arab nations have embraced rejectionism far too long, but today, new breezes—fresh breezes—are blowing in the Middle East."

"It has been said, 'There is a time for war and a time for peace.' This, my friends, is a time for peace."

This, from a Muslim?

This, from the Custodian of the Two Holy Mosques?

Al-Qassab fumed. A bomb was too good, too quick and painless for such a man who epitomized the very definition of apostasy. Such a man deserved instead to be hanged. Or better yet, beheaded in the public square.

It was too late for that, of course. Yet for a moment, however fleeting, al-Qassab wondered if he'd been too hasty. Perhaps instead of killing Haqqani, he should have insisted the good doctor perform one more surgery, place one more bomb in one more *shahid*—in al-Qassab himself. True, he would never get close enough to the king, to such a *kafir*, to such an infidel. But oh, to walk into a crowded synagogue three days hence, on the Jewish Sabbath, and blow himself and all those around him into eternity.

Al-Qassab savored the fantasy, then cursed himself for it. The plan that he and the Turk had developed was sound. If it worked, it would change the Muslim world forever. But he had to stay focused. There was so much that could still go wrong.

100

Marcus called the war room.

"We found Haqqani," he said.

"That's tremendous," said Roseboro. "Where?"

"In an apartment on the Mount of Olives."

"Is he talking?"

"No, he's dead."

"How long?"

"An hour at most."

"How?"

As Tomer and Kailea, now both in the flat with him, looked around the room—being careful not to impede the work of the crime scene investigators—Marcus relayed what he knew.

"Did you find Haqqani's phone?" Roseboro asked.

"No," Marcus said. "The Israelis are tearing the place apart, but they haven't turned up the phone. Still, the Raven is working with the NSA to scour his call log. Apparently, Haqqani received one message and sent another. One was this morning before dawn. The other was a few hours later. Both were to the same number in Pakistan. We're not sure yet to whom, but the Raven is working on it."

"So al-Qassab and the bomber—or bombers—are still out there," Roseboro said.

It wasn't a question. It was a statement of how much trouble they were still in.

"Where's POTUS now?" Marcus asked.

"Boarding the motorcade—the next stop is the Holocaust memorial."

"Then the Temple Mount?"

"You got it."

Marcus sighed. "All right. I'll keep you posted."

He hung up the phone. Kailea and Tomer had finished looking over the flat. Now they were staring at the lifeless body of Haqqani, surrounded by a pool of crimson.

"Who owns this place?" Tomer asked the commander.

"A dentist," he said. "Someone named Daoud Husseini."

"What do we know about him?"

"Lives here with his wife and kids, who are apparently abroad at the moment. Brother lives downstairs. The clinic is on the first floor."

"Have you contacted him?"

"We're trying."

"What do you mean, *trying*?" Tomer shouted. "Get him on the phone. I want to talk with him—*now*."

"We've called him repeatedly," a detective replied. "He's not responding."

"Maybe he's on the run," said the commander.

"Or dead," Kailea added.

"Or maybe the dentist has moved al-Qassab to another safe house," said Marcus. "I mean, whoever this Husseini guy is, he probably knows the city and the country like the back of his hand. Once the surgery—or surgeries—were complete, Husseini would be a lot more helpful to al-Qassab than a Pakistani from London, right?"

"Maybe so," said Tomer, turning to the commander and asking questions in rapid-fire Hebrew, then relaying the answers to Marcus and Kailea in English. "Husseini has another clinic. Maybe we can find more clues there."

"Where?" Marcus asked.

"The Old City—the Muslim Quarter," Tomer said.

"How close to the Temple Mount?" Marcus asked.

"A few hundred meters, if that."

"Then let's move."

The three raced down the stairs. Marcus jumped into the driver's seat of their sedan while Kailea tossed him the keys. With lights flashing and siren blaring, Tomer took the lead. En route, they heard him issue orders over the radio to forces in the Old City. They were not to move on the clinic or even make their presence known. They were, however, to block every street and alleyway leading to the clinic and put a drone—not a helicopter—over the building to provide live images. Simultaneously, two tactical units were to take up positions one block north and one block south of the clinic. "And put the bomb squad on standby."

Yasmine Mashrawi adjusted her veil and kept her mouth shut.

She just wished the shoemaker would keep his shut too.

She had never been to Yad Vashem, Israel's national Holocaust memorial and museum. She'd never had any interest, and even if she had, she couldn't imagine her husband, much less her father, permitting such a thing. Hussam was a kind soul, quiet, and might not have really minded, she thought. But her father was a proud and public man. It would never do for his youngest daughter to be studying the suffering of the Jews from so long ago when Jews were making her own people suffer right here and now.

Still, she found it fascinating to watch the coverage of the Saudi monarch walking through the museum with its director, asking questions alternatively about why the Nazis had slaughtered so many Jews and how scholars could be certain the number was really six million. That was the one question the shoemaker had applauded, until the king clarified his question by asking the museum director how he could be certain that even more Jews hadn't been killed.

101

Amin al-Azzam glanced at his watch, then back at the television.

Now genuinely worried that his son-in-law still had not joined them, he found himself frustrated that no one had a mobile phone. Unable either to call or text Hussam, he would have to resort to old-school methods. Discreetly calling his young veiled assistant over to him, he asked her in a whisper to scour the grounds and buildings for Hussam. He warned her to do nothing that would alarm the Secret Service or the Shin Bet, and certainly not to tell anyone what she was really doing. If asked, she was to say she was just checking on everything at the request of the Grand Mufti.

"Report back to me in no more than thirty minutes, whether you find him or not," he whispered, careful not to attract the attention of the others. "But if you do find him, tell him I must see him at once—it is of the utmost importance."

Mohammed al-Qassab could not watch this trash any longer.

Yad Vashem?

Had the leader of the Sunni Islamic world completely lost his mind?

Barely able to control his rage, yet unable to scream or break things for fear of being overheard by neighbors, the Syrian decided to change out of the paramedic's uniform and take a shower. First, however, he unzipped his backpack and took out the Uzi submachine gun. He double-checked to make sure the magazine was properly loaded and set everything on the master bed. Then he pulled out the various phones in his bag and checked to see if he had any messages waiting. Fortunately, there were none. No one was supposed to be in touch with him anyway, not even Hamdi Yaşar, not even on the satphone they used all the time. There was little or no chance of anyone intercepting their messages or tapping into their calls, but this was no day to take chances.

Realizing that he had not yet checked the roof, he poked around the flat until he found a closet off the living room with a ladder leading up to a hatch. Switching on the closet light, he climbed the ladder, unlocked the hatch, and opened it ever so slightly. Rather than linger, however, he turned on the video function on one of his phones, raised the phone above his head, and captured a 360-degree view. Then he lowered the hatch and played back the video while still standing on the ladder in the closet.

To the east was a direct and gorgeous view of the Haram al-Sharif, the golden dome, and the famed Mosque in the Corner. To the west, the most prominent building was the tower of the Church of the Holy Sepulcher. In every other direction, he saw rooftops covered with water tanks and solar water heaters, a forest of radio and television antennas, satellite dishes, and clotheslines, though with all the rain of the past few days, there were few articles of clothing hanging on any of them.

It was from the roof that al-Qassab wanted to see the explosion, and just as Hamdi Yaşar had promised, it was an ideal vantage point. All the television networks would replay the close-up images of the detonation over and over again. Certainly Al-Sawt would. Yaşar would make sure of it. The most gruesome images would be immediately uploaded onto YouTube and Twitter by jihadists around the world. He would savor all those in due time. But there was something intoxicating to al-Qassab about the prospect of actually watching the explosion from just a few hundred meters away—hearing the blast, feeling the shock wave—so this was where he would be when it happened.

Leaving the hatch unlocked, he climbed down the ladder and headed back to the living room. The ceremony at Yad Vashem was wrapping up. Adding insult to injury, the Saudi king had just laid a wreath before the Eternal Flame in the Hall of Remembrance, telling the Zionist criminals that "your pain is our pain, and together we must work to heal old wounds and build a new world of peace and security."

Tasting the bile in his mouth, al-Qassab raced to the toilet and slammed the door behind him. He stood there, his head down, taking deep breaths until the wave of nausea passed. Then he turned on the shower and stepped inside, calculating just how much time he had left. The delegation still had to exit the museum and load back into the motorcade. Then there would be a fifteen- or twenty-minute drive to the Old City, followed by a walk up the ramp, through the Mughrabi Gate, and onto the Haram al-Sharif. All told, he figured he had a mere forty-five minutes until the moment of truth, and he was electrified.

102

Marcus screeched to a halt in front of the Damascus Gate.

Tomer was already out of his car and running to the checkpoint. Kailea followed close behind. Marcus needed an extra moment to turn off the engine and grab his keys, but he soon reached the checkpoint as well. Other emergency vehicles were converging on the site, but Tomer had ordered everyone else to keep their sirens off.

"Who has been through here in the last few hours?" Tomer asked the officer in charge.

"No one," the young man replied. "We sealed it off, just as we were ordered."

"You're absolutely certain no one came through? No one at all?"

"Well, there was a heart attack. Some paramedics came through to help."

"You saw the victim?"

"No, the medics told us about it."

"How many were there?"

"Two."

"Arab or Jewish?"

"Jewish, of course."

"How do you know?" Tomer demanded.

"They were Magen David Adom. They spoke Hebrew. They were Jewish, believe me."

"You checked their IDs?"

"Of course."

"You say they spoke Hebrew?"

"Yes."

"Did they have accents?"

"One was a *sabra*, for sure."

"And the other?"

"I don't know, probably an *oleh*," the officer said.

"What's an *oleh*?" Marcus asked.

"An *oleh chadash*—a new immigrant," Tomer said.

"What country was he from?" Marcus inquired.

"How should I know?" said the officer.

"I mean, what was the accent? Russian, French, Arabic, Persian . . . ?"

"English."

"What kind of English?"

"*English* English."

"British, American, South African, Kiwi, what?"

"*British*," the officer said, then looked around at the rest of his unit, all of whom nodded that it had been British English.

"That's got to be him," Marcus said.

"Maybe," Tomer said. "I'm calling in the army."

"No," Marcus shot back. "We move in heavy, and he's going to hear us coming."

"The place could be booby-trapped."

"With him inside?" Marcus asked. "Why rig the doors with explosives if you're planning to escape?"

"Why assume he's planning to escape?"

"Look, we don't have time to argue," Marcus insisted. "If you send in the army, somebody might get trigger-happy. We can't afford to take that risk. We need this guy alive and talking, and we need to get him fast."

Tomer wasn't convinced.

"Look, Agent Curtis and I will go in first," Marcus offered. "If we blow ourselves to smithereens, then send in the bomb squad to make sure there's no other booby traps. But if we live, we get al-Qassab. Okay?"

"You sure?" Tomer asked.

"I'm sure," said Marcus.

"What about you?" Tomer asked Kailea.

"Where he goes, I go," she replied.

"Fine," Tomer said. "But you're both crazy."

The Israeli headed through the Damascus Gate with Marcus and Kailea in tow, both wearing body armor but no helmets. As they moved through the maze of narrow alleyways, Tomer radioed for a sitrep from the drone, in English for the Americans' benefit. He was told there was no one in the alley that led to the clinic and only one entrance. "No back door?" he whispered. "You're sure?"

The answer came back affirmative—the surveillance unit was sure.

"Do we have sharpshooters in place?" Tomer asked next.

"You told us to keep a low profile, nothing visible—so no," he was told. "Should we put them in place?"

Tomer turned to Marcus, who was hearing through his headset everything the Israeli was hearing.

"No—a sniper shot would kill him," Marcus whispered back. "I'm telling you, we need this guy alive. Al-Qassab is the last chance we have to find out how many bombers there are, who they are, and where."

103

They reached the blockade around the corner from the clinic.

Two dozen heavily armed commandos from Mishmar Hagvul—the Israeli border police—were waiting for orders to move. Behind them were officers from the sapper unit, already fully dressed in their bomb detection and defusal outfits.

Marcus drew his Sig Sauer. Kailea drew hers. Tomer would have none of it. They were going to need heavier firepower than that. He grabbed M4 assault rifles from two of the commandos, handed them to his American colleagues, and ordered the commandos to hand over their spare magazines, as well. They did so, and Marcus returned his pistol to his shoulder holster.

Tomer then took an M4 and ammo for himself. He explained to the commandos what was about to happen. He radioed the same information to the mirror team at the other end of the street. They all made sure they were on the same frequencies. Then Marcus called Roseboro to quickly bring him up to speed.

The moment he hung up, they moved out.

Marcus led, taking care not to move down the center of the alley. Instead, he hugged close to the buildings on the right side of the alley to cut down both the line of sight and angle of attack if al-Qassab was watching from one of Dr. Husseini's windows. Kailea was right behind him. Tomer brought up the rear. With no time to spare, there was no point making a slow approach, so Marcus broke into a sprint.

Seconds later, they were at the door of the dental clinic. All the lettering on the windows was in Arabic, which Marcus could not read. When Tomer confirmed this was the place, Marcus reached for the door handle and turned. It was locked. Tomer handed him Semtex plastic explosives and a detonator. Marcus attached the Semtex to the handle, inserted the detonator, and unspooled enough cord for him to back off a safe distance to the left of the door. Kailea and Tomer moved back an equal distance to the right. Marcus silently mouthed a countdown from three.

The explosion was instant and deafening. It didn't simply blow the door off its hinges; it disintegrated the door entirely. None of them were wearing goggles, but Marcus bolted inside anyway, working on the assumption that anyone on the other side of the door had to have been badly injured or at least had his ears blown out. Either way, he'd have the element of surprise.

Sweeping the M4 from side to side, Marcus saw no one in the waiting room. He headed down the main corridor, keeping his weapon pointed straight ahead. Using hand signals, he directed Kailea and Tomer to check the offices and exam rooms on the left and right. Each shouted, *"Clear!"* as they did.

At the end of the hall, Marcus found four bloodied bodies in the break room. Keeping his weapon trained on them in case it was a trick, he immediately called his colleagues to join him. Kailea guarded their six, keeping her weapon trained back up the hallway, while Tomer entered the break room and checked each person for a pulse.

"They're gone," he said. "Double-taps to the head."

"Nine-millimeter?" Marcus asked.

Tomer nodded. "Yeah."

"Same as Haqqani?"

"Looks that way."

"That's gotta be al-Qassab," Marcus said. "How long ago were they shot?"

"Not long," said Tomer. "Bodies are still warm."

"Then he could still be in the building," Kailea said.

"Find the stairs," said Marcus. "Come on—let's move."

104

Al-Qassab had just stepped out of the shower when he heard the explosion.

As the building shook, he knew instantly what was happening. The Zionists had found him, and they had breached the door. The only question was how many commandos were pouring into the building and whether more were fast-roping from helicopters onto the roof.

Grabbing his Glock 9mm pistol, he came out of the bathroom stark naked. Reaching for the backpack on the bed, he pulled out his spare set of clothes. One of the Kairos operatives had stolen an Israeli police uniform, complete with utility belt, holster, boots, and sunglasses. Al-Qassab quickly put them on. He also grabbed a wallet and false set of papers from his backpack and stuffed these in his pockets, along with the satphone and the mobile phone set up to detonate the bomb inside Hussam Mashrawi.

Putting his pistol in the holster and spare magazines in his belt, al-Qassab now snatched the Uzi and raced to the closet. He climbed the ladder, pushed the hatch up, and thrust the barrel of the submachine gun into the chilly morning air, expecting to engage with Israeli forces. He spun around to the left, then quickly to his right, but to his astonishment, there was no one on the roof at all.

It could be a trap, he knew. There had to be snipers hiding on adjacent roofs, but so what if there were? A head shot would be fatal, but it would also be instant and thus far better than being captured and tortured and then paraded before the media as the first Kairos operative ever apprehended, and by the Zionists, no less. Tossing the Uzi through the hatch, he finished climbing the ladder, crawled onto the roof, and picked up the weapon again. Scanning the nearby rooftops and matching the scene in his mind with the video he'd taken earlier, he quickly mapped out a route and began to run.

Marcus slowly crept up the stairs.

He was moving more carefully now. If there were people on the second floor, surely they'd heard the explosion. If it was al-Qassab, he was armed and dangerous and waiting for them.

While Marcus wanted the man alive, he knew that might not be possible. If the man was wearing a suicide vest, Marcus would have just one shot—a head shot between the eyes—to take him out before he could push the button and detonate the bomb. If al-Qassab had actually undergone surgery to implant a body cavity bomb inside his chest, he might have a second or two more before the man could hit his speed dial and trigger the explosion. Unless he'd hit the speed dial already.

Wishing he had a stun grenade, but realizing time was of the essence, Marcus stopped creeping up the stairs. He sprinted up the remaining steps, pivoted around the corner, and burst onto the second floor with sound and fury. Why wait? Why give al-Qassab any extra time to think or act?

Sweeping the M4 from left to right, Marcus found no one in the hallway. He heard a television to his left and decided to break right, into the master bedroom, in case the running TV was designed to lure him to the left. Staying low, he kicked in the slightly open door, sweeping the weapon from right to left this time. Again he found nobody. Instead, he saw a half-empty backpack on the bed. Moving to the bathroom, he could see the steam, the water on the floor, and the discarded paramedic's uniform. He checked under the bed and in the closet but found no one. It was clear. He was about to shout that when he heard Kailea yell from the living room.

105

Fearing the worst, Marcus raced to the living room.

When he got there, he immediately saw the open closet door, the ladder, the hatch. Kailea had already scrambled up to the roof.

"*I see him,*" she shouted and took off in hot pursuit.

Marcus quickly climbed the ladder and was soon sprinting to catch up, even as he radioed to Tomer and the team that they were heading east over the rooftops. They were moving too fast to open fire, but so was al-Qassab. Darting around water heaters and under clotheslines, Marcus was rapidly gaining on Kailea, and they were both closing the gap with the Syrian. Moments later, Tomer radioed to say he, too, was now on the roof. He was pushing hard to catch up and ordering Mishmar Hagvul forces near the Temple Mount to get to the roofs and start coming toward them from the east.

Up ahead, Marcus saw al-Qassab jump from one building to another, but when he hit the roof, he didn't keep running. Instead, he dropped to one knee, swung around, and opened fire on Kailea. She immediately dove for cover, as did Marcus. Kailea was closer to the Syrian and returned fire. Marcus didn't have a clear shot. Kailea was directly ahead of him, about ten or twelve yards, crouched behind an air-conditioning unit. Marcus could hear the bullets pinging off the metal unit.

Glancing to his right, he saw a path to another AC unit and bolted for it. The movement drew al-Qassab's attention and his fire. Marcus could hear rounds whizzing past his head and did a Pete Rose, diving headfirst and landing on his stomach behind the unit just as the Syrian unleashed two automatic bursts.

At the same moment, Kailea leveled two bursts from her M4, then followed those up with a third. That drew al-Qassab's focus back to her. As she popped out a spent mag and reloaded, the Syrian lit her up with everything he had in a fresh magazine.

Sensing his opportunity, Marcus gripped his M4 close to his chest, leaped to his feet, sprinted toward the building's edge, and jumped across an alleyway. He made it, but just barely, and was fortunate to land on his feet. A row of a half-dozen large water coolers obscured al-Qassab's view to the south. That—combined with another three bursts of return fire from Kailea—gave Marcus the time and cover he needed to arc around several air conditioners and get in position behind the Syrian.

He briefly debated shouting a warning and giving the man a chance to surrender but quickly abandoned the thought. If the man did have a suicide vest or a body cavity bomb, the warning would give him the time he needed to blow himself up. Both Marcus and Kailea were likely far enough away to survive the blast, but that wasn't the point. As Marcus had told Tomer repeatedly, they needed this guy alive.

Just then, however, he heard Kailea radio that she'd been hit. He was about to ask how badly she was hurt when to his right he spotted a team of Israeli commandos climbing onto the roof and heading in their direction. They were at least a football field away, but Marcus worried when they got within range, they would shoot to kill, no matter what Tomer had told them.

Out of time and options, Marcus lifted the M4 carbine, trained the infrared laser sight on al-Qassab's right shoulder, and squeezed the trigger. The .223 round spat out of the barrel at a velocity of 2,970 feet per second. A fraction of a second later, Marcus saw a puff of pink mist. He saw the man lurch forward and collapse to his left side. Then al-Qassab emitted a blood-curdling scream that could be heard across the city.

"Tomer, al-Qassab's down—I'm moving to him," Marcus shouted into his headset. *"Get to Kailea and make sure she's okay."*

106

Word came back almost immediately.

Kailea was not okay. She'd been hit in the left leg. The bullet had torn through her femoral artery, and she was in danger of bleeding out. Tomer reported that he'd already ripped off his belt to create a makeshift tourniquet. But he ordered a chopper to land—or at least hover—near his position and medevac the woman out immediately.

Even as Marcus heard the words and tried to process the severity of his partner's wounds, he was racing toward al-Qassab. When he reached the Syrian, he aimed his automatic rifle at the man's head and kicked the guy's weapon out of reach. Behind him he could hear the Israeli commandos coming up fast. When they arrived, he held up a hand and ordered them to back off and give him space to operate. Then he tossed his own M4 to the closest soldier and told another to grab the Uzi.

With the immediate environment secure, Marcus speed-dialed the war room and let Roseboro know al-Qassab was wounded and in custody.

"Is he talking?" Roseboro asked.

"He will," Marcus replied. "Where's POTUS?"

"They're all at the church."

"Did they hear the gunfire?"

"The principals didn't, but the agents posted outside did."

"What about the press?"

"I don't think so. Everyone covering the church visit is deep inside the cathedral at the moment."

"All right. I'll call you back the moment I have something."

"Great work, Ryker—really."

"Don't jinx it, Carl. We're not out of this thing yet."

The Grand Mufti's assistant, breathless and pale, returned to the office.

The staff was still glued to the continuing live coverage of the most powerful Muslim in the world, a hajji from Mecca, walking through a church building that not a single one of them had ever been to or even considered going to, although the historic site was close to where they were sitting now. Indeed, the group was so captivated by the unfolding drama, no one noticed their colleague slipping back into the room.

"Well?" al-Azzam asked in a whisper.

"The Secret Service said he left," his secretary said quietly.

"What do you mean, *left*?"

"Departed the plaza, left the premises—gone," she said.

"That's impossible. He's supposed to be running the whole event."

"That's what I said. But apparently he told one of the agents that his wife was having an emergency, and he had to go. He said you were in charge, and he'd call you on a landline the moment he got the chance. The agent gave me this."

From her purse, she pulled out a lanyard. The Grand Mufti took it in his hands and stared at the printed name under the plastic. Sure enough, it read, *Dr. Hussam Mashrawi, Executive Director—VIP / ALL-ACCESS PASS.*

Al-Azzam's face grew pale. "Get Yasmine on the phone," he whispered.

The assistant obeyed immediately. She picked up the landline and dialed the Mashrawis' home number by heart. After ten rings, she shook her head and hung up.

"Try her mobile."

Again the assistant picked up the receiver and dialed from memory. This time Yasmine answered on the second ring.

"Hello, Mrs. Mashrawi, I have your father on the line."

The Grand Mufti breathed a sigh of relief and took the receiver. "Sweetheart, is everything okay?"

"Yes, of course," she replied.

"Are you at home?"

"No, with some neighbors."

"Doing what?"

"Watching the coverage, what else?"

"Is Hussam with you?"

"No, why would he be?" she said. "Isn't he with you? Your big moment is coming up. I'm so excited to see it."

"Has Hussam called you today?"

"No."

"Texted you?"

"No, he had to leave his phone at home. Didn't you all?"

Al-Azzam ignored the question. "When was the last time you saw or spoke with him?"

"This morning, just before he left for the mosque. Why?"

"No reason, I suppose. Just a misunderstanding."

"What kind of misunderstanding?"

"The kind that happens when we don't have our mobile phones. Don't you worry. I love you, but I'm very busy, and I have to go now."

"Okay, Father—I love you, too."

Al-Azzam hung up the phone. He could see in his assistant's eyes that she was desperate to know what was going on, but he didn't know himself. He motioned for her to join the rest of the group; then he turned and looked out the window.

Something was wrong. Very wrong. And the old man suddenly feared he knew what.

107

Marcus hung up the phone and slid it into his back pocket.

A medic with Mishmar Hagvul offered to give the Syrian sedatives. But Marcus shook his head. Relieving this man's pain was not the way to make him talk. Instead, Marcus walked over and drove his left boot down on al-Qassab's right shoulder. For a moment, the man went rigid and made not a sound. But only for a moment. Then he unleashed a shriek that didn't seem human.

"Good morning, Mohammed," Marcus said, pressing down even harder.

"*You're making a mistake!*" the man screamed at the top of his lungs—in Hebrew, no less. "*I'm Jewish. I'm an Israeli!*"

The commander of the Border Patrol translated the lines for Marcus, then laughed out loud. "This man is not Jewish, and he's certainly not an Israeli."

"But I am, I am," al-Qassab now said in English but with an Israeli accent.

The commander scoffed. "Agent Ryker, I grew up in this country. I've been with the Border Patrol for more than twenty-five years. This man may know Hebrew, but he is an Arab, not a Jew."

"Well, I guess there's a simple way to find out," said Marcus. "Strip him."

The commander's eyes went wide, as did those of the writhing prisoner.

"Strip him now, and we'll know for sure."

The commander shrugged when he saw where this was going. He waved over his deputy and several other men. In the end, it actually took six Israelis to keep al-Qassab pinned down. But they stripped him, all right, until he was completely naked. When they saw that he was not circumcised, they had their answer. This was no Jew. But Marcus was relieved for a far different reason. There were no signs on al-Qassab's stomach or chest that he had recently undergone surgery. That meant he wasn't about to blow up. But it also meant there was still someone out there who was.

"Search the pockets," Marcus ordered the commander, pointing to al-Qassab's pants, "and put this man in cuffs, both hands and feet."

When the commandos found the mobile phone, Marcus nodded to it, and one of the soldiers handed it to him.

"Listen," Marcus told his prisoner, "we know you're Mohammed al-Qassab. We know you're Kairos. We know you entered the country last Friday, just after 3 p.m., on a direct flight from London. We found your safe house on the Mount of Olives. I was there. I saw the body of Ali Haqqani. I saw what you did to him and to the dentist, Daoud Husseini, and to his assistants and the paramedic."

A look of shock flashed across the man's face.

"That's right, Mohammed—I know exactly what you've been up to," Marcus continued as the winds began to pick up and al-Qassab shivered in the cold. "You ordered Haqqani to do surgery on your *shahid*, to plant a bomb in his chest and sew him back up. And then you didn't need the good doctor anymore, so you wasted him."

Marcus squatted down until he was inches from the Syrian's tormented face.

"Now I want you to listen very closely, because I'm only going to say this one time. Do you understand me? I'm going to give you one chance to tell me the truth. If you tell me what I need to know, we'll put a blanket over you and give you some morphine for the pain and put you in a warm car and take you someplace where we can chat further in a calm and civilized manner."

Marcus paused for effect, then lowered his voice as he continued.

"However—and this is the important part, Mohammed—if you refuse to answer my next three questions, or if I believe you're not telling me the truth, then I'm going to forget about your shoulder. I'm never going to give you morphine. Instead, I'm going to put a bullet through your right kneecap. If you still won't talk to me, I'll put a bullet through your left kneecap. And then we'll reassess how we're doing. Got it?"

Al-Qassab had stopped screaming. He was fighting to maintain some last shred of dignity, but time was not on his side, and despite the defiance in his eyes, he knew it.

"Question number one," Marcus said. "How many people here in Israel have a body cavity bomb surgically inserted into some part of their body?"

He waited a few seconds, then proceeded.

"Question two—what are the names and exact locations of each of the bombers at this moment?"

Again, Marcus paused for a few seconds.

"Question three—how do we override the system and prevent the bombs from exploding?"

For an instant, Marcus thought the man was actually going to answer him. Al-Qassab looked away, staring up at the sky and then down at the roof they were on. Then he looked up with vengeance and spat in Marcus's face.

Marcus instinctively recoiled, then calmly wiped away the bloody saliva with his sleeve. "Wrong answer, Mohammed."

He stood, drew the Sig Sauer from his shoulder holster, and wedged his foot beneath al-Qassab's bloody shoulder. Leaning back and lifting his leg, he forced the man over onto his stomach. Then, as the Israeli commandos looked on in shock, Marcus leaned down, put the barrel of the pistol behind al-Qassab's right knee, and squeezed the trigger.

A descending Black Hawk helicopter drowned out the shot.

And the scream.

There was no clear place to land, and Marcus doubted the roof of the adjacent apartment could withstand the chopper's weight. Instead, it hovered about thirty feet above the roof. Two ropes dropped from the open side door. Two medics fast-roped down to the roof, and the soldiers still in the bird lowered a stretcher to them.

Marcus watched as the medics checked Kailea's vital signs. He saw them give her an injection of something and hook her up to an IV. They carefully lifted her onto the stretcher and strapped her in. Soon the soldiers in the chopper were hoisting her up and bringing her on board. The two medics were hoisted back up as well, and they were gone.

Al-Qassab was still screaming. Marcus was about to reengage him, but his phone rang.

"Ryker—go."

"Agent Ryker?" said the muffled voice at the other end, barely above a whisper.

"Who is this?" Marcus asked, not recognizing the number on the caller ID.

"Agent Ryker, this is Amin al-Azzam."

"Your Excellency?"

"Yes, yes, I need to speak with you."

"Well, I apologize, but this is not a good time. Can you call back in a few—?"

But the old man cut him off in midsentence. "No, you don't understand, Agent Ryker. This is a matter of the utmost urgency."

"So is this, Your Excellency. Really, I will call you back—"

But again al-Azzam cut him off. "My son-in-law is missing."

"Dr. Mashrawi?"

"Yes."

"What do you mean, missing?"

"He cleared through security early this morning. But no one has seen him for the last few hours, and we haven't been able to find him. I've sent my people throughout the grounds, but there's no sign of him. Now one of your agents says he's left."

None of this was making sense, and al-Qassab would not shut up. Marcus checked his watch, motioned for the commander to watch the prisoner, then pressed the phone to his ear, plugged the other ear with his finger, and walked away fifty feet or so to try to hear better. "Left?" he asked. "Left where?"

"Left the grounds, into the Old City. My aide just handed me Hussam's security lanyard. She says Hussam told one of your agents he had to attend to an emergency with his wife."

"Your daughter?"

"Exactly."

"What's wrong with her?"

"That's just the thing, Agent Ryker. I called Yasmine. She's fine. She's at a neighbor's, watching the coverage of today's events. She says she hasn't seen or heard from Hussam since he left for work, early this morning."

Again Marcus glanced at his watch. In his earpiece, he could hear the traffic picking up. POTUS and his colleagues were wrapping up their visit to the church. They were preparing to move to the Temple Mount. Marcus still had an enemy combatant to interrogate, and time was running out.

"Look, Your Excellency, with all due respect, I don't have time for a game of hide-and-seek. The entourage is leaving the Church of the Holy Sepulcher right now. They should be to your location in ten minutes. Now . . ."

"Agent Ryker, listen to me," the Grand Mufti nearly shouted through the phone. *"Hussam is not only missing. I believe he may be the bomber you're look-ing for."*

109

The hair on the back of Marcus's neck stood erect.

"How do you know we're looking for a bomber?" he asked, so completely unprepared for, and chilled by, what the man had just said.

"Come now, Agent Ryker, your agents have been up here for days. I hear what they talk about, no matter the hushed tones. I know what happened in London and in your own capital. I know what Kairos has threatened, and I see the extraordinary lengths you all are going to in order to make this summit secure."

"Then why help us?"

"I promised you I would."

"But your entire life has been spent resisting the so-called Israeli 'occupation' of your land and the 'oppression' of your people."

"Never violently—not ever and not now. I am a devout Muslim and a fiercely loyal Palestinian, Mr. Ryker. I want justice for my people. I have never hidden that objective from you or from anyone. But with everything in my soul I oppose the use of violence to achieve my goals."

"So just to be clear, you're accusing your own son-in-law of working for Kairos?"

"It's not an accusation; it's a dread fear."

"Because he's stepped into a prayer closet and you haven't seen him for a while?"

"No, no, of course not—*listen to me, Agent Ryker. You must listen.*"

"I am listening, Your Excellency, but you have to make it fast."

"Remember last Wednesday? Hussam went to the dentist to have a root canal."

"So what?"

"Maybe he did have a root canal. Maybe he didn't. I don't know. But I know he had surgery that day that was far more extensive than he let on."

"Go on."

"He didn't come to work that day or Thursday or Friday. I went to visit him twice. Yasmine was beside herself. Hussam was on very strong pain-killers. He would try to sleep but wake up screaming, take more medicine, then pass out. It went on like this for days. When he finally came back to work on Saturday, he could barely walk, barely stand. I finally sent him home. But all this for a root canal and the extraction of a wisdom tooth? No. I've had my share of root canals and other dental work, but I've never experienced anything like that. Daoud is highly competent. And Hussam is in excellent physical condition. He isn't typically affected by pain. He barely takes aspirin, even for a headache. I'm telling you, Agent Ryker—this wasn't dental surgery. Hussam had major surgery of another kind on Wednesday, and I fear he is planning something terrible."

"Wait, wait," said Marcus. "Who did you just say?"

"I said I fear Hussam is planning something terrible."

"No—before that. You mentioned a name."

"Daoud?"

"Right, and the last name?"

"Husseini."

"The dentist?"

"Yes, he's our family dentist, and I'm telling you, there's no way he . . ."

The Grand Mufti kept talking, but Marcus no longer could hear him. He had not even considered a connection between Hussam Mashrawi and Daoud Husseini. But that's whose clinic he'd just been in. That's whose apartment on the Mount of Olives Haqqani and al-Qassab had been staying in. That was the man he'd found shot to death in the break room just minutes before.

"Listen to me very carefully," Marcus said, interrupting the Grand Mufti. "I need you to order every single one of your staff off the Haram al-Sharif immediately. No one stays behind but you. No exceptions. Do you understand?"

"Yes, but—"

"No—there's no time to argue or discuss this," Marcus told him. "Is your staff gathered with you now?"

"Yes, well, in my office. I'm in Hussam's office down the hall."

"Okay, I'm going to call the special agent in charge, and he's going to facilitate the evacuation of everyone up there. But I want you to stay in your office and near your landline. I'll have some agents stay with you. Inside as well as out in the hall in front of your door. Do you understand?"

"Yes."

"Don't tell anyone on your staff what is happening or why. Not a soul. We don't know who else may be in on this, but we have to move quickly."

"Yes, yes, I'm with you—I just pray to Allah that I am wrong."

Marcus was praying too, but he was quite certain the Grand Mufti was right.

110

Marcus speed-dialed the war room.

The director of the White House advance team answered.

"Joe, I need Carl."

"He stepped out."

"Where?"

"I don't know. He said he'd be right back. Want me to reach him on his cell?"

"No, no, I'll do it," Marcus replied. "But listen—we've got a situation developing."

"Yeah, we just heard you nabbed al-Qassab. That's fantastic."

"Maybe not—where's POTUS at this exact moment?"

"Heading to the Temple Mount. They're almost there now. Why?"

"We have reason to believe there may be a suicide bomber up there. I'm still trying to get more details, but we can't take any chances. You need to get your people off the site as quickly and quietly as you can."

"That's Carl's call, not mine."

"And I'm sure Carl will make it, but we don't have time to wait. And while you're at it, cut the live video feed—make it seem like a technical problem and tell the media your guys are working on it and should have it fixed in no time. You got that?"

"I do, but you don't really have the authority to—"

Marcus hung up and speed-dialed Roseboro's mobile phone. Again he got no answer, so he called Geoff Stone, who answered immediately.

"Geoff, are you with the secretary?"

"Yeah."

"And POTUS?"

"And the PM and the king—why?"

"Where are you?"

"We're just entering the Temple Mount now."

"Okay, look, Geoff, you need to get the principals into the secure holding room as quickly as possible, and you need to keep them there and harden up the detail. No one comes in or out until you hear from me or Carl. And I mean no one. You got it?"

"Why? What's going on?"

"Dr. Hussam Mashrawi may be the bomber."

"The executive director of the Waqf? That's impossible."

"That's what I would have said, but his own father-in-law is accusing him."

"The Grand Mufti?"

"Crazy, I know."

"How do you know it's not a ruse?" Geoff asked.

"I don't—not yet—and that's why I don't want POTUS or the other principals anywhere near the Grand Mufti or Mashrawi until we can figure this thing out. In the meantime, brief the detail leaders but not the principals. Get them in the holding area, lock them down, and put your best guys in front of the door. I'm going to send you a photo of Mashrawi right now. Forward it to all the agents. If he's spotted, he must be ordered to stop, strip to the waist, and lie down on his back, faceup. If he fails to comply in any way, shoot to kill. But under no circumstances get anywhere near him."

"Understood," said Geoff.

"All right, get to it." Marcus ended the call and speed-dialed Roseboro again. But there was still no answer.

Yasmine was watching live coverage of the arrival on the Haram al-Sharif.

Suddenly the screen went black.

A moment later, all she and her hosts could see was a test pattern. The shoemaker cursed and grabbed the remote. He began flipping through one news channel after another—first the Arabic ones, then those in Hebrew, and finally the European and American news networks. When he realized that all of them were showing the same test pattern, he switched back to the Al-Sawt channel. The anchors in Doha were apologizing for a glitch in the feed and promising to get it fixed as quickly as possible. In the meantime, they turned for comment to two Qatari political analysts on the set with them, both of whom began blasting the Saudi monarch for "betraying the Palestinian cause" and "defiling Islam" by trying to "normalize relations with the criminal colonialists occupying Palestine."

Peter Hwang picked up the receiver and hit line four.

"Ops center, Hwang."

"Pete, it's me," said Marcus from half a world away.

"Marcus, you okay?"

"Yeah, I'm fine. It's Kailea I'm worried about."

"The chopper just landed at Hadassah," Pete said, referring to Israel's premier hospital on the west side of the capital. "They're wheeling her into surgery as we speak. She was shot in the leg, and the bullet tore the femoral artery. Lost a lot of blood. They think they got her there in time, but we'll know more in a few hours."

"Good—now, look, Pete, I need you to do me a favor."

"Of course, whatever you need."

"I'm going to hang up the phone now. But in two minutes, I need you to call me back. Okay?"

"Sure, but why?"

"You'll understand then, but right now I've got to go."

111

Marcus shoved the phone in his pocket and ran back to al-Qassab.

He found Tomer Ben Ami standing over the Syrian. Blood was pouring from al-Qassab's knee, and no one had given him any medical attention because Tomer had ordered them not to. He knew what Marcus was trying to do, and he approved.

Al-Qassab had stopped screaming. Gritting his teeth and writhing in agony, he was nevertheless trying his best not to make a sound. But he gasped as he saw Marcus approaching and drawing his pistol.

"All right, Mohammed, you ready to try this again?"

The Syrian said nothing and turned his head, refusing to look Marcus in the eye.

"How many of your operatives have a body cavity bomb surgically inserted into them here in Israel?" This time Marcus chose not to pause between questions. "What are the names and exact locations of each of the bombers at this very moment? How can we prevent the bombs from exploding?"

Marcus chambered a round. The sound of him doing so turned al-Qassab's head. Marcus raised his eyebrows.

"I'm waiting," he said.

But the Syrian did not reply.

"Fine, Mohammed—just don't say you weren't warned."

Marcus again pressed his boot on the man's bleeding shoulder and pressed down until he convulsed in pain. Then Marcus kicked the man in the ribs and tried to roll him over, but this time al-Qassab refused to budge. Marcus looked at Tomer, and Tomer ordered the commandos to roll the naked man onto his stomach. The moment they did, Marcus pressed the barrel against al-Qassab's left knee.

"Last chance, Mohammed," Marcus said.

"Okay, okay, I'll talk," the man suddenly growled. "There's only one bomber."

"Man or woman?"

"A man."

"Where is he?" Marcus demanded.

The Syrian said nothing, so Marcus pushed the barrel deeper into the back of the man's knee.

"I don't know," al-Qassab said. "I gave him three options where he could strike. I don't know where he is right now."

"What's his name?"

"I don't know that either."

"You really want this bullet?"

"It's true, I swear; it's true—he was recruited in Jenin and trained by one of our operatives on the West Bank. I only met him when the Pakistani performed the surgery on him. But I wasn't told his name, and I didn't ask."

Marcus was skeptical, but with the clock running, he moved on.

"How can we override the system?" Marcus asked.

"You can't," the Syrian replied.

"There's no way to defuse the bomb?"

"Once it's been implanted, it cannot be deactivated. It cannot even be removed from the *shahid*—if someone tries, it will go off."

"Then how can we stop him?"

The Syrian said nothing, so Marcus stood upright and slammed his boot down on the man's shoulder once again. This time al-Qassab could not stop himself. He cried out loudly, and Marcus pressed down even harder.

"You can't," the man cried. "You can't stop him."

"But *you* can, right?"

Nothing.

"*Right?*" Marcus asked again, applying still more pressure to the shoulder wound.

"Yes, yes, I can—*only* I can," the man gasped.

"How?"

"How what?"

"How can you reach him?"

There was a long pause.

"Forget it, Mohammed. I have no time to play games with you," Marcus yelled.

Then he bent down and shoved the Sig Sauer into the back of the man's left knee again. Before he could fire, however, the man blurted out the answer.

"*The phone,*" he yelled. "*The one you took from me—the man entered his own mobile number in my speed-dial system. Call him, and I will tell him to stand down.*"

"What's the number?" Marcus said, turning back to al-Qassab.

"I told you it's on speed dial—I don't know the actual number."

"Fine, what's the speed-dial number?"

"*Five,*" said the Syrian. "*Call him, and I'll tell him to stand down—I promise. Just give me morphine and make the pain stop.*"

112

Marcus looked at al-Qassab's phone.

He stared at the number five key. But just then his own phone rang. Marcus removed the gun from the back of the Syrian's knee, stood, pulled his own phone from his pocket, and took the call.

"Hey," Marcus said, turning to look at the Dome of the Rock.

"It's me," said Pete. "What do you need?"

But Marcus didn't respond to Pete directly. "Really, just now?" he said instead, loud enough that the Syrian and Tomer and all the commandos could hear him. "Where?" He paused, then added, "What did he say?"

Again Marcus paused, pretending he was listening while actually paying no attention to Pete's confused questions.

"Okay," he said finally. "Keep him isolated. If he tries to move toward you, shoot to kill. Got it? Good. I'll be there in five minutes."

Marcus hung up and shoved his phone back in his pocket. Then he knelt down again and looked into al-Qassab's frantic, bewildered eyes.

"Game's up, Mohammed—Israeli forces just stopped your pal Hussam

Mashrawi," Marcus said. "He was walking across the plaza on the Temple Mount, toward the holding room where he was to greet the president, the prime minister, and the king. Fortunately the soldiers noticed he was limping and perspiring, even in this cold. So they stopped him and forced him to strip down, and guess what they found, Mohammed? They found a bloody bandage taped to his chest. And under that, a six-inch scar. And once they told him we had you and your phone in custody, Mashrawi began crying—sobbing like a little girl. He confessed to everything, Mohammed, and he laid all the blame on you. Said he'd had to leave his own phone at home because of the last-minute security protocols. But he said you had the other phone, and all you had to do was press speed-dial number five."

Al-Qassab stopped struggling, stopped trying to get away, and all the color drained from his face. "I don't believe you," he said after a long silence.

"I couldn't care less what you believe, Mohammed," Marcus replied, standing again. "It's over. Your boy's in custody, and he's talking—talking up a storm—about everyone and everything he knows about Kairos. And by the way, he's begging the Israelis to remove the bomb from him."

Suddenly al-Qassab let loose with a torrent of profanity that caused Marcus to actually take a step back from the man. His face was dark red, almost crimson, and he was screaming at the top of his lungs like a man possessed. Marcus didn't understand a word he was saying. It was all in Arabic.

Tomer translated some of it. "He says he knew Mashrawi was a coward. He says he was always against choosing him, that he told Abu Nakba that Mashrawi was not really one of them, that he never should have been trusted for a mission as important as this, that the man never truly believed in jihad, that Mashrawi is a liar and a traitor and a *kafir*."

"A *kafir*?" Marcus asked.

"An infidel," said Tomer.

Marcus turned, looked al-Qassab in the eye, and smiled.

"*Why?*" the Syrian roared in English. "*Why are you smiling?*"

Marcus shook his head. "Because until this moment, Mohammed, I didn't know for sure whether Hussam Mashrawi was really your bomber. And we don't have him yet. But I guarantee you we will."

113

Marcus's personal phone rang again.

It was Roseboro.

Carl explained that he'd been in a SCIF—a sensitive compartmented information facility—updating the director of the Secret Service back in Washington on the latest developments. Marcus quickly filled his colleague in on the latest and told him about the order he'd given Geoff Stone to evacuate the Temple Mount.

"I heard about that," Roseboro said. "But there are two problems."

"What problems?"

"POTUS and the PM. They were furious at the idea of an evacuation and countermanded the order."

"You're not serious."

"One of the agents told POTUS that Hussam Mashrawi might be the bomber but that Mashrawi hadn't been seen in hours and might, in fact, have departed the Temple Mount," Roseboro said. "When POTUS heard that and relayed it to the PM and the king, all three men said they wanted to proceed. Secretary Whitney cautioned against it, saying they should at least wait in the holding room until the situation became clearer."

"Did they listen to her?"

"So far."

"Thank God," said Marcus. "That may be the only reason they're all still alive."

"Where are you now?" Roseboro asked.

"On a rooftop in the Muslim Quarter."

"What's being done with al-Qassab?"

"Tomer and I are going to take him into custody. I'll keep interrogating him and see what more I can get."

"No, that can wait—have Tomer bring you here. I want you to brief the president on what you've learned and just how dangerous the situation really is."

Marcus agreed, and soon he and Tomer had turned custody of al-Qassab over to the Mishmar Hagvul commandos and were racing across the rooftops to the two aluminum ladders the commandos had used. The two men quickly scrambled down and sprinted through the *shuk*, then through another labyrinth of alleyways until they reached a now even more heavily fortified checkpoint onto the Temple Mount.

They showed their IDs and explained what was happening, but that wasn't enough to allow them to enter. The commander of this checkpoint explained that he'd been given strict orders to allow no one in or out of the Temple Mount.

Marcus was furious at the thought that he was being blocked by his own order. Pulling out his phone, he speed-dialed Roseboro, explained the delay, and handed the phone to the commander. Still, the commander refused to budge.

Tomer lit into him in Hebrew, but the commander only dug in his heels. So Tomer pulled out his own phone and dialed the personal number of Asher Gilad, director of the Mossad. Tomer spoke in rapid-fire Hebrew, then a moment later hung up and called another number. This time, he spoke more slowly, though still in Hebrew. The conversation lasted for almost a minute. Then Tomer handed the phone to the commander, and fifteen seconds later, the commander ordered his men to stand back and let Marcus and Tomer pass.

"Who was that?" Marcus asked as they cleared through the stone archway and enormous green wooden doors and stepped onto the Temple Mount together. "Who did that soldier just talk to?"

"His prime minister."

Ahmet Mustafa ordered all of his senior advisors out of his office.

The moment they were gone, the Turkish president went to his wall safe, unlocked it, removed the satellite phone that Hamdi Yaşar had given him months before, and called the Al-Sawt producer in Doha.

Yaşar answered on the fourth ring.

"What is going on?" Mustafa demanded. "Why can't I see what is happening on the Haram al-Sharif?"

"I don't know," Yaşar replied. "My guys say it was not them."

"Was the feed cut? Did Israelis cut it? Why?"

"I said I don't know," Yaşar repeated, the tension thick in his voice. "Look, I've got to go. I'll call you when I know more."

"Where are you going?" Tomer asked. "The holding room is this way."

"I'm not going to the holding room," Marcus replied, heading the opposite direction down the colonnade. "Not yet."

"Then where?"

"To see the Grand Mufti."

Tomer caught up with him just as Marcus burst past two Secret Service agents into the front doors of the administrative offices of the Waqf and headed down the hall toward a dozen more heavily armed U.S., Israeli, and Saudi security men. When he got to the door of the office, he did not stop to knock but entered without warning.

114

Startled by the sudden intrusion, Amin al-Azzam rose abruptly to his feet.

"Put him in handcuffs, now," Marcus ordered.

Confused by the unprecedented demand, none of the six IDF soldiers standing guard moved. Tomer repeated the order in Hebrew. Only then did the commander of the squad order his men to comply.

"What is the meaning of this?" the Grand Mufti complained.

"Strip him," Marcus ordered. *"You heard me. Do it. Quickly."*

The soldiers and the two DSS agents standing post in the room were wide-eyed. But again, Tomer repeated the order in Hebrew.

"This is outrageous," the Grand Mufti shouted. *"Get your hands off me. I demand to—"*

But Marcus cut him off. "Your Excellency, you've accused your own son-in-law of being a suicide bomber. Yet by all indications, Dr. Mashrawi left the Temple Mount hours ago. How do we know you're telling the truth? I have to be sure you're not a threat."

At this, al-Azzam stopped resisting, though he turned his head away from Marcus and the others as the soldiers followed their orders. Marcus hated having to do this but was relieved when there was no evidence that the Grand Mufti had recently had surgery of any kind.

"Okay," he said softly. "Get him dressed again. Let's go. *Move.*"

A minute later, the cleric was back in his robes.

Marcus looked him in the eye. "I'm sorry," he said. "We had to know for sure."

Al-Azzam said nothing.

"He hasn't called?" Marcus asked.

Al-Azzam shook his head.

"And you still have no idea where he is?"

"Wouldn't I tell you if I did?"

"That's not an answer, sir."

Al-Azzam glared at Marcus, but Marcus stood his ground. He was genuinely sorry that such measures had to be taken. But the situation was extraordinary. There had been no other option, and both men knew it.

"No," al-Azzam finally replied. "I don't."

"Fine," Marcus said, turning to the two DSS agents. "Keep him comfortable, but keep him away from the phone—you guys answer any calls that come in—and he doesn't leave this room or see anyone else unless you hear from Tomer or me."

The agents nodded. Tomer signaled the Israelis to lower their weapons, which they did. Then Tomer followed Marcus out of the office, back down the hall, and across the plaza as Marcus explained his plan.

Even before they reached the holding room, they were met by two dozen Israeli commandos guarding the perimeter. The commander checked their IDs, then radioed their presence up the chain of command. It took two full minutes—time they did not have—but finally both men were allowed to proceed.

115

President Clarke stood up when the two men entered the room.

He looked furious.

"Agent Ryker, what the hell is going on here? The world is watching this delay, and it's undermining the entire point of this peace summit."

"I understand, Mr. President, and I'm sorry it had to be done," Marcus said. "But it's time to proceed."

"What do you mean?"

"We're ready for the three of you and Secretary Whitney to tour the complex, take the photo, and make your remarks," Marcus said. "And afterward, of course, we will take His Majesty to the mosque so he can have some time alone to pray."

The holding room was silent. Besides Marcus and Tomer, only eleven other people were present—POTUS and the head of his Secret Service detail; the Israeli prime minister and his bodyguard; King Faisal, the head of the Royal Guards, and his intelligence chief, Prince Abdullah; Secretary Whitney and Agent Geoff Stone; and Senator Dayton and Annie Stewart.

Suddenly the senator spoke up.

"Marcus, you know I have the highest respect for you, but I'm confused," Dayton began. "I share the president's frustration, and I want this summit to proceed and to succeed as much as everyone in this room. But if you tell us it's not safe out there, then I'll believe you. Don't tell us what we want to hear. Tell us the truth."

"Yes, Agent Ryker, tell us the truth," Prince Abdullah added. "What is really going on out there?"

Marcus looked at Clarke, who nodded his consent.

"Very well," Marcus began. "Ali Haqqani is dead. Mohammed al-Qassab is wounded but in custody. We've just confirmed the Grand Mufti is not the bomber and poses no threat. And we're now convinced that Hussam Mashrawi *is* the bomber. We're also certain that you all are the target and that Mashrawi intends to rush you and detonate himself the moment you all appear together at the photo op with the Grand Mufti in front of the Dome of the Rock. The problem is, at this moment, we don't know where Mashrawi is. Personally, I believe he's still here, somewhere on the Mount."

"That's impossible," said Prime Minister Eitan. "Our people—and yours—have been over every square meter of this place and there has been no sign of him."

Marcus was about to reply, but Tomer spoke first.

"With respect, sir, no one knows this place better than Hussam Mashrawi. I believe Agent Ryker is correct. Mashrawi is here, somewhere, lying in wait."

"Then why in the world would you send us out there?" the president asked.

"To flush him out, sir," Marcus replied.

"I'm sorry?" Clarke said in disbelief.

"Sir, you're insistent on doing the photo op," Marcus explained. "That's your prerogative. So let's go do it. If I'm wrong and Hussam is not here, then there's nothing to fear. The summit will proceed apace."

"But what if you're right?" asked Secretary of State Whitney.

"Then we'll stop him before he can get close to any of you, and I assure you, we'll take him out."

For several moments, the holding room was silent again.

Then Clarke said, "Agent Ryker, would you give us a minute?"

"Of course, sir."

Marcus and Tomer turned and stepped out of the room. As they did, Marcus called the war room and briefed Roseboro.

"Yeah, I heard the whole thing," the deputy director replied.

"How?"

"Agent Stone switched on his radio the moment you walked into the holding room. I heard every word. Everyone in the war room did. You're insane. You know that, right?"

"Have you got a better option, Carl?"

"No," Roseboro said. "As a matter of fact, I don't."

116

Annie Stewart watched in fascination as the principals discussed Marcus's plan.

To her astonishment, the one most in favor was the Saudi monarch.

"Mr. President, like I told you, we absolutely must not let ourselves be intimidated by the jihadists," King Faisal told Clarke. "Too much is at stake, and we must all rise to the challenge. Agent Ryker is correct. It is time for all of us to go outside with courage and determination. We will meet the Grand Mufti. We will shake his hand. We will take the photo in front of the Dome of the Rock. We will give our remarks. And in so doing we will show the entire world that with the able assistance of the American people and government, the Kingdom of Saudi Arabia and the State of Israel can and will make peace. We can do what all the naysayers think is impossible. We can set a powerful example for the rest of the Arab world, including the Palestinians, and there is no force on the face of this earth that can stop us."

The Israeli prime minister nodded quietly and offered his hand to the king. The Saudi looked surprised at first, but only for a moment; then he took Eitan's hand and shook it firmly.

"His Majesty is absolutely right," Eitan affirmed. "I have full confidence in our combined security forces, and I can't think of a better way to send a message of peace and regional cooperation to the world than if we go out together right now, or a worse message to send than if we remained in this holding room for a minute longer."

Clarke broke out into a broad smile and slapped both men on the back. "I couldn't agree more," he said. "Let's do this thing."

Secretary Whitney did not look happy, Annie noticed. Even Senator Dayton looked skeptical. But the decision had already been made. Word was radioed to Ryker and Tomer Ben Ami, who were standing outside in the colonnade, surrounded by dozens of agents and special forces operatives, that the principals were ready to proceed. Ryker radioed back that he just needed a moment to brief all the forces on the plaza on the exact plan and the precise rules of engagement.

"Get ready to switch the video feed back on," Marcus told Roseboro by radio.

As he walked outside, scanning for Mashrawi, Marcus could hear Roseboro relaying the message to the control room—a satellite TV truck parked just inside St. Stephen's Gate to the Old City, also known as Lions' Gate.

When they reached the Dome of the Rock, Marcus asked a staffer from the White House advance team for a roll of duct tape. Then he counted off thirty yards from the front door of the dome, ripped off two long pieces of tape, and created an X on the stone plaza. Shifting rightward, he did it again and again until there were eight Xs marked in equidistant intervals around the octagonal building.

As Marcus did this, Tomer repositioned Secret Service and Shin Bet agents and Saudi Royal Guards, backing most of them far away from the Dome. At Marcus's insistence, Tomer placed no agents in the corridor between the entrance to the Dome of the Rock and the risers where three remotely controlled broadcast television cameras stood on tripods. Marcus wanted nothing to obstruct the TV cameras' view. He also wanted to lure Mashrawi out into the open.

Then Marcus ordered each pair of sharpshooters and spotters to fixate on one of the eight gates that provided access to the plaza in front of the Dome of the Rock. He ordered an additional team of sharpshooters to keep a close eye on the front doors to the Al-Aqsa Mosque. Two final teams were to play free safety, as it were, watching for anything the others might miss.

From their vantage points on the roofs of the mosque, the administrative offices, and various other buildings, the shooters and spotters could plainly see the duct-tape Xs. Over his wrist-mounted radio, Marcus told them that if Mashrawi appeared, they were not to shoot him unless given a direct order by himself or Tomer or unless Mashrawi began rushing the principals and crossed the perimeter marked by the Xs. Marcus required each man to verbally acknowledge that he had both heard and would comply with these new rules of engagement. They all did.

Marcus then asked several Saudi agents—all Muslims—to enter the Noble Sanctuary and guard the entrance from the inside, just in case Mashrawi had hidden himself indoors. Finally, Tomer radioed the guards at each of the eight entrances—inside and outside—to leave their posts and reassemble under the colonnade by the administrative offices. This effectively left all the gates open to Mashrawi. It was an enormous risk, but Tomer and Roseboro had reluctantly agreed to it.

Once this was done, Marcus took one last look around the plaza.

"We good?" he asked.

"I can't think of anything else," said Tomer.

"Then let's go—it's showtime."

117

Marcus walked to the door of the dome and stood to its right.

Tomer took up his post to the left of the door.

This gave them a 180-degree view of everything in front of the entrance, including the risers and the cameras. Everything behind the dome was being covered by snipers and other agents.

"Carl, restart the live video feed," Marcus said into his wrist-mounted radio.

Ten seconds later, Roseboro radioed back to say it had been done. "Smile, Marcus," he said. "You're being broadcast to the entire world."

Marcus did not smile. Through his Ray-Ban sunglasses, he tensed, waiting for Mashrawi to emerge, even as the White House press secretary stepped up to the bulletproof podium positioned in front of the magnificent gold dome and spoke into the bank of microphones.

"Ladies and gentlemen, the president of the United States, Andrew Clarke, and his esteemed partners for peace, the prime minister of the State of Israel, Reuven Eitan, and His Majesty, King Faisal Mohammed Al Saud of the Kingdom of Saudi Arabia."

The several dozen staffers who had not, in the end, been ordered to evacuate applauded loudly from somewhere off to Marcus's left, near the Al-Aqsa Mosque.

"They are joined by His Excellency, the Grand Mufti of Jerusalem, Amin al-Azzam; the U.S. secretary of state, Margaret Whitney; and the senior United States senator from the state of Iowa, Robert Dayton."

"Start the music," the director of the White House advance team said over the radio.

A moment later, a band and honor guard comprised of U.S., Israeli, and Saudi military musicians entered the plaza and began to play the Saudi national anthem.

From his right, Marcus could now see the six principals emerging from their holding room, strolling down the colonnade and smiling and waving to their staff and to the cameras as they approached their positions. Marcus, however, ignored them all. He was certain Mashrawi was coming. But when? And from which direction?

"Hatikvah," the Israeli national anthem, was the next to play, followed by "The Star-Spangled Banner." As the anthems played, each leader took his or her assigned spot behind the podium. Their bodyguards stepped aside, three to the right and three to the left, out of the view of the cameras and careful not to obscure Marcus's or Tomer's views.

President Clarke strode to the podium, cleared his throat, and spoke first. His remarks were brief. Two minutes, if that. He heralded the historic nature of the day, thanked the Israelis for hosting the peace summit and the Saudi king for his "courageous decision" to come and "break ancient taboos" and pursue a "new birth of peace and freedom" for Arabs and Jews and "all the people of the Middle East."

Prime Minister Eitan was next. Given the extremely sensitive nature of an Israeli Jewish prime minister speaking on the Temple Mount at all, much less in front of one of the most revered sites in all of Islam, he wisely kept his remarks even more brief. He simply thanked the president and the king for their "bold pursuit of peace" and welcomed both to "the Holy City," noting that "nowhere on earth are religious freedom and tolerance more revered or enjoyed than here in Jerusalem, beloved to followers of our three great monotheistic faiths."

King Faisal Mohammed spoke last. He stooped as he stood before the podium and with tears in his eyes spoke the longest. He thanked "Allah, the beneficent, for granting me this dream of my entire life, to come to al-Quds and stand where Muhammad—peace be upon him—and Jesus and so many of the great prophets once stood." He described how much he looked forward to praying in the sacred Al-Aqsa Mosque. He thanked the president and the prime minister for their gracious hospitality.

And then Hussam Mashrawi stepped onto the plaza.

118

Marcus didn't see him first.

One of the spotters did, informing the team over the radio. Mashrawi was emerging from behind them, through an entrance known appropriately as the Gate of Darkness, located on the north side of the plaza. The spotter explained he was dressed in his clerical robes, did not have a security lanyard around his neck, and was walking with a slight limp.

The king, unaware of what was happening, continued to speak.

The spotter provided continuous updates to Marcus, Tomer, and the rest of the security teams as Mashrawi approached from the back side of the dome. He walked slowly and maintained the same steady pace, making no sudden moves.

When he came around the left side of the shrine, Marcus finally saw him. The two men stared at each other as Mashrawi passed by a grove of olive trees. He was still about a football field away, and Marcus ordered everyone to hold all radio traffic.

The king, looking directly into the main television camera, still didn't know Mashrawi was approaching. But there was a buzz coming from the staffers, some of whom were beginning to move back toward the presumed safety of the mosque.

"Shooters, mark your target, but hold your fire," Marcus said into his wrist-mounted microphone. "And watch for a diversion."

The satphone rang.

President Mustafa answered it immediately.

"Are you watching?" asked Yaşar.

"Of course," the Turkish president replied, sitting transfixed by the image on the screen on the side wall of his office.

"Do you see the man coming into view right now on the far right side of the screen?" Yaşar asked.

"The cleric, in the robes?"

"That's the one."

"What about him?"

"That's our man."

"Stand by—something is happening," said one of the Al-Sawt anchors.

"If you're just joining us, King Faisal of Saudi Arabia has been speaking in front of the Dome of the Rock for the last several minutes," said his colleague. "But just now the king has stopped speaking. It's not entirely clear why he—"

"Wait," noted the first anchor. "Someone's approaching."

"Who is that? A security man?"

"No, no, it's a cleric of some kind."

"Let's see if we can get a close-up of the man who has just stopped the king's speech in midsentence."

Yasmine Mashrawi gasped.

"Hey, that's your husband," the shoemaker said.

The chief of the Royal Guards took a step toward the king.

Marcus saw the motion out of the corner of his eye yet never took his focus off Mashrawi, who he estimated was now no more than a few yards away from one of the Xs on the pavement.

"Your Majesty, welcome to al-Quds," shouted a beaming if somewhat–glassy-eyed Mashrawi. *"What a joy and an honor to have you here, to have all of you here, in one beautiful and sacred place."*

At this, Marcus stepped directly into Mashrawi's path, between the approaching cleric and the Saudi king. He shouted to the man to stop right where he was.

"It's okay," Mashrawi shouted back. *"It's me, Agent Ryker. It's Hussam."*

Marcus had not drawn his weapon yet. But Tomer now came up beside him, ready to draw his. Mashrawi kept walking. Not quickly. He still made no sudden movement. He simply continued walking toward them at precisely the same speed.

"Dr. Mashrawi, this is your last chance," Marcus shouted at the top of his lungs. *"Stop right where you are. Do not approach another foot."*

"I don't understand," said the shoemaker. "Why are they telling him to stop?"

"Don't they know who he is?" asked the man's wife.

Yasmine, too, was confused. Just then, however, she remembered the phone in her hand, looked down at it, and flipped it open. As she did, she tried to remember precisely what her husband had told her. Was she to call him the moment she saw him on television or only when Hussam was in the same shot as the president, the king, and the prime minister? She rested her finger over the 5 button and looked back up at the screen.

Was it time? she wondered. *Was this the moment?*

119

Mashrawi didn't stop.

The man was steadily approaching the X. Any closer and a sniper was going to take him out. Marcus suddenly wondered if he had calculated enough distance. What if the bomb the Pakistani had implanted in this man was more powerful than the one in London? Could it kill them all, even from there?

"Snipers, hold your fire," Marcus ordered over his radio. "I've got this."

"I don't understand," Mashrawi shouted. *"Whatever is the problem, Agent Ryker? You know me. You vetted me. You invited me to be here today."*

As Marcus tried to figure how best to respond, knowing his every move was being broadcast to the world, Mashrawi kept talking.

"I apologize—to all of you—for being late. But as you know, Agent Ryker, I have not been myself since my dental surgery on Wednesday. I have been on heavy painkillers, and they have been hard on my stomach and my heart."

Mashrawi crossed the X and kept coming. Five feet closer. Ten feet. At fifteen feet, Marcus drew his weapon and aimed it at the man's forehead. Tomer did the same. And Mashrawi suddenly stopped.

"*You didn't have dental surgery, Dr. Mashrawi,*" Marcus shouted back.

"*What are you talking about? Of course I did. Ask my dentist. He removed one of my wisdom teeth, and he did an emergency root canal.*"

It was a bizarre conversation to be having on live television, especially given the high-powered people behind him and all those watching in capitals around the globe. But Marcus continued.

"*Is Daoud Husseini your dentist?*"

"*Yes, that's him. Call him. Ask him. He will verify everything.*"

"*I don't need to call him.*"

"*Why not?*"

"*I just came from his office—he's dead.*"

Mashrawi looked shocked. Marcus couldn't tell if the reaction was genuine or feigned, but it struck him as genuine.

"*Your friend Mohammed al-Qassab shot him in the head,*" Marcus continued.

"*Who?*"

"*Your Kairos handler.*"

"*My what? What in the world are you talking about, Agent Ryker? What nonsense is this?*"

Marcus ignored the question. "*Dr. Haqqani is also dead.*"

"*I don't know who that is.*"

"*Yes, you do. He's the man who performed your surgery. The man who implanted a bomb inside your chest cavity. The bomb you came here today to detonate.*"

"*You've lost your mind, Agent Ryker. I have come to do no such thing. Now please, put that gun away and let us continue this historic event. You're embarrassing yourself and your country.*"

"*It's over, Hussam,*" Marcus replied. "*Al-Qassab told me everything. I arrested him thirty minutes ago. It's time to surrender before anyone gets hurt.*"

Mashrawi's expression suddenly changed. He looked like a caged animal. He scanned the crowd. He spotted the sharpshooters with their rifles pointed at him. He saw other agents now with weapons drawn. And he turned to the cameras.

"*It is all lies,*" he shouted. "*Everything this man says, it's all lies.*"

Then he appealed to the Saudi king.

"*Your Majesty, this is the persecution we have suffered as devout Muslims, as good Arabs, as faithful Palestinians. Don't believe these men. They are liars. They don't want you to make peace. They want to foment war between us, a religious war that will rage for a thousand years.*"

Mashrawi began to move again. He began to walk forward. Again Marcus shouted at him to stop immediately or he would be shot dead.

"*Do you see this, Your Majesty? Do you hear them, the unbelievers trampling on our holy grounds? I am not a suicide bomber. I am not a terrorist.*"

Marcus took three steps forward and then stopped. "*Then prove it, Dr. Mashrawi—to me, the king, and the entire world, right now.*"

"*Just tell me how, Agent Ryker. Nothing would make me happier than to prove you wrong, to humiliate you before the entire world. Do you think I'm wearing a suicide vest under these robes? Is that what you think?*"

"*Take off your robe,*" Marcus shouted.

Mashrawi did. "*See, Agent Ryker—no vest.*"

"*Take off your shirt,*" Marcus replied.

Mashrawi stood there for a moment, defiant. But then, to Marcus's surprise, he unbuttoned his light-blue oxford dress shirt and threw it to the ground. Now he was standing only in a white T-shirt and a pair of tan khaki pants.

"*What should I do now, Agent Ryker?*" the cleric sneered. "*Shall I strip naked for you, for the whole world? Is this how Muslims are to be treated here on our sacred space? Is this what the American peace plan means for Palestinians? More humiliation, more degradation?*"

120

Yasmine's anger boiled.

The sight of her husband being humiliated by this American agent was more than she could bear. It was all she could do to restrain herself and not throw the phone in her hands across the room, shattering it in a thousand pieces. And why not? There was no point calling now, she knew. Her husband was not going to the VIP reception, and neither was she.

For the first time, Marcus genuinely doubted himself.

What if the Grand Mufti was lying? What if al-Qassab was setting him up? What if the plan had never been to kill President Clarke and the others but to embarrass and discredit them?

The chilly December winds were picking up. Yet as cold and alone as he was, his hands were perspiring. His heart was racing. For one of the few times in his life, Marcus was scared—scared of being wrong, scared of all that would mean for his country. Still holding the Sig Sauer in his right hand, he removed his left hand and wiped it on his trousers. As he did, he suddenly felt the phone in his pocket—the phone they'd taken off of al-Qassab.

"Take off your T-shirt, and put your hands in the air," Marcus ordered.

"Why should I?" Mashrawi angrily shouted back.

"Look, Hussam, this can all end peacefully," Marcus said. *"Now, as a show of goodwill, I'm going to put my gun away, to show you I mean you no harm."*

Mashrawi glared back at him with hatred and defiance in his eyes. Marcus could see the man was plotting his next move. Slowly he put his gun back in his holster. Tomer, standing directly beside Marcus, glanced at him like he was crazy. Marcus didn't care. He was convinced the man was going to charge them, and soon. Yet it also occurred to Marcus that al-Qassab could not have the only phone to trigger the detonation. Someone else had one too. Not on this site. It had to be someone watching on television. Why else was Mashrawi so confident? Marcus had just told him he had al-Qassab in custody. He'd just told Mashrawi that they knew he was the bomber. Why else, then, would he be preparing to charge?

If Marcus was wrong, of course, then he didn't want to imagine the fate that awaited him. Not only would he be fired. He'd be humiliated in front of all his colleagues. He'd never work in law enforcement again. Worse, the president of the United States would be discredited in front of the entire world.

If Hussam Mashrawi was the bomber, he would want the bomb to go off as close to POTUS, the PM, and the king as possible. Which meant that at that moment Mashrawi would be praying that whoever was going to dial that phone was preparing to dial it now.

Marcus slowly slipped his left hand into his left pant pocket and took hold of al-Qassab's phone. With his eyes still locked on Mashrawi, he just as slowly pulled it out, then let his hands drop to his sides in such a manner as to hide the phone from Mashrawi's view. As he did, he once again ordered Mashrawi to remove his T-shirt and then raise his hands over his head.

Mashrawi didn't move.

"Look, Hussam, I put my gun away. I don't want to hurt you. I certainly don't

want to kill you. None of us do. Now, just take off your shirt—slowly—and prove to everyone that you don't mean us any harm either."

Mashrawi glared at Marcus. For a moment he remained motionless, but how long was that going to last?

Marcus gripped the mobile phone, knowing he held the man's life in his hands. If Mashrawi did not surrender, Marcus could not hesitate. He had taken life before to protect the innocent. He was ready to do so again. But he desperately did not want to. Each time he did cost him something precious, something he could never replace, and silently he prayed he wouldn't have to do it today.

One thing was certain. If he had to kill Mashrawi, Marcus knew he would be sending the man straight to hell. Forever. No way out. No second chances. Not now. Not ever. In most life-and-death situations, he had no time to think about such things. Events just happened so quickly, and all he could do was react according to his training. Kill or be killed.

But now he was staring into the man's eyes, looking into his soul, wondering if it was damned or might somehow yet be redeemable. Now Marcus had the rare luxury of contemplating the terrible implications of what might be coming.

Yet he resolved not to hesitate. If he had to act, he would. What happened next was between Mashrawi and God. The man had to make his own choices.

If it came down to a decision between ending the life of a man willing to commit murder or allowing that man to murder those whom Marcus was sworn to protect, Marcus knew he would make the same decision every time, without pause.

There was nothing more to say. Marcus stood his ground, silently pleading for Mashrawi to obey his order and save his life and perhaps his soul. But suddenly Marcus saw something shift in the man's eyes. They narrowed, ever so slightly. Two fingers on Mashrawi's left hand twitched.

This was it, Marcus knew. He'd spent a lifetime studying killers. Mashrawi was about to make his move. So Marcus made his.

With his eyes still locked on the Grand Mufti's son-in-law, Marcus pushed number five. If he was wrong, nothing would happen. Only the snipers would be able to save them. But he was not wrong.

As if in slow motion, Marcus saw Mashrawi's head lean forward. He saw the man's right foot come up. Marcus shouted into his wrist-mounted microphone, *"Cover!"* Then he turned and pulled Tomer to the ground just as Mashrawi started charging toward them. With a crazed look in his eye, he was shouting, *"Allahu akbar!"* at the top of his lungs.

The snipers never fired a shot. No one did. They never got the chance. For in a flash of blinding light and a deafening boom, Hussam Mashrawi detonated before their very eyes.

121

For several seconds, Marcus could see nothing.

The air was thick with smoke. He could hear nothing but a high-pitched ringing in his ears. The wicked stench of burned flesh permeated the mountain. But eventually Marcus raised his head and scanned the ghastly scene.

Bits of limestone and body parts were raining down from the sky. Where Mashrawi had been standing, there was nothing but a smoking crater. To his right, Marcus could see the TV cameras had been completely blown off the risers. Behind him, Marcus saw bodyguards lying on their protectees. No one was moving, and for a moment, Marcus feared they were all dead.

Crawling off of Tomer, he asked the Israeli if he was okay but wasn't sure the man could hear him, since he could barely hear himself. He asked again. Tomer didn't immediately respond, not verbally, anyway. But slowly he began to move his arms and hands and was soon brushing off the debris that had fallen on him and waving away the smoke and ash still heavy in the air.

Marcus climbed to his feet and pulled Tomer to his. The Israeli began coughing violently. Marcus did a quick check to see if Tomer had sustained any serious injuries. He certainly had numerous cuts on his face and hands. They both did, but beyond that they weren't bleeding, and best of all, they were alive.

When Tomer stopped coughing and said he was fine, Marcus slapped him on the back and staggered through the haze toward the entrance to the Dome of the Rock. As he did, he saw others finally beginning to move. The chief of the Royal Guards was helping the king to his feet. Several Secret Service agents were doing the same for President Clarke, as were the Shin Bet with Prime Minister Eitan. A moment later, Marcus spotted Geoff Stone helping Secretary Whitney to her feet. They, too, were alive, as were the Grand Mufti and Senator Dayton, both of whom were already back on their feet.

But Annie was not. Marcus rushed to her side. She was breathing, but her hands and arms and face were covered with contusions. She was lying on her back, faceup, her eyes closed, and Marcus wondered if she had been knocked out by the blast.

"Annie, can you hear me? It's me. It's Marcus. Do you know where you are?"

She did not reply, did not even move, and he felt a rising panic. She couldn't be dead. Not Annie. Not after all she had already come through. Marcus had already lost too many people he was supposed to protect. He could not bear to lose another.

Taking one of her hands with one of his, he gently wiped ash and bits of rock from her eyes and mouth with his other.

"Hey, you all right? Can you hear me? Come on, Annie, wake up."

Marcus's hearing was beginning to return, and soon he could hear the urgent radio chatter coming through his earpiece. He heard Roseboro dispatching more agents to create a protective cordon around POTUS and to seal off the gates to the Temple Mount immediately. A moment later, he was informing the team to clear the courtyard on the north side of the plaza because Marine One was inbound.

Dayton spotted them and ran to their side. He took Annie's other hand, pushed several strands of blonde hair out of her eyes, and pleaded with her to wake up, promising her that everything would be okay, that everyone was safe, that everyone had lived, and that she would too.

Soon, the distinctive green-and-white Sikorsky helicopter came into view, and what hearing Marcus had recovered was deafened by the roar of its rotors. Finally, just as Marine One touched down behind them, Annie's eyes fluttered open. The senator kept talking to her, though it was impossible to hear him.

Marcus tried to call over the radio for medical assistance but couldn't be heard. Yet as the principals and their bodyguards were being helped into the president's helicopter—and two more identical Sikorskys approached from the south—a team of IDF medics came running over to Marcus's side. They, too, did a quick check to see if Annie was bleeding anywhere but her face, arms, and hands and confirmed that she was not. They checked her pulse, gave her several shots, and hooked up an IV. As a precaution, they also put her in a neck brace, slid a wooden board under her, and strapped her down just in case she had a neck or back injury.

The moment POTUS and the other principals were aboard, Marine One lifted off, flying away in a rotating formation with the other two Sikorskys, creating an airborne shell game designed to confuse any more would-be assassins as to which chopper the president and the others were actually in. When they were gone, an IDF Black Hawk helicopter roared into view. As it landed, the medics carried Annie directly to it and carefully loaded her on board. The senator climbed in next, never leaving her side.

Marcus did not climb in. He wanted to, but it was not his place. His friends were in good hands now, but he still had a job to do. He was moved as he saw Annie's eyes fill with tears. She was not only conscious now but slowly taking in the enormity of what had just happened.

"*Thank you,*" she silently mouthed to him over the cacophony, as the side door of the chopper slammed shut.

Marcus stepped back several yards. He watched as the Black Hawk lifted off the plaza, hovered about forty feet off the ground, rotated slightly toward the southwest, and then streaked off across the skyline of the Old City, toward Hadassah hospital.

"You're welcome," he said under his breath as the chopper vanished into the December clouds.

Just then, Tomer came up behind him and put his hand on Marcus's back. "Hey," the Israeli said.

Marcus turned. "Hey yourself," he replied.

"You all right?"

Marcus thought about the question but had no idea how to answer it. He thought about losing Elena and Lars. He thought about losing Nick and Carter Emerson and almost losing Pete and Jenny Morris. He pictured Kailea Curtis taking a bullet and Annie Stewart being flown off the Temple Mount. He thought, too, about the look in Maya Emerson's eyes the last time he'd seen her.

"No," he confessed. "But I will be."

EPILOGUE

Thunder boomed over the Holy City.

Lightning flashed across a dark and ugly sky. Israeli, Saudi, and American flags whipped fiercely in the winter winds outside the parliament building, and a great downpour commenced and didn't let up.

Inside the central chamber, the aging Saudi monarch climbed to the rostrum with the help of an aide.

As he was introduced by the Speaker of the Knesset, every elected member not only stood but roared in thunderous cheers and applause—all, that was, but the twelve Arab parliamentarians. Immediately they began shouting curses and epithets at the king at the top of their lungs, unfurling banners written in Arabic, Hebrew, and English that accused the king of "betraying the cause of Palestine" and bringing "disgrace on the House of Saud and the whole of the Arab people and the Muslim world."

Seeing such rage in their eyes, Marcus, Geoff Stone, and two other DSS colleagues—all of whom were standing post behind where Secretary Whitney was seated—immediately hardened up their defenses around the secretary, even as their Secret Service colleagues tightened up around Clarke, who was sitting directly beside Prime Minister Eitan. In the end, it was a raucous but short-lived protest. Israeli security removed the twelve from the chamber, and things began to settle down.

When Agent Stone finally took two steps back from Whitney, Marcus and his colleagues followed suit. It took a few moments for his adrenaline to settle, but even as the Speaker apologized to His Majesty for the "brazen show of disrespect," Marcus was having trouble making sense of what he'd just witnessed.

The protestors were not part of Ismail Ziad's government. They were not members of the Palestinian Authority's legislature. Everyone who had just been removed from the chamber was both an Arab and a full Israeli citizen, with all the rights of every Jewish citizen of the state. Each was a Sunni Muslim, a member of one of several Muslim-majority political parties in Israel. Each had been duly elected to the parliament by fellow Israeli Arab citizens in the only true democracy in the Middle East. Certainly none of them were fans of Reuven Eitan's right-wing government; that much Marcus got. But why, as Sunni Arab Muslims, were they so vehemently opposed to the king of Saudi Arabia coming to Jerusalem to make peace? Wasn't this move toward peace a good thing, he wondered, something to which one should aspire, not rebuke?

As he scanned the room for other possible threats, Marcus looked across the gallery, packed with members of the American and Saudi delegations, foreign ambassadors to Israel, and myriad other VIPs. He scrutinized the faces of the dozens of reporters present and the camera operators and producers as the entire session was being broadcast live around the planet. Even without the drama of the previous day, the world would have been riveted on this city at this unique moment. But in the aftermath of the unprecedented suicide bombing on the Temple Mount, Marcus had no doubt that viewership in the U.S. was going to break every ratings record imaginable, not just on cable networks but on the Big Four broadcast networks as well. What he found truly extraordinary was the fact that viewers in the Kingdom of Saudi Arabia, and in most Gulf states—with the exception of Qatar—were able that day to watch live images from the Israeli parliament for the first time in their lives.

The Israeli president had already delivered his speech. So had Prime Minister Eitan, and—just moments before—President Clarke. Now they were all about to witness something few, if any, had ever dreamt possible: the king of Saudi Arabia, the Custodian of the Two Holy Mosques, addressing the legislature of the world's only Jewish state.

Clearing his throat, then taking a sip of water, King Faisal Mohammed Al Saud held the lectern tightly, steadying himself as he looked into one teleprompter, then the other, and gathered his strength.

"In the name of God, the Gracious and Merciful," he began.

The line was in Arabic, but Marcus had spent enough time in the Arab world over the years to know what the first sentence of every speech by every Arab Muslim leader meant.

The next line, however, was in Hebrew, and everyone was stunned.

"Anee ba b'shalom."

Marcus had no idea what it meant, but it must have been good, for the Israelis erupted, rising again to their feet and giving the monarch an ovation that lasted at least two full minutes, maybe more. Amid the cacophony, a Knesset staffer whispered in his ear, "The king just said, 'I come in peace.'"

Now the monarch switched to English.

"Mr. Speaker, Mr. Prime Minister, Mr. President, esteemed dignitaries, friends: Yesterday we witnessed a gruesome act of evil, the work of those who would not only oppose peace but also seek to kill all who would dare to make it, and do so in the name of my religion. But that was yesterday. Today, here and now, I tell you I reject such outlaws of Islam. They do not represent my faith. They do not represent me, my family, or my creed. And they do not represent my people."

Again the applause was thunderous.

"I come to you today—as the great Anwar Sadat of Egypt once did; as Jordan's great King Hussein once did—to forge a peace between our nations, a friendship between our peoples, and a hope for our region and for the world. I come to honor those who came before me—to build on what they accomplished, not threaten or undo it. And I come with the prayer—earnest and heartfelt—that if our two countries can find the courage to make peace, then perhaps my fellow Arabs will be inspired to join us, from Rabat to Ramallah, from Algiers to Abu Dhabi, from Muscat to Manama. . . ."

Line after line electrified the room. Yet Marcus would not remember all the king said. He was not there, after all, to listen to the Saudi leader's address but to protect the American secretary of state. He doubted many others, aside from diplomats and historians, would remember the words either. What they would remember—so long as the peace process stayed on track and soon came to resolution—was the gesture and the spirit from which it came.

Back in the secure holding room, after the king was finished, Marcus stood near Secretary Whitney as the principals thanked one another for their remarks, discussed their next meeting at Camp David in early January, and took photos together. He was struck by the genuine camaraderie he was witnessing. Gone was the initial awkwardness the leaders had experienced in their first hours together. On the Temple Mount, they had been through a terrifying ordeal, and staring down Hussam Mashrawi's attack and surviving it had bonded them in a way the Kairos leadership could scarcely have imagined. That wasn't to say the road ahead was clear or straight. These were profoundly different men from profoundly different backgrounds who faced immense obstacles before an actual peace treaty could be forged. Yet more than anything else, what was fusing them together and what might very well enable them to cross the finish line against all odds could be summed up in one word.

Iran.

For the Israelis, there was very little downside to negotiating a treaty with the Saudis. The two countries had never been in direct warfare with each other. They had no outstanding land disputes. What's more, both sides could declare how much they wanted to achieve a fair and comprehensive peace agreement with the Palestinians with precious little chance of having to make good on the pledge anytime soon.

That said, Riyadh had far more at stake in reaching out to the Israelis, and everyone in the room knew it. Everyone from al Qaeda and ISIS to the Muslim Brotherhood to Qatar to the Turks would be working to undermine the new

Saudi stance. Still, the existential threat posed by the regime in Tehran was dramatically reshaping the geopolitics of the Middle East. The ayatollah's race for nuclear weapons and the missiles to deliver them—and his funding of every terror group in the region from Hezbollah to Hamas to the Houthis—was forcing every Arab leader in every Arab capital in the region to fundamentally rethink who was a friend and who a foe. Clearly, His Majesty had concluded he no longer had the luxury of treating the Israelis as an enemy. The two nations had to become not just friends but strategic allies if the Iranian threat was to be neutralized. But would anyone now come to the Saudis' side? Would the Bahrainis? Would the Emiratis? What about the Moroccans and the Omanis? Or would Riyadh be forced to go this one alone? And if so, at what cost?

Marcus heard in his earpiece that the presidential motorcade was ready to depart. Final instructions were being issued to both the Secret Service and DSS agents in the room to prepare to move the American principals out of the holding room in the next few minutes. Yet just then, to Marcus's surprise, one leader after another came over to him to personally express thanks for saving their lives. True to form, perhaps, the Israeli prime minister was the most formal and thus somewhat awkward in conveying his appreciation. The Saudi monarch, on the other hand, was the most effusive, hugging Marcus and kissing him on both cheeks and inviting him to come back to Riyadh to see the king when everything quieted down.

"There are things to say," His Majesty said quietly. "Things I would prefer to say only to you."

Touched, Marcus nodded. Though he could not imagine any scenario in which his supervisors at the Diplomatic Security Service—much less the Central Intelligence Agency—would let him travel to the kingdom alone for a private parley with a foreign head of state, he kept such thoughts to himself and simply thanked the king for his kindness.

The last to come over was Clarke. "You did good, Ryker," he said with a smile. "You turned out not to be a traitor after all."

"Thank you, Mr. President," Marcus replied, laughing despite the pain from all the cuts and contusions on his face and neck.

Clarke asked how Agent Curtis was doing.

"Quite well, sir. I spent several hours with her at the hospital last night and saw her briefly again this morning. She's going to be just fine."

"That's good to hear," Clarke said. "And Miss Stewart?"

"Annie's doing great as well. She and Agent Curtis were actually on the same floor, so as luck would have it, I got to spend time with them both."

"Glad to hear it. When will they be released?"

"Annie was released about an hour ago, and Agent Curtis is being released as we speak. Lord willing, they're both going to fly home later tonight. I promised to be with them to make sure they're okay."

"And they're both up for flying so soon?"

"These are two tough cookies, Mr. President."

"They must be."

For a moment, the president seemed as if he was going to go back to chatting with the other principals before heading to his motorcade for the quick trip to the airport. Instead, however, he stopped himself. "You folks want a ride home?" he asked Marcus.

"I'm sorry?" Marcus replied, not sure he could have possibly heard the question right.

"I'm asking if you, Miss Stewart, and Agent Curtis would like a ride home," the president repeated. "After all, I assume your destination is Washington, and as it happens, I'm heading there myself. I'd be honored to have you all as my guests, if that would interest you."

"Wow, Mr. President, I'm not sure what to say."

"Say yes."

"Well then, yes, I'd love a ride home," Marcus said. "I'm sure the others would too. I'll need to get permission from the head of my detail, but . . ."

Clarke laughed. "I'm the head of your detail, Ryker. Permission granted."

And so it was that some ninety minutes later, Marcus Ryker was sitting aboard Air Force One with Annie Stewart, Kailea Curtis, and Senator Dayton, soaring over the Mediterranean and homeward bound, recounting with laughter and a few tears the drama they had just lived through and wondering what the future held for them, for their country, for the region, and for the world.

A NOTE FROM THE AUTHOR

The Jerusalem Assassin is entirely a work of fiction.

It is true that I once worked for an Israeli prime minister, though that was for a very brief time and occurred some two decades ago.

Yes, I may be one of the few—perhaps the only—novelist to have traveled to the Kingdom of Saudi Arabia to meet with and spend hours in conversation with senior Saudi officials and members of the royal family.

It is also true that just prior to the release of my previous novel—*The Persian Gamble*—I had the opportunity to meet in the Oval Office with the president of the United States, the vice president, the secretary of state, and the national security advisor and discuss then, and in other meetings, a number of themes in this book.

That said, I want to be clear: the characters herein are made up from whole cloth, figments of my fertile imagination. They are not meant in any way, shape, or form to represent real people, living or dead. The dialogue herein is also completely fictional. There are no actual quotes from any real person I may have met or read about.

On one level, this novel contains a number of worst-case scenarios. That is, high-ranking American diplomats are assassinated. Various world leaders—including the head of a NATO ally—are involved in funding the launch of a new and deadly terrorist organization. Palestinian leaders continue rejecting all efforts to forge a real and lasting peace treaty between their people and the people of Israel. The list goes on. While all of these plot elements are plausible, they are not predictions of what I believe will necessarily happen in the near or distant future—only fears.

And let me hasten to add that I certainly pray that no harm ever befalls the brave men and women involved in peacemaking efforts in the Middle East, as befalls some of the fictional characters in these pages.

On another level, of course, this novel certainly contains elements of wishful thinking. That is, as both a dual U.S.-Israeli citizen and an evangelical from a Jewish heritage, I pray every day for the peace of Jerusalem, just as commanded in the Scriptures. What's more, as a resident of Jerusalem, I long for the day when another Sunni Arab leader demonstrates the boldness and the courage of Egyptian president Anwar Sadat and Jordan's King Hussein by choosing to make peace with the State of Israel, and that the leaders of Israel show the wisdom and the discernment to make it easier— not harder—for such a day to come and come soon.

Will the Palestinian leadership continue to resist every effort to bring about peace? Perhaps, but I genuinely hope not, because I want to see peace for their sake and for ours. Will the Saudis see it in their national interest to make peace with Israel, even if the Palestinians maintain a rejectionist posture? Perhaps someday, and I genuinely hope so, though we all know there are many forces inside the kingdom and throughout the region who will try to thwart such moves should they ever be actively contemplated, much less acted upon.

This is one of the reasons I love to tell stories. For writing a novel is not fortune-telling or prophecy. It is the act of exploring my nightmares and my dreams. It is the art of trying to capture the imaginations of readers around the world and take them into a world I hope might be one day, and a world I hope never comes to pass.

ACKNOWLEDGMENTS

Ever since I was eight years old, I have wanted to write novels or screenplays. I have yet to write a movie or television script, but this is my fifteenth novel and I want to express my deepest appreciation to those who have helped make this one a reality.

Scott Miller has been my agent and my good friend since agreeing to represent my first novel, *The Last Jihad*—he and the Trident Media Group are without a doubt the gold standard in the world of literary agents.

The Tyndale House publishing team is the finest in the business—Mark Taylor, Jeff Johnson, Ron Beers, Karen Watson, Jeremy Taylor, Jan Stob, Elizabeth Jackson, Andrea Garcia, Maria Eriksen, Caleb Sjogren, Danika King, the entire sales force, and all the remarkable professionals who make Tyndale an industry leader. And a special shout-out to Erin Smith for her wonderful copyediting assistance and especially to Dean Renninger, who continues to design amazing covers for my novels.

Our award-winning PR team—Larry Ross, Kristin Cole, and Kerri Ridenour and their colleagues—is first-rate and a joy to work with.

Nancy Pierce and June "Bubbe" Meyers are my rock-star teammates at November Communications, Inc.—they continue to handle everything from my schedules to flights to finances and a great deal more, and with them I am in very kind and capable hands.

Every year that goes by, I am even more grateful to my parents, Len and Mary Jo Rosenberg, and to all of my extended family and Lynn's, for their love and grace, wise counsel and prayers, and all the fun and laughs we have together.

The same is true of our four sons: Caleb—and his beautiful wife, Rachel—Jacob, Jonah, and Noah. I am proud to be your dad and love all the adventures and challenges we face together.

Most of all, I want to thank my dear wife, Lynn. She was just eighteen when we met at Siberacuse—I mean, "No Excuse"—er, rather, Syracuse University. I was only nineteen. Through those long, bitter central New York winters, we became the best of friends and then fell deeply in love. We married in her adorable little church in Point Pleasant, New Jersey, on June 30, 1990—just weeks after her graduation—and this year we will celebrate our thirtieth wedding anniversary. I've said it before but I happily repeat myself: Lynn is my best friend in the world and there is no one whose love or advice or affection and companionship I could possibly cherish more than hers. May the Lord give us another thirty years—and many, many more.